P9-CQP-507

Wildwood Boys

Other Works by
James Carlos Blake

Borderlands: Short Fictions
Red Grass River
In the Rogue Blood
The Friends of Pancho Villa
The Pistoleer

Wildwood Boys

A NOVEL

JAMES CARLOS BLAKE

William Morrow
An Imprint of HarperCollins*Publishers*

This is a work of fiction. Names, characters, places, and incidents either are the product of the author's imagination or are used fictitiously. Any resemblance to actual events, locales, organizations, or persons, living or dead, is entirely coincidental and beyond the intent of either the author or the publisher.

WILDWOOD BOYS. Copyright © 2000 by James Carlos Blake. All rights reserved. Printed in the United States of America. No part of this book may be used or reproduced in any manner whatsoever without written permission except in the case of brief quotations embodied in critical articles and reviews. For information address HarperCollins Publishers Inc., 10 East 53rd Street, New York, NY 10022.

HarperCollins books my be purchased for educational, business, or sales promotional use. For information please write: Special Markets Department, HarperCollins Publishers Inc., 10 East 53rd Street, New York, NY 10022.

FIRST EDITION

Designed by Nancy Singer Olaguera

Printed on acid-free paper

Library of Congress Cataloging-in-Publication Data has been applied for.

ISBN 0-380-97749-4

00 01 02 03 04 QW 10 9 8 7 6 5 4 3 2 1

For JoAnna

Blessed be the merciless, for they shall see
God's enormous shrug.
—George Garrett, *Entered from the Sun*

The man in the violent situation reveals those
qualities least dispensable to his personality,
those qualities which are all he will have to
take into eternity with him. . . .
—Flannery O'Connor, "On Her Own Work"

Contents

I
The Clan

1839–1862

Saint Louis days

Will Anderson had always felt that life should own more excitement than a farm could ever afford. He'd begun to resent farming from the time he was old enough to be charged with the morning milking, and by the time he was steering a plow he abhorred the yeoman's life. His brothers laughed whenever they heard him cursing in his struggles to harness a recalcitrant mule, and they told him he'd best get used to it. It was not that he was averse to hard work but that he was possessed of a romantic disposition. As he grew toward early manhood he labored the days long and then lay awake nights and pondered possibilities until he fell asleep with fatigue. He thought the city might be the thing, though he knew little of cities except that they were not farms.

He was not yet eighteen the night he forsook his Kentucky home. He made directly for the neighboring farm of the prosperous Kiner family and sneaked through shadows blinking with fireflies and up to the house past dogs that knew his scent. At Martha's window he hissed her awake and asked her to go with him and be married and live in Saint Louis. She was a shy but comely girl who generally preferred the company of books to social entertainments, but one day she'd accompanied her sisters to a county fair and was introduced to

Will Anderson, and they'd neither one had eyes for any other since. Her father had repeatedly told her she was pretty enough to make an advantageous marriage and that the Andersons were hardly removed from hardscrabble, but like Will himself she was of a nature more fanciful than practical, and she knew in her heart that no greater excitement would ever come her way than this young man at her window.

They made off in the bright haze of a gibbous April moon, giggling like children, mounted double on the big mule he'd stolen from his father, though he did not see it as stealing but as compensation due him for all the young years of labor he'd given to the farm. He would not, however, take any of her father's animals without permission. They carried few clothes and one blanket, a coffeepot, a fry pan, a small bag of books, and the zither she would not abandon and bore slung upon her back.

"Damn, girl," he whispered as they made away, "I guess I ought've took Daddy's wagon too, just to tote all your goods. This poor mule ain't never carried such a load."

She hit him on the back with her fist and said, "It's not *that* much."

They took as well the small dowry her father had been putting aside toward the gainful marriage he envisioned for her, and which money she knew to be cached under a flat stone in the springhouse. Will had yielded to her reasoning that it was their proper due. "*You're* the husband I choose," she'd whispered. "It's yours by all justice of the heart." She was a reader of poetry, this Martha Kiner. He'd had to grin as he said, "All right, then."

They were wed in Hickman, then ferried over the Mississippi and followed the river road to Saint Louis. They took lodging in a boardinghouse. She wrote to her parents to explain how deeply she loved this young Anderson who set her heart to dancing every time she looked on him. In return came a brief note from her father: "You ever come back here I'll whip you to the assbone. He comes back I'll feed him to the hogs."

Though Martha assured him her father would not come looking for her, he thought it prudent for them to change addresses and take another name for a time—Jackson, like Old Hickory, whom he'd long admired. She nevermore wrote to nor heard from any bloodkin but her elder sister Sally, who also lived in Missouri but far off on its western border. Sally had married a stage driver named Angus Parchman six years earlier and gone with him to work a farm he'd inherited in Jackson County. But not even her sister would Martha ever see again.

He thought he should learn a city man's trade and so took a position as apprentice in a hatter's shop. But he soon came to detest Saint Louis for its crowded sidewalks and bullying policemen, its ceaseless clamor of wagon traffic and steamboat whistles and bellowing humanity, its multitude of alien stinks. Even the smell of horseshit seemed somehow foul to him when it came off Saint Louis streets. But most of all he hated the city's incipient population of foreigners, in particular its Germans.

"There wasn't near as many Dutchmen yet in that town as you got today," he would later tell his sons, "but there was already enough so you couldn't help but run into some of them every time you stepped out in the street. Couldn't help but hear them neither. It was 'Dutchland this' and 'Dutchland that' everywhere you turned your ear. What galled me the most was them all the time saying the U S of A is a backward country because some of the states got slavery, saying Missouri ought be ashamed of itself for being one of them. Bunch of damn foreigners—*squareheads*—calling *us* backward and right in our own country! I tell ye, boys, a man can get his fill of such talk pretty damn quick. Goddam Dutchmen. It was in Saint Louis I first heard it said the Dutch are like farts because they most of them loud, they ain't about to go back where they came from, and loud or quiet they every one of them stinks to high heaven. Gateway to the West, my sorry ass!—Saint Louis is the Gateway from Dutchland is what it is. I seen it happening way back then."

His bitterness toward the city's ways and foreigners was made worse by his day-long confinements in the hattery. He rarely saw the sun. The shop reeked of solutions used in constructing the hats and he began to suffer chronic headaches. His muscles ached for proper use. One day a man who worked at the table next to his and had been employed in the shop for more than a year—an amiable fellow, but increasingly given to tics and soft mutterings as he worked—

went crazy in his own home. He refused to get out of bed one morning, and when his wife asked what he thought he was doing and why he wasn't getting ready to go to the shop, he simply and mutely stared at her. Frustrated to anger, she grabbed him by his sleepshirt and tried to pull him bodily from the bed. He in turn grabbed her by the neck with both hands and throttled her. The whole episode witnessed by their spinster daughter who ran shrieking from the house to cry murder in the streets.

Will Anderson read all about it in the newspaper. According to the report, lunacy was not uncommon among hatters and was thought to be inspired by prolonged exposure to the chemicals of the trade. Will had now been at hatmaking for several months and this revelation explained everything to him about his headaches—and it put him in a rage. This damned Saint Louis! That damned hat factory!

The following morning he stalked into the manager's office and closed the door behind him. He announced he was quitting and demanded the pay he was due. The manager was an Acadian come to Saint Louis to make his fortune, but he bore no love for Missourians and believed Will to be one. He said workers were paid for a full week's labor only and Will would have to finish out the week if he expected any wages.

Will knew the man kept money in his desk and he stepped around to search for it and extract what was rightfully his. When the manager roughly shoved him back and said, "Get out from here, Jackson—you damned puke!" his only thought was to put a quick end to it before the man made outcry. He snatched up a heavy iron desk ornament in the form of a rearing horse and crowned him with it. The manager's eyes rolled up as if he would inspect the damage from inside his skull and he fell with the inimitable languor of the dead.

Will's heart was thrashing in its cage as he stared at the bloodstain blooming darkly on the carpet under the man's broken head. But his apprehension quickly gave way to righteous anger—the man had tried to cheat him, after all. He hurriedly searched the desk and found more than fifty dollars in paper and specie and stuffed the money in his pockets. Then went to the door and paused there to ease his breathing. Then opened it and turned to call back into the room, "All right, then, Mr. DuBois, I'll fetch that catalog from the mercantile directly, sir." Some of the hatters looked up from their blocks and molds with the barest curiosity, then gave themselves back to their work. Will shut the door and left the shop. An hour later he and Martha were clear of Saint Louis and bound back to the farming life.

TRUE CALLING

He told Martha he'd been obliged to take his rightful pay from DuBois by force and so thought it wise if they now called themselves Tyler, just in case the law should come searching for him with a trumped-up warrant or some such. She regarded him with narrowed eyes but asked no questions.

They homesteaded in Marion County and raised corn and swine. A clearwater stream wound through a copse of cottonwoods in the swale below their cabin and the deer that watered there provided plentiful fresh meat. He tried his hand at muletrading in the nearby hamlets but proved no match for the sharps. He sadly confronted the possibility that a farmer was all he was or ever would be.

Martha was rosy in her first pregnancy now, and as he came in from the field at sundown he would hear her singing to young Bill forming up in her belly for entry to the world. She played her zither after supper. He smiled on her contentment and held her close in the night, embraced the easy rise and fall of her breathing, felt the steady beat of her heart in her breast. And yet he yearned for something more—not for more money or goods or property, but for a life less ordinary, for an excitement he couldn't give name to.

One Saturday he delivered a wagonload of pigs to the Palmyra market and then took his ease in a tavern with three men of recent acquaintance. In the course of their convivial drinking, he learned they were all in agreement with him that farming was dull use of a man's life. Among them was a graybeard named Sutpen who now leaned forward on his elbows and asked Will if he was interested in going with them to Iron County to retrieve some horses. Will asked whose horses they were, and the man smiled and said there was some question about that but they intended to resolve it. Will looked from one grinning man to another and said, "I see." He sipped his whiskey and gave the matter regard. The risk and hazard of the proposal sped his blood. Risk and hazard, yes. He filled the cups around and said, "You boys count me in." And thus discovered his true calling of horse thief.

They never rustled more often than once every two months, and sometimes three months would pass between forays. They usually rode in the dark of a new moon, they never stole in their own county, they never raided the same county twice within the same year, no matter how rich the region's pickings. They never took but a portion of a herd, rarely more than two dozen head at a time, the better to contain the animals as they galloped them back to Marion County. Because Will's place was the most isolate they always took the horses there and corralled them in a clearing a good mile deep into a hickory grove behind his house. They would rework the brands and sell the animals singly or in pairs to various neighbors and acquaintances whose love of a bargain outweighed whatever vague suspicions they did entertain. Sometimes a dealer would buy the whole lot, asking only the direction it would be wisest to take the horses for resale and tipping his hat with a wink when they pointed the way opposite from the horses' origin.

To let even part of his small acreage go fallow or to quit raising pigs might have roused speculation about his means of livelihood—musings that might reach ranchers of adjoining counties who had lost horses, that might pique the curiosity of agents of the law—and so Will Anderson, known as Tyler in Marion County, continued to work his farm even though he could have supported his family on the proceeds of the horse deals. His partners did the same.

THE FAMILY

Martha was at first sorely vexed to learn of the new risk he had introduced to their lives but she soon enough struck a truce with this circumstance she could not have altered by any rhetoric. She had anyway always known that life with Will Anderson, long or short, would be venturesome, had known it since the night of their elopement from Kentucky. She conceded that the man was but following his nature and no good could come of her resistance to it.

For his part, he no longer resented farm life so utterly, now that his family's keep did not depend on it and its tedium was relieved by the rustlings. Now he knew contentment to sit in his rocker of a warm evening, smoking his pipe and hearing the strings of Martha's zither and watching baby Bill—christened William T.—crawl about the porch trying to catch fireflies with his hands, the child's eyes remarkable for their bright and ceaseless curiosity as well as their rare coloring, the hazel irises rimmed by a thin band of bright blue.

In years to come Will would on various occasions tell his first-born son the story of his birth on the coldest day in local memory, the second of February, 18 and 40, a Sunday. "A regular winter day just all of damn sudden went about four times colder," Will Anderson would say. "Birds fell out of the sky froze solid as rock. Wasn't much snow but there blew a norther to tear the hide off a goat. Lord, the wind! The roof sounded like it was in pain. There was frost all on the inside walls. We had the fireplace booming and still we were freezing. You were blue as a virgin's vein and not yet a day old but you never made a sound, just squinched up your face and seen the thing through. I knew then you were a hardcase and I told your ma so. When the wind finally let up, it sounded like war the way the trees were popping. I stepped outside and the first breath of that cold air was like getting hit across the nose with a scantling. The wind had pulled a door off the barn and the cow for some dumb-ass cow reason wandered out to the trace and just stood there and froze to death on its feet. I couldn't so much as put a nick in her hide with my bowie. Tried to quarter her with an ax but it was like hacking at an oak stump. Had to build a fire under her to thaw her sufficient to chop her up bit by bit. Talk about *cold*! Was that way for six days before it got usual winter again."

A year after Bill was born came Robert, who in his fifth month was carried away by some nameless disease. Then came Tommy, who at age two and with a stick provoked a huge colony of ground wasps that enclad his head like a snarling yellow hood and stung his hands and scalp and every exposed portion of him including his eye-balls and the tongue of his open shrieking mouth and he died even as little Bill and his pregnant mother came running to flail at the yellowjackets and carry the boy away to the house. The head and hands of the small corpse his father buried under an elm were bloated and darkly purple.

Martha next delivered Jim and she and Will smiled to see four-year-old Billy keeping watch over his baby brother and instructing him in the names of things in the world. When Mary was born the following year Will Anderson held her as though she were made of the rarest glass and Martha beamed at his happiness in a daughter. Then came Josephine, then Jenny the last, and all three sisters would come to dote on Bill and Jim and feel both pride and rue in the knowledge that none of them would ever meet a man the equal of their brothers.

Bill grew up a child of nature, observing intently its ways and creatures, the wind and clouds, the currents and moods of rivers. He taught himself stealth and moved through the brush like shadow. He learned to shoot at a young age and was a deadeye naturalborn. What he did not teach himself about horses he learned from his father. And all that he came to learn and know he taught to his brother as well.

He made claim from boyhood to understand the thoughts of dogs and to be able to talk with them through mind language, although he sometimes spoke to them aloud, if only because some things—reprimands, for example, and jokes—were simply of better effect when heard with the ears and not just the mind. At first his father had wondered if Bill was touched. But the boy seemed sensible enough in all other ways and the elder Anderson had anyhow encountered enough lunacy in his life to know a serious case from a harmless one. Still, he couldn't help but shake his head each time he saw Bill sitting eye to eye with one or another of their hounds and nodding and smiling as the dog worked its ears and brow and now and then wuffed low and showed a broad grin.

Martha's love of books did not slacken over the years, and their house held an uncommon lot of volumes for that part of the world. She taught the children early to read and to letter. Their basic texts were the Old Testament and the first through the fourth of McGuffey's *Eclectic Readers,* but their readings included as well Sarah

Josepha Hale's *Poems for Our Children,* Washington Irving's *Sketch Book,* and the aphoristic wisdoms of *Poor Richard's Almanack.* As they got older they graduated to Shakespeare's sonnets, the *Lyrical Ballads* of Wordsworth and Coleridge, and the works of a more recent writer named E. A. Poe, whose macabre and melodious poetry Bill Anderson thought wondrous. His mother frowned on Poe's morbid cast of mind and claimed to regret having bought the books at even the bargain price of five cents each.

In the family library too was Webster's *American Dictionary of the English Language* and Bill loved to pore over it in search of recondite words with which to affect airy learning. "You are an olfactory offender," he would accuse his brother—and laugh while Jim angrily riffled through the dictionary and his mother smiled over the cookpot. "Looks like precipitation might be erumpent today," he would say as he leaned on his ax and studied the clouded sky and his father would glower and tell him to talk plain goddammit or keep his lip buttoned.

They were mad for music, this family Anderson, though Bill would never learn to play any instrument other than his father's Jew's harp and some few chords on the harmonica, which instrument his brother played with enviable ease from the time he was five years old. His father also a harmonicist and a fair hand with the fiddle, though his wife liked to joke that the best thing about his fiddling was that it kept the field rats from the house. She herself adept with the zither passed through generations of her family and which she taught her daughters to pluck as her mother had taught her in Kentucky. Saturday evenings the Anderson porch would sway with music born in Appalachian hollows, with melodies sailed over from Britain's misty isles. The livelier numbers set them to turns of stepdancing on the porch planks, the plaintive tunes to harmonizing on ballads of lovers long gone, of honor defended and died for, of foggy rivers and wandering ghosts and deepwood mountain homes, of bloodfeuds and murder and the hangman's rope.

THE PARTNERS

In their first eight years of rustling Will Anderson and his partners but thrice failed to get horses, each time caught in the act and each time holding to plan and abandoning the horses and splitting up in all directions and each man of them making his way back home on his own. Then came a night when they were driving a dozen ponies out of Clark County and were suddenly beset by pursuers. Sutpen the graybeard was shot from his mount and the attitude of his tumble was sufficient testament that he was dead. The escaped three later learned that he'd been stood in an open upright coffin in front of a Kahoka general store with a sign on his chest: "Do you know this man?" But none did identify him and after a few days the stink demanded interment. His surviving partners lifted a cup in his memory and continued to rustle, just the three.

The following year a posse fell on them as they were driving a pilfered herd up from the riverbreaks of Saint Charles County. The partner named Harris had his mount shot screaming from under him and was captured. Will and Nordstrom, the other partner, got clear, but Will wondered aloud if Harris would hold to their common pledge never to give up the names of the others. Nordstrom said he had been friends with Harris most of his life and knew for a fact the man would hang before betraying a partner.

Three days later in the early dawn one of Nordstrom's neighbors who had often bought horses from him and Will came riding up to the Anderson house at a gallop. Will stepped out on the porch to receive the man's breathless report that a party from Saint Charles County had showed up at Nordstrom's farm in the night and dragged him from his bed and hanged him for a horse thief. Hanged him from a shade oak flanking the house, bootless and in his underwear. The vigilantes were cooking breakfast over open fires when the Marion County sheriff arrived to find Nordstrom still suspending crooknecked and frog-eyed in full view of his sobbing widow and two young children. When the Saint Charles men explained the matter to him, he said he couldn't much fault them for hanging the man, then told them to take the body down and lay it out in the house.

"Them boys're looking for you too, Will," the neighbor said. "Asked after Will Tyler by name. The sheriff said he'd bring them here just as soon as he had him some breakfast."

Bill Anderson was then eight years old and this his first inkling of his father's true and perilous trade. He was deeply impressed by Will

Anderson's self-possession in the face of this news which he received as though it were not news at all. The neighbor's face by contrast was antic with fear and the boy could sense danger closing fast. He felt himself grinning with a novel excitement he could not have described but did evermore want in his life.

At midmorning the hanging party arrived to find the place deserted but for its livestock, and none of the abandoned beasts did say whither the man Tyler and his family had fled.

THE VETERAN

They settled in Randolph County, a mile west of Huntsville and hard by Black Owl Creek branching off the east fork of the Chariton. The countryside was thick with river willows and cedar brake, hardwood forest, glades with rich yellow grass as high as a horse's belly. Bears rambled in these woods, wildcats prowled the shadows. The last of the local wolves raised distant wail in the night's deep reaches. Herons stalked the creeks and owls hooted in the dark trees and swooped in hunt through the hollows. Here had Will Anderson's two brothers, Jessup and Hayes, come to settle a few years ago after they'd finally had enough of their bullying father and struck out from Kentucky. And here Will found a tract of good bottomland bordering his brothers' farm.

His younger brother Hayes was gone away to the war in Mexico when Will and his family arrived in the heat of mid-summer. Hayes had taken a Boone County woman to wife in his first year in Missouri but before they'd been wed five months he was widowed by the cholera. His bereavement was such that when the war broke out in the spring of '46 he gave a deaf ear to Jessup's arguments against enlistment and went for a soldier. He rode to Texas to join up, rather than enlist with Bill Doniphan's Missouri volunteers, for he wanted no comrades but strangers. He did not write even one letter in his absence, and now the war was nearly six months concluded and still no word had come from or about him. Whether he lived or lay dead in Mexico's alien ground remained mystery.

Jessup was delighted to have Will for a neighbor and helped him to construct a family cabin and a barn. The brothers often visited back and forth, and as they puffed their pipes and passed a jug between them in front of a fire built high against the icy winter evenings, they sometimes mused about heading west into the vast new territories taken from the Mexicans. At first they refused to believe the tales they heard on every trip to town about the gold strikes in California, the ready wealth to be reaped there. But still the stories came, and they began to ask each other if they weren't fools not to go claim their own portion of riches. Martha sometimes heard them as she sat at her sewing or at writing a letter to her sister in Jackson County. Her lips would draw tight at their foolishness but she'd hold silent and tell herself it was just talk, that at least he wasn't out doing something to set the law after them again.

They had been living on the Black Owl more than a year and the autumn trees were turned yellow when Hayes came home. His empty right sleeve was folded and pinned to the shoulder of his threadbare dragoon's tunic. His face was sickly hued and skeletal under a scraggly beard. His hair hung in tangles from under his hat. He nodded on being introduced to Martha and the children. Bill Anderson was enthralled by this uncle who had warred in a foreign land and whose eyes looked aged beyond his years by all the things they'd seen. Hayes kept a whiskey jug at hand as he sat on the porch with his brothers and he often sipped of it. Jessup gestured at the armless shoulder and said he guessed the mash helped some with the pain. Hayes shrugged and said, "I guess."

At supper he spoke only in response to direct address and said no more than necessary. He was indifferent to conversation and shrugged at most questions put to him. He did not care to say where he had been for the year and a half since the end of the war or how he had lost his arm nor anything at all about his time in Mexico. He was unaffected by his brothers' jokes and efforts to make him smile. In days to follow he was content to keep to himself and the comfort of his jug. Jessup and Will soon tired of trying to animate his spirits and thereafter let him alone.

Only in the company of young Bill and little Jim was Hayes inclined to talk. The boys would go to his house and ask if he cared to go fishing with them and he always did. They were usually accompanied by several dogs and Hayes was much amused by Bill's supposed ability to converse with them. A yellow curdog named Quick once sat and stared at Hayes intently and then turned to Bill and wuffed low and the boy looked into its eyes for a moment before making a gesture of dismissal and the dog trotted over to a shady spot under a tree and settled itself with its muzzle on its paws.

"That yeller say something about me?" Hayes said, his expression both suspicious and amused.

"Well, sir," Bill said, "he believes you're about the saddest man he ever saw."

"Is that right?" Hayes said. He looked over at the dog and it cut its eyes away without moving its head. "Well, truth be told, that son of a bitch don't look so all-fired jubilant to me neither."

The boys laughed with him and the yellow dog raised its head and itself appeared to smile.

He never spoke of his lost bride but talked mostly of the war, of having seen the elephant, as the expression of the day had it. While they sat on the creekbank and watched the stick floats bobbing on their lines he told of the battle of Monterrey, of the boom and blast of artillery and of house-to-house fighting and men shot and bayoneted and blown to portions. Told of screams and smells that might have issued from hell's own butcher shop, of blood running in the cobbled streets. Three days the battle endured, and when it was done he was one of the fortunates yet intact and without serious wound. That night he and some of his fellows celebrated in a cantina. In his joy at being alive he whooped and discharged a pistol into the ceiling and the ball ricocheted off the iron brace of a viga and angled down to strike the arm he rested on the dusky shoulders of a señorita and shatter its humerus like a thing of glass. The surgeon had been obliged to amputate at the shoulder. He said the missing limb sometimes itched him so bad he thought he might go insane for not being able to scratch it. He still couldn't stand the thought of his arm rotting in Mexican ground, and he regretted not bringing it back to bury in America.

One day Hayes revealed to the boys a Colt revolver he'd stolen from an ordnance wagon for no reason but conviction that the army owed him something for his disfigurement. A huge thing more than fifteen inches long and weighing close to five pounds fully charged with .44-caliber conical balls, it was hardly less than a hand cannon.

"A Texas Ranger named Walker helped Colonel Colt to design

it," Hayes told the boys. "It'll blow the most of a man's head off. If you run out of rounds, why, you can bust a skull with it sure as a hammer."

He handed the piece to Bill. "I can't work that loading lever with just one arm," Hayes said. "You might as well have it." Bill cradled it in both hands and marveled as if upon some holy object.

Years of the Argonaut

Another winter passed and now nothing would do for Jessup and Will but to go to California and claim their share of gold. Martha argued vehemently against the enterprise. She had made wide allowance for Will's inclination to horse theft but this ambition was too reckless for her to accept without protest. Just because every fool and fool-killer in the country was going to California was no reason for them to join the parade. She asked what they knew about prospecting, asked Will how she was supposed to manage the farm without him as well as care for two-year-old Josephine and newborn Jenny. Will let her talk herself tired and then said Hayes would stay on the place with her and pointed out that Bill was almost of a size to do a man's work and six-year-old Jim was already tending to various main chores. She couldn't believe he was leaving her to care for a farm and five children and one of them an infant and another not much more and nobody to help her but a one-armed and half-distracted man devoted to the jug. But she could see that her husband was decided, and so at last she only sighed and said no more about it. Three weeks later Will and Jessup struck out for the Santa Fe Trail and four years would pass without a word from either.

Hayes proved surprisingly adept at working a variety of tools with his single hand, and though he sipped from his jug all through the day he seemed never to be drunk. Young Bill demonstrated his sufficiency to grown man's work of every kind and Jim and Mary worked hard as well and their mother never rested and the farm fared better than any would have guessed. The cornfield throve and the pigs fattened properly. In season they harvested the corn and shocked the stalks, put up yams and turnips and potatoes in the root cellar, butchered hogs and smoked the meat. Evenings after supper the family came together on the porch for music and song. Uncle Hayes delighted them all with his nimble stepdancing to the strains of Jim's harmonica and Bill's Jew's harp and Mary's able thumping on a washtub bottom.

Sometimes of a late afternoon Bill took the big Walker to the creek to practice. When he shot a bird or squirrel the creature simply vanished and nothing remained but scattered feathers or bits of bloody pelt. He taught his little brother to shoot the Walker too, though it was all young Jim could do to aim the piece with both hands, and the recoil each time flung the gun high over his head and usually threw him down. Their uncle regarded their shooting with approval and took pulls from his jug and now and then told them another story of the war. He told of men dying in greater numbers of fever than by enemy hand, of men so sick with the "blues" they did shit themselves to death. The whole time he was in Mexico there was no escaping the stink of human shit. He told of Mexican coronets playing the no-quarter tune called "Degüello" all through the night before the fight at Monterrey. Men stopped their ears with plugs of tobacco to keep from hearing it another minute. "You never heard nothing like that cutthroat music," he said. "Freeze the hair in your ass."

Three years passed and half of a fourth. One cool autumn Sunday Uncle Hayes went to the Black Owl by himself to sit under the drooping willows and drink from his jug and skip stones across the water. When they found him four hours later he was facedown on the bottom of the creek in a depth of barely three feet. Young eels swam through his early grayed hair wavering in the current. The jagged bone jutting from below his elbow told the story: he'd fallen in and broken the arm and been unable to push himself up to breathe. Bill dug his grave in the shade of a cottonwood and Jim and Mary fashioned a cross from two barked pieces of wood and his mother read over the gravemound from the Psalms.

There came an early thaw that spring and the days warmed fast. On a brightly blue May morning Jim Anderson saw a man mounted on a sagging horse plodding across the meadow toward the house and even before the rider drew close enough to make out his face he thought he knew who it was. Now the dogs came aware of the stranger and rose up out of the new grass in a clamoring rush and Jim called them to come back but they ran on until Bill came out and whistled them down. The pack came loping back with tongues lolling and they sat before him and Bill told them with his eyes not to bark at that man ever. They cocked their heads and he said, "It's Daddy is why." The dogs resettled on the grass and watched the man come on and none did yap at him again.

Bill called into the house and a moment later the family was gathered on the porch and staring out at the approaching rider. A low breeze was at his back and they caught his smell while he was yet at a distance. He dismounted at the porch steps and the ruined horse that was naught but hide and bone blew tremulously and Will Anderson looked up at them all in turn with eyes blackly hollowed by every sort of exhaustion. His clothes were torn and caked with dirt and his own accumulated exudates, his boots held together with wire, his hat absent its rear segment of brim.

Martha Anderson went down the steps and took him in her arms. He hugged each of his children in turn and Bill saw that the others' eyes too went tearful with the reek of him. They did not know that this hard smell was not entirely of the filth of his rags and unwashed flesh but was also the very smell of rage, of festering anger, a scent Bill and Jim Anderson would come to know well in men other than their father in the years ahead.

"Jessup's dead" were his first words. His voice raspy and unfamiliar. "Took sick on the Mokelumne placers two winters ago and died in a fever."

He scanned the area and Bill knew who he was looking for. "We anyway never got us one bit of gold except for what we took from a Chinaman's teeth one time when he was drunk and Jessup lost that at dicing the same night." He turned to his wife and said, "If I ever had a worse idea than going to California I can't remember what it was. Where's Hayes?" And learned then that his only other brother in the world was in his grave.

He spoke no more of California. He'd told the truth about not acquiring even a speck of gold but for the Chinaman's teeth, but he never told of the bandits who fell on him and his brother in their camp in their second year of working the placers. They shot Jessup dead and would have killed Will too if he hadn't jumped in the river and been carried downstream to safety, although he barely escaped drowning and then nearly died anyway of the ague he contracted from the icy water. He did not tell of the long months of sickness and then being penniless in San Francisco and turning in desperation to the robber's trade and being as often beaten and robbed himself as he did beat and rob others. He joined with a pair of partners and thought he'd struck it rich the night they robbed the counting room of a gambling hall and got away with thousands of dollars. But when they reined up at the outskirt of town to apportion the loot, one of the partners shot the other dead off his horse and tried to shoot Will too but only killed his mount from under him before making away with all the money. Back at thieving and robbing on his own, he was captured one night by a party of city vigilantes. He would have been hanged but for a ship company's need of work crews to put its vessels right for voyages round the Horn. The company was hard pressed to find willing workers in that city of goldseekers and businessmen and grifters and thieves, but the owner had influence with the vigilante committee and they would sometimes provide him with criminal labor for a fee. And so Will was bound over to the ship company to serve a sentence of eighteen months, and in that time he toted and caulked and hammered and sawed and sanded and painted while others in California sought for gold or robbed it from those who'd found it. These things he never told.

Over the following days his talk was all of Kansas territory. On his way back from California he had come on a fine tract of homestead land some hundred miles east of Missouri. It was set near Agnes City, a few miles removed from the Santa Fe Trail, well-wooded and richly topsoiled and cut through by a swift creek. He was decided they would move there. Martha could not refrain from asking why. How much better could that portion of Kansas be than the good bottom they had on the Black Owl? He said he just knew it was better and would brook no further argument.

And so they removed to the Kansas tract Will had set his eye upon. They built a dogtrot cabin and a stable, put up fences, planted corn and raised pigs. And by the end of the year Will Anderson was again at doing what he had in truth moved to Kansas to do—stealing horses. This time with his sons at his side and learning the rustler's trade. California had convinced him for good and all that a man ought to stay with doing what he could do best, and that bloodkin was the only partnership for it.

BLEEDING KANSAS

The farm was as always good cover for the rustling, and by the rustling they did prosper. In the same year the Andersons moved to Kansas, the Kansas-Nebraska Act was passed and new settlers were pouring into the region. The increase in traffic along the Kansas portion of the Santa Fe Trail was the boon to horsethieving Will Anderson had thought it would be. By the time they had been in Kansas a year, he was taking Bill and young Jim on late-night raids of waystation corrals and grazing pastures, sometimes of the local ranches that provided horses to the stage and freight lines. They took as many as two dozen head each time and moved them fast across the southern backcountry along old stock traces and over isolated prairie and along the Marais des Cygnes River and in a week had them in Bates County, Missouri, and sold off to ready buyers who asked no questions except "How many?" and "How much?"

Every raid gave Bill Anderson a quivering thrill as they cut out the horses and made away with them in a raise of dust. He loved the look of their manes and tails lifting in the night wind, the sounds of their deeply sonorous breathing and the drumming of their galloping hooves. He delighted in their wonderful variety as they raced under the stars—bays and duns and buckskins, blacks and claybanks, sorrels and paints, horses blazed and raindropped, skewbald and mottled and ass-spotted, all kinds. Every rustling made his blood jump with the chance of being found out, with the possibility of violent encounter. He laughed at the wild grin of his brother Jim, hardly more than a child and already more seasoned to risk than most grown men. They naturally took the very best of the animals for their own, the fastest and boldest. Bill was proud of the big sable stallion he named Edgar Allan, and Jim had taken for himself a speedy Appaloosa he called Buck.

They were good at their work and were rarely discovered. In the few instances when they were caught in the act and pursued, they usually had only to fire a few rounds behind them and their chasers would fall away, especially on hearing the blasts of Bill's big Walker. When the chasers proved brave and returned fire and continued to come for them, they would let the horses go in one direction and themselves veer off in another, racing into the darker cover of the woodlands, galloping through the shadows of the river traces with their hatbrims folded back in the wind and the cries and gunfire of their hunters growing faint behind them until the only sounds they heard were their own laughter and the clattering of their horses' hooves.

Even on the rare occasion of an unsuccessful rustle, when they got back home they would sit out on the porch and recount to each other the grand fun they'd had. Bill and his father would pass the jug between them, but even young Jim, from the time he was twelve, was permitted a small cup of whiskey as his earned right for engaging in a man's work. The females of the house would be abed but awake and listening to them—Martha with her head full of fears for the future, Mary and Josie and little Jenny holding each other close, their eyes wide, their hearts thumping with thrill and envy.

They did not go uninformed during their Kansas years, these Andersons. Newspapers and the talk of neighbors at barn dances and village stores, the conversations of strangers in the little towns they passed through on their hundred-mile rides back from horse sales in Missouri—through such sources did they keep up with the news of the day, most of it about the antagonisms attending the matter of slavery and Kansas's own part in the issue. The Andersons well knew of the clamor attached to the territorial election of '55 when the Federal government allowed Kansas to decide for itself to sanction or reject slavery. They'd heard tale upon tale of abolitionists come all the way from New England in pretense of being settlers but in truth only to vote in league with the nigger-stealers and the damned Dutch—hypocritical interlopers who held themselves morally superior to every man of southern ancestry and yet were avid to spill blood, the proof of it in the Bible shipments they received from back East that in fact were crates of Sharps rifles.

No Anderson had ever owned a slave or would, but Will had early implanted in his sons an aversion to bullies of any stripe, and the boys shared in his resentment of these outsiders from half the continent away who would force their beliefs on Kansas. The Andersons were gladdened by news of the hordes of Missourians who crossed into Kansas to outdo the free-stater vote. "Ruffians" the abolitionists called them, and northern newspapers routinely referred to Missourians as depraved "pukes" hardly fit to be called human.

There were fewer than three thousand eligible voters in Kansas on election day and over six thousand votes were cast. The Andersons were elated when the southern vote carried the day. And then shortly thereafter were enraged once again when the free-staters formally denounced the new legislature and called for another election. The Kansas government-elect said the matter had been settled and suggested the northerners go back to New England where they damn well did belong. But the abolitionists refused to yield. They established a headquarters in the town of Lawrence, elected their own governor and legislators, and solicited still more Yankees to the territory.

Hostilities naturally increased. The following spring the Andersons smiled at reports that ruffians had swarmed into Lawrence—"Yankeetown," the pro-slavers called it, "Boston Colony"—and destroyed the printing presses of both newspapers as well as looted stores and fired several buildings, including the governor's house and the three-story Free State Hotel. They laughed when they heard about the southern congressman so infuriated by a northern senator's scurrilous denunciations of the South that he had stalked into the Senate chamber with club in hand and right there on the floor beaten the man to bloody insensibility. But they didn't laugh when they heard that a self-anointed messenger of God named John Brown and several of his sons and followers had descended on five pro-slavery Kansans in the dark of night and cloven them to death with broadswords.

"Claymores they used—Sweet Mother Mary!" Will Anderson remarked to his boys about the John Brown murders. "I hope the son of a bitch does hang, but I have to say he knows how to get his point across. *Fear*, boys—that's half the fight right there. Make the other fella more afraid of the awfulness of what you'll do him if he falls in your hands than you are of what he'll do to you. That's the secret, and crazy old Brown knows it. Same with the Indians. Damn Indians known it since forever. It's what scalping's all about, burning at the stake, all them redskin ways of killing."

His sons thought this a novel advisement but would in time come to know it for common credo in this brute portion of the republic.

And so, five years before Fort Sumter, the war was already under way along the Kansas-Missouri border. "Death to all Yankees and traitors in Kansas!" was the cry of pro-slave Missourians. And the Kansas free-staters did bellow in response: "War to the knife and the knife to the hilt!" Strangers approaching each other on lonely border roads would clutch their weapons and ask, "Free state or slave?"— and the answer could provoke mortal dispute. In newspapers across the country the region now bore the name of "Bleeding Kansas."

In these early years came into being the dread jayhawkers— organized bands of hardcase Kansas vigilantes who preyed upon southern sympathizers on both sides of the border. Among the most notorious of their chieftains were a vicious little man named Charles "Doc" Jennison—a bona fide physician who wore absurdly high-crowned fur hats to make himself appear taller—and a wildbearded half-mad Campbellite preacher named James Montgomery. But the most powerful and reviled of all jayhawkers was James Henry Lane, "the Grim Chieftain," a redhaired political opportunist who would be elected one of Kansas' first two senators. He was a fiery orator whose speeches were said to make dogs howl, children wail, women break into tears, and men of Kansas avid to kill and plunder in Missouri. It was Jim Lane's declared intention to root out all things disloyal to the Union, "from a Durham cow to a Shanghai chicken." But so utter was his hatred of Missourians that he preyed on them all alike, believing that any who claimed to be pro-Union was a puke lying in his teeth.

The Andersons got letters from Martha's sister Sally Parchman telling of the terrible troubles in Jackson County, of fierce skirmishes between Missouri guerrillas and damnable Kansas jayhawks, of sometimes hearing the gunfire of such fights not a mile from their own farm. She told of shot-dead bodies of strangers stood in a line of upright coffins on town sidewalks that they might be recognized by kin and claimed. Of the burnings of houses and oubuildings, now by this band of nightriders, now by that one. Of the theft of livestock and crops, of torchlight lynchings. Her fear of the jayhawkers, Sally wrote, grew greater by the day. And her hatred.

By the summer of '58 there were four abolitionists for every pro-slave resident in Kansas. In a new election overseen by Federal troops the territory voted itself free. But the election did nothing to dissuade the vigilantes of both sides from raiding back and forth across the border, burning what they could and stealing whatever they might make off with, sometimes leaving men sprawled dead in their own fields or hanging from the trees.

Animosity toward Missouri was now so intense that the Andersons made a secret of their origins. "Used to be nobody's damn business where a man was from," Will Anderson said, "but the times being what they are, it's the first thing anybody wants to know anymore. From now on, somebody asks, we're from Union Kentucky." He looked hard at Bill and Jim. "The border scrapping's got nothing to do with us, you hear? Nor the big war that's coming. It's a war between rich factory owners and rich cottongrowers and we ain't either one or ever will be. Piss on the Yankees twice as much, but piss on the Virginia bigwigs too. It's their fight, not ours. The only thing the war's going to mean for us is better business. There's going to be more call for horses and they'll bring a better price. We don't stand to do nothing in this war but make money."

And so, when the nation went to war with itself in April of '61, the Andersons stayed put.

WAR NEWS, PROSPERITY, A TRIAL

A rustling foray never kept Will and the boys away from home for more than a few days before they were back with new stock to hide in their woods corrals—but with the advent of the larger war, Will would no longer leave his wife and daughters at home by themselves for as long as it took to get the herds to Missouri and come back. Although it was riskier to sell the rustled stock so close to home, there was no shortage of customers in the region. Newcomers were settling within a day or two's ride of the Anderson farm, and these homesteaders wanted good horses and few were particular about where they came from.

While the Andersons prospered in Kansas, the news from Missouri was mostly worse. The Yankees had an iron grip on Saint Louis and its huge arsenal—and had the fierce loyalty of its population, especially its Germans. The Union held the state capital. It had strong garrisons at all the key railheads and river ports. The Federal army had put the state under martial law and its citizens were required to "swallow the dog"—to swear loyalty to the U.S. government—and to post bonds in guarantee of their oaths. It was clear that the Union's grip in Missouri would not be easily broken—and clear as well that Missouri's allegiance in the war was fiercely divided. Although most Missourians were of southern ancestry, many of them were pro-Union. Neighbors all over the state had become bitter antagonists. Most wanted nothing more than to be let alone, to stay out of the war altogether. They might as well have wished for wings to fly themselves above it.

The only glad news from Missouri was of General Sterling Price and his State Guard, who that summer won a major battle against the Union at Wilson's Creek. But that good tiding was offset by reports of Jim Lane's jayhawkers. At the rich Osage River town of Osceola, they murdered citizens accused as friends of the Confederacy. They robbed the banks of their every dollar and loaded a train of wagons with all the property they could bear away. Three hundred jayhawks got so drunk they had to be carried on the wagons as well. As they made off, the reivers put the town to the torch and every building but three was burned to ash.

"We did good to come this far west," Will Anderson told his sons as they raised a cup to each other in celebration of Christmas Day. "Nobody in Missouri or within fifty miles of this side of the border is safe from that damn war. We did good to come this far west, I say."

His forecast of high profit proved true, and they were not shy about spending it. Will gave Martha a regular and handsome allowance to buy whatever pretties she desired for herself and the girls when the family went to town on Saturday mornings. The Anderson men now kept themselves in good boots and clothes, and Bill proved something of a dandy in his predilection for shirts with pleated fronts and ruffled cuffs and in his strutting delight in a broadcloth cloak he wore even to barn dances.

Jim japed him for his sartorial flamboyance but secretly conceded that Bill cut a dashing figure and now turned even more pretty heads than before. The brothers looked much alike—both lean and near to six feet tall, sharp-featured, their black hair down to their collars—but Jim envied Bill his easy way of looking at girls so that they'd smile even as they blushed and turned away and then kept sneaking glances at him.

They bought saddles, knives, firearms—were particularly taken with the .36-caliber Navy Colt revolver, a marvelous engine of uncanny accuracy. Weighing little more than half as much as the gargantuan Walker, it felt to the Andersons as light as a toy, and they could work it like a magic trick with either hand.

If any among the Agnes City storekeepers wondered about the source of the Anderson affluence, they kept their curiosity to themselves.

One Saturday morning as the family was getting ready to go home, a drunken muleskinner passing on the sidewalk muttered an indecency to Mary Anderson as she was stepping up into the wagon—and he made things worse for himself by patting her haunch. Mary turned to kick at the man, and Bill and Jim both started around the wagon to get at him, but Will had just come out of Mercer's Hardware and seen what happened and his newly purchased pickax was already describing an arc as he swung it with both hands. The curved iron blade drove through the man's spine and various vital organs and emerged through his front ribs to transfix him to the wagon sideboard. The wide-eyed corpse hung limply pinioned and dripping dark blood and drew gawkers and blowflies while the constable was searched out and fetched. Although several bystanders supported the family's account of the incident, Will Anderson was charged with murder and made to stand trial.

This was a time when Missourians stood little chance in a Kansas courtroom, but the Andersons had now long been passing for Kansans and were known to most storekeepers as free-spending patrons. The killed man, on the other hand, was a stranger for whom no witness could testify. It was rumored he was a border ruffian. Most of the jurymen, moreover, were fathers of daughters. They deliberated twenty minutes and voted for acquittal. That evening, the Andersons celebrated into the late hours with whiskey and music, dancing and song. And though Bill Anderson would forever be a Missourian in his bones, he would henceforth feel very much a man of Kansas too.

THE BERRY BOYS

Best friends to Bill and Jim Anderson were the Berry brothers—white-haired Ike, the elder by a year, and roanhaired Butch who had a way-ward eye. They were fellow Missourians out of Ray County whose family had arrived in this part of Kansas a few years after the Andersons, their father bent on getting clear of the violence back home. But two weeks before Butch's sixteenth birthday, Alston Berry went by himself into Emporia to pick up some harnesses he had ordered from Saint Louis, and in the course of things he found himself in a saloon where he entered an affray with three men later identified as jay-hawkers of Jim Montgomery. He was carried home in the blood-stained bed of his wagon and holding his bowels to himself where a jayhawker blade had slashed his belly. Their mother repositioned the entrails as she best could and sewed the wound closed and prayed over him and expected him to die. But he did not, and three months later he still lived, though the wound would never heal. Some days it seemed to be improving and then a few days later it would worsen once again. Yellow pus and watery blood seeped constantly from the suture. His pain rose and ebbed by intervals but was unremitting. It precluded him from sitting up for more than an hour at a time or sleeping through the night. Bedsores rooted into his back and but-tocks. The stench of the wound was unabating and different from the stink of the bedclothes, which his incontinence persistently soiled and which the two Berry sisters were ever washing and drying and chang-ing. He wasted to a coal-eyed skeleton hung with waxy skin. His voice was a raw croak each time he told his family he was shamed by his lack of courage to shoot himself and end the ordeal for them all.

The Berry boys made quiet inquiries, and over time they learned the names of the trio of jayhawks who had ganged on Alston Berry. On a dark night a month after their father's maiming, they hid them-selves in the bushes beside the Emporia house of one of those men. When he passed by a lamplighted parlor window they fired their

Sharps rifles and the thunderous muzzle flares illumined the bushes and the pair of .52-caliber bullets removed the top portion of the man's head and slapped it across the wall in a scarlet paste of hairy bone and brain. As the brothers ran through the shadows to their tethered horses they heard the rising screams of the man's wife and children.

Three weeks later they set up in the brush alongside the trace leading from Americus to the wooded cabin of another of the three jayhawkers. When the man came riding along in the last of the evening twilight they hupped their horses out onto the trail and forced him to rein up. The man thought they were highwaymen and said they would be fools to rob one of Jim Montgomery's men. If they had any sense at all they'd ride away right now and never show themselves to him again. Angelfaced Ike Berry smiled at him, his lank pale hair hanging to his collar. "Mister," he said, "we *promise* you won't never see us again." Then brought his Sharps up and shot him in the belly and the man went off his mount as though he'd been yanked from behind by a pullrope. They walked their horses to where he lay moaning in the grass, hugging himself tight, his knees drawn up. Butch Berry had his five-shooter in hand. He said "Hey!" and the man cast his eyes up and Butch shot him in the head.

The third man they were denied. He was killed in a drunken brawl in Topeka before they could attend to him.

Will Anderson was much impressed by the Berry boys' revenging of their daddy. He suggested they join him and his sons in the horse-brokering business. The Berry boys didn't have to think about it. They said they'd be proud to ride with them. Then proved quick to learn the trade and fearless in the practice of it.

Shortly after the first frost of autumn Alston Berry woke his wife with a strangled cry in the middle of the night and she fired the lamp in time to see his last breath rising palely on the chill air. The Andersons helped to bury him under a wide oak overlooking Wabaunsee Creek on a day denied all color by a leaden sky. Ike Berry read the passage from Matthew his mother had selected wherein men are reminded that the Almighty makes His sun rise on both the evil and the good and sends down His rain on the just and the unjust alike.

The next day the Widow Berry announced she'd had enough of

Kansas and Missouri too and was going home to Cross County, Arkansas, where she was born and still had plentiful kin. She would take both daughters with her. The Berry boys bought a covered wagon and an ox team and paid for a place for it in a small well-guarded train taking hides and corn and other goods to Saint Louis for shipment down to New Orleans. Their mother would sell the wagon in Saint Louis and then steam down to Memphis and ferry over to Arkansas. On a cold blue November morn, Ike and Butch stood at the trailside and waved goodbye to their mother and sisters as the teamsters cracked their whips and the train clattered into motion and the Berry boys never saw their women kin again.

A SISTER IN LOVE

As he'd grown to manhood Bill Anderson had naturally become acquainted with various farm girls of the region and he now and again enjoyed sportings with many of them. On two occasions, however, each with a different girl, an outraged father had suddenly come stalking into the barn in a rush of curses and brandishing a shotgun, and Bill had both times been obliged to take flight with pants in hand—once leaping from the loading door to a full hay-wagon below, the other time shinning down a ready rope, both times his good Edgar Allan saddled and waiting behind the barn. He was twenty and the girl fifteen on the second of these instances and it had been a very near thing. He forevermore would carry five blue shot-scars on his right buttock as a consequence of it. He enlisted his brother's raw doctoring skills to extract the pellets and repaid him for the service with a detailed account of the adventure.

Jim was sixteen by then and still untried with a woman, and he ached to remedy that sorrowful state. It happened that Bill had recently met a pair of sisters in Agnes City and needed somebody to occupy the one while he gave his attentions to the other, and so the first time he got together with the Reedy girls his brother was with him. Jim had afterward blathered about the experience so happily and at such length as he and Bill rode for home through the sunrise-reddening woods that Bill finally reached out and yanked his brother's hat down over his eyes and said that if he was going to keep talking so damn silly he might as well look it too.

They had been paying periodic visits to the Reedys for nearly two years now. The sisters had survived a smallpox plague in childhood that struck their whole family at once and carried off their father and enfeebled their mother and robbed her of all interest in the remaining world. The disease had left the girls with badly scarred faces, but they were both fullbreasted and slim of waist and so enthusiastic for sexual play that Bill and Jim hardly noticed their disfigurements. The girls helped their mother run a small cafe in Agnes City and lived with her in the upstairs flat. Every now and then Bill would get word to them that he and Jim would be in town on a given evening, and after the cafe closed and their mother shut herself in her room for the night, the girls would slip out and meet them in the alley below. They would repair to a spot beside a creek in the nearby woods and there put down blankets and share a bottle and generally have a fine time until just before dawn when they'd put their clothes back on and kiss goodbye until their next tryst.

Each time the brothers returned home from one of these all-night gambols, everybody at the breakfast table knew what they'd been up to. Their mother would fix them with accusatory tightlipped stares while their father grinned and usually made some remark about the rough day's work ahead for anybody who might not have had his proper rest the night before. Their eldest sister Mary could never help smiling either, even as she shook her head at them, and twelve-year-old Jenny would grin and waggle an admonishing finger.

Of their sisters, only Josephine, now fourteen, was unamused by their tomcat times in town, though she never expressed her disapproval vocally but rather by ignoring the two of them utterly for the duration of the breakfast meal.

On the dawn following their most recent night of sporting with the Reedys, the brothers arrived home still chuckling about their good time. They continued to talk about the frolic as they unsaddled Buck and Edgar Allan and rubbed them down and forked hay into their stalls and occasionally glanced toward the house lest their mother or one of their sisters be coming to fetch them and overhear their salacious talk and jesting. As they started out of the stable they heard a soft rustle around the corner and they pulled their Colts and ran out and saw Josephine dashing for the woods with her skirt hiked to her knees.

"I guess she got an earful," Jim said.

Bill Anderson stared out at the woods where she'd vanished into the shadows. "I guess," he said. He holstered his pistol and headed for the woods.

Jim watched him go. The whole family had long known that Bill and Josephine shared a singular kinship that excluded the rest of the world, but only Jim knew just how special that kinship had become.

From the time she was an infant Josephine had taken a special comfort from Bill that no one else could give her, not even their mother. She could be strident with crying and refusing Martha's teat and then eight-year-old Bill would take her up in his arms and she would immediately fall quiet and stare up at him in bright-eyed rapture. From earliest childhood she owned an independence of spirit and freedom of expression that sometimes prompted Will Anderson to threats of stropping her with a belt for her sass, though he never made good on them. Her mother, however, did sometimes order her to stand with her nose in a corner as a penance for her disrespect. Josephine could be scathing with her sisters, could drive Mary to a shrieking rage and little Jenny to tears—and yet every neighbor child learned early that to speak ill of either sister in Josie's earshot was to risk a severe thrashing.

Her only object of veneration was ever and always Bill. She loved Jim dearly and was never a smart-mouth with him except in obvious playfulness that he clearly enjoyed, but whenever Bill was nearby she had eyes for him alone. As she grew older she hurried through her daily chores so she could offer to help with his, or at least sit by and watch him tend to them. She hung on his words, was avid to learn whatever he would teach her about the ways of the woods and skies and rivers, about animals and people, about the Walker Colt she so admired. No discussion on any point however trivial could start up at the supper table but she would immediately cast her vehement opinion on Bill's side and only his raised finger signaling her to hush would save her from yet another session in the corner.

She liked to show him how strong she was by toting his tools or, as she grew bigger, by helping him to heft rocks or trim timber for a new fence. She showed off her good wit by memorizing some of the poetry he liked so well. He might be shirtless and dripping sweat and hammering out a red-hot horseshoe and she would sit close by and entertain him with renditions of his favorite poems. He would pause in his labor and applaud her at the end of each performance and she would beam proudly. Sometimes he joined her in the recitations as he worked, and sometimes Jim would be working with him and would chime in as well, all of them dramatically intoning passages about Poe's Annabelle Lee or Coleridge's Ancient Mariner.

Whenever he finished with some stretch of hard work she hastened to him with a towel and would insist on drying him herself. She could not get enough of touching him. From the time she was a small child she missed no opportunity to sit on his lap and cling to his neck and put her head on his chest. She had only just learned to walk the first time he placed her feet on top of his and danced her about the porch. She was four years old when he set her astraddle in front of him on a horse and held her tight to his chest as they galloped over the countryside and she had laughed with exultation as her hair flew back in his face. By the time she was twelve she could ride better than any woman and most men in the region, but she still delighted to have Bill swing her up in front of him on Edgar Allan and hold her tight and go riding tandem.

Although physically brave, she was from earliest childhood given to inexplicable anxieties. She was only five when a fierce winter storm woke her one midnight and upset her so much that she eased out of the bed she shared with her sisters in the loft and silently descended the ladder into the room where her parents slept and went out into the freezing wind in the dogtrot and then into the other room that contained the kitchen and the dining table and where her brothers slept on narrow bunks against the wall. She got under the covers with Bill and there slept snugly with her face nestled against his neck. The next morning her big sister Mary joshed her for a fraidycat and everybody grinned but she didn't care.

She thereafter made her way to Bill's bed every time she wakened in a late-night fright. Will and Martha were aware of this new practice from its start but only shrugged at it since the comfort she took from a night with Bill seemed also to ease her usual fantods and make her less inclined to sassiness—sometimes for weeks at a time. If cuddling to her big brother could calm her that much, it was fine with them. For his part, thirteen-year-old Bill didn't mind at all. "That girl puts out heat like a pony stove," he said at the breakfast table one morning after an ice storm had howled at the doors and windows through the night. He smiled at her and tousled her hair. "You're better than my own private hotbrick, girl." She grinned and grinned. But even when spring and summer came on, the nights were never too warm to discomfort him when thunderclaps brought her scooting to his bunk.

In the years after they moved to Kansas she continued to make her way to Bill whenever she had such fearful night wakings, and their parents seemed still to think little of it. Then one morning at breakfast Will Anderson looked up from his ham steak and corn-bread just as Josephine leaned over the table to refill his coffee mug and the front of her dress drooped to disclose small but ripely rounded breasts with nipples like raspberries. He cut his eyes to his breakfast to hide his rush of embarrassment. Later that morning he asked Martha how old the girl was now and was surprised to hear she was already thirteen—and then envisioned her breasts once again and marveled that thirteen was all she was. He didn't know what to think. In this day and part of the world, wives of sixteen were not uncommon, brides of fifteen hardly unknown. Martha sensed what was troubling him and confided that she had lately begun to wonder about Josie's habit of going to Bill's bed whenever she had the nightspooks.

"She's a child no longer, William," she said. "And Bill's for some time been a man. It ought to quit."

He could only nod in agreement and mumble that he'd talk to Bill about it.

A few days later when he and Bill were splitting logs, Will Anderson loudly cleared his throat and spat and looked all about to ensure they were alone and then told Bill about his mother's concern regarding Josephine.

"What it comes down to is, she ain't a little girl no more," he said. "It ain't fittin, Billy."

Bill leaned on his ax and looked perplexed. "Oh hell, Daddy, Momma doesn't think . . . I mean, Sweet Jesus, Joey's my little *sister.* I'd never *in hell* . . . you know . . ."

"Well of course not, goddammit. It's just your momma thinks . . . well . . . it ain't fittin. You know? It ain't"—he gestured vaguely—"*fittin.*"

Bill tamped the ground with the nose of the ax head. "No . . . I guess it ain't."

"I know she's special to you and it's hard to deny her," Will said. "She's always been prone to the jimjams but she takes ease from you and Lord knows she's one to have her way or know the reason why. I don't understand the first thing about her and won't pretend I do. Mary's always done like she's been told and never been one to back-sass, and little Jenny the same. But that Josephine, I swear . . ." He shook his head and again made the vague gesture.

"I'll tell her quit it," Bill said.

The next day as he was reinforcing a cracked windlass post she sat on the well rim to keep him company and he told her about his talk with their father.

"I guess they're right," he said, keeping his attention on his work as he talked but sensing the intensity of her gaze. "You ain't a baby anymore, you know."

He chuckled to try to make light of the matter but she was having none of it. She irritably brushed her brown hair from her eyes as if it hampered understanding.

"I can't go and hold to you the next time I wake up scared in the dark?"

"They don't think you ought," Bill said.

"What do *you* think?"

He turned and looked at her. She would always lack the social grace and the conventionally rounded prettiness of her big sister Mary, who was the only blonde of them. And she was certainly not the naturalborn beauty or charmer that little Jenny had already proved. But she was keenly striking in her dusky complexion and leanly supple form, her dark violet eyes. Since early girlhood she had carried a mysterious air that unsettled him even as it quickened his blood whenever she stared at him intently. As she now did.

He gave his attention back to the windlass post and said, "I think it's how it's got to be, Joey." He was the only one she permitted to call her by that nickname.

As he hammered a support board in place against the post he could feel her gaze still on him. Her fingers lightly brushed his forearm under his rolled sleeve but he kept his eyes on his work. When he looked up a minute later she was headed back to the house.

A few weeks later there struck a mean storm in the night and he was wakened by the crash of thunder. He listened to it for a brief while and then had just fallen back to sleep when he was waked again, this time by the press of Josephine against his back. He turned to face her and she hugged his neck tightly and her freshly washed hair was in his face and he could feel her trembling under her thin nightshirt.

"I told you quit this," he whispered.

"I just got to hold to you, Billy," she said. Her breath was warm against his neck. Their voices so low they could barely hear each other.

He raised his head and looked over at Jim's bunk and concentrated intensely but did not sense that his brother was awake.

"You're way too grown up to be scared of a storm, goddammit."

"I'll get back to my bed before anybody else wakes up," she said. "I can make myself wake up real early, you'll see."

"Joey . . ."

"*Biiillll.*" She hugged him tighter, snuggled closer into him.

Now one of her hands left his neck and gently stroked his face. He was still cleanshaved back then and her fingers felt cool on his cheeks and jaw. Then she searched out his hand and brought it to her hip and she whispered, "Hold to me, Billy. I'm scared."

He held her.

She sighed softly. "That's nice."

"Hush up," he whispered. He stroked her back and gently patted her bottom. "Go to sleep."

But they neither one went to sleep and after a time her hand was into his underclothes and found him as it had found him for the first time some months before. And just as he had not pushed her hand away then or any of the times since, he did not push it away now but only lay there in quickened pulse with her hand on him and felt her smiling against his neck.

"I know you like it," she breathed into his ear, her fingers moving gently on him. She kissed his cheek and caressed his neck with her free hand and just as they had first done those months ago they kissed softly and couldn't help smiling as they did. His hands went under her shirt and he felt of her small breasts and fondled her bottom and it was all they could to keep from giggling out loud with their pleasurable play.

It never went beyond that. He was sworn to himself never to let it go beyond the kissing and stroking and he would forever be true to the vow.

For her part, she at first seemed content enough with the limits he put on their game. But then came a new winter and she began easing to his bed sometimes even when she was unspooked. He had to make her promise not to do it more than once a week. By the light of the moon at the window they could see their breaths mingling palely. They huddled under his quilt and petted and kissed until they fell asleep in each other's arms. And then true to her word she always woke well before dawn and slipped away to her own bed as noiseless as a shadow.

One night when they lay together she whispered, "Let's do it, Billy."

He raised up on an elbow and gaped at her in the darkness. "What?"

"You heard."

He put his hand to her face and held it and whispered fiercely, "Never, never, *never*. Understand me, girl? *Never*."

"I saw Ike Berry and Ida Mullen doing it one afternoon on a horseblanket by the creek where I'd gone to get dandelions. I watched from the bushes. It looked fun."

"Nev-er!" he said through his teeth.

She had him in her hand and gave a quick hard squeeze and he gasped loudly and she giggled and they quickly clapped a hand over each other's mouth and he felt her grinning under his palm. They lay utterly still and listened and heard Jim toss and snort and mutter unintelligibly in his sleep and again settle into a deep and steady breathing.

She eased his hand away and whispered, "Why not? I love you, Billy. I'll never love no other man, not ever."

"*No.*"

"Why not?"

"It ain't done! Can't you get it in your wood head? It's the worst thing in the *world* a body can do is lay with his own blood. And don't make like you didn't know that. You *know* it."

"Even if they love each other more than they love anybody else or ever will?"

"Yes! Yes, *even.* Especially."

"How come?"

"Oh *Jesus* . . . It just—look, we're not going to do any such a thing, you and me, not *ever,* and that's an end of it."

She moved her hand on him and put her mouth to his ear and whispered, "Don't you *want* to, though?"

Yes he did—and he felt damned for the desire. And further damned for cavorting with her in even such restrained fashion as they did cavort. And damned worst of all by the perverse circumstance of being free to lay with women he loved not at all but denied by the laws of man and God from lying with the one he adored. He cared not a whit what might happen to his own soul—he was anyway no believer, not like his mother—but, because no one could say for certain what lay beyond the grave, he would not jeopardize the soul of his sister. And more than that: he would not risk implanting her with a child. An unmarried woman with child was a pariah, the child itself a pitiful woods colt. And still more than that: he had heard—as who had not?—so many terrible stories of children begat of incestuous coupling. Idiots condemned to a life of drooling witlessness and wallowing in their own filth and evermore requiring tending as closely as babes. Some born fingerless or clubfooted or blind, some with a roofless mouth or with the sexual organs of both male and female or with some other of a thousand horrifying afflictions. How could any woman who bore such a child—and it a bastard, to boot—not feel entered into hell even long before she was dead? He would not now or ever endanger his sister that way.

"I said that's an end on it, Josephine."

And it was. She knew better than to press an argument beyond his evocation of her Christian name.

Still, they had continued with their occasional nocturnal play through the rest of that winter and into the new spring and were so clever and careful about it that no one else in the family did suspect. Except Jim, who had come awake late one winter night and heard their low hissings and smothered giggles from Bill's bunk in the darkest corner of the room and felt his heart sink with misgiving. But as he strained his ears to catch bits and pieces of their low whisperings, he came to comprehend the limits of their game. He felt sorry for them for reasons he could not have made clear even to himself, but he had not told Bill—and never would—that he knew.

Thus, on the morning they spied Josephine running for the woods after she overheard their banter about the Reedy girls, Jim well understood why Bill sighed as he did and then went to the woods after her.

He found her in the meadow, sitting crosslegged at the creekbank in the shade of an oak. She was pitching pebbles into the water and did not look at him when he sat down beside her. Dragonflies wavered over the grass. The air smelled of creekwater and moss. A family of mockingbirds shrilled at them from their cottonwood nest. Sunlight filtered through the leaves and mottled the water surface and flashed on her hair.

She kept tossing pebbles. For a time he watched the splashes and the ensuing ripples, and then he began to skip stones along the surface with sidearm throws. After a particularly good fling that skipped a stone seven times he grinned and said, "Oh yes indeed!"

She snorted in disdain and searched the ground to both sides of her and found a small flat rock and tried its heft, then crooked her finger around it just right and got up on her knees and the tip of her tongue showed between her lips as she cocked her arm and threw. The stone left a trail of eight dimples on the surface before it sank.

She turned to him with a grin so beautiful his chest filled with fluttering birdwings.

He shrugged and said, "You always been better at it than me."

She quit the grin and studied him in her unnerving way and he looked off to the creek to elude her eyes.

"I don't know them Reedy girls you and Jimmy were talking about," she said, "but I hate them more than I can say. I guess there's others I could hate just as much for the same reason except I just don't know about them."

He turned to her and put his hand to her cheek and she held it there and nuzzled it.

"I hate that you can do with them what you can't with me," she said "I hate it, Billy. I *know* it's wrong, what I want, but I don't care and I wish you didn't either. But I'll always do like you say." She kissed his palm. "And I'll always and always love you."

He would know a number of grown women in his life who did not possess even a small portion of the grace his middle sister owned at the age of fourteen.

"I'll always love you too, girl," he said, and even as he made the declaration he recognized its unalterable and crushing truth.

A BETROTHAL

While Josephine could not reveal to anyone but Bill her desire for him—and therefore suffered her heartsore yearning in secret—her elder sister, just turned seventeen, was also in love that early spring and fairly beaming with the rapture of it. Culminating a whirlwind courtship of barely a month, Mary Anderson was now engaged to one Arthur Baker, a fine-featured and well-spoken man fifteen years her senior, a childless widower whose wife of eight months had been killed two years before in a fall from a horse. He and Mary had been introduced at an Agnes City dance and by evening's end he was already wooing her. He had since come calling at least two nights a week. When he tendered his proposal in the shadows of the Anderson porch on a soft evening winking with fireflies, she had no doubt about accepting.

Though he could play no instrument of music Baker sometimes joined in the Anderson harmonizings. Only once did he yield to their urgings to take a turn at stepdancing and then proved so comically awkward that none of them, not even reticent Martha, not even Mary herself who revered him, could keep from laughing at the spectacle he presented. The women apologized profusely but the Anderson men laughed and laughed and he was so thoroughly abashed he would never again trip the boards and they would never again ask him to.

Despite his ungainliness as a dancer, Arthur Baker was the sort of husband Will Anderson desired for all his daughters—a man of property. Baker's father had bequeathed to him a sprawling farm maintained by capable hired hands and he was in addition the sole proprietor of a prosperous supply store at Roan Creek Crossing on the Santa Fe.

He was not without formal schooling, albeit his learning was chiefly in the principles and tools of commerce. On his first visit to the Anderson farm he was asked by Bill who his favorite poet was and smilingly answered that he wasn't much of a one for poetry and preferred to leave that dainty subject to the ladies. His grin faltered under Bill Anderson's suddenly narrow gaze but Mrs. Anderson cleared her throat loudly and gave her son a look. Bill Anderson sighed and said "Never mind" and thereafter paid little heed to him until the time to come when he would kill him.

For her part, Martha Anderson commended Mary for her choice of husband and was unfailingly polite to Arthur Baker. Among themselves the other four Anderson siblings believed their mother secretly saw Baker for the same stiff-collar bore they did.

One evening while Mary sat out on the porch in Baker's company, the rest of the family was indoors preparing to make music, Will Anderson and his sons and daughters whispering jokes about Baker's collars and bowler hats and his ridiculous dancing. Finally, Martha made a shushing gesture at them and said, "Stop it, all you. The heart can't help what it wants."

The remark brought them up short in their tittering—and prompted a glance between Bill and Josie that did not escape Jim's notice. They all knew she was right. Mary had not lacked for prospects before meeting Baker but none of the suitors had struck her fancy. Yet neither was it in her nature to marry someone simply for the comfort of his holdings. There was no question she loved this man and no matter she hardly knew him. That none of them could understand why she loved him was no argument against the truth of it. The wedding was set for the second Sunday in June.

YANKEE CAVEAT

APRIL 21, 1862

IT IS REPRESENTED ON RELIABLE AUTHORITY . . . THAT BANDS OF . . . GUERRILLAS, MARAUDERS, MURDERERS, AND EVERY SPECIES OF OUTLAW ARE INFESTING TO AN ALARMING

EXTENT ALL THE SOUTHEASTERN PORTION OF JACKSON
COUNTY. . . . MURDERS AND ROBBERIES HAVE BEEN COMMIT-
TED; UNION MEN THREATENED AND DRIVEN FROM THEIR
HOMES; THE U.S. MAILS HAVE BEEN STOPPED; FARMERS
HAVE BEEN PROHIBITED PLANTING BY THE PROCLAMATION OF
A WELL-KNOWN AND DESPERATE LEADER OF THESE OUT-
LAWS BY THE NAME OF QUANTRILL, AND THE WHOLE COUNTY
DESIGNATED REDUCED TO A STATE OF ANARCHY. THIS STATE
OF THINGS MUST BE TERMINATED AND THE GUILTY PUN-
ISHED. ALL THOSE FOUND IN ARMS AND OPPOSITION TO THE
LAWS AND LEGITIMATE AUTHORITIES, WHO ARE KNOWN
FAMILIARLY AS GUERRILLAS . . . MURDERERS, MARAUDERS,
AND HORSE-THIEVES, WILL BE SHOT DOWN BY THE MILITARY
UPON THE SPOT WHEN FOUND PERPETRATING THEIR FOUL
ACTS.

JAMES TOTTEN
BRIGADIER GENERAL
CENTRAL DISTRICT, COMMANDING

RUMORS OF QUANTRILL

The larger war was now more than a year under way and the bush-
fighting along the Missouri border was reported to have grown
meaner. The Berrys occasionally rode to the Anderson place of an
early evening and joined them on the porch to share in a jug and the
latest news before taking supper together. On this occasion they were
speaking of the new company of border scouts the Federals had
formed, the redlegs, so named for the color of their Moroccan leggings. The outfit's captains were George Hoyt—a lawyer who had
vainly defended John Brown at his trial—and the hated Doc Jennison, who'd recruited many of his old jayhawker comrades to the
redlegs with him.

"I never thought I'd hear of a worse pack of bastards than those
reivers of Jim Lane's," Will Anderson said. "But I'll kiss all your
asses if these goddam redlegs ain't the ones."

"It was redlegs hung Ellsworth Mallory in front of his wife and
children down in Cass County last month because he wouldn't tell

where Quantrill was hiding," Jim Anderson said. "In the past two weeks they burned a half-dozen farms in Jackson for the same reason. I can't help but wonder if those farmers just wouldn't tell on Quantrill even if they knew where he was, or if they were just more scared of what *he'd* do to them if they did."

They had first heard of this man Quantrill two months ago and heard much more of him since. Of the various guerrilla bands harrying the Federals and jayhawkers along the border, his had been the most effective, his name become the most widely revered by Missouri rebels, the most despised by Union loyalists. Bushwhackers they were called, because the bush, the wildwood, was their hideaway, and their preferred tactic the ambush.

"I heard he ain't even from Missouri," Ike Berry said. "From Maryland is what I heard."

"I recent heard how come he hates the damn jayhawkers so much," Butch Berry said. "You all know why?"

Will Anderson snorted and said, "That's like asking do we know how come somebody don't like the smell of shit."

"Him and his big brother were headed for California when jayhawkers fell on them on the Santa Fe," Butch said. "Montgomery men. They shot him up bad and killed his brother and robbed them of everything, including their clothes and boots. Left him for dead, they did. But some old Indian come along and found him and saved his life. After he healed up he grew a beard for a disguise and took a false name. Pretended to be a Unionist and searched out Montgomery's party and joined up with them. He recognized those among them who killed his brother and he found out the rest of them over time. They say it took him months, but he killed every last one of them sonofabitches one by one when there was no witnesses about. More than twenty all told. That's how I heard it. Then he went on back to Missouri and started his band of raiders and been giving the Feds hell ever since."

Will Anderson spat over the porch rail. "I've heard that story. Sounds sham to me." He turned to Bill Anderson who sat puffing his pipe. "You reckon?"

Bill shrugged and stared out into the gathering gloom and at the first visible winks of starlight. His favorite dog Raven lay at his feet.

"Well, it's for sure no sham that neither the Federal regulars nor the jayhawkers have been able to run him to ground for all their trying," Jim said.

"He rode into Independence with not more than a dozen men and that town just full of Yankee soldiers," Ike said. "He took a ball in the leg and they shot his horse from under him and *still* he got away. Now that's a fact. A month later he had near sixty men in his company."

"For a fact he's raided into *Kansas*," Jim said. "Rode into Aubrey and shot up the place and stripped it clean and then took breakfast before he rode out again."

"I bet he didn't ask for hardboiled eggs," Butch said. "He already got him two goodsize ones."

"I've heard tell the Feds three or four times got him surrounded and were sure they had him and he gave them the slip every time," Ike said. "He and his boys have made off into the wildwood afoot as often as ahorse but they got away just the same."

"They ain't about to catch him," Butch said, "not out in the bush, and not with all them farmers helping to hide him and his boys. Feeding them, keeping them posted on where the Feds are."

"They're paying for it, though, them folks helping him," Will Anderson said. "The goddam Feds are coming down harder on them all the time."

"Momma believes Aunt Sally and Uncle Angus are maybe helping him," Jim said. "Aunt Sally doesn't come right out and say it, but I guess she's got to be careful what she puts in a letter. Can't know for sure who might read it sometime."

"Those Parchmans be damn fools to mix with bushwhackers," Will Anderson said.

"The harder the Feds come down on them who help Quantrill, the more run off to join him," Butch said. "Hell, they're singing songs about him."

"You all know he was a teacher?" Ike said. "They say he can speak in Latin. He can give a big long speech of Shakespeare as easy as you can sing 'Sweet Betsy From Pike.' "

"I know it," Jim said. "But I never knew a teacher who can shoot like they say he can. They say he can throw up four bottles at once and pull his pistols and bust all four before they hit the ground. I'd say that's some shooting."

"*I'd* say it's no damn wonder he's captain of that bunch of long riders," Butch said. "I mean, hell, the smartest, the best shot. Can ride like a damn Comanche they say."

"He's been a regular soldier too," Ike Berry said. "Before he become a bushwhacker. He was at Wilson's Creek with Pap Price. At Lexington too. They say he handled himself real admirable in both of them bad fights."

"Bad is the least thing those battles were," Jim said. "Wilson's Creek always did sound like windblown hell the way I've heard it."

Bill Anderson stood up and stretched hugely and gave a great yawn. He looked down at Raven who sat up and fixed his eyes on him. "I believe you are correct," he said to the black dog. He smiled around at the others and said, "Raven says all you boys sound like you found *religion.*"

For a moment they simply stared at Bill looming over them tall and lean in the thin yellow light from the porch window and then they all looked to the Raven dog that sat openmouthed with a dog grin. And then Will Anderson let out a great guffaw—and then they were all of them laughing and making jokes about a religion called the Sacred Church of Quantrill.

A few evenings later when the Berrys made their next visit and while the sky was yet daylit Bill Anderson left the porch and went around behind the house and then returned with two empty bottles in one hand and two in the other. He was wearing his Navies on his belt.

He stood well away from the porch so they all might have clear witness. He flung up his arms and all four bottles sailed high in the air and he drew the revolvers and there was a quick sequence of pistol cracks echoed by bursts of glass and no bottle did hit the ground whole.

The men cheered and whistled, stomped their boots on the planks. Behind them the Anderson girls had come out to watch and they applauded wildly while their mother stood in the shadowed doorway behind them unsmiling and with her arms crossed tightly over her breast.

Bill Anderson swept off his hat and bowed like a cavalier, then grinned around at them all and intoned, "The Holy Order of William T. Anderson welcomes ye one and all."

REQUIESCAT

Came an April daybreak when Martha Anderson was beset by a pain in her stomach and the affliction worsened through the morning. In the late forenoon Mary noted the strain in her mother's face and asked what was wrong. Martha gestured irritably and said she felt like she had a big bubble of gas in her belly she couldn't get shed of. Josie joked that she sure hoped for a warning before that gas came loose so she could quick scoot out of the kitchen. Mary gaped and said, "*Jo-sie!* You *aw*ful thing!"

Young Jenny giggled and Josie grinned at her and then said to her mother, "You reckon all that gas might come busting out so loud Daddy and the boys'll hear it at the corral and think it's a Yankee cannon firing at them?"

Jenny squealed with mirth behind her hands and Martha gave Josie a look of mock outrage and took a playful swipe at her with a dishrag and they all giggled even as they blushed.

Martha's pain persisted and by that afternoon she was sick at her stomach and began to feel weak and feverish. Her joints hurt. She had never been ill in her life and was as much vexed as distressed by this sudden malady. At supper that evening she ate but two bites before rushing from the table and out the door to throw up over the porch rail. The girls put her to bed and bathed her face by candlelight with a cool washcloth. Jenny offered to read to her from the Bible or a volume of poems but Martha waved away the idea. They placed a bowl close to hand and she was sick into it several more times that evening before she finally fell into a sweaty and fitful sleep.

They could fix on no cause for her sickness but the cup of milk she had taken that morning shortly after rising. No one else had drunk of that morning's milking. Now Will Anderson wondered if their cow might have fed on snakeroot.

"We ain't hunted out that damned snakeroot in a while," he said. "Could be some sprouted since we last cleared it. Son of a *bitch*!"

He went out to the barn and closely inspected the cow by the light of a lantern and determined that the animal was indeed infected, its milk poisoned. In the house they heard the shotgun blast. Will reappeared at the door and told Bill and Jim to bury the animal first thing in the morning. In order that his wife might rest more comfortably with the bed to herself he would sleep in the barn that night.

Martha began to moan in the later hours and the girls took turns sitting at her bedside and mopping the fever sweat off her face and neck. When Bill and Jim came into the room at daybreak she looked ghastly. Her mouth was tight with pain and she lay with her eyes closed and her hands pressed to her stomach. Her breathing was strained. The girls were redeyed and Bill and Jim offered to tend their mother through the morning so they might get some rest but the girls said they could manage all right. Will Anderson came in the house and stood over the bed and looked down at Martha for a time without saying anything and then he went out again.

She nevermore opened her eyes nor spoke another word. Just before noon she died.

Will took the front door off its hinges and set it on a pair of sawhorses in the center of the room and the brothers raised their mother's body from the bed and gently laid it on the cooling board. The men then went out and the girls set to washing and preparing their mother. They put her best dress on her and smoothed her features and brushed her hair and folded her hands on her breast. The brothers took turns digging the grave in the shade of a sycamore while Will constructed a coffin in the barn.

The only ones to join the family at the wake that evening were the Berry boys. Jim Anderson had carried the news to Arthur Baker, who sent his condolences and an explanation that he did not wish to intrude on the family's private grief and so would for a time refrain from visiting. Mary thought he was being overly solicitous, but Will told her the man was just being considerate and not to trouble herself about it.

At daybreak they placed Martha in the coffin and the men carried her out to the grave and settled her in it. Will deferred to Bill in the reading from the Psalms. He then spaded earth over the coffin until it was covered and then Bill and Jim took over and finished filling the grave. At the head of the gravemound they implanted a simple wooden cross which Will Anderson would replace in another week with a gravestone bearing an inscription he himself chiseled into it:

Martha Anderson
1823–1862
Beloved Wife and Mother

Following the burial the Anderson girls wept and comforted each other, but by sundown they had quit their tears and were busy with preparing supper for their father and brothers and the visiting Berry boys. The men passed the afternoon sitting on the porch and pouring cups from first one jug and then another and they now and then spoke in low voices of the war news from the border. When they came to the table all of them were slackfaced with drink. The Berrys were not such practiced imbibers as the Andersons and Ike periodically and abruptly would sway in his chair. Butch had difficulty finding his mouth with his fork and portions of his supper streaked his shirtfront. Despite themselves the Anderson men grinned at the Berrys' bewhiskeyment. Even the girls had to bite their tongues against smiling and all three blushed at their own failure to hold to a proper solemnity.

Midway through the meal Will refilled the men's cups and doled a splash of whiskey to each of the girls, even a wee one for Jenny, and then raised a toast to the memory of Martha Anderson and they all drank to her. By the time they were done with supper Will was telling affectionately funny stories about his twenty-three years of marriage to Martha and they all laughed at every tale. He was in the middle of another when he suddenly fell silent and looked all about as if thinking to catch sight of her somewhere in the room. Then stood and took his jug outside and told no more tales of her that night or ever again. The others traded looks over the table. Bill raised his brow in question at Mary. She leaned over the table and whispered, "We ought just let him be for now." They all nodded. Soon the girls were chatting in low voices about Mary's upcoming wedding and the pairs of brothers talking of the latest rumors of Quantrill.

And so their lives went on. Mary Anderson wrote a brief letter to their Aunt Sally in Missouri informing her of Martha's death. But in the following days widower Will became less inclined to conversation. He turned laconic, was distant at the family meals, detached even from talk of Mary's impending marriage. He had always enjoyed his jug at the end of a day's work but he now nipped from it the day long. They had sold all the horses from their last raid and Bill and Jim were keen to rustle up some more, but when they asked if they should get the Berry boys and go on a foray, Will Anderson said no, they'd wait a while yet, and he gave no explanation. The brothers grew disheartened at his seeming lack of interest in everything but his jug and his own morose company. Mary said he was still grieving. She said that whenever she watched him sitting in his porch rocker and staring out at nothing, she could just about see the sorrow holding to him like a chilly mist. They just had to wait a while longer, she said, before he'd get back to being his old self. But none of them had known him for a sentimental man, and so all of them were surprised by the might of his loneliness in a world lacking Martha Anderson.

A PROMISE BREACHED

Two weeks after Martha's burial Arthur Baker still had not come calling nor even sent word of when he might. With the wedding date barely six weeks away Mary wrote to inform him that he should again resume his visits and she looked forward to his help in completing the nuptial plans. Three days later one of Baker's hired men arrived with a sealed letter. The horseman spurred off again without asking if he should wait to carry back a reply.

Mary thumbed off the wax seal right there on the porch and laughingly spun away from Josie who wanted to read on tiptoe over her shoulder. But as her eyes sped down the page her smile withered. She looked up at the others, her face gone slack—and then hastened to read the letter again, her aspect abruptly desperate, as if she might have misunderstood it the first time. Then let the paper fall and rushed sobbing into the house.

Josie picked up the letter but Will Anderson snatched it from her. He read it slowly, then muttered "Shit" and handed it to Bill. Jim and Josie pressed in at his sides but Jenny was yet too short to see that high and said, "Let *me* see," and he lowered the letter to his belly so that she might read it too.

My dear Miss Anderson—

This is a most difficult Letter. In this bleak Period of Mourning, following the sorrowful Occasion of your dear Mother's Demise, I have had ample Time to reconsider carefully our Proposal to wed,—and the sore Truth of the Matter, dear Lady, is that I am as unready for Matrimony as a Man can be. You deserve the best of Men, which, I readily confess, I am not. Perhaps, one Day, should Fortune smile upon me, I might be worthy of the Affections of Someone at least in Part so fine and noble as Yourself. At Present, however, I lack such Worthiness. It is, therefore,—and with the deepest Regret,— that I hereby make formal Renunciation of our Betrothal.

I most deeply and humbly apologize for any Distress this Decision may impose upon you,—and I beseech you to be assured that my Affections toward you are, and have always been, most truly honorable and sincere.

> I remain,
> your humble Servant,
> Arthur I. Baker

"What in the *world* is he talking about?" Jenny said.

"The man's changed his mind about getting married," Jim said.

"I know *that*," Jenny said. "But how come?"

"Because he's an asshole," Josie said.

"Mind your mouth, Josephine!" Will Anderson said.

"Worthless shithead," Bill Anderson said softly.

"I believe I'll go whip his ass," Jim Anderson said.

"Do it, Jimmy," Josie said. "Go over there and kick him in the plums—if he's even *got* any damn plums, which I truly do doubt."

"*Josephine!*" Will Anderson said. "I won't have a woman of this family talking low."

"Well dammit, Daddy, it's just exactly what somebody ought to do to him!"

Will Anderson glared at her. Jenny put an arm about Josephine's waist and whispered, "Quit now."

Will Anderson hawked and spat. "He's a weak excuse for a man, all right, and I'm sore disappointed to learn it," he said. "But I ain't never in my life held with forcing a man to marry a woman except if he got her in the family way, and all this one's done is change his mind about getting married. He gave his word and broke it and proven himself for a shithead, and I'm sorry for Mary—Lord knows I am—but it ain't a thing to draw blood over."

It was the most they'd heard him say at one time since they'd buried their mother. They had grown used to his taciturn and melancholic mood, but his voice now seemed strained, as if he didn't believe his own words, as if he were uncertain of purpose, he who had not hesitated to impale a man with a pickax for touching his daughter.

Will Anderson rubbed his face and sighed tiredly. "I ain't been keeping out of the war with the Union just to get into one with some peckerwood for crawfishing on a marriage promise," he said. He fixed Bill and Jim with a stern look. "We couldn't win it no way. If we kill him we'd have to stand trial or run. The man's got friends all over and the jury'd be full of them. And I've run enough. So that's an end on it."

Mary Anderson wept all that day and night, but by the following morning she had settled her mind about the situation and penned a brief note to Arthur Baker without salutation or signature:

> The sooner you drop dead, the sooner you will go to hell—and the sooner I will rejoice.

Thus did the matter seem concluded. Until a Sunday evening two weeks later when the Berry boys came by with an interesting tale to tell. They had recently made a visit to Miss Juliette's house of pleasure in Emporia some thirty miles southeast of Agnes City, an establishment they deemed to be worth every mile of the ride. The Anderson brothers were known to Miss Juliette's girls too, having patronized the place now and again for a change from the Reedy sisters. It was only natural that the whores the Berrys consorted with— a frolicsome pair named Ida and Brenda—would inquire after Bill and Jim, and only natural that the girls, vast repositories of gossip and rumor, had heard of Arthur Baker's jilting of Mary Anderson. They thought it was a damn shame, the fella asking Mary to marry him just because he was having a tiff with another girl and then throwing poor Mary over when he made up with the first one, who happened to be the sole daughter of a rich daddy and whose only brother was a born halfwit. Thus did the Berrys learn of Arthur Baker's betrothal to Clara Segur, daughter to John Segur, a horse rancher in Lyon County. Three weeks ago, Segur had invited all his friends to his ranch for a picnic in Baker's honor and there announced Clara's engagement to him.

As Ida and Brenda told it, Baker had started courting Clara back in autumn, but he hadn't yet proposed to her when they had a quarrel of some kind in February and stopped seeing each other. That was when he met and began calling on Mary Anderson. The gossip conveying from the Segur ranch was that Clara knew he was visiting some girl who lived near Agnes City, but she thought he was only trying to make her jealous. When she heard about his engagement to the Anderson girl, however, she thought he might be angry enough to go through with it if she didn't act fast, so she wrote him a long and sweetly apologetic letter. Shortly afterward came her daddy's picnic and his announcement of the engagement.

"This is the same fella who wrote to Mary he's unready for marriage as a man can be," Jim Anderson said sardonically. "Bastard went and got engaged to that other girl before he'd even broke it off with Mary."

"I never met the shithead myself," Butch said, "and he best hope I never do."

They were sitting on the porch, each man sipping from his own jug, and they were all a little drunk but for Will, who was very drunk, having been drinking since morning. Now his face was drawn, his eyes gone narrow and bright and fixed on some outraging vision in his head.

"There's more," Ike Berry said. "Somebody asked Baker where you all were from, and he said Kentucky, but somebody else said you were from Kentucky like Abe Lincoln was from Atlanta. Said he knew for a fact you all were from Missouri and so he could hardly blame you for lying about it. The way the story goes, Baker was mighty put out. He said marrying into a family of pukes would've been the most shameful thing he ever did."

For a moment no one spoke, and then Jim Anderson said, *"Pukes?"*

They held silent again for a time before Will Anderson said, "His wife's got no sisters and but one brother and him a softbrain. So I guess everything belonging to his new daddy will be his some day."

His words were slurred but clear enough. The others exchanged looks.

"All that good horseflesh this Segur fella's got," Will said, "it'll someday belong to Baker, won't it?" He took a deep pull off his jug. "Well, I believe we maybe ought slide on down there and lay claim to some of those horses Baker's due to inherit. I believe it'd be nothing but proper settlement for the man's goddam breach of promise."

His grin was reflected in every face.

A FORAY

They did not wait for a moonless night nor even until they were sober. Will had intended to accompany them, but he was so rough in bridling his horse that he frightened the animal and the spooked horse shied hard and knocked him down. He had to be restrained from attacking it with his fists. Bill and Jim ushered him back to the porch and sat him there and put a jug in his hands and assured him they could manage the rustle without him. Then they were mounted and on their way.

The Berry boys knew where Segur's ranch lay and the four of them rode hard to the southwest under a high half-moon of polished silver. They passed a bottle among them as they rocked along in their saddles and they drank and made jokes and laughed into the warm night wind pushing back their hatbrims.

Just before midnight they crested a low hill and hove up and saw below them a moonlit herd they guessed to number a hundred head milling on a grassland the Berry boys said was Segur's north pasture. They spied no campfire to indicate a guard camp. Had they been less drunk they would have scouted for guards more carefully. If they'd spied any, they would have sent one man around to the far side of the herd to create a distraction and lure away the lookouts while the other three swiftly cut out horses from the unguarded side and made off with them. If necessary, the decoy could have fired in the air to frighten the remaining herd into stampeding and occupy the guards in rounding it up while the gang got away clear. That's how they would have done it had they not been quite so drunk.

They hupped their mounts forward and rode down to the herd and began to cut out horses. They were laughing and loudly admiring the fine quality of the animals when Butch shouted, "Riders!"

They were ten or more, at a distance of about a half-mile and coming at full stride in the moonlight over a bare western rise.

"Damn," Bill Anderson said, suddenly much sobered. He heeled Edgar Allan around to the east and yelled, "Go!" As they galloped away they fired in the air to spook the herd into a clamoring stampede for the open range to the south. Most of the pursuing riders swung off to chase down the horses, but some kept coming behind the rustlers.

Far ahead, the low silhouette of a line of hills showed blackly against the weaker darkness of the sky and Bill Anderson led them toward it. Pistolshots cracked behind them. He heard Ike Berry yell and turned to see him slowing up and looking rearward. Jim's horse had been hit and had slowed to an awkward stagger—and now he slid off the saddle just as the Buck horse collapsed. Butch Berry had already turned around and was headed back.

Bill and Ike reined up so short their horses almost sat. They watched Butch and the pursuers closing on Jim from either side.

"They're coming hard," Ike said.

"Shoot the horses!"

They opened fire on the four chasers as Butch slowed his horse and leaned from the saddle with his hand outstretched and Jim caught it and swung up behind him. The lead chaser was almost on them, his pistol sparking—and then his mount abruptly plunged groundward and both horse and rider went flailing past them in a shrieking raise of dust.

Then Butch was heeling his horse past the sprawled animal kicking crazily on its side and he just missed trampling the felled man gaping up at him as they went by.

Bill and Ike kept shooting at the other chasers and another horse went down and its flung rider somersaulted over the ground with arms and legs slinging every which way. As Jim and Butch galloped past their brothers the last two chasers chose the wiser course and quit the contest, turning away and ducking low in their saddles while Bill and Ike fired at them with their second pistols.

"Let's go!" Bill hollered, and they set out after their brothers.

RESPITE

"You *sure* it was Bobby Raines?" Bill Anderson said.

"As sure as it's you standing there," Jim said.

"He know you?"

"He knew me. It was all over his face he knew me."

"In moonlight? As fast as it went?"

"If I knew him, Bill, he knew me."

They were camped by a narrow creek in a dense woods some dozen miles eastward of Agnes City. After crossing the hills aflank of Segur's rangeland they had borne north for this good hiding place and arrived as the red sun rose up hugely on their right. Now shafts of dusty yellow light leaned through the looming elms and sycamores, and the brothers had seen to their lathered horses and let them water at the riverbank. They had carefully explored the animals for wounds and discovered that Butch Berry's horse had a ball in its chest. The round wasn't deeply embedded and Butch extricated it with a pocketknife and then packed the lightly bleeding wound with a bandage of river mud.

The Bobby Raines they spoke of had been a wrangler for some years on a ranch west of the Anderson farm. Both Anderson brothers were acquainted with him and they had all taken an occasional mug of beer together. A year ago he received notice that his father had died and left him the family farm and so he'd headed back home to Texas. They had not thought of him since—not until last night, when he had stared up wide-eyed at Jim and Butch even as he crabcrawled out of the way of their horse.

"I guess he couldn't tolerate Texas," Bill said.

"Don't rightly blame him," Butch said. "Our daddy used to tell this story where he woke up drunk one morning and didn't know where he was. It was so hot and dusty he couldn't hardly draw a breath. He thought he'd died and gone to hell but turned out he was only in Texas."

"Maybe he'd ruther wrangle for wages than bust his back on a farm," Jim said. "Even his own."

"Can't fault him for that either," Bill said.

"Of all the shit luck," Ike said. "The only fella of them who knows you is the one to get a good look. Will he let on to Segur, you think?"

"Why wouldn't he?" Bill said. "We're only somebody he drunk beer with. Segur pays him."

"What do we do, Bill?" Jim said.

"Stay put," Bill said. "I'll wager there's a bunch of Segur's boys headed for the house this minute."

"Daddy'll tell them a tale," Jim said, "but they won't believe the first word of it."

"No, they won't," Bill said, "but they got no quarrel with Daddy. They might stay close by the house for a day or two watching for a sign of us. If we wait them out they'll get bored and go home."

"They're bound to tell Sheriff Horner about this," Ike said, referring to the sole lawman in Agnes City.

"So what if they do?" Bill said. "It's only Bobby's word against all ours. We got no worries with the sheriff."

"You really think they'll head on back when they don't find us at home?" Jim said.

"They won't hunt too long for fellas who didn't get away with even one damn horse," Bill said. "From now on he'll put more men on night watch and we'll keep our business north of Americus. That's all that'll come of this."

So they stayed put. Later in the day Ike shot a large doe just a few yards into the trees and Jim helped him to drag the carcass into the clearing. They butchered it and roasted it over a low fire and gorged themselves to greasy satisfaction on the backribs and cut the rest into strips for smoking. That night the moon was hidden in thick clouds and Bill rode out alone and far into the open country. He bypassed the first two farms he came upon, regarding them as too near their camp. Ten miles farther on, he came to a ranch where he spied a cor-

ral containing several fine horses. Just before dawn he was back in
camp with a fine blood bay to replace Jim's appaloosa. He'd even
prowled into the barn and found a saddle for the animal.

They passed that day and the next telling stories, napping, tending to guns and horses. They bathed in the creek, washed their
clothes and hung them to dry on the trees. At daybreak of their third
day in hiding, Bill sent Butch Berry to the Anderson farm to see how
things stood.

THE SEGUR PARTY

He had sobered but little when Mary came running from the springhouse to inform him of the riders. Sprawled in his porch rocker he
squinted in bemusement as she stood over him babbling excitedly.
Then he heard the hooffalls and looked to where she was pointing,
where the trace debouched from the woods, and saw them coming
out of the reddening trees of the late afternoon. More than a dozen
and most with a rifle in hand.

He stood up and felt a nudge at his side and there was Josephine
with his twinbarreled shotgun. "I checked it's loaded," she said low-
voiced. Behind her back she held Bill's fully charged Walker, its massive heft familiar for her shooting lessons with it.

He held the shotgun crosswise at his thighs like an ax-wielder
paused in his labor and watched the riders coming at a trot, every
man of them looking sharply about for telltale of lurking ambush.
He did not recognize any of them and thought they might be jayhawkers who had found them out for Missourians. Two broke off
from the group and hupped their horses to the barn to have a look
within.

Josephine felt Jenny press up close and she cut her eyes to her little sister and whispered, "We ain't scared even a little bit and don't
you let them think we are."

The riders reined up in a loose line in front of the house so each
man's view of the door and windows was unhampered. Their horses
blew and stamped nervously. Most of the longarms were Sharps and
there were several Texas Colts in evidence among the belt weapons.
Every gaze was wary and hard, but Will Anderson saw no killer's

eyes among them. He intuited they were not jayhawkers but a posse of local lawmen and ranchers with a rustling grievance.

"You be Will Anderson?" The man to speak sat his horse directly before the porch steps. He was lean and gray but not much weathered and wore a closely trimmed mustache.

"Who's asking?" The man slipped the barest bit out of focus and Will forced his face to convey alertness, the better to conceal the whiskey haze in his head.

"John Segur. I own a place south of here, down near Americus. Rustlers tried to cut out some of my horses last night and my men chased after them. Two of my boys got their horses killed. One of them is laying paralyzed in the legs from the fall he took. Bobby here"—he pointed to a young man with an arm splinted and in a sling—"got a look at two of the thieves. One he don't know but one he does. If you be Will Anderson, the one he knows is your son, the one they call Jim."

Segur paused as if he would hear Will Anderson's protest but Will held silent. He kept his eyes on Segur and his only thought of the moment was that if this man told him either of his sons was dead he would blast him to hell in two halves and damn what came next. Now the men who had gone to the barn rejoined the party and one shook his head at Segur.

"I guess your boys ain't home," Segur said. He fixed a narrow look on the dark open doorway for a moment, then said, "Can you say where they might be?"

Will Anderson slowly shook his head. He felt the porch sway slightly with the gesture.

"Texas!" Josephine said. "They been in Texas for weeks and weeks so it wasn't them."

John Segur turned to her. She spat and fixed him with a cold stare. His aspect stiffened.

"I don't care a damn what reason a man might have for thinking he can steal from me," he said. He glanced at Mary and she felt herself flush with angry humiliation. His horse tossed its head to shake off a deerfly and he reined it still and patted its neck. "Artie Baker told me he suspicioned your boys were horse thieves and it appears he was right. If they're still around, you tell them I been to the law and there's warrants for them. If they got any sense at all they'll clear out and truly go to Texas or back to goddam Missouri where they come from. That's all the warning I'll ever give them."

He reined about and hupped his mount forward and his men followed after in a clattering lift of dust. Then they were into the woods and gone.

Josephine stalked the porch and muttered curses and felt the Walker's weight in her hand like a mean dog straining at its leash. Mary held Jenny to her. Will Anderson stared into the yellow dusthaze lingering at the edge of the woods. The hoofbeats of the parting horses had faintly quivered the planking under his bootsoles, but even after the riders were gone he felt the trembling yet.

WHISKEY AND BLOOD

His night was sleepless. He sat on the porch with the shotgun propped close to hand and a jug on his knee and stared out at the blackness sparking with fireflies. His thoughts caustic and fearful. He told himself to refrain from rash act, that he'd had enough of rashness in his life. To hell with Baker and with Segur too. Yankee sons of bitches didn't rate notice and never mind their goddam mouths. . . . Unless they did harm to his sons . . . If they put the law on his boys . . . But they'd have to catch them first, and that would be a job. . . . Nothing mattered but that his sons avoided harm and capture. The family could resettle elsewhere. . . . Texas . . . Texas was the place.

Such were his ponderings in the passing night as he drained one jug and began on another, waiting to be informed if his sons were dead or alive, seized or at large.

At daybreak Mary came out with a cup of coffee and set it beside his rocker, but when she returned a half-hour later with a tinplate of ham and cornbread the coffee stood cold and untouched.

"Daddy, eat something."

He gave her no notice. She took up the coffee and left the food in its place by his chair and sometime later found the tinplate spotless and knew one of the dogs had been at it. Sometime later, Josie came out to look at him and then went back in the house and told her sisters there was nothing to do but to let him be. They heard the resentment in her tone. A father ought not to get drunk when he was the only man around to protect his daughters.

Josie had looped a cord through the Walker's trigger guard and the weapon hung ponderously from her neck like an awful responsibility. Mary was three years her elder but was feeling like a child beside her. The three of them took turns sitting by the front window where they could keep an eye on their father even as they watched the trail at the edge of the woods in hope that their brothers would show up and in fear the Segur men would come back.

Will Anderson's bewhiskeyed mind is a whirl of visions to which attach no clarities of thought, although each image is starkly vivid and each in its turn evokes a sovereign sentiment. Now he sees Segur sitting his horse and flanked by his henchmen, again hears him make threat on his boys, and again tastes a bilious resentment through the mash on his tongue. Now he catches sight of Bill and Jim hanging by their necks from a tree in some desolate landscape ruled by crows and again feels his heart flail with fear. He envisions young Martha in the moonlit window of her parents' house saying yes she will go with him and be married in Saint Louis, and his chest goes hollow as a waiting grave. He once more perceives Arthur Baker courting Mary under the Anderson roof and telling his smiling lies, again sees the man's letter and its oily mendacities, and again seethes in his injured honor. One vision follows another before his inward eye, round and round and then round again, all through the morning as he takes drink on drink.

The sun is at its meridian when one of the passing images fixes in his head as suddenly and securely as the bobbling ball falls into a slot on the turning roulette wheel. The vision is of Arthur Baker. Will Anderson sets down his jug and stares hard at the trees beyond the sunbright cornfield but he is seeing only Baker. But for Baker's lies to Mary she would not be in her misery. But for the injury to her heart, his sons would not have set upon stealing Segur's horses. But for that rash rustling foray, Bill and Jim would not now be wanted men and in peril of their lives, nor he himself feeling his world spun out of control. . . .

The force of this besotted epiphany suffices to launch him from his rocker and he totters for an instant at the earth's wild reel beneath him. Then steadies and grabs up the shotgun and lurches down the steps and rushes staggering to the stable. Mary cries from the window for him to come back. Jenny's face is wide-eyed and gaping beside hers. Josephine bounds to the door, sensing in her soul some vague but horrible misfortune to come from whatever manic mission he is bent on, some catastrophe to befall them all unless he is stopped right now. In her terror she raises the Walker in a two-hand grip and puts the nub of the front sight on his distancing back and cocks the piece. She hears her sisters shouting at her as she holds the trembling gunsight on him and feels the trigger under her finger. And then he is into the stable and she lowers the revolver and thumbs down the hammer. Her sisters gape on her with horror—then rush to her to hug her tight. They are clutching to each other as his horse bursts from the stable with his heels in its flanks. He heads for Baker's house with shotgun in hand and no thought at all but that if Segur is there he will kill him too.

Arthur Baker's farm lies a mile north of his Santa Fe Trail store and some dozen miles from the Anderson place. On this midday he is in his upstairs den attending to some business papers, pausing now and then to reflect on lovely Clara and his wedding to her just five days hence. Now he hears a pounding of hooves drawing nearer and his curiosity is piqued, for his farm is a placid place where even a galloping horse is a rare excitement. He goes to the window and sees a rider trailing a plume of dust and coming hard down the road. A pair of men digging postholes pause to stare after the horseman in the risen haze. The rider turns off the road and onto the lane to the house and Baker now recognizes Will Anderson and sees the shotgun in his hand—sees him rein up almost directly below his window and slide out of the saddle and lose his footing and go sprawling and one of the shotgun's barrels discharges its crunching load into the side of the house and Baker feels himself flinch and his breath wedges in his throat.

Will Anderson scrambles to his feet, snarling and cursing, and lurches out of sight under the porch roof. Near to panic, Baker hastens to the guncase against the wall and takes up a singlebarrel shotgun and checks the load, which almost falls out of the breech for the violent trembling of his hands. He steps into the hallway as a downstairs door crashes hard against a wall in a thunderous shatter of glass. A high shriek from the housekeeper and low cursing from Anderson. Baker's legs tremulous as he waits at the top of the walled and L-shaped stairway. Anderson's maledictions louder, his boots stomping on the lower leg of the stairs. He appears on the middle landing with the shotgun at his waist and looks up and his red clenched face loosens in surprise to see Baker standing there with his own shotgun at the shoulder.

The walls jar with the blast of Baker's weapon and the compact load of buckshot enters Will Anderson at a point between the left shoulder and the neck and breaks apart the clavicle and several upper ribs and bores through the torso at an angle traversing an assortment of organs including the heart and both lungs and bursts out just above the right hip to splatter a thick mortal portion of him over the wainscoting. Will in a spasm jerks the trigger of the other barrel and detonates a fistsized hole through the landing wall and then his shotgun clatters as he topples backward to sprawl head-down on the lower stairway, his eyes wide but forever done with seeing. Blood rolling from his gaping wounds and sopping his hair and cascading down the steps to shape a bright gleaming pool on the wooden floor. All amid the housekeeper's continuing screams.

RIDDANCES

Butch Berry sat his horse and kept hidden at the edge of the woods as he regarded the Anderson house across the open patch of ground this warm and cloudless midday. Smoke swirling from the kitchen chimney. Chickens pecking in the dirt and the pigs snortling in the wallow. Will's rocker stood empty on the porch. Butch thought the elder Anderson might be sleeping—or passed out, the way the man had been drinking lately.

He had been riding hard all morning since departing the camp at daybreak and had not yet eaten. He hoped the girls had something tasty simmering in the cookpot. He chucked his horse forward and out of the woods and rode up to the house.

He hallooed loudly and dismounted at the front porch and slung the reins round a post. As he started up the steps two men came out the door with cocked pistols pointed at him. Another showed himself at the window and held him in his riflesight. Butch Berry stood fast.

One of the pistolmen ordered him to cross his arms and then took his revolver off his belt and then reached down and removed his bootknife as well. Voices rose up behind and he turned to see a group of men gathered at the door of the barn and looking at him, all of them armed with long guns and one with his pant leg cut open to the knee and showing a bandage above his boot.

The man who'd disarmed him now prodded him into the house with a pistol muzzle at his spine. In the center of the lamplit room a body lay on planking set across sawhorses. It took Butch Berry a moment to recognize the colorless waxen face as that of Will Anderson, who now bore but a vague resemblance to the living man. His hair looked stiff and mudcaked and then Butch understood that the crusting was dried blood.

The sisters were seated on the other side of the body and all three staring at Butch—Jenny weeping softly and Mary redeyed and drawn, Josephine tightlipped, her aspect more outraged than bereaved. Moonfaced Sheriff Horner of Agnes City, a man of amiable and fair reputation, sat over coffee with two men at the table on which lay Bill Anderson's Walker Colt with a cord looped through the trigger guard. One man lean and grayly mustached. The other Arthur Baker, whose eyes could not hide his fear.

The lean man pushed an empty chair out from the table with his foot. "Sit," he said. "We got a proposition for the Anderson boys. You and your brother too. Hear it out careful and then take it to them."

By sundown he was back at the camp. As soon as they saw his face the Anderson brothers knew the tiding was bad.

The news of their father's death stunned them all the more for Arthur Baker being the instrument of it. That clumsyfoot fop of a storekeeper.

"Sheriff Horner's calling it self-defense plain and simple," Butch Berry said.

Bill Anderson poked at the fire with a stick, his face a wavering red mask in the firelight, his brother Jim's the same.

"I guess I know what you boys are thinking," Ike Berry said. "It's only natural. For a fact, me and Butch didn't let them sonofabitches slide who cut up our daddy. But this is different. They got your sisters there. They got your daddy who needs burying."

Jim Anderson spat into the fire.

"Ike's telling you right," Butch Berry said. His wayward eye seemed more pronounced in the firelight.

The Andersons exchanged a look in which each recognized in the other's eyes how much the world was changed by the fact of their father's removal from it. And in that look they pledged to set the matter right in its proper time.

They sent Butch back that evening with acceptance of Segur's offer—backed by Sheriff Horner's assurance—of their safe passage to come home and bury their father and then go away to Missouri with their sisters and whatever belongings they cared to take with them. The rustling warrants on them would be put aside. In exchange, the Andersons agreed never to return to Kansas. As the Berry boys were now known members of the rustling party, they too had to swear they would keep out of Kansas henceforth.

Butch was on the porch the next morning with the Anderson girls, the sheriff and Segur when Bill and Jim appeared out of the woods and rode up to the house. Arthur Baker was in the barn with several of his armed men about him and would not show his face throughout the proceedings.

The Anderson family's two wagons—one covered and one not—stood before the house, each already hitched to its brace of mules and bearing what possessions the sisters had selected to keep, and so the remaining business did not take long. There was little talk beyond the girls' weepy greetings as they embraced their brothers. Bill informed the sheriff that he would not dishonor his father by burying him in Kansas but would take the body back to Missouri.

The sheriff squinted at this news and took a quick look back into the house where the body yet lay on the planking. "It's a long ways to Missouri and he's already dead two days."

Bill Anderson looked at him without expression. The sheriff shrugged. "Hell, he's *your* father."

The Anderson brothers rolled the body in a blanket and tightly tied off the ends of the shroud and carried the corpse to the wagon in which Josephine sat and they laid it on the open bed. Josie leaned down to whisper in Bill's ear, then Bill looked at Segur on the porch and said, "I'll have that pistol you spirited out of the house."

Segur stood with his thumbs hooked in his belt and regarded Bill without expression. Sheriff Horner cleared his throat loudly and spat off the porch. Segur glanced at him, then shrugged and stepped down and went to his horse. He probed in the wallet behind the cantle and withdrew the big Walker and handed it to Bill who passed it up to Josephine. She checked to see that all the chambers were charged and then held the piece in both hands with the muzzle skyward and looked to the barn and said, "Sheriff, why don't you call that Baker fella to step up to the door there a minute?"

The sheriff's mouth and Segur's too came ajar. She showed Bill a quick grin and then laid the pistol beside her. He chuckled and got into the wagon and took up the reins and slapped them over the mules' haunches and the wagon lurched into motion with loud creakings and clatter. Jim brought the covered wagon up behind, Mary and Jenny seated beside him, and the Berry boys followed on their mounts and with the Anderson horses on lead ropes.

"Where's the dogs?" Bill said low to Josephine.

"Raven got hold of one of them sonofabitches by the leg and wouldn't let go till they shot him," Josephine said. "They shot Mariner too. I guess they shot them all."

The Segur men watched them go by. In the first moments the only sounds were the rattlings of the wagons and the falling of hooves. Then someone hollered, "And *stay* gone, you goddamn pukes!"

Much guffawing and epithets and curses, a chorus of derision raining on the Anderson party as their wagons headed for the woodland trace. The brothers Anderson and Berry bit hard on their fury and kept their eyes ahead, refusing to give any show of insult or even of hearing. Mary and Jenny sat close together and admonished each other to be brave.

Only Josephine would not endure their taunts. She turned around on the wagonseat and yelled, "Everybody knows there's three kinds of suns in Kansas—sunshine, sunflowers and sons of bitches—and none of you look like a sunbeam or a blossom to me!"

A few of the men laughed at her spunk, but most were enraged by the profane mouth on this slip of a girl and they came back at her with a torrent of the rawest cursing. One man flung a stone and it came near its mark, whacking on the inner side of a wagonboard and ricocheting against the shrouded body of Will Anderson. Josie clambered into the bed and grabbed up the rock and flung it back with fine form, scattering the bunch of them like spooked birds.

"Jesus! Little bitch can *throw*!"

Some of them started hustling after more stones, but from the porch Sheriff Horner hollered, "No rockfighting, goddammit!" The men said "Ah sheriff" and grudgingly lobbed their rocks aside.

As the wagon turned onto the trace, Josephine stood swaying in the jolting bed and bellowed, "*Shitheads!* Kansas *shit-heaaads*!"

Then their wagon was around the bend and behind the trees and Bill said, "All right, girl—hush up and sit down before you fall and bust your ass. I guess you told them."

She settled back onto the seat and snuggled against him and held his arm tightly with both of hers. "I know you just want to be sure me and Mary and Jenny are safe someplace before you and Jimmy come back here and kill that Baker son of a bitch," she said, this Josephine Anderson who was fourteen years old.

"Listen to *you*—such a young girl talking about killing."

"I can't help it I'm a girl, and killing is just exactly what he's got coming. And I'm not *that* young."

He looked at her sidewise and smiled.

"We're not done with Baker, are we, Billy?"

"*We*? Well, *we* gave our word not to come back to Kansas."

"Don't shine me, Billy Anderson. I know as good as you a man's word only holds when he gives it to a man worth having it."

He chuckled. "That's what Daddy always said. I didn't know you ever listened to him."

She glanced back at the body in the wagonbed and said softly, "I listened sometimes." Then smiled at Bill again.

"I don't know how come you keep grinning like there's something to be glad about," he said. "We got a shotdead daddy here and we've been run out of our home."

"Kansas ain't *home*," she said, "and getting run out of it is no punishment as far as I'm concerned. It's got too many Kansans in it is the trouble."

"You've spent more of your life in Kansas than you ever have in Missouri," he said.

"So what? It's not how long you been someplace that makes it home. You think the people been in hell a thousand years would feel like they were leaving home if they got out tomorrow?"

He laughed. She hugged his arm and kissed him several quick times on the side of his face. "Oh Billy, I was *so* scared for you. I thought maybe they got you."

"Hey girl," he said, turning to look back at Jim and his sisters in the other wagon some dozen yards behind and the Berrys riding side by side a little behind Jim.

Josephine glanced back at the others too, then fixed Bill with a look and said mockingly, "Oh Bill, I'm just *so ashamed* for kissing my brother."

He had to grin.

She kissed him on his ear and his cheek and the corner of his mouth. Then hugged herself to him with her head on his shoulder and hummed softly as the wagon jounced on.

ON THE LONE PRAIRIE

By their second day on the winding trace the stink was risen and it worsened swiftly in the swelter of this prairie summer. Two days later it was grown so foul they wore bandannas over their noses like a theatrical troupe playing at bandits but the measure was of little effect. The wagonbed was enclouded in a blackgreen storm of flies. The Berry boys daily rode farther behind and to north or south of the trace, depending on which way the wind was carrying. The Anderson girls pleaded with their brothers to bury the corpse anywhere along this remote landscape and be done with it.

"I told those Kansans I'd bury him in Missouri and I mean to do it," Bill Anderson said.

To lessen the chance of encountering jayhawkers—who more and more were said to be robbing and murdering not only secessionists but even Unionists who could not solidly prove their loyalties—they were keeping off the Santa Fe Trail and making their way by an old stock trail a few miles to the north. This route was safer than the main road but also rougher and thus slower going, and the plodding pace prolonged their ordeal with Will Anderson's rotting remains.

Came a noonday when they encamped for dinner and none could eat for the gut-twisting stench.

"It's only a few days more to the border," Bill said. But his tone lacked its earlier timbre of sworn purpose.

"Oh hell, Bill," Jim Anderson said, slinging away his untouched beans and refitting the bandanna on his face, "I guess we made our point by not burying him back there. That's what counts."

"They'll never know if we don't get him all the way to Missouri," Ike Berry said.

"Jesus, Billy," Josephine said, "if I have to breathe this stink another day I believe I'm going to start throwing up forever."

"Billy . . ." Mary began, and Bill Anderson threw up his hands and said, "All right then, all right! Get the damn spades."

The men shed their shirts and worked in pairs under the hard sun, taking turns at digging a deep grave a few yards off this isolate trail. There were no other witnesses to the proceeding in this vast emptiness but the swirling flies and a dozen watchful crows lured by the aromatic deliquescence staining through the blanket. When the grave was ready, they lifted the body out of the wagonbed and lowered it into the hole and hurriedly covered it over. They crafted a cross of broken scantlings and cord and planted it firmly at the gravehead, and then Mary read from Ecclesiastes:

"To every thing there is a season, and a time to every purpose under the heaven:

A time to be born, and a time to die; a time to plant, and a time to pluck up that which is planted;

A time to kill, and a time to heal; a time to break down, and a time to build up;

A time to weep, and a time to laugh; a time to mourn, and a time to dance. . . ."

"Well," Jim Anderson said when she was done, "I'd say he pretty much knew most of those times."

"He sure knew the time for dancing," young Jenny said.

"He was good about the times for laughing too," Ike Berry said.

"It didn't say anything in there about a time for getting drunk and a time for cussing, did it, Mary?" Bill said. They all laughed.

"He knew about a time to kill," Josephine said seriously. "Remember how he did to that sorry muleskinner who tried to grab up under Mary's dress?"

"Lord Jesus," Butch Berry said, "I always did love that story. That's something I would of paid to see three or four times."

"You only had to see it once to not forget it," Jim Anderson said.

Where the corpse had lain on the wagonbed it left umber stains bearing remnant stench. Though the girls would scrub the boards with brushes and lye they would never fully remove imprint or odor. For a long time after, people who walked by this wagon would catch a low scent from they knew not where and would have a sudden intimation of the grave.

They moved on. Fierce flaring sun on limp yellow grass. A fine dusthaze under a sparsely clouded sky of palest blue. They were most of a day crossing a range overgrown with young sunflowers risen to the wheel hubs like a bright yellow tide. Then they were once again on green shortgrass prairie but now the country assumed a gentle roll and was marked by brushy rises and a scattering of hardwood groves. The following day an unbroken line of woodland hills rose into view on the forward horizon like a shadowed landfall surfaced from a jade sea.

"Missouuuri, Missouuuri, bright *lannnnd* of the west," Josephine sang happily.

They were yet a half-day from the state line when a low cloud of dust appeared in the distance on the Santa Fe road. The cloud was moving west—and then seemed to hold in place, and then began to swell. Butch Berry chucked his horse up beside Bill's wagon and said, "Whoever they are, they're coming."

The Andersons reined up the wagon teams and watched the riders come. Ike held close to Jim's wagon. Every man of them had a pair of charged revolvers hidden under his coat and Josephine had the Walker ready on the seat beside her and under a fold of her skirt. The only weapons in evidence were the knives in the men's boots and two Sharps carbines, one propped beside Bill against the wagonseat,

one lying across Mary Anderson's lap. In the covered wagon lay Will
Anderson's old doublebarreled shotgun.

The approaching riders shaped into dark figures against the risen
glaring dust—then into view came a Union banner batting at the fore
of a column of two dozen cavalrymen.

The column reined up alongside the trail and their following dust
came billowing over them and hazed the air yellow. A lieutenant
heeled his horse up to Bill's wagon and said, "Scouts spotted you."
He said it like an accusation. He sported a bare wisp of blond mustache and could not have been more than twenty years old.

He eyed the men thinly. Then took in the girls and smiled and
said, "Ladies," and tipped his hat. Mary and Jenny showed him their
best smiles. Behind his back the men at the front of the column leered
and pointed and blew kisses at the girls. Josephine started to make a
rude gesture but Bill caught her hand and gave her a look. She made
a face at him, then folded her hands in her lap and stared out at the
prairie.

The lieutenant asked who they were.

"Loyal Union Kentuckians bound for home," Bill said. "Three
years was all of this damn Kansas we could stand. If it's not a windstorm pulling your house apart and carrying off your corn into the
next county, it's outlaws stealing your stock or Indians sneaking up
from the Nations to steal whatever you ain't nailed down or locked
up. It's not a thing to look at out here but sky and grass till you think
you'll go crazy for the sight of a hill. No sir, you can have all this
empty Kansas and ye welcome to it."

"Give me the Ohio Valley every time," the lieutenant said,
almost smiling—and then his look again narrowed. "Union Kentucky, you say? How is it you men aren't in uniform?"

"We aim to be," Bill Anderson said, "just as soon as we get our
sisters to our uncle's farm. I got to say, Lieutenant, when we spied
your dust we had a bad moment. We thought you might be bushwhackers. It's why we're keeping off the main road. We heard there
was bushwhackers raiding all over yonder part of the Santa Fe road
and we sure's hell didn't want to run into any. It's a comfort to know
you fellas are about."

The lieutenant spat. "Bushwhackers! Those cowardly sons of—
Excuse me, ladies. Those curdogs haven't got the sand to set foot in

Kansas. Not again." His gaze shifted to the covered bed of the trailing wagon and he nodded at it and said, "I'll just have a look."

He hupped his horse to the rear of the wagon and leaned to peer within and satisfy himself that it held no munitions or other contraband. He reached inside and took up the old shotgun and assayed it with an indulgent smirk and then put it back. Mary and Jenny looked at him through the front flaps of the wagoncover and he again smiled and nodded. Mary's smile at him was radiant. Bill Anderson was impressed by how well she played her part.

The officer advised Bill that they'd be safer traveling on the Santa Fe than out here. "When you make the Leavenworth road you should take it to the fort and attach to the next army wagon train bound for Saint Louis. Be a lot safer for you traveling with the army than trying to get across that damn Missouri on your own."

"I'll take it as sound advice," Bill said, "and I thank ye for it."

The lieutenant again smiled at Mary and touched his hatbrim. "Ladies."

He reined his mount around and circled his hand over his head and started back for the main road and the column came about to follow him. As the soldiers made their turn near the wagon, many of them called endearments to the girls through the rising mist of yellow dust.

"You blue-assed monkeys!" Josephine shouted into the rumble of hooves.

"Josephine!" Bill said.

She turned to say that's exactly what those Yankees were and saw that he was grinning at her. So was Butch Berry.

"Josie, I swear your mouth is going to get you hanged one day," Mary called from the other wagon.

"Get us *all* hanged," Jim Anderson said.

Josephine affected to yank up on a noose around her neck and crossed her eyes and bulged out her tongue and despite themselves they all had to laugh.

NIGHTCAMP CAPERS

They moved on, keeping to trails off the main road. They didn't know where they crossed into Missouri but by early afternoon they knew they were there. The country was as lovely as the Anderson brothers and Berry boys remembered it but it was also different in that two of the four farms they passed in sight of during the day seemed clearly to be abandoned—both of them with fences shambled, their cornfields trampled and going to ruin, one house bearing a blackened roof and wall and the barn half-burned as well. At one of the two places that showed smoke at their kitchen chimneys a trio of men with faces deepshadowed under their wide hatbrims and each with a rifle in hand had stood out in front of the house and watched them go by and none of the three lifted a hand or in any way made recognition of the greeting Butch Berry shouted in hope of being asked to stop and take dinner. At the other inhabited farm, no one came out to the porch or even showed himself at the door in response to Jim's halloo. Only a pair of stave-ribbed horses and a tattered mule in the corral showed curiosity at their passing. The eerie silence was broken solely by the rattle and creak of the Anderson wagon and the snortings of the animals.

They put down for the night in a hickory grove watered by a narrow serpentine creek. Doves crooned in the creekside brush. The setting sun loomed enormous, the trees afire in its fierce orange flare, the air itself gone gold. A flock of cranes made for its evening roost in a slow working of white wings against the redstreaked purpling sky. The men saw to the horses and mules and got a fire crackling and fashioned a spitframe of sturdy greensticks on which to suspend the cookpot. They would sup yet again on jackrabbit stew. Ike and Jim had earlier shot six of the bony things and Josephine now made quick work of skinning and quartering them. Jenny and Mary seasoned the meat in a medley of root vegetables, then hung the cookpot over the fire and the campsite was soon suffused with a savory redolence.

When they had finished with supper, the moonless night was fully commenced, the sky a thick encrustation of stars. A comet streaked and vanished, its origin and destination both beyond reckoning. They pointed out to each other the Bear and the Archer and the Bull. They speculated whether any of the winking lights they looked on did hold life. Only Butch Berry thought it possible, but Mary Anderson chided him for a blasphemer.

"The Bible doesn't say a thing about God creating anybody else in His own image anywhere but on earth," Mary said.

"It don't come right out and say He didn't either," Butch said, who wasn't at all sure what the Bible said about anything. "See the endtail star of the Dipper yonder? Could be there's a campfire on it and some fella and his sweetheart are sitting beside it right this minute and they're looking at some bright star and wondering if there's any life on it and the star they're looking at could be the very one we're sitting on."

The others chuckled at this notion—and at the moony gaze he seemed unaware of repeatedly fixing on Josephine across the campfire as she studied the night sky. Now she saw his look too and turned her face to the shadows to hide her angry blush.

"Could be the fella on that star's saying to his sweetie that for all they know there's some rascal sitting here next to *his* sweetheart and looking at *their* star and wondering if there's any life on it," Jim Anderson said.

"Like two mirrors facing each other," Jenny said. "Showing each other back and forth and back and forth and on and on forever." She was hugely taken with this conceit. The others grinned at Butch Berry's face reddening more deeply than the firelight could account for.

Only in the past few days had they become aware of his eye for Josephine. Those of them in the second wagon would smile and nudge each other and jut their chins at him gawking on her as he trotted his horse on the off side of Bill's wagon and a few feet back of it, the better to look on her without her knowing it. Sometimes she turned and caught him at it, and then he was always quick to tug down his hat to shade his embarrassment and rein back to the rear of the party. After a time he would ease up close to her wagon once again.

At first Mary had not been sure how to feel about this turn. At one of their stops to water the animals, she took Bill aside and asked what he thought of it. "She's *fourteen*," she said. "Hardly more than a little girl."

"Josephine's never been a little girl," Bill said, "and Butch ain't barely four years older than her. Let it go how it goes." In truth the circumstance unsettled him, but he would not question himself too closely as to why.

The last to ken to Butch's smitten condition had been Josephine herself. At the evening camp two nights ago she was puzzled by his offer to skin the rabbits for her. She thanked him but said she could tend to them just fine. He stood there and looked around as if in search of something else he might offer to do for her but Mary shooed him away so they could get on with fixing supper. And then last night when Josie was chopping kindling for the cookfire he offered to relieve her of the chore. This time she took a good look at his face and realized what was happening. She felt her own face go hot and said, "I know how to use a damn hatchet!" The sharpness of her tone drew everybody's grinning attention and Butch hastily retreated to the far side of the campsite to make a show of checking his horse's shoes.

Next morning as they rattled along the trail Bill said to her, "Looks like somebody's set his cap for you."

"Well he best set it for somebody else," she said. She glanced back to see if he was riding near enough to hear her and almost hoped he was, but he was farther back at the moment and talking with his brother.

"He's capable," Bill said. "That off eye's never hindered him a bit that I know of."

"It's got nothing to do with his eye," Josie said. She hugged to his arm and put her head on his shoulder. He thought she might say something more about the matter but she didn't. He had told himself she would soon enough show interest in other men, yet couldn't help smiling with the knowledge that so far she did not—and then chided himself for a selfishly confused man.

Now the party had had enough of astral speculations and of japing at Butch. Bill took the Jew's harp from his pocket and began to twang upon it. Jim unwrapped his harmonica from its bandanna and blew a few quick trills to clear it and they set into a rendition of "Oh! Suzannah."

Ike Berry offered his arm to Mary and she curtsied and took it and they stepped away from the fire and began to swing around and kick their heels, their hair tossing. Butch was hesitant to ask

Josephine to dance, unsure if she knew his feeling toward her and certain that if she did she must be displeased by it, to judge from her tight face and recent aloofness. But Josie would not deny herself a dancing turn just because of the cow eyes this silly boy kept making at her. She put out her hand to him and said—loudly, that no one might mistake the gesture—"Well come on, boy—it ain't but *dancing*!"

Now Mary let Jenny take a turn with Ike and after a time the Berry boys switched partners. Unlike his younger brother, Ike was not a good dancer but was an immensely enthusiastic one. Mary once said that dancing with him was like holding tight to a real drunk man trying to find his way out of a burning house. Josie couldn't help laughing the whole time she swung round with him. Butch at times took over from Jim on the harmonica and Ike would spell Bill on the Jew's harp, and in this way did every man have a turn with each of the sisters. Josie beamed when it came her turn with Bill, and she would not surrender him for the rest of the evening.

Every night of this journey the Anderson girls had slept in the wagons—Mary and Jenny in the covered one, Josephine in the open bed. The Berry boys would unfurl their bedrolls under the covered wagon and the Anderson brothers would put down under the other and the men took turns of two hours each at keeping watch through the night. At their first nightcamp, Josephine had sidled up to Bill and asked in low voice if she might make her bed next to his under the wagon and he had refused, saying he didn't want the Berry boys to draw any wrong conclusions. She said the Berry boys were their friends and friends wouldn't draw any such conclusions, and if they did then they weren't true friends. He said he wasn't going to argue with her about it and that the matter was at an end. She had not broached the subject since.

They had so far been fortunate in the weather, but on this evening, shortly after Jim relieved Bill on the night watch, a wind rose up from the south and carried on it a cool sweet scent of rain. The trees began to toss. The stars dimmed by portions and then faded completely behind a gathering of clouds. The campfire coals flared redly under the gusting wind and sparks leapt and swirled and streaked away crimson into the night. Jim put on his slicker and sat upwind of the fire to avoid the sparks. Now the southern sky came alight in a shimmering white cast of lightning and fell dark again and there followed a low roll of thunder.

Under the open-bed wagon Bill Anderson had been asleep but a few minutes when he woke to a soft pressure against his back, a warm breath at his neck. He rolled over and raised on his elbow and looked at the shadowed shape huddled to him. "Don't even try to tell me you're still afraid of storms."

"It's even worse out in the open like this," she said. She hugged his neck and pulled closer against him with her face to his chest. "There's not even a roof or a wall to keep it off." They spoke in whispers.

"Joey . . ."

"*Biilll.* Just let me stay till it's done with."

"You're no more scared than I am. It hasn't fallen the first drop of rain. That storm's a ways off and might not even touch us."

Another show of sheet lightning quivered in the southward sky and a moment later came the resonant rumble. Though the lightning was no brighter and the thunder no louder than before, Josephine's clutch on his neck tightened and she made a tiny whimper.

"You little faker," he hissed.

"Billy, be nice. Even if I wasn't scared—and I truly am—but even if I wasn't, I don't want to get all *rained* on. Do you want me to get all rained on?"

"*Rained* on? I got a notion to drown you in yonder creek."

"*Shhh!*" She put her fingers to his lips. "You'll wake everybody." She gave quick kisses to his ear, his cheek.

"Jim'll anyway be off watch before too long."

"He can fit on the other side of you. I'll just scootch way over here"—she squirmed backward with a wriggling of her hips but kept her tight hug on his neck so that he moved over with her before he was even aware he'd done so. "See? He's got lots of room there."

She found his hand and put it on her hip. She stroked his face lightly.

"Joey . . ."

"Shhh." She slid her hand to his chest.

"*Josie . . .*"

"Oh Bill, *stop*. Everybody knows I come and hold to you when it's bad storming."

His hand was insubordinate to his protest and pleasurably roamed the swells and slopes of her. "The Berry boys . . . they don't—"

"Oh hush about them."

She kissed his neck and worked his buttons and then had him in hand and he ceased all remonstration. Pulsing in her gentle grasp. Both of them caressing now, stroking with a familiar pleasure, kissing lightly. He finds her shirt already unlaced to admit his hand. Her breath hisses as he fingers the tightened nipple—and then a deeper gasp as his hand seeks under her skirt. Her hips arch upward in a response as ancient as the race itself, her breath swiftening, her excitement fervoring his own. He tenses and puts his face in her hair and moans softly, and she smiles as she kisses him. They put a hand to each other's mouths and taste their own pungent selves on the other's fingers. So practiced are they in such frisking that no one hears them at it. They fall asleep embraced.

The storm but grazed their camp with a brief windblown drizzle as it passed them by. Its lightplay and thunder were fading to the west when Ike Berry sleepily relieved Jim Anderson of the camp watch. Jim went to the open wagon and squatted to arrange his bedroll and saw Bill sleeping spoonfashion with Josephine. In that moment they seemed to him like children, both of them, as unsinful and unmindful. He looked back at Ike and saw him whittling on a stick by the low light of the glowing coals. He carefully eased himself down beside Bill so as not to wake him and for a while lay there feeling content for reasons he had no interest in even trying to name. And then was himself sleeping.

He woke with Bill still bedded at his side. The sky was darkly gray but cloudless, yet beclung with a few tenacious stars. The campfire stoked now, wet wood smoking and softly popping. The coffeepot on a firestone, lid chittering and issuing steam. Butch Berry sat cross-legged and watched Josephine prepare a pan of cornbread. She neither looked his way nor spoke to him as she worked.

Bill stirred. Yawned and stretched. Raised himself on his elbows and peered past Jim to the campfire scene. He smiled sadly and whispered, "Poor damn Butch."

She carefully set the pan of batter to bake on the firerocks and put the coffeepot aside to ease its boil. Then turned and saw her brothers watching her. And smiled widely and said, "Breakfast, you slugabeds."

WEST MISSOURI

They pressed ahead on abandoned tracks and weedy traces toward a red new-risen sun. Low reefs of pink-veined purple clouds showed on all horizons. They intercepted the Santa Fe Trail where it curved up from the south and they kept to it as it made for the Blue River and they encountered no other travelers. A hawk followed them for a time, spiraling overhead. Husky crows taking respite in the trees along the roadside chuckled low in remarking these passing pilgrims. When the river came in sight Bill reined his team off the road and Jim brought the covered wagon behind. The wagons jounced and yawed over the uneven ground and then onto an old stock trail leading into the brushland.

They were bound for the Parchman farm, which Aunt Sally in her letters said was on Brushy Creek at a point some ten miles north of where the Santa Fe met the Blue. In addition to these spare but sufficient directions, they had also found in their mother's letters a photograph of Aunt Sally and Uncle Angus. They were posed stiffly and in their Sunday finest before a studio backdrop of a sunny beach fronting a whitecapped ocean. This couple who, like the kin who owned their picture, would never in their lives behold a sea. An inscription on the back of the photo informed that it had been made in Westport in the year of '58.

The region they now moved through was a patchwork of thickets and hardwoods and hollows scattered over open country with more rise and fall to it than they had seen in Kansas. They rolled past wooded hills and brushy swales, forded darkwater creeks overhung with sycamores and willows. Josephine had been six years old when the family left Missouri, and the past eight years had made vague her recollections of it. As their wagon jostled over the rugged trail she gaped on the passing country and told Bill she loved this rough old Missouri that made Kansas look boring as a bare table.

They nooned at a stony creek shaded by cottonwoods and they roasted for dinner a dozen plump quail Butch Berry had earlier taken down with birdshot loads in Will's old shotgun. Roasted too some sweet potatoes and ears of corn, and their gusto in the meal was in no wise lessened by having to pause in their chewing to spit shot like it was seed.

That afternoon they drove through sunny meadows of grass as high as the mules' bellies and around narrow stony ravines and through shadowy stands of trees so close together that they had to perform intricate maneuverings of the wagons and the wheelhubs did often scrape bark. Yet none of them minded the slow going. The afternoon was warmly pleasant and the air sweet with the scent of grass and wildflowers. Josephine hummed and sang softly and now and then licked her finger and wriggled it into Bill's ear and said, "Here's another Wet Willie for you!" He every time threatened to break her fingers off if she didn't quit and she every time tittered happily. At one point she jumped off the wagon and quickly gathered a purple cluster of sweet william from a patch growing alongside the trail. She said it was her favorite flower because it had his name. He affected to protest but did not stop her from braiding them into his hair.

They were passing through a hackberry grove when they caught a thin stink of decayed flesh mingled with a strong smell of burnt wood. They emerged into a clearing where stood the blackened ruins of what had once been a farm. All that remained upright of the house were one charred wall and the stone chimney. Where the barn had stood was a black carpet of ashes shedding lightly into the breeze. Next to it a skeletal bovine carcass with rotted skull and ribcradle exposed to the placid sky. A fat crow picked at the scraps of hide yet on the bones.

The men stepped down. Josephine with the Walker in both hands started to follow after Bill but he told her to stay and watch her sisters. She made a face but did as he said.

They treaded carefully through the ruins but saw nothing resem-

bling human remnant. Then came on three gravemounds in the
shade of the trees behind the remaining wall of the house.

"Whose doing, you think?" Jim said.

Bill Anderson shrugged. "There's so many bunches of jayhawks
and Union milish and Federals, hell, it could've been any of them."

"Could be these were Unions and it was Quantrill done it," Ike
Berry said. "Or maybe some other band of bushwhackers."

"I ain't going to stand here feeling sorry for anybody who
might've been Union," Butch Berry said.

"This place wasn't Union," Bill Anderson said. He stooped
beside a shrub at the foot of an oak and extricated a blue cap with a
black visor and a U.S. Cavalry insignia on its crown. There was a
hole in the side of the cap and a dark stain they all knew to be
blood. On the band along the inside of the cap was inked the name
GALLAGHER.

"Yankee bastards," Ike Berry said. "At least one of them got put
down."

"Wish to hell they'd all been," Jim Anderson said.

"Hold that thing out here, Bill," Butch Berry said. He dug a
block of matches from his jacket pocket and broke one off and
struck it alight in a burst of sulfur and put the flame to the cap. Bill
Anderson held it by the bill until it was fully ablaze and then let it
fall. They watched it burn till only the visor was intact and then Ike
Berry put his bootheel to it and ground it in the dirt.

They moved on. Advancing upcountry through a midafternoon of
wavering heat, they late in the day arrived at Brushy Creek. They
checked the line of the lowering sun and agreed that their course had
brought them more to westward than they had intended. So they
turned east and held to a narrow road along the creek and in a cool
hollow of tall cottonwoods and limp black willows.

At sundown the entire reach of the western sky was a riot of
crimson streakings. The trees seemed afire and were clamorous with
roosting birds. They spied a thin wavering line of chimney smoke a
half-mile to southward and figured it for the Parchman place. They
got onto a branching wagontrack off the creek road and followed it
through another shadowy hollow. Now there was a stone fence on

one side of the track and a rail fence on the other, and then they were out again into the gold light of evening, and there the farm was.

A short lean man with a bucket of water in each hand was hobbling up from a narrow creek at the bottom of a shallow slope, heading for the house, when the clatter of the coming wagons raised a pair of yowling red hounds on the run from under the porch steps. The man let the buckets drop and he hurried to the house in an awkward half-crippled scurry and snatched up a longrifle from where it leaned against a porch post.

Bill Anderson reined up. The mules stamped in their traces and laid back their ears at the clamoring closing dogs. Sharply as a quirt snap Bill ordered "Quit!" and the dogs instantly fell mute and nearly tumbled over each other, so abruptly did they arrest their charge. They gawked inquisitively at Bill and offered tentative tailwags. Bill smiled on them and said, "It's friends, you jughead sons of bitches." Their tails blurred.

In front of the house the little man stood with the rifle at his hip. "Who's there?" he called raspily. "Name yeself!"

Even at this distance and though the man seemed of more wizened aspect than he showed in his studio portrait of four years earlier, Bill Anderson recognized Angus Parchman. "Say now, Uncle," he called, "do you intend to put holes in your own wife's bloodkin?"

Now a stout gray woman came rushing out the door and down the steps and handed her own rifle to the little man as she passed him by. Aunt Sally with her arms wide, hurrying to them and weeping in her joy, saying "I know you! I know you!"

AT THE PARCHMAN FARM

She did in fact know much about them, all of it by way of correspondence with their mother over the years. She had always been avid for news about her nephews and nieces, and in her letters Martha had always reported their doings and misdeeds. "I could've described all of you to a hair before ever I set eyes on you," Aunt Sally said at the supper table that first night. "Mattie loved telling me what you looked as you were growing up."

They had never before heard their mother called Mattie. The

sobriquet conjured visions of her as a young girl who had not yet even imagined her children to come.

Sally Parchman smiled at the Berry brothers. "She mentioned *you* boys now and then. I knew you on sight by that buttermilk hair, Ike Berry. And you, young Butch . . . well, I recognized you right off too."

Butch redfaced and nodding. He knew what she meant but was too polite to say. She'd known him by his wayward eye.

When she received Mary's letter last month telling her of Martha's death she had wept through the night. She'd written in response but was not now surprised to learn Mary never got the letter.

"It's a wonder *your* letter made it to the Raytown postmaster," Aunt Sally said. "Hardly any mail ever gets through along the border anymore, what with one wildbunch or another robbing the carriers all the time."

Bill Anderson recounted to his aunt and uncle the circumstances of his father's death. As he told of Baker's jilting of her, Mary's face reddened and Aunt Sally reached over and patted her hand in sympathy. He told of their failed try at rustling Segur's horses as redress, but he did not reveal that it wasn't their first essay at horse theft— and neither did any of the others volunteer this information to the Parchmans. He concluded with an explanation of the bargain he'd made with the sheriff in order to retrieve his father's body and collect his sisters.

Uncle Angus cursed all Kansans for low bastards. He said he meant no disrespect to their father's memory, but a man seeking after requital was making a bad mistake to try to get it when he was drunk and a double bad mistake to try to settle things on the other fella's property, where the other fella had all the advantage. "I guess he wouldn't of done it that way if he hadn't been bad drunk to start with," Angus said sadly. "Being bad drunk is the mother of wrong ideas." His tone suggested personal acquaintance with this truth.

Bill Anderson said he didn't doubt his daddy would agree with him. He said he hoped they weren't imposing themselves on the Parchmans by coming to them without notice. Uncle Angus waved a dismissive hand and Aunt Sally said of course they weren't. "Good lord, boy," she said, "you're *family*. All of you got a home here for as long as you want it—and I mean you Berry boys too."

The Parchmans were childless, although they had produced two children, the first a girl named Delia, the second a boy called Bellamy who was born dead. Their graves lay side by side in the shaded earth of a maple stand behind the barn. After she delivered Bellamy, Sally went barren, a turn made the worse by little Delia's death at age four.

"She got took by the Saint Vitus dance," Aunt Sally said. "She laid in bed for three days, burning up and twitching all over and crying with the pain until finally her little heart just quit. These twenty-four years now it's been just me and the mister."

The mister himself faring none too well. Returning home on the Raytown Road one afternoon last winter, Angus Parchman had been set upon by a band of jayhawkers led by none other than tall-capped Doc Jennison. The little redbeard had demanded to know Angus' allegiance, but would not accept his sworn word that he was a loyal Union man. He said the fine for telling a lie to an agent of the Federal government was one horse and saddle and ordered him to dismount and hand the reins over. Angus protested and Jennison didn't say another word, he just pulled a pistol and shot him in the chest. Angus would forever remember the ball's breathtaking punch and the sudden tilt of the sky. Next thing he knew, he was lying bootless in the bed of a wagon and being driven to a Raytown doctor by a family who had found him left for dead in the road. He'd been shot in the chest and in the knee—he'd not even been aware of receiving the second wound—and he was weeks in recovering sufficiently to get back on his feet. But he would evermore limp and his lungs had since been prone to chronic inflammations that made hard labor of breathing. Sometimes the infections were so severe he would nearly drown in his own mucus.

"Jennison was right about me lying, of course," Uncle Angus said in his wet rasp. "I ain't no more a Union man than that red hound yonder. I've hated hawkers from the start, I'll have you know, but truth to tell, all I wanted was to stay clear of the whole thing if I could. Then I run into Jennison and he sure enough made a true believer out of me—made me truly believe I'd like to see every last jayhawker dead and him the deadest one."

"You still staying clear of it, Uncle?" Jim Anderson said. "Or have you maybe got into it some kind of way?"

Aunt Sally cleared her throat loudly even as she held her attention on her supper and Angus glanced at her and then looked at each of the men in turn, as if he had something more on his mind but was unsure if he should say it. Then said: "I think you boys ought to give close thought to something before you decide to stay here with us. Might make a diff—" He was abruptly beset by a fit of coughing that raised the veins of his neck and darkened his face and filled his eyes with tears.

The fit passed but left him gasping and hawking bloody sputum into a bowl at hand for just that purpose. Aunt Sally said, "You rest yourself, Angus."

Their farm was so far from the main road and so deep in the bush, Aunt Sally said, that they had never yet been visited by Union forces. But that didn't mean it couldn't happen tomorrow or the day after or the day after that. Jayhawkers and militia and Federal troops were constantly scouring the region in search of guerrillas. "This is your home if you want it to be," she said. "You boys can stack another pair of bunks atop the two already in the kitchen and the girls can put pallets in the loft above our room. But you ought to know it can get mean if the Unions come by. You have your sisters to think of."

"Your sisters, that's right," Uncle Angus said breathlessly. "Can be awful mean country. Just look how it's done me."

"Well sir," Bill Anderson said, "it was jayhawkers killed the Berry boys' daddy and it was a son of a bitch protected by Kansas vigilantes that killed ours. Pardon my language, Aunt Sally. What I mean is, I guess we know something about how it can get mean."

The three sisters nodded to assure their aunt and uncle that they too knew about meanness.

"I guess you do at that," Uncle Angus said. "So I'll just say welcome to home, all you."

In the months since Uncle Angus' maiming, the farm had fallen into disrepair and now the Anderson and Berry brothers applied themselves to replacing fallen fence sections and the railings on the corral, to reshingling the barn roof and restoring to soundness the hog pen, the corn crib, the henhouse and its run, the springhouse. They rebuilt the jakes. They baled hay, gathered ready corn, plowed the fields, completed construction of the smokehouse their uncle had begun. The Anderson girls were also a boon to the place—so many able female hands made short work of domestic chores, and the men were fed plenty and well. The daily dinner was a sumptuous affair.

The Anderson and Berry boys were all now cultivating mustaches. The first time Josephine sneaked a kiss with Bill since he'd begun to grow his, she joked about the feel of it. "It'll take some getting used to," she said. He leered melodramatically and affected to twirl its ends, and she laughed and kissed him again.

On several occasions—sometimes in the bright light of day, sometimes in the night's deep hours—they heard shooting, each time near enough to make them pause at their labor or at their meal or sit up in their beds and listen hard for notice of danger closing on them. But it never did.

"You see the meanness?" Uncle Angus said one day when they spied a distant smoke spiral. "Two families we used to know just yonder of the creek woods got burned out in the past year. Jayhawkers got one and the state militia the other. Now there's another put to the torch."

"How come they burned them out?" Butch Berry said. "Were they helping bushwhackers?"

"That's what was said," Uncle Angus said. "That's what the Feds always say." He spat and turned back to work, ending the conversation.

In their first days on the farm, all the young men had at one time or another raised the subject of Quantrill, but neither Uncle Angus nor Aunt Sally showed any interest in discussing him. The brothers believed the Parchmans knew more about the bushwhackers than they were letting on, but if the odd couple did not want to speak of it, there was nothing to do but be polite and respect their wishes.

They'd been at the farm nearly two months when they told Uncle Angus they would be going away for a time. The supper meal was done with and the girls were in the house, helping Aunt Sally with her spinning and sewing, the men out on the porch, a jug making the round.

"The farm's in good order now and you'll have the girls to help you keep it up," Bill Anderson told his uncle. "Jim and me are obliged to you for giving them a home. It's a comfort to us to know they'll be with you till we get back. Could be we'll be back directly, could be a while longer, all depends."

Angus' face made no secret of his surprise. "Well, you'll pardon me for asking, but where all are you going?"

"We figure it's better we don't say," Bill said. "That way, nobody can ever hold you to any part of it."

"Oh horseshit!" the old man said. His gaze narrowed. He glanced at the open window and then said in lowered voice, "It's that Kansas business, ain't it?"

The Andersons and Berrys traded looks and then all of them grinned at Uncle Angus. "We ain't told our sisters nor Aunt Sally exactly where we're going either," Bill said, "but I guess they probably got as good a notion as you."

"Well, you boys got to do what you got to do and I'll not ask ye anymore about it," Uncle Angus said. He coughed hard, hawked, spat over the railing. "Just don't think you fool me. I know none of you cares even a little bit for farming, and if it wasn't this Kansas business taking you away it'd just be something else." He hacked hard and spat again. "Hell, I never liked farming neither—that's exactly why I spent the years I did driving a stagecoach. You know, I used to be sorry I hadn't gone to fight the Mexicans, and I'd be lying if I said I still wasn't. Now we got this new war, and I mean to tell you, if I wasn't so stove up nor so damn married—" He was taken with a fit of coughing so intense it seemed to them all he might pitch out of his chair. Gradually the fit subsided and he was left gasping and wiping at his tearful eyes. "Ah hell, it's what I get for flapping my mouth so much." He took a long drink.

"You know, boys, I believe if Uncle Angus was a younger man he'd be riding with some wildwood bunch this minute," Butch Berry said.

"Hell, he'd be riding at Quantrill's right hand," Jim Anderson said.

"You all saying it, not me," Angus said, grinning in the weak light.

They sat on the porch a while longer and said little else. They drank and stared out at the darkness and listened to the steady drone of insects, the rustle and swoop of owls hunting in the near woods, the sudden quick cries of prey caught up and carried off in the night.

Before dawn they had their mounts saddled and ready. The women had prepared small bundles of food and the men tucked these into their saddle wallets. They shook hands with Uncle Angus and then hugged Aunt Sally and each of the girls in turn. Butch stood before Josephine an awkward moment before smiling wryly and showing her his palms in a slack invitation to hug that expected rejection. She stopped his breath when she stepped into his arms and even deigned to put her hands lightly to his back. "You watch after my brothers good, you hear?" she said.

"I promise," he whispered. His voice tight at the feel of her, his heart jumping at being asked to do something for her. He wished she'd ask for more, wished she'd ask him to bring her the man's ears, his balls, anything she wanted.

"Go on, boy," she said, patting his back and stepping away. He tipped his hat and went to his horse.

Then she was clinging hard to Bill's neck and whispering in his ear, "I could go with you. I can ride, I can shoot—you know I can, you taught me."

He held her and stroked her hair, spoke in low voice that none else could hear. "Your sisters need you to keep them brave."

"I know it's true but it feels like a trick to keep me here," she said. "Will you be back soon?"

"Soon as we can." He felt her tremble under his hands. "If you cry now, I'll be disappointed."

"I don't *cry*," she said, stepping back so he could see her tearless eyes.

He stroked her cheek, then turned and mounted up. She blew him a kiss and he smiled and winked. Then hupped his horse away and the others followed after him.

LEX TALIONIS

They rode out of Missouri and into Kansas, staying well south of the Santa Fe, traveling by routes remote and roundabout. They at vari-

ous times saw raised clouds of dust in the distance but could not
have said if they were looking on troop detachments or wagon
trains, bands of vigilantes or spiraling dust devils come together in
the vagaries of the summer wind. Their nightfires leaned and swirled
in the prairie breeze. The high and fattening moon paled the luster of
the proximate stars but the lower skies sparkled in a rich stellar spill.
The orange sun rose at their backs and they rode after their quartet
of elongate shadows to overcome them at noon and then play them
out behind as the day drew down to reddening eve.

On their fourth morning in the saddle a brown cloud rose off the
distant southern expanse and gained height and breadth as it closed
on them. They covered their lower faces with bandannas against the
storm but the dust whipped under their hatbrims and burned into
their eyes. The horses shrilled into the wind. The world grew
enmurked in a rushing tide of dust that blurred visibility to a few
yards around and rendered their figures ghostly. The noon sun was
an umber wafer in the hazed sky. The storm persisted into the late
afternoon and then suddenly quit. The dust fell away and the prairie
once more rolled out to its horizons and the sun was restored to
incandescence in a clear and blue-pink firmament. But Butch Berry's
mount was gone blind in one eye and all the horses were in bad temper the rest of the day. For hours thereafter the men were coughing,
and even after they crossed the Dragoon River at sundown and made
camp for the night, they were still spitting mud.

The following day found them in a vast field of sunflowers as tall
as the horses' chests and the party looked like four small ships with
equine figureheads making way through a saffron sea. They struck
the Marais des Cygnes that afternoon near the Lyon County line and
followed the river upstream past a hamlet of name unknown to them
and that evening crossed the Santa Fe Trail in the light of the moon
and camped in a grove of cottonwoods.

At daybreak they set off into the woodlands west of the river,
pacing themselves so they would not arrive at their destination
before sundown. A pearl moon round and low against the blue sky
in the west. They held to a wagontrace that would pass them north
of Agnes City. They reined up to watch hawks hunting on the grassland, and then again to study the cumulus clouds and tell each other
the things they saw in the altering shape of them. In the late forenoon

they turned off the trace and made their way through the trees so the Anderson brothers could have a true last look at their home of former days when their parents were yet alive, days not three months past but feeling to the brothers as distant history. They sat their horses at the edge of the still woods and saw smoke rising in a straight line from the kitchen chimney, watched a man in red long-handle sleeves and suspenders working at splitting logs, his grunts and the whunks of the ax mingling with the steady crying of a baby from within the house. They watched unseen and wordless and after a time reined around and returned to the trace and resumed their westward progress.

Bill asked the Berry boys if they wanted to go by their old place but neither one did. "Doesn't feel to me like we ever even lived there," Butch said. Him neither, Ike said.

Just after sunset they came out of the woods and onto a narrow but well-defined lane. The gathering twilight rendered their faces indistinct under their hatbrims. The soft air was plaintive with the calls of mourning doves. Less than a hundred yards to northward was the boundary fence of Arthur Baker's farm. The outbuildings already dark but for a weak light at the open barn door. The main house showed bright yellow windows.

"Place does look peaceful and prosperous, don't it?" Ike Berry said. He spat.

They had reviewed their plan once more as the sun lowered, and now Bill Anderson sat his horse and stared off at the Baker house for a long moment before turning to the others and saying, "Let's do it."

Arthur Baker had never met either of the Berry boys, so they'd flipped a coin to decide which of them would go to his door, and Ike won. He followed the lane along the fence to the open gate of the Baker place and then turned onto the wagon path to the house. He dismounted at the porch steps and went up to the front door and worked the iron knocker. A Negro manservant came to the door and eyed him narrowly by the light of an oil lamp in hand. Before Butch could ask for Arthur Baker, the man himself appeared, wiping his chin with a napkin and saying, "Who is it, Grover?"

Ike Berry introduced himself as Alston Berryman and claimed to be assistant to a wagontrain boss. He said they had a train from

Independence due to arrive at the Baker store at Roan Creek Crossing within the hour.

"Some of the families who signed on at the last minute are in want of essentials," Ike said. He patted his shirt pocket and said, "I got a list right here. You can make yourself a nice dollar, Mr. Baker, if you can provision us this evening. Better for my boss too, since it'll be quicker to supply them at your store tonight than at Council Grove tomorrow. That Council Grove station's always so damn busy it takes near half the day to get your goods and move on."

"Mind your language, young sir," Arthur Baker said. "My wife is within."

Such exigencies of the wagontrain trade were familiar to store owners all along the Santa Fe, and as men of business they knew that profit did sometimes present itself at an awkward hour. Baker said he would be ready to go in a few minutes and left Ike standing on the porch in wait.

A farmhand brought a pair of saddled horses around to the front of the house. Now Baker returned with a husky young man whom he introduced as his brother-in-law George. The boy's mouth had a peculiar cast and he stared at Ike with a curious aspect, and Ike figured him for the softbrain Segur son he had heard about. Baker stood in the door with his hat in hand and called into the house: "We're away, dearest."

A woman with thick auburn hair bunched and ribboned at the back of her neck came hurrying from the other room, holding her skirts hiked slightly before her. She went to Baker and hugged herself to him. Ike Berry was struck by her prettiness. Over Baker's shoulder her gaze fell on him for a moment where he stood at the bottom of the porch steps. But her eyes were as unintelligible to him as a foreign language and he had no notion what she might have thought of him, if anything at all, before she cut her look away.

Baker kissed her on the cheek and assured her he would be gone but briefly. The three men mounted up and hupped their horses out to the gate and turned to the south. Ike Berry looked back at the house and saw the woman still standing in the brightly lighted doorway and looking after them. He felt a moment's touch of pity—and then the sentiment was fled and he did not look back again.

* * *

They trotted their mounts down the moonbright lane, the night now fully risen around them. Ike and Baker rode abreast, the softbrain slightly behind. Fireflies wavered on a gentle nightwind and flared greenly yellow against the blackness of the flanking brush. Baker breathed deeply and said, "It's a lovely evening, don't you agree, Mr. Berryman?" Ike Berry allowed that it was. The softbrain was humming a tune unheard before by anyone else in the world.

The lane from Baker's house ended at his store on the Santa Fe, a short mile from the house and a stone's throw east of Roan Creek. When they got there, the trail showed naught but moonlit emptiness in both directions. To the south, the country was scrub prairie and the only trees were thick and deeply shadowed growths of willows along the creek.

"Your train looks to be farther behind than you figured, Mr. Berryman," Baker said, sitting his horse and peering down the eastern stretch of road. The softbrain leaned forward in the saddle and whispered into the ear of his sagging horse and giggled softly as if sharing with the animal a special joke.

"They'll be along directly," Ike said. He dismounted and hitched his horse and took a piece of paper from his pocket. "We can start pulling together some of these necessaries while we wait on them."

Baker and the softbrain stepped down from their saddles and up onto the porch and Baker worked his key on the lock and they all three went inside. The storekeeper lighted four lamps at various points in the store for ample illumination. The place was full of an assortment of smells but the dominant odors were of coal oil and new leather and freshly sawn lumber. The walls held shelves of canned goods and were hung with harnesses and wagon parts and a variety of farm implements. There were bins and kegs and sacks of every sort of supply necessary to long-distance wagon travelers. The main counter was set toward the rear of the store and faced the front door. Behind this counter were still more shelves of goods as well as the canted door to the cellar where the whiskey barrels were stored.

Baker went behind the counter and hung up his coat and tied an apron around his waist. "All right, then," he said, fitting a pair of spectacles to his face, "let's see that list."

Ike Berry handed it over and the storekeeper studied it a moment and then called out, "Three twenty-pound sacks of sugar." The softbrain hastened to that part of the store where the sugar was kept and piled three sacks one atop the other and then hefted the stack back to the front of the store as easily as if it were of feather pillows and set it on the counter.

"Two twenty-pound . . ." Baker began, and then fell mute at the sound of hooffalls that drew up in front of the store. It sounded to be more than one rider but none reined up before the open door. The chinking of bridle rings carried into the store and a horse blew hard. The small front window showed no one.

Baker took off his eyeglasses and Ike Berry knew he was reckoning where the riders had come from. The road and the open country around them had lain deserted but minutes before. Only someone who'd been hidden in the trees nearby could have arrived at the store so soon after they themselves entered.

"Probably some of the fellas from the wagon train," Ike Berry said. But he was a bad liar and Baker's eyes cut to the door and his hands went down behind the counter.

Bootfalls thumped on the porch and Ike turned to see the Anderson brothers come through the door with revolvers in their hands. He flung himself against the wall and both Andersons fired at the same time and Arthur Baker yelped and the shotgun he'd started to bring up from under the counter discharged like a thunderclap before the barrel even cleared the countertop and the load blew through the counter's front panel and gouged the floor planks and some of the shot ricocheted and sang off a row of spades hung on the wall. Baker ducked below the countertop and Jim Anderson shot at the softbrain and missed as the boy dove behind the counter too. For a moment no one moved. Then the cellar door creaked and the Andersons rushed forward as the door slammed shut and they heard the barlatch within slide home.

They went behind the counter and saw that the door was shaped of thick heavy planking with gaps of perhaps a half-inch between planks. They exchanged looks and shrugs and then Jim Anderson bent and put his eye to one of the gaps. The cellar was in full darkness but he could hear a low whimpering and a soft pained grunting. He straightened up an instant before the shotgun blasted and its load slammed against the door and several pellets raised splinters as they passed between the planks and peppered the ceiling.

Jim fell back against the counter, mouth ajar. Ike Berry laughed and said, "Boy, you damn near got some more holes in your face."

"What the hell's going on?" Butch Berry said, peering in at the door. He was keeping watch for interlopers and had already put his own saddle on Baker's good roan mare.

"Let's take off the damn hinges," Ike Berry said.

"No, wait," Bill Anderson said. He looked around him and holstered his Colt. "Let's weight it down."

Hefting in concert they set several crates of heavy tools and a large anvil atop the slanted door. No two men pushing together from the awkward angle below could now have raised the door.

Then they doused the store with coal oil. Soaked all of the floor and splashed all the shelves and walls. Drenched everything of cloth. The smell was smothering. They stood just outside the front door and Butch Berry broke a lucifer off a match block and struck the match alight and put it to the remaining matches and the bunch of them burst into flame. But before he could toss the torch inside, Bill Anderson caught his hand.

"It was *our* daddy the man killed," Bill said. He carefully took the incendiary from Butch and then looked at Jim and his brother nodded and Bill lobbed it through the door.

Fire sprang from the floor and streaked to all corners and ran up the walls to the rafters. In less than a minute the interior of the store was infernal. Flames billowed from the door and drove them off the porch. They mounted up and set themselves to watch every side of the building in case the two within might yet escape by some hidden exit. But there was no hidden exit and in quick order the outer walls were sheeted in fire, the roof ablaze, flames flailing and leaning in the wind, the surrounding night illuminated by a quivering jaundiced dreamlight shot through with black shadows. The front window burst with the heat and they drew back still farther to calm their horses and avoid being blistered. Now came several muted thumps in succession and they knew the fire had found the whiskey stores. Flaring embers went streaking on updrafts into the black nightsky. Twenty yards from the house and through the cacophony of crackling wood and breaking glass and popping tins they faintly heard the screams of the pair trapped in the cellar.

"He shouldn't have brought the softbrain," Bill Anderson said loudly to be heard above the sparking crash of roof timbers. In the wavering firelight, each man looked to the others both horrified and exultant.

From the cellar of the burning store came a muffled report. No sounds now but the rendings and mastications of the fire.

"Shotgun," Bill Anderson said. "Heat must've fired it. They're done for sure—let's go." He touched his heels to Edgar Allan and they galloped away.

None of them would ever know that Arthur Baker's charred bones would be found in the ashes with the shotgun muzzle between his teeth and his blackened skull absent its rear portion. Or that the hardmuscled halfwit in a frenzy of terrified digging with bare hands did manage at the last to burrow through the cellar wall and out of the fire raining upon him. Without witness save the indifferent moon and stars he crawled through the grass, a smoldering half-cooked effigy of humanity, crawled all the way to the creek and there lowered into the shallow water in effort of easing the unreckonable pain which he could not even give proper cry for the seared ruin of his voicebox. Those who found him at daybreak and raised his yet living remains from the water could not bear to look on him. He was nearly two days more in dying, the cords sometimes standing on his neck but his screams no more than raspy hisses to his last breath. A hapless child of God, not the first to perish horribly in this region of the republic in these crimson years of malice, and far from the last.

II
The Company

1862

FLIGHT

They rode hard under the high moon and met no other travelers on the road but twice caught sight of wagon train campfires. Nightguards sat their horses near the road in the ghostly moonlight and watched them go by. They crossed the Marais des Cygnes in gray dawnlight and at daybreak they left the Santa Fe in favor of downcountry traces. They fed on jerky as they went, at times halted to take water at the creeks they crossed and let the horses recruit themselves.

That afternoon they came on a medicine man driving his wagon in desultory route over the countryside to stop at isolate farms and hawk his various elixirs. The huckster allowed that hard experience with towns had taught him the wisdom of plying his trade among folk of less suspicious nature. The bright pink splotches on his face and the backs of his hands bespoke recent burns, and portions of his raw face were yet pitted blackly. None of them had seen a man tarred and feathered but they'd heard stories, and they were curious about particulars such as how much it hurt and how long it had taken to pluck and peel himself clean, but basic politeness kept them from asking. In the course of their exchange, they discovered that the fellow had whiskey in his stores and they bought a jug.

They rode on. Under a cloudless blue sky they once more traversed a lake of sunflowers and then debouched onto a prairie of green and yellow grasses leaning in a soft wind. Their shadows drew up from behind and passed under their horses and lengthened before them as the sun lowered at their backs to enflame the western sky. Each man followed his own shade into the rising darkness. Just before nightfall they put down in a hickory grove. They made a fire and supped on the last of their jerked meat and passed around the whiskey jug.

At first light they were moving again, in no hurry now and walking their horses as often as not. Midmorning they struck the Dragoon and followed it east to a shallow ford above its juncture with the Marais, and in the early afternoon they arrived at Pomona hamlet. In the town's sole cafe they made short work of platters of beefsteak and fried potatoes, then went to the general store and bought a supply of coffee and beans and jerky. They camped that evening in country owning no distinction but grass and lying flat to every point of the compass and cast pale blue in the light of the gibbous moon. A wind rose out of the south and their fire twirled and lunged in the vagrant gusts and loosed chains of sparks to vanish in the darkness. A distant coyote raised a high lonely cry to be echoed by another from a far corner of the night. The tethered horses nickered and stamped nervously and the men called soothing words to them. Butch Berry pulled up a handful of grass and went to his new mare and fed her from his palm and told her there was nothing to be spooked about. He'd named her Jay and the others had smiled that he hadn't dared to give her but a portion of Josephine's name.

They bore northeast all the next day under a sky endless and empty but for the ferocious sun, the air unstirring, and settled for the night beside a creek in Johnson County, within sight of the Santa Fe and of a wagoncamp's firelights a half-mile downstream. After supper they lay back and studied the waning moon and spangled sky and Butch Berry well endured the others' grinning remarks about the possibility that some poor fool on one of those stars might be sitting at his own campfire and looking up at the gleam of earth and wondering if some sorry specimen like himself was sitting here and pining for a sweetheart who didn't much pine for him.

A STREET AFFRAY

Noon of the next day saw them trotting into Olathe, a prosperous town of some eight hundred souls. Ike Berry had persuaded the others that they would long rue the day if they neglected this opportunity to take dinner at Coogan's Restaurant, reputed to serve the best fried chicken in Kansas. They trotted their mounts down the main street through a boisterous traffic of wagons and horsemen and found the eatery on a street off the courthouse square. They hitched their horses at the sidewalk post and went inside.

The room was loud with talk and the clatter of dishware, the air hot and rich with savory aromas. They took a table near the back wall but with a clear view of the front of the room. A half-hour later the table was covered with platters of chicken bones amid congealing white gravy and remnants of roast potatoes and biscuits. They paid the bill and were contentedly at work with toothpicks as they exited to the sidewalk.

Six men stood beside the horses and one had unhitched Ike Berry's gray and held it by the reins. One brandished a two-barrel shotgun and the others except one had pistols in hand. They were all young except the one holding no firearm, and they were all looking at the Andersons and Berrys and none of them smiling.

"That's him right there, Sheriff," one of them said to the older man. Red hair showed under his hatband and his face was rife with raw sores and he was pointing at Ike Berry. "That's the one rode in on the gray."

"This your horse, son?" the sheriff asked Ike. He wore heavy drooping mustaches and there was about him an air of tiredness.

"Surely is," Ike Berry said. He spat away his toothpick and looked narrowly at the young man holding the horse by the reins. "You catch this fella trying to steal him?"

"I asked Junior to hold him till Mr. Porter has a look at him," the sheriff said. "I sent a man to fetch him from the Jefferson Hotel. Won't take but a minute to settle this."

"Settle *what*?" Bill Anderson said. "Who's Porter?" A small audience of townfolk was assembling to both sides of them on the sidewalk.

"Harrison Porter," the sheriff said. "Owns a ranch north of

town." He nodded at the redhead deputy. "Cyrus used to wrangle for him and was out there when a bunch of horses got stole last year. One of them was a gray with a white stocking just like this one here. It was Mr. Porter's favorite pony and Cyrus is sure this is the one."

"The animal have a brand?" Bill Anderson said.

"H with a P pressed to it," the sheriff said.

"You can see that's exactly what this was," Cyrus the redhead said, pointing at the gray's haunch, "before somebody tried to make it look like a double B. Jackleg piece of work, you ask me."

"Look here, Sheriff," Bill Anderson said, "I got a herd of cows a mile south I got to get to Kansas City. I don't have time to waste. Henry here's been with the outfit about six months and I haven't known him for a thief yet." He turned to Ike Berry. "Tell me true, Henry, you steal that horse?"

"*Hell no,*" Ike Berry said. "That badface peckerwood is crazy. I bought the horse off a fella in Emporia three months ago."

The redhead spat and scowled. "I'll just bet you did. If you ain't a Missouri horsethief I'll kiss your ass."

"You can kiss my ass anyhow, you ugly sonof—"

"Hush up!" the sheriff said. "Both you."

The word "horsethief" went muttering through the spectators and there came a clear utterance of "pukes."

The sheriff glared at the onlookers. "You people get on about your business." The assembly retreated a small distance in both directions but did not disperse.

"I guess you got a bill of sale," the sheriff said.

"Damn sure do," Ike Berry said. "It's with my possibles at the cow camp. I'll just go and get it."

The sheriff told him to stand fast. Ike sighed hard and shook his head in the manner of one sorely burdened by unfair accusation. The sheriff peered down the street and said, "What's taking that fool so long to get Porter? I can't give him the simplest damn job—"

"Tell you what, Sheriff," Bill Anderson said, stepping off the sidewalk and taking his horse's reins from the hitch post. "*I'll* go get that bill of sale myself and we'll get this done with." He stepped up onto the saddle and said to Ike Berry, "You best be telling the truth, Henry. I don't find that bill in your possibles I'll know you for the horsethief they're saying you are."

"It's there," Ike Berry said. "I ain't no damn rustler."

"And you boys," Bill Anderson said, pointing at his brother and Butch Berry. "Who gave you leave to stand around here admiring the ladies? I want you back with the herd right now."

Some of the onlookers chuckled at Jim Anderson's and Butch Berry's looks of disappointment as they stepped down off the sidewalk and mounted up.

"I'll have your man over at the jail," the sheriff said. He pointed down the street. "Just around the corner there."

Bill Anderson unholstered and cocked a Navy and pointed it at the sheriff's face and said, "I'll have him now."

Mouths came open—and Jim leaned down and grabbed the shotgun from the startled deputy. Ike laughed and hopped off the sidewalk, snatched away his reins and stepped up onto the gray. Butch held a revolver on the others and said, "Turn loose of them, boys—now!" Three of the deputies let their guns fall—but the redhaired deputy jerked up his pistol and fired at Bill Anderson and passed a ball through his hatbrim. Butch shot the redhead in the face and the man sat down hard on the sidewalk with a black hole under his eye and a look of profound astonishment and Bill shot him above the same eye and he pitched onto his back like he'd been yanked by the collar.

The onlookers scattered amid women's shrieks and the shrilling of horses lunging against their posted reins and the patrons gathered behind Coogan's big window ducked out of sight. The deputy called Junior fired twice at Ike Berry and both times hit his horse and Ike managed to jump clear as the gray buckled under him with a rasping grunt. Jim Anderson discharged both shotgun barrels and the buckshot stripped Junior's lower leg to the shinbone and ricocheted off the sidewalk in a spray and shattered Coogan's window and a falling shard gashed the arm of a woman crouched inside. Sidestepping the frighted horses, the sheriff saw Butch Berry loom before him and shot him in the side. Butch clutched hard to his saddlehorn as Ike shot the sheriff in the arm and in the hip and the man went down. Ike grabbed the reins of a tall buckskin and swung up into the saddle and Bill yelled "Go!" and they put heels to their mounts and sprinted away in a hammering of hooves and flying dirtclods.

They pounded like racers past an encamped wagon train just outside of town and every settler's face was agape in the billow of their trailing dust. They rode at full stride until they were miles from the town, then reined up on an open rise and stared hard behind them but saw no sign of chasers. Each saw on the others' faces his own wild grin.

"You holding all right?" Bill Anderson asked Butch.

Butch took his bloody hand from his side and considered his wound. He nodded.

"Then let's move," Bill said.

A DECISION

They rode through the rest of the afternoon and into the rising dusk and made camp alongside a creek in a dense wood. They could not have said whether they were in Kansas or Missouri. They'd shot a pair of rabbits and dressed and split them, and the four halves were now roasting on spits over a wavering fire, juices dripping and hissing.

Butch Berry sat shirtless with his back against an oak trunk and his bloody side to the light of the fire, Ike and the Andersons squatting beside him. The round had only scraped his ribs, and the wound looked more like a nasty cut than something done by a bullet. Ike was the best of them with needle and thread and he set to sewing up his brother.

"You were lucky," Jim said. "Couple of inches over and it might've been serious."

"If I was lucky," Butch said, "it would've missed me."

As Butch endured his brother's rude surgery with grit teeth and low profanities, Bill said he wasn't sure if they should return straightaway to the Parchman farm. "I mean, what if there's trackers coming behind? We got Aunt Sally and the girls to consider."

"That's right," Jim Anderson said. "We don't want to lead some posse to the farm and them think it's a haven for outlaws. Kansas sonsofbitches would fire the place in a minute."

Ike paused in his stitchwork. "I'm with you boys," he said. "I say we keep a distance from the farm for a time."

"So where do we lay up?" Jim said. "We can't stay here for long. It's Union men patrolling all up and down this border."

"Ain't you boys always said we'd get a fair welcome in Ray County?" Bill Anderson said to Ike.

"Damn right," Ike said. "We had plenty of good neighbors back there. We won't ever lack for a full plate of dinner nor a dry place to sleep."

"Let's do it," Jim said. "Only let's make a stop in Kansas City. They say that town's got sporting ladies to make Helen of Troy look like a mangy dog."

"All right, then," Bill said. "Ray County it is—by way of Kansas City."

Ike resumed his surgery and Butch took up his muttered cursings. In truth, none of them was eager to get back to a life of farming, not even Butch, whose reveries entailed vague wooings of Josephine on his return to the Parchman place.

Bill uncorked the jug and took a pull. He passed the whiskey to Jim, who had a drink and then held the jug out to Ike, who again left off from his sewing. "You know," Ike said, "I was just wondering if I did in that sheriff. I hit him twice but I don't believe I hit him mortal."

"No question we did in the badface," Bill said. He took off his hat and poked a finger through the hole in the brim. "I want you all to look here what that jackleg did to my hat."

"I know I made a cripple of that one deputy," Jim said.

"Maybe the sheriff bled to death," Ike said. "You reckon?" He took a drink and passed the jug to Bill.

"You all don't quit this gabbing and give some attention here," Butch Berry said, "*I'm* like to bleed to death. And how about letting the only wounded man here have a pull off that damn jug."

Ike Berry affected to harken to some distant sound. "You boys hear something? Like some naggy woman at complaining?"

Bill Anderson smiled and cupped a hand to his ear. "More like a baby mewling, I'd say."

"I don't know," Jim Anderson said. He cocked his head in an attitude of hard listening. "Sounded to me like some little girl crying. Maybe skinned her knee, something like that."

"You sorry sonofabitches, all you," Butch Berry said. And grimaced with the pain of joining in their laughter.

KANSAS CITY

They rode into Kansas City on a night of sodden rain. Its official name was City of Kansas and would remain so for another twenty-seven years, but even now everyone called it Kansas City.

The enclouded sky looked like violet smoke in every shimmer of haze lighting. The rain had fallen steadily through the day but was now eased to a drizzle. Federal soldiers everywhere in black slickers, horsed and afoot, resembling conjured shades bound for dire and dark appointments. The wagon traffic heavy despite the inclement weather, muleteers cracking whips and cursing at teams lunging against loads bogged in the mud. Blazing yellow doorways of saloons and bawdy houses open wide and issuing a cacophony of music into the night. Strains of piano and fiddle and banjo, songs abused at a bellow. Laughter of every sort—high and happy, hoarse and lewd, shrill and near to demented.

They trotted past a clutch of onlookers withstanding the weather to witness a pair of men grappling clumsily in the mud and cursing in gasps, vowing each to kill the other, though neither man was sober enough to stand unassisted or armed with more than bare hands and bad intention.

They stalled their horses in a livery and gave the boy instructions to feed the animals and rub them down. As they slogged across the street toward the nearest saloon they were hailed by a pair of cajoling young women leaning out of a brightly lighted second-floor window. The girls wore ribbons in their hair and lip paint bright as blood and yellow pantalettes of thin cotton that clung to their haunches like fruitskin and they wore nothing else. They held one hand to their breasts and blew red kisses at them with the other. Ike Berry waved vigorously in return and slung kisses back with both hands. The girls laughed and turned around and waggled their bottoms at them and withdrew into the room.

"Sweet baby Jesus," Ike said. "I believe I'm in love."

The din pressed on them like a thing of substance as they shouldered through the crowd and up to the bar. Men conversing in yells, greeting each other in hollers, bellowing profanities in earnest and in jest. There were two pianos, one to either side of the room, each playing at full volume and each a different tune. A half-dozen young women in uplifted ruffled skirts were bouncing about on a small stage in rude and risqué semblance of French-dancing, singing with no hope of harmony to an audience whooping its admiration and lobbing coins onto the stage in proof of it. The air of the place was humid and hot as breath, woven with the smells of smoke and whiskey and lamp oil, of men long between baths, of perfumes and powders and pomades.

They stood drinking and admiring the huge gilt-framed copy of *The Rape of the Sabine Women* hung above the backbar mirror. They pointed out to each other various of the painting's notable qualities—mostly pertaining to its bounty of female nakedness. When they had exhausted their store of art criticism, they stood with their backs against the counter so they could study the room.

They drank, sang along to the piano tunes, pitched coins to the dancers. A half-hour later each of them went upstairs with a whore. When they reconvened at the bar, Ike and Jim were manic with delight and couldn't stop talking about the goodlooking cyprians they'd sported with. Bill said his girl had lacked a proper enthusiasm, but this failing had been somewhat offset by her breasts, as lovely as any he'd ever known. "All in all," he said, "if she gave me back one of my two dollars and I gave her a feather up the ass, we'd both be tickled."

Asked about his girl, Butch shrugged and said she was all right but nothing special. The others traded looks and smiled in their sad knowledge that he was in love, a sore affliction that can imprison a man in thoughts of the beloved and make dull for him all readier pleasures, a condition the more vastly pitiful when a man's love was unrequited, which they knew his to be.

They moved on to other establishments. At the saloon next door they had a drink and then another just to be sure the first one did its duty. Then to another emporium, and then another, and they took a drink at every saloon they entered and tapped their feet to the music of piano or fiddle or a string band entire. In every place they went they called for favorite tunes, Ike exhorting for renditions of "Darlin

Corey," Jim Anderson for "Shady Grove." In this manner did they work their way down one side of the street and back up the other.

They took rooms in a hotel that night, and in the morning had a breakfast of beefsteak and eggs in a raucous restaurant full of teamsters and roustabouts and Union soldiers. Then the Berry boys and Jim Anderson went off to the docks to look at the steamboats and watch the passengers boarding and debarking, and Bill went in search of a bookstore. He inquired of a storekeeper on Grand Avenue who was sweeping the walkway fronting his establishment and the man directed him to a place called The Bookworm, just around the corner. Every wall of the store was covered with shelves from floor to ceiling and every shelf was spilling with books.

As he browsed, other customers came and went, almost all of them women and all of them piqued by the rough aspect of this lean and handsome presence whose muskiness pervaded the room and whose idle glances their way sent their own eyes blindly scampering over the stacked titles before them. He settled on a collection of Poe's tales. At the front desk, the aged and bespectacled proprietor with skin the color of watery milk consulted the inside of the front cover for the book's penciled price. "Strange fella, this one," he said.

Bill jutted his chin at the book lying open in front of the man and said, "What about him?"

It was a copy of Shakespeare's sonnets. "He's another," the old man said, and they both laughed. He went out with both volumes under his arm.

A FERRY CROSSING

The next day they moved on, following the river road to eastward along the top of a low pale bluff. The caramel-brown Missouri was in full view below them, gently rippled and a hundred yards wide at this stretch. The high ground gradually declined and some miles farther on they spied a ferry landing and whooped at their good timing—the ferry was on the near side of the river and taking on passengers. They paid a dollar apiece to hup their horses aboard in a clattering of hooves and join three other horsemen and a family with a wagon and a two-mule team. The vessel was a capacious log-and-plank construction and was operated by a heavy-muscled man in a sleeveless yellow duster, assisted by his wife and a pair of strapping sons both in their early teens. As soon as they were aboard, one of the boys set the stern rail in place and cast off the mooring ropes and the family went to work with the push poles.

The current along this stretch was slow but strong enough that the family crew had to pole at an upriver angle to compensate for it. The Andersons and Berrys patted their nervous horses and whispered to them. Up close the river was even darker brown than it had looked from the bluff. It smelled of raw earth and rotted vegetation. One of the passengers, an old man holding to the bridle of a horse as gray as his beard, remarked that Big Muddy was sure the right name for it.

"Like they say," a horseman in a well-tailored suit of white linen remarked, "it's too thick to swim in but not enough to walk on."

The family consisted of a man and wife, their fourteen-year-old son and two small children. The man was explaining to the ferryman that they were bound for Iowa. The marauding along the border was worse than ever, he said, and they'd had the ill fortune of living on a farm hard by a favorite route of the guerrillas. The wildwood boys had time and again cleaned them out of everything there was to eat, and finally the man and his family could endure it no longer and so they would spend the rest of the war at their cousins' farm near Ottumwa.

"Ye can count yourself lucky if all they done was steal your food and if it was only bushwhackers to come down on ye," the third horseman said. He wore a black wool cap and a much stained tan coat. An ulcerous red sore the size of a silver dollar ate into his cheek just above his mustache. "A party of bushwhackers showed up at my uncle's farm in Cass County and said they needed his wagon, and when he tried to stop them from taking it they shot him in the leg. Not two weeks later, a party of jayhawkers—jayhawkers, mind! *Unionists!*—come along and stole every animal on the place. My uncle kept telling them he was Union but them hawkers called him a puke liar and come yay close to hanging him."

"Damn well what he deserved," said the old man. "Union trash is all the same, be it jayhawk, bluebelly or dumbshit farmer."

The blackcapped man gawked at him—then started toward him. "Why, you secesh son of a bitch . . ."

The old man hopped back and stooped and snatched a knife from his boottop.

"Stand fast!" From under his duster the ferryman produced what for an instant seemed a pistol of gross proportions—and then clarified itself as a two-barreled shotgun, each muzzle as round as a shot glass, the barrel sawed off not twelve inches from the breech and the stock cut down to a pistol grip. Not a man on board was ignorant of the weapon's capacity to clear most of them from the deck with one yank on its triggers. The ferryman held his push pole in his other hand, but without his effort joined to theirs the rest of the family had to labor harder to try to keep on course for the opposite landing.

"Put up that cutter," the ferryman said. The old man took a moment to further consider the gaping muzzles of the shotgun, then shrugged and slipped the blade back into his boot.

"I don't care a damn who's a niggerlover and who's secesh but I won't stand for fighting on my vessel," the ferryman said, looking from the graybeard to the Unionist. "You want to fight, wait till you're on the other side or I'll put you off right here in the river."

He ordered the old man to take his horse to the rear of the ferry and told the Unionist to position himself at the front. He returned the shotgun to whatever holstery he'd arranged under the duster, then renewed his poling and the ferry began to recover the distance it had lost to the current. He glanced now and again at the antagonists to be sure they kept apart.

"Hoo," Ike Berry said with a grin. "Thought for a minute we'd have us an entertainment."

They were standing at the starboard rail and still joking quietly about the near fight when the water alongside them broke with a splash and showed a passing of something pale gray before closing up brown again.

Butch Berry pointed. "You all see that?"

"Catfish," Bill Anderson said. "Looked good size."

"They say there's some cats in this river bigger then me," Ike Berry said. "Butch caught one in the Crooked River one time weighed onto eighty pounds, but it was a baby compared to what they say's in here."

"You ain't telling us a thing we don't know," Jim Anderson said. "Back before we moved to Kansas, Daddy and us saw a catfish they caught over in Glasgow that weighed three hundred pounds if it weighed an ounce. Whiskers on it like ropes. They hung it up on the dock and sawed its belly open and all manner of things came out. Some animal—maybe a dog, maybe a coon—it was hard to say because it was mostly digested by then, but I ain't ever forgot the smell. There was a hat in there. A tin cup. There was a saddle stirrup with the strap still on it. Remember that fish, Billy?"

"It wouldn't have surprised me to see the rest of the saddle fall out of that thing's stomach," Bill Anderson said. "The rest of the *horse*."

They debarked into Clay County—the graybeard, the last to come off the ferry and spitting at the sight of the blackcapped man already well down the road—and an hour later arrived at the town of Liberty. The western sky was reefed with clouds afire at their core. They went into a restaurant and took a supper of cabbage and ham and then rode on again. They kept to the road in the gathering twilight until just before nightfall and then turned off onto a wagontrace flaring with fireflies and rode a quarter-mile farther and made their camp in a clearing. The air was softly fragrant of the day's warmed grass.

They raised a large fire and settled themselves around it. Bill Anderson got out the volume of sonnets and selected one at random. " 'Shall I compare thee to a summer's day?' " he began. But the Berry boys were unfamiliar with Shakespeare and his language, and Jim had never been partial to the Bard despite his mother's insistence on his glory, and by the time Bill arrived at the closing couplet—" 'So long as men can breathe, or eyes can see, / So long lives this, and this gives life to thee' "—Ike was hissing and Jim was calling for the hook. Later and privately, Butch would confess to Bill that he hadn't understood all of the poem but he liked it anyway, don't ask him why.

"You and me, Butch," Bill would tell him with a grin, "we got the true poetry in our souls. Our jughead brothers got nothing in theirs but stringband music."

Ike insisted that Bill read something with a damn *story* to it, by Jesus. So Bill opened the Poe collection and leafed through its pages, scanning the opening lines of each tale in search of the one most promising. The night around them had drawn closer, the shadows gone deeper. An owl made hollow calls in the high darkness.

Bill settled on a tale, took a sip of whiskey to lubricate his tongue, and began to read, captivating his audience with the very first sentence:

"The thousand injuries of Fortunato I had borne as I best could, but when he ventured upon insult, I vowed revenge. . . ."

RAY COUNTY SOJOURN

They rode the next day through thickly wooded country yielding sporadically to grassy prairie redolent of dog fennel, meadows brightly white with Queen Anne's lace. That afternoon the clouds grew thick and dark and came together in a high purple roil that spread across the sky and swallowed the sun and then loosed a hard windless rain to soak them in minutes and turn the ground to sucking mud. The rain ceased before sundown and they dried their clothes that night by the heat of a crackling fire billowing smoke for the wetness of the wood.

The next day they arrived at the Berrys' former home, a farm a few miles south of Burns Hollow. They took dinner with the Crashaws, the people who had bought the place from Alston Berry and who greeted the Berry boys like their own homecome sons. When the Crashaws heard of Alston's hard death at the hands of the jayhawkers, the woman wept and the husband's face drooped. "I never been one to say to nobody I told ye so," Mr. Crashaw said, "but I told Alston it were a bad mistake to go to that damn Kansas."

They slept in the barn that night and then the next day politely took their leave, claiming they had various other families to visit. The truth was that they would have felt obliged to lend a hand with chores if they'd stayed with the Crashaws any longer than one day— and farm work was what they sought to avoid for a while. They made a comfortable camp for themselves on the Crooked River in the woods about a half-mile from town.

There was a dance in the public square the following night. The

Berrys had been popular boys and their old neighbors were glad to see them. The brothers were obliged time and again to tell of their father's killing and of the vengeance they had exacted, to inform of their mother and sisters having gone away to Arkansas. Every recounting of Alston Berry's murder roused in their listeners a new round of imprecations toward all Kansans in general and the damned jayhawkers especially—and prompted yet more backslaps and proffered jugs in admiration of the way the Berry boys had set- tled the account.

Ike and Butch introduced the Andersons all around. With so many of the town's able men gone to soldiers, there were plenty of unattached women to notice the handsome strangers, and in the course of the evening Bill and Jim danced with them all. They reeled and waltzed and squaredanced, the fiddlers sawing and grinning as the caller sang out his commands:

> Haint been drunk since away last fall,
> swing your partner and promenade the hall!
> Promenade eight till you get straight,
> swing that gal like you're swinging on a gate!

The question of whether they would return to work their uncle's farm or join the army was sometimes posed discreetly by men who offered them a jug, and sometimes more directly by the girls they danced with. It was a matter the four had discussed among them- selves, and their unanimous inclination was neither toward farming nor soldiering but for renewing their rustling enterprise. It would not do, of course, to make public this ambition, and so their ready answer was that they had come to Burns Hollow to report the news of the Berry family and as soon as Ike and Butch were done with vis- iting old neighbors they were all four off to enlist in Sterling Price's Missouri Brigade. The venerable name of Old Pap had the expected effect of making the men nod with satisfaction and brightening every girl's eyes.

Over the next weeks the Andersons attended still more dances. They called on young women and sipped lemonade with them on front porch swings. They went on picnics in the company of one or another pair of pretty sisters, sometimes accompanied by the Berry boys and their own fetching companions. As his ladyfriend peeled a boiled egg for him in the shade of a maple one fine afternoon, Ike Berry kissed her ear and made her giggle and blush and slap at him playfully. Ike winked at the others and said, "Now don't this just beat purple hell out of pushing a plow?"

When they were not dallying with girls, the Andersons and Berrys were often fishing on the banks of the Crooked River or sitting in the taverns, drinking and playing cards, chatting with the locals. They always fished from the same spot on the river where the Berrys had caught the monstrous catfish they'd told of. They would set out the baited lines and lie down in the shade of the trees and pass a jug around and tell each other that life was a pleasant enough arrangement for men who knew how to deal with it. On their best day they caught nine catfish but were agreed that the biggest of them would not have scaled much above thirty pounds. Ike and Butch could only mutter in embarrassment. "Biggest ones must've all been caught while we were away in Kansas," Butch said.

The tavern talk was chiefly of the war and the region's good fortune to date. No local farm had suffered much beyond losing some of its stock to a few raiding redlegs and to thieving squads of passing militia. No one had yet been murdered, praise Jesus, although in the instance of stealing Walter Finley's horses a redleg bunch had clubbed him down with riflebutts when he protested the theft and Walter's wit had been somewhat dulled ever since.

One night after a dance, Bill and Jim offered to take a pair of blonde sisters home on horseback by the light of a low full moon. The girls swore to secrecy the giggling friends they'd come with in a wagon and then swung up behind the Andersons on their mounts. They hardly protested when Bill and Jim suggested they stop by the riverside and enjoy the sweet night. At a distance from each other, the couples spread blankets on the shadowed bank of the river running silver in the moonlight. Bill told his girl that if he was destined to die while serving with Old Pap he wanted this moment to be his last memory. Then began softly to recite Poe's "Dream Within a Dream." By the time he reached the part about golden grains of sand slipping through his fingers " 'While I weep—while I weep!' " the girl was hugging him around the neck and then he could speak no more for her kisses in his mouth.

Even as Bill was enjoying the girl he could faintly hear his brother at the other blanket: " 'For alas! alas! with me / The light of life is o'er! / No more—no more—no more—' " And then heard clearly the clink of a buckle. And then soft pantings that shortly grew to gasps.

Oh Mister Edgar, Bill thought, your poetry is more potent than you know. The girl smiled up at him in the glow of the moon and stroked his newly grown goatee, her pleasure bright in her eyes.

They afterward helped the girls to readjust their clothes, to re-tie shirtlaces and smooth their skirts. They had to make do with their fingers for hairbrushes. When they finally got them home, there was a light burning in the front window. They reined up at a distance and the girls gave them quick goodnight kisses and slid off the horses and made off in the moonlight like raiders stealing up on an enemy fortress. As they ambled back to camp the brothers agreed it had been almost too easy.

Such pleasant days and nights do fleetly pass. They had been in Ray County nearly a month when Bill Anderson began to feel uneasy about his sisters having no protection but frail Uncle Angus. And his apprehension had been heightened by reports of an increase in Federal outrages against border folk suspected of secessionist leanings. His distaste for farming suddenly seemed to him poor reason for having put his sisters at such risk.

They were lazing on the bank of the Crooked one early afternoon, their catfish lines out, when he suddenly sat up and said, "Boys, I'm for heading back."

"About damn time," Butch Berry said. He flung the coiled slack of his handline into the river. "I've *been* for heading back."

"Well I'm ready too," Ike said. "Some of these folk have begun to wonder out loud if the war'll be over and Old Pap Price retired to a rocking chair before we go off to join the fighting like we said. I believe we're starting to be looked on with a suspect eye."

"When do we go, Billy?" Jim Anderson said.

An hour later they were saddled and saying goodbye to the Crashaws and then riding hard to the south.

NEWLY TURNED GRAVES

The tangerine sun was almost descended to the treetops and the air was hazed in gold as they closed to within a half-mile of the Parchman place. When they saw there was no show of chimney smoke above the trees in the direction of the farm, they halted and looked at each other, then chucked up their horses and went forward with pistols in hand. The birds were holding silent, the only sounds the fall of hooves and the low chink of harness metal.

They advanced in pairs along the narrow trail through the heavy woodland, Bill and Jim in the lead, the Berry boys some twenty yards behind and watching their backs and all of them alert for ambush. Where the path entered Parchman property it was flanked on one side by a stone wall and on the other by a fence of split rails.

They reined up at the edge of the farmyard and looked upon a place made shambles. The barn was a charred ruin with three black walls still upright and casting long shadows. The house was intact and looked unburned in any of its visible parts, but the front door hung askew on its lower hinge and the window shutter was fallen onto the porch and the porch roof was partly collapsed at one end where the support post had been knocked away. The corn crib was absent several of its side slats and stood emptied. The hog pen railings were down, and most of the rails of the horse corral. There was no stock in sight, no sign of the red hounds. Bill put his index fingers to the corners of his mouth in some secret fashion and let a whistle so high that none but dogs could hear it, but no dog answered his call. Beyond the outbuildings, portions of the cornfield had been burned and much of it trampled by horses and most of it lay in a blackened tangle of broken stalks and ears.

"Sonofabitches," Butch Berry said. He hupped his horse out of the trees and headed for the house at a lope. Bill Anderson heeled Edgar Allan after him. Ike and Jim came behind at a slow trot, warily scanning to right and left as they advanced into the open.

Bill and Butch dismounted at the house and went up the porch steps with their Colts cocked. Every item of furniture lay broken. The floor was littered with clothing, some of it the Parchmans', some belonging to the Anderson girls.

"Josephine!" Butch Berry shouted. He hastened to the door of the kitchen room and looked within, then went to the loft ladder and climbed it high enough to see that no one lay hidden or dead up there. He came down and kicked the wall, then stalked to the door and yelled, *"Josie!"*

"Quit hollering," Bill Anderson said. "If they were around they'd let us know."

Butch glared at him, then stepped to the railing and spat. Despite his rebuke, Bill did not fault him for his rage. His own chest was weighted with a dread fury, his breathing tight, his grip aching on the Colt. He studied the sky—bloodcolored in the west, deep purple to eastward—and held hard to the thought that somewhere beneath it Josie was this minute alive and hale and telling her sisters to be brave or she'd without mercy ridicule them to their brothers.

Jim came around the corner of the house. "Billy, come look." His face bespoke bad news. As they followed him to the burned barn, crows cawed in the higher branches and a nearby mockingbird echoed them in a fair mimicry.

In the twilit maple grove beyond the blackened barn walls were four fresh gravemounds, one to either side of the pair of small graves holding the bones of the long-dead Parchman children, the other two a few yards farther away and side by side. Of the mounds flanking the children's graves, one showed fresher, more recently turned earth than the other. The pair of farther graves were more recent as well.

Ike was squatted by the darker of the nearer gravesites and working a handful of its dirt, assaying it as a man might the soil of a field for planting. The grave bore a wooden cross into whose horizontal piece was awkwardly carved the name of Sally Parchman and the year 1862. The cross on the neighboring grave informed that it was Angus Parchman's. The two farther crosses carried the names of Tobe and Baldwin and no other information. Butch blew out a long breath and Bill leaned against a tree.

"This one wasn't dug even a week ago," Ike said of Sally Parchman's grave. "Probably right after the place was raided." He duck-walked to the grave of Angus Parchman and scooped some of its dirt and felt of it. "This one's about a month old."

"Hell, Old Angus probably died just after we left here," Jim Anderson said.

Ike stood up and brushed the dirt from his hands. "I wouldn't reckon the raiders for burying Sally, so had to've been the girls." He glanced from one Anderson brother to the other. "I'd look on it as good news. They're likely gone to someplace safe."

"Who in the hell is Tobe and Baldwin?" Jim Anderson said. "Who buried *them*?"

Ike shrugged.

Butch said he'd had enough of this jabber. He wanted to go looking for the girls right away, but Bill said they should wait until morning. "If they're hiding in the woods, they won't see it's us," he said. "They might think it's raiders and keep hid from us. We could pass right by them and never know it. Better we wait till morning, and then we'll ask at every farm roundabouts. Could be they're sheltering with one of them"

Butch Berry cursed and spat. Then raised and dropped his arms at his side in a gesture of capitulation.

REDLEGS

They tethered the horses alongside the house and put down their bedding amid the ruined furniture within. The pantry of course stood bare. The root cellar too had been cleaned out. But the creek was still running clear and so they had plenty of fresh water. They went out to the trampled cornfield and by the weak light of a crescent moon collected a dozen intact ears and roasted them for supper over a firepit they dug in front of the house. They took turns keeping watch on the porch steps through the night and each man in his turn heard the others tossing on the floor in fitful sleep.

Bill Anderson's was the last watch before dawn. He sat on the porch steps and observed the eastern sky as it lightened to gray above the silhouetted treeline. Somewhere a cock crowed and he wondered if the rooster was one of theirs that had escaped the raiders. The trees began to take form in the receding darkness. As the eastern sky reddened he set about raising a cookfire. He thought he would go into the woods and see what he might shoot for breakfast. He checked the Navy's loads and tucked the pistol in his waistband and started for the near woods just the other side of the creek.

Midway between the house and the creek the ground sloped down, and he had just reached the crest of the incline when his left arm was slapped forward and he heard the rifleshot as he spun half-about and went tumbling down the slope.

He lay stunned and staring up at the crimson sky. Shouts in the distance. A pounding of coming hooves and an outbreak of gunfire. His brother shouting, "*Billy*—where you at?"

He tried to sit up but could not—and his arm came awake to such pain that he cursed through his teeth. The house was thirty yards away and from this angle he could see only its roof. It sounded as if the attackers had reined up short of the house, had likely taken cover at the barn and the corn crib. The gunfire was furious. A horseman loped over the crest of the slope and saw him and heeled his mount into a sprint directly at him. He drew up his knees to make himself smaller and he fired up at the animal as it bore over him.

His next awareness was of looking the horse on its side in the risen dust, shrieking and coughing blood and trying vainly to regain its feet. The rider lay a few yards beyond the animal and was making his own efforts to rise. Bill locked his teeth against a dizzying pain and propped himself on his right elbow, the Colt still in his hand. The man sat up and looked at him. Bill cocked the piece and adjusted its angle and fired and the ball struck the man in the face and he flung backward and lay still. Bill saw now that the man wore red gaiters.

He fell back. The sky looked askew and the cracking and the popping of gunfire seemed louder now and to be coming from every direction. And at some remove but closing fast came yet another assembly of gunfire and with it a howling to prickle the scalp. Then the red sky reeled and the wild cries seemed as close to his ear as the screams of the crippled horse and then he saw and heard nothing.

WILDWOOD BOYS

I am a poor wayfaring stranger
traveling through this world of woe.

Yet there's no sickness, toil or danger
in that bright world where I go.

He was unsure if he was dreaming the music or was awake and
actually hearing the song and the plunking banjo strings, if his eyes
were open to darkness or simply closed.

Going home to see my mother,
going home no more to roam.
Going across the River Jordan,
I'm forever going home.

His head felt thick and heavy and it was a moment before he
became aware of its pulsing pain. And of the pain in his arm. He
was lying on his back and his eyes were closed. The strength
required to open them seemed more than he could muster and he did
not even try.

I know dark clouds may gather round me,
I know my way is hard and steep.
But I must ride the road before me,
and travel far before I sleep.

Other voices now. Some loud and nearby, some at a distance, all
of them a garble. A hornpipe ditty. Laughter. Nickerings and snuf-
flings of horses, jinglings of bridle rings. His eyes still closed, he put
fingers to his head and the sensation was of guiding someone else's
hand. He felt gingerly of a bandage there. Then explored his arm and
found that it too had been attended and was bound. His right thigh
ached as well but it was unbandaged and felt dry to his fingers and it
could stand the hard squeeze of his hand and so he knew the leg was
both unbloodied and unbroken.

"Welcome back to the world, friend."

He opened his eyes to the underbranches of a maple tree and
through them saw fragments of bright blue sky wisped with white.
Sitting crosslegged on the ground beside him was a hatless smiling
man with a sandy pompadour, rampant chin whiskers and shaven

cheeks. He had been scribbling in a small notebook and now closed it and put it and his pencil in a shirt pocket. Then turned and called to someone, "It's Lazarus returned to the living."

Jim Anderson appeared and hunkered beside Bill and smiled at him. "How you doing, Billy?"

"Well," Bill said, "I don't exactly know." His own voice sounded strange to him.

"You hurt anyplace other than your head and arm?"

"Leg. It's not broke."

"Hell, you'll be all right," Jim said. "Bullet bit your arm but didn't break bone. I thought you'd been shot in the head, but W. J. says it looks more like the horse kicked you. Musta stepped on your leg too is why it hurts."

"*Who* said?"

"William J. Gregg," the goateed man said. "I used to go by Bill but every other man in the country's named Bill anymore so I started going by W. J. Don't ask what the J. stands for because I've never told or intend to." He carried a revolver on each hip and another tucked in the front of his pants and his gray shirt was oversized and showed four large pockets with a bright pink rose embroidered over each of them. A huge ensheathed bowie was tied to one leg and he carried a Green River knife in a boottop. "You're lucky, friend. A right horsekick can bust your brainpan sure as a bullet."

"Listen, Billy," Jim said, "the girls are all right. They're in Westport."

"The girls? Josephine?"

Jim nodded. "All of them."

"They're at the Vaughn place," Gregg said. "With the sisters to one of our boys."

Bill looked at him. "Who in hell *are* you?"

"Quantrill men."

"They saved our ass, Bill," Jim said. His voice tight with excitement, eyes aspark. "They put down all them sonofabitches—*fifteen* of them!—and didn't lose a man doing it."

"Truth be told, we put them all down but two, and you got one of them," Gregg said to Bill. "Could be the other got away. We'll know soon enough."

They helped Bill to sit up with his back against the tree, pain flaring in his skull with every movement of his head. Someone handed him a canteen and he took an avid drink. He saw the banjo picker sitting on a porch step, saw the farmyard full of men and horses. The horses were superb breeds and better groomed than their wildlooking riders, whose aspect was of displaced pirates, deserters of the Mother Ocean fled to a life ahorse.

Every man looked to be as heavily armed as Gregg and most of them wore baggy shirts of a cut like his, some in a like gray color, others in butternut or brown or dark yellow, each shirt with a different embroidery but every stitching fanciful. Bill had thought his own hair long for brushing past his collar, but the hair on some of these men hung in wild tangles to their shoulders. Most sported beards and mustaches but many seemed too young yet to do so. He saw Ike Berry talking with someone who looked no more than a child, whose three Colt revolvers on his belt appeared hugely outsized against his small stature.

"That sprout you're eyeballing is Riley Crawford," Gregg said. "Not yet fifteen years old. His momma brought him to us a couple of months back and told us a tale we've heard a hundred times before. Jayhawkers fell on them and called her husband a liar when he said he was on their side and then hanged him. They fired all the buildings and burned the cornfield. Took shameful liberties in handling the mother and daughter both. Young Riley went at one of them with a grub hoe and got his front teeth knocked out. They drove off the stock and stole all the goods and carried them away in the Crawfords' own wagon. Left the momma and children with not a thing to eat. Not a shovel to bury her husband. They dug the grave with their hands and a tree limb. The woman decided to take the girl and go live with kin in Illinois, but first she borrowed a wagon and brought the boy to us. Told the captain if young Riley was old enough to bury his murdered daddy he was old enough to kill the likes of them who murdered him. The captain said he couldn't refute her argument. You wouldn't think so to look at him, but that child has since killed some dozen Union men and I don't misdoubt he'll dispatch a few more before he's through. The jayhawks made a mistake not to kill him when they had the chance."

"Which one's Quantrill?" Bill said, scanning the faces of the milling men.

"He ain't here, I asked," Jim Anderson said. "He's off with the rest of the company."

A trio of guerrillas was leading a line of thirteen horses into the woods and each horse held a bloodyshirted body draped over the saddle. One of the horses bore two bodies. Every dead man wore red leggings.

A dapper man with a feather in his hat and a neatly trimmed imperial now joined them, and Gregg introduced him as George Maddox. Maddox said the redlegs would be thrown in the river to float downstream and be fished out by whoever might want them.

"What happened to Uncle Angus and Aunt Sally?" Bill Anderson said. "What happened here?" He gestured at the surrounding ruin, and the effort dizzied him.

"Old Angus coughed to death a while back," Gregg said, "but Sally Parchman, I'm sorry to say, was killed by militia bastards who came raiding a week ago. The girls said it was an accident, but it don't hardly lessen the sin."

Ike Berry heard this as he walked up. "Riley says not a man of that milish bunch is still breathing," he said.

"Somebody informed those shitheads we were here," Maddox said. "We got people making inquiries and we'll soon enough know who it was."

"You all were here?" Bill said. "I mean, before?"

"Many a time," Maddox said.

"We reckoned Uncle Angus was helping you all, but he never would say," Jim said.

"He was a good man for keeping his mouth shut," Maddox said.

"I only wish we'd still been here when these bastards showed up," Gregg said.

"I mean," Bill said, "have you all been here since we been gone?"

They had, Gregg said. About three weeks ago they'd come to Parchman's to tend their wounds and rest up after a bad fight in Cass County. It had been their meanest skirmish yet—against a Federal force outnumbering them three to one. They'd left sixteen dead and hardly a man came away unbloodied. Quantrill himself took a ball in the leg. When they got here, they found the Anderson girls in residence with newly-widowed Sally. "Sally always was a fine one for the surgeon's trade, even in her mourning dress," Gregg said.

"Your sisters were quick apprentices as well," Maddox said, "especially the darker one, the middle one—Josephine, is it?"

"She's good at anything she puts her mind to," Bill said. His own voice sounded to him as though it were coming from somewhere else. The pain in his head was grown larger.

"She's a caution is what she is," Maddox said. "She was ladling water to some of the hurt boys one time and Andy Blunt gave her a little grab of the hind end as he was passing by. Well sir, she whacked him with that ladle so hard he spun about like a drunk wondering which way's home. Swole his eye up like a plum. Gave us all a good laugh."

"Andy's a fine fella and didn't mean any disrespect," Gregg said. "He was just feeling frisky is all. Soon as he got his wits back he apologized to the girl and you could see by her face she was sorry she'd hit him—or at least that she'd hit him so hard."

"Good thing for that fellow she wasn't chopping wood when he put his hand to her," Jim said.

"The girls said you fellas had gone to Kansas to settle a matter," Gregg said. "They were hoping you'd be back before we left." Bill and Jim exchanged a guilty glance.

They had been at the farm two weeks before Quantrill could ride again, and then scouts brought word of a Federal cavalry company that was questioning farmers in the area and burning out those who couldn't prove they were Union. The Feds were reported to be fifty strong, and there were only twenty-four guerrillas at Parchman's, including a pair of men too badly wounded to get on a horse. But Quantrill figured he had the advantage of surprise and better knowledge of the country, so they mounted up, leaving their two wounded in care of the women. They found the Yanks camped on the Blue and hit them at first light and dropped more than a dozen before the others went racing back to their post at Independence. Quantrill then split up his party, taking half the men with him to rendezvous with the rest of the company, sending Gregg and the others back to the Parchman place to watch over their wounded and the women until their brothers got back.

"We were on our way here when we came on a party of milish driving stock," Gregg said. "Twenty-two of them and each one is this minute stoking a furnace in hell. After we put them down, we saw the horses and mules had Angus Parchman's brand, and we came here quick as we could, and, well, this . . ."—he gestured at the burned and broken outbuildings, at the trampled and partly fired cornfields—"is what we found."

"The girls had already buried our two boys and Sally Parchman," Maddox said. "We figured it was best to take them up to the Vaughn place for safekeeping, then come back to see if you boys showed up. I'd say we got here at a good time."

"There they be!" somebody shouted.

"That's the redleg's horse! You owe me a dollar, peckerwood!"

A pair of horsemen were coming down the trail at a trot, the lead rider husky and cleanshaved, his short blond hair showing bright in the sunlight as he took off his hat and wiped his brow. The other man was leading a saddled horse by its reins and Bill Anderson saw now that he was Butch Berry.

THE STONEMASON

The blond man was handsome in a hardfaced fashion. He dismounted and smiled around at his fellows' congratulations for hunting down the runaway redleg. He told Butch Berry to put the redleg horse with the rest of the captured mounts and Butch said yes sir and grinned at his brother and the Andersons as he moved off. The blond man came over to them, slapping dust from his shirtsleeves.

"Boys," Gregg said, "meet George Todd." He introduced Todd to Ike Berry and the Andersons. Todd nodded and fixed an appraising look on each newcomer in turn. The hands thumbed onto his pistol belt were large and strong, the hands of a stonemason, which had been his trade before the war. He'd told little else of his past except that he had been born in Canada. But there were many rumors about him, including one of a murder warrant in Wisconsin for having throttled a man in a fight over a woman.

"What do you think?" he asked Gregg. "They be bushwhackers?"

"I believe they'll do fine," Gregg said.

Todd considered Bill Anderson's bandaged arm and head. "This one don't look to be doing so fine right now."

"I figure he can lay up at the Vaughn place till he's hale," Gregg said.

Todd looked at Jim Anderson and then back at Bill. "You boys got some hardbark sisters. Good girls, the lot."

"We know it," Jim Anderson said.

"All right then, mount up," George Todd said. He turned and called out for men named Younger and Pool to take the point.

Jim and Gregg helped Bill Anderson to his feet. He tested his injured leg, found that it would bear his weight, and limped over to Edgar Allan. He had to use his right hand to hold to the saddlehorn as he stepped up onto the horse. It was a tricky maneuver but he managed it, though the effort broke a rush of sweat on his face and made him go even lighter in the head.

"Mr. Todd!" Calling out as he came riding toward him was Riley Crawford. Todd smiled and took something from his pocket and tossed it underhand to the boy. Riley Crawford caught it and looked on it and his grin revealed a black gap where his front teeth had been.

"I want you all to take a good look at that," Butch Berry whispered to his brother and the Andersons. "I was right there when Todd took it off the redleg."

They watched Riley Crawford remove his hat and lift from around his neck a long necklace of thin rawhide that appeared to be strung with pieces of dried fruit graduating in hue from black to brown to rosy nearest the rude clasp fashioned from a pair of ladies' hairpins. It took a moment for them to realize he was holding a collar of human ears. With his knife tip the boy cut a hole in the ear Todd had just presented him, then held the thing to his mouth and said, "How you like it down in hell, redleg?" He laughed and strung the ear onto the rawhide thong and reclasped it and slipped the necklace back over his head. The horrid garland hung to his belt buckle. Grinning like a goblin with a new trinket, he reined his horse about and hupped away.

Butch Berry laughed as if he'd been told a good lewd joke, and Todd called out, "Let's go!"

They navigated along wildwood routes the Andersons and Berrys had not known to exist, holding to deer traces and hog runs wending through the high grass and the thickest and most deeply shadowed portions of the wildwood, and they sometimes had to hug to their horses' necks to dodge the low overhang of tree branches. Wherever the trails widened sufficiently the riders formed a double column. The Berrys rode directly ahead of the Andersons, and behind Bill and Jim came Gregg and Maddox. The guerrillas bringing up the rear of the column also drove the bloodstained and still-saddled redleg horses. Because the Union army allotted its best horses to the eastern war zones, Yankee mounts in Missouri rarely met guerrilla standards of horseflesh. Redleg horses, however, were mostly stolen Missouri stock of superior breed, and the guerrillas usually kept for themselves any they captured.

The latesummer air now thickly hot. Bill Anderson's arm throbbing intensely. His leg ached to the bone. The back of his eyes sparked with white pain at Edgar Allan's every stride. His hat did not fit his bandaged head and so he had folded it and tucked it under his cantle.

As they rode, Butch Berry told of how he and George Todd had chased down the redleg who tried to get away. The man made the mistake of bearing for the open country to the southwest rather than heading up the Kansas City Road. When they came in sight of him out in the flats like that, Todd abruptly reined up and slid off his horse, unsheathed and cocked his Sharps carbine, and laid the barrel on the saddle to steady his aim while his mount stood still as a statue. The Sharps could drive a one-ounce bullet through four inches of oak at a thousand yards and had a range of up to a mile. He shot the redleg off his horse at full gallop at a distance Butch reckoned as three hundred yards.

When they got to him he was facedown and still alive. The round had passed through his right side and destroyed a lung, to judge from all the blood he'd coughed up. Todd dismounted and rolled him over with his foot and Butch saw that he wasn't much older than himself and didn't look all that scared. He tried to say something but began to choke on his blood. Todd drew his revolver and leaned down and shot him in the heart from so close up the boy's shirt smoked with the powder scorching.

"Then he lops his ear off as easy as picking a flower," Butch said. He looked back at Gregg and said, "How come he gave it to Riley?"

"The sprout's been cutting ears from his first day with us," Gregg said. "Got the idea from tales of the Mexican War. Heard that Texas Rangers used to take the ears and noses off the Mexicaners they killed. Todd, he'll sometimes dock an ear but he won't *wear* it, and I don't much blame him. Says he'd feel like a damned heathen. So he gives them to young Riley."

They had closed to within a half-mile of Westport when Todd halted the column. They could see the haze of the town's chimney smoke above the trees. Bill Anderson was now so feverish he believed they had been riding most of the day, though in fact they'd been ahorse little more than an hour. His skull felt immense, his brainpan asmolder. His vision was skewed and his hearing muffled. His nerves felt dulled, as though he were wearing heavy clothes and gloves. He was vaguely aware that a horseman had appeared out of the trees along the trail ahead and was talking to Todd. Then clearly heard someone say that the Unionist farmer who'd brought the militia down on the Parchman place had been found out by Quantrill and was this minute hanging big-eyed and bootless from a rafter in his own barn. Now somebody was tugging his sleeve. To turn his head required prodigious effort. He saw Jim looking at him strangely and moving his mouth but the only sound he heard was a low hum. Then he felt the ground tilting under Edgar Allan and himself pitching toward it.

He woke on a soft bed in a lamplit and sparsely furnished room. His head hurt with every heartbeat. His vision was slightly hazed, but he saw clearly enough the ladderback chair set within easy reach of the bed and hung with his gunbelt and the two Navies. Through a thinly curtained window paled with diffused moonlight came the sounds of hoofcloppings and rattling wagons passing in the near distance. He heard the strains of a fiddle playing low somewhere. Smelled coal oil and soapfresh sheets and the sunlight in which they had been dried. Became aware that he was shed of his stink, had been bathed and bandaged afresh, was wearing but a nightshirt.

The door softly creaked open. A lean woman stood in silhouette against the brighter light of the hallway behind her and then stepped inside and closed the door and came rushing across the room in a swishing of skirt to descend upon him and tightly hug him. He breathed the smells of her skin and hair and felt her wet cheek on his face. Then her lips were on his and he knew them for Josephine's.

THE VAUGHN HOUSE

Set on the Santa Fe about three miles south of Kansas City, Westport was an outfitting post for wagon parties heading west. The town was centered on an intersection of streets lined with stores and shops and offices, with liveries, eateries and saloons. It included a few residential streets and a scattering of isolated homes along its outskirts. The Vaughn estate stood about a half-mile south of town. The family patriarch, a wealthy shipping contractor and fervent secessionist, had together with his wife succumbed to diphtheria the previous year. They were survived by a pair of daughters, Hazel and Annette, and a son named Jimmy, who early in the spring had gone to join Quantrill.

The Vaughn house was a spacious three-story structure on an iron-fenced and thickly wooded twenty-acre property fronted by the Westport Road. It was boundaried on its other three sides by heavy woodland. The grounds were kept by a man named Finley and his Negro helper Joshua. They also tended the large stable of horses and mules set far behind the main house and in whose lee lay a well-worn trace into the woods, a path by which parties of guerrillas could come and go unseen. With his prematurely gray hair and pronounced limp—the Vaughns had told townfolk he'd been born crippled—Finley seemed an innocuous figure, but in truth his knee had been wrecked by a jayhawker rifleball during the territorial border war, and both he and Black Josh were men of Quantrill. As they played their public roles of hired men and protectors of the Vaughn girls, they made careful account of Federal and militia movements along the local roads and regularly informed Quantrill about them.

This was where the Anderson girls had been brought to be sheltered. The Vaughn sisters received them with smiles and kisses and warm embraces and the girls had all taken immediate like to each other. And in a second-floor bedroom of this house was where—not a week later—Bill Anderson found himself ensconced on the night he regained consciousness and received Josephine's happily tearful kisses before again falling asleep.

When he woke the next morning the room was brightly sunlit. His fever had broken, and he was greatly relieved by the restored clarity of his vision, his abated pains. Josephine, fully dressed and with her hair veiling one side of her face, slept beside him. He smiled on her and gently brushed the hair from her face and saw her cheek was swollen purple. His instant impulse was to wake her and demand to know who'd struck her—then find the bastard and kill him without discussion.

But now came giggling from the door and he saw Mary and Jenny standing there and grinning widely—and felt himself smile at them in return.

"Hey, Billy," Jenny said, "you sure look funny with that wrap around your head and those whiskers on your chin."

Then they were sprinting across the room and clambering onto the bed and hugging and kissing him and both talking at once and Josie was startled awake by their jostling and happy squealing and she told her sisters to be careful of Billy's wounds, dammit.

The girls kept interrupting one another as each delivered a breathless narrative of the militia raid on the Parchman farm. He was able to understand that the two wounded guerrillas had been in the barn and that Josephine came by her bruised cheekbone when she tried to protect one of them and a militiaman flung her aside and her face struck a stallpost. Aunt Sally had tried to shield the other wounded man with her own body by lying atop him and hugging him tight to her, but the soldiers rolled them over and one of them shot the bushwhacker in the back even as Sally clutched herself to him. Mary and Jenny thought she was trapped under his weight, but when they heaved the body off her they saw the bloodstain on her breast and saw her dulled eyes and they burst into tears with the realization that she was dead of the same bullet that killed the guerrilla. When the militiamen realized what they'd done, they made away fast.

"We'd buried Uncle Angus but a few weeks before," Josephine said, "and here we were burying Aunt Sally too. *And* two murdered boys. That's all we did the day after those bastards came—dig graves and put people in them."

"Josephine, watch your mouth," Mary said.

"If they weren't the worst days of my life," said Jenny Anderson, twelve years old and without inkling of the future, "I can't imagine what might be."

"Did Josie tell you about Uncle Angus?" Mary asked Bill. "He started coughing one night like always, only this time he couldn't stop and he fell dead right there at the supper table."

"Poor Aunt Sally," Josie said. "She didn't cry a whole lot, but from the minute Uncle Angus died she started looking really *old*."

Bill asked where Jim and the Berry boys were now and Mary said they'd gone with the bushwhackers to meet somewhere with Quantrill. They'd asked Jim to stay, but he was set on joining with the others in whatever mischief they had planned. Besides Bill, the only men on the place were Finley and Black Josh.

Then the Vaughn sisters were knocking at the open door, and the Anderson girls said for them to come in and meet Billy. At nineteen, Annette was almost two years older than her sister, was shorter and tending to plumpness, but she owned an exceptionally lovely face. Hazel was pretty and warm-eyed and softspoken, well-breasted but leanhipped as a boy.

It seemed understood by everyone that he was Josephine's special charge. After he'd been introduced to Hazel and Annette and had given Mary and Jenny several more one-armed hugs and permitted them to pepper him with still more kisses, Josie shooed them all out of the room, telling the tittering Vaughn girls they'd done enough gawking at her brother in his nightshirt, he wasn't no coochie show.

When the others were gone he asked who had bathed him and dressed him in the nightshirt. "Well, who you think?" she said—and only the faintest blush showed through her smile. "And let me just say I have smelled things dead a week that didn't stink as bad. I about needed a chisel to get some of that filth off you. But I kept the door closed the whole time so nobody else could, you know, get a peek at you all bare-assed."

He couldn't help but laugh. He asked if the Vaughn girls knew she'd slept in his bed last night, and she said they did now. They had a brother of their own, the Vaughn girls, also named Jimmy, and they just loved him to pieces. She didn't have the slightest doubt that if Jimmy Vaughn was wounded and needed close tending, either one of his sisters would sleep beside him in order to be as close as they could to take care of him.

"I don't think Annette or Hazel either was looking too terribly shocked this morning, do you?" she said.

"Don't mock your older brother."

"Oh, pardon *me,* Squire Anderson," she said, and smiled brightly. She went to the window and drew back the thin curtains and stared out at the sunbright day chittering with birdcalls.

"Did you see Butch?" he said.

She quit her smile and looked at him.

"I had the feeling he was real eager to see you."

She gestured irritably. "The bunch of them were only around long enough to carry you up here and eat some supper. He acted so nervous the whole time, he made *me* nervous, and I hate that. I said I was glad they'd got back from Kansas all right, but you'd of thought I was *singing* to him, the way he kept looking at me." She made a face of slackjawed witlessness.

"He can't help it. He's a smitten man."

"Well he can just get *un*smitten."

"You know what he named his new horse?"

"Jim told me. So what? It's not my name."

"You're not going to give that boy the first chance, are you?"

She fixed him with a look of such sudden anxiety it made his heart sway. A look seeking fearfully to know if that was what *he* wanted her to do—to give Butch Berry, or any other man, a chance.

He wanted to tell her what he knew was right, to tell her yes, yes, of course she should, she *must,* give some fella the chance to prove worthy of her affections, some fella she could marry and make a family with, have a normal life with. He wanted to tell her that he himself was selfish beyond redemption and damned for his sinful desires, to tell her they must nevermore touch each other as they had, to tell her that Butch was as good a man as any and far better than most and would always love her and could always protect her.

Standing at the sunlit window and staring apprehensively at him, she looked as beautiful as he had ever seen her. And he thought: No, God damn me, *no.*

She smiled as if she'd heard him. Then came to him and brushed the hair from his eyes with her fingers and kissed him lightly on the cheek and said, "I bet you're hungry."

He said he could eat a live mule down to its shoes. He felt strong enough to get dressed and go downstairs to the dining table but she wouldn't hear of it, not on his first morning in her care. She helped him to sit up and positioned pillows at his back, then fashioned a sling for his arm, then went off to get his breakfast. While she was gone he checked the Navies hung on the chair beside the bed and found them fully loaded.

She returned with a tray holding a platter of ham steak and fried eggs and potatoes, a bowl of cream gravy, a basket of biscuits, a smoking mug of coffee heavily sugared the way she knew he liked it. She tucked a napkin into the collar of his nightshirt, then cut his ham for him into bite-sized pieces.

While he ate she told of the night a large company of men rode up to the Parchman house and she had no idea who they were and had the big Walker ready until Aunt Sally got a good look at the men through the window and told her to put the thing away, the men outside were friends. "You could of knocked me over with a sparrow feather when she said it was Captain Quantrill and his men and I heard her calling them each one by name."

They'd just come from a bad fight somewhere, and over the next days she and her sisters learned to feel bones and tendons to see if they were intact, to cleanse wounds with carbolic solution or turpentine oil, whichever was to hand. Suturing a wound required less skill than sewing a dress, except that a dress never flinched nor cussed when you ran a needle through it. She'd been the one to repair Quantrill's calf wound and he thanked her for work well done.

Bill asked what she thought of the man. She pondered a moment, then said, "He's real polite—and real educated. You should hear the way he talks sometimes. And he must be truly brave—the others look at him like they can't wait for him to tell them something dangerous to do so they can prove to him how brave they are too. He's handsome, I guess—but not as much as you."

In the time the guerrillas were on the farm she and her sisters got acquainted with most of them. Some were every bit as polite as

Quantrill, but some so terribly shy around girls she sometimes wanted to pat them like you do a nervous dog and say hey boy, easy now. Only a few were so coarse that Quantrill had to warn them to mind their language and manners in the presence of the ladies. She said Mary had gone sweet on a boy from Layfayette County named Tyler Burdette. "Jayhawks killed his daddy and his big brother," she said, "and then the Feds tried to make him enroll in the state militia, so he went off and joined the bushwhackers. It's a sad tale, but so many of the boys tell a like one."

Bill said he'd heard a tale about her and a fellow named Andy Blunt. "I hear you gave him a lesson in manners."

Josephine abruptly laughed into her hands. "God, Billy, for a minute I was afraid I'd knocked his brains out his ear."

When the bushwhackers rode off and left them with two badly wounded men to care for and no protection but themselves, she hadn't been afraid. "I just wish I'd kept the Walker in the barn instead of in the house. When the militia showed up I didn't have a chance to get it." The Baldwin boy she tried to protect was already so badly wounded he likely would've died in another day anyway and the soldiers didn't have to shoot him again, the cowardly shits. The knock she took on the stallpost left her fairly addled until the soldiers were gone, and then the first thing she saw clearly was Mary and Jenny crying over Aunt Sally.

"But they didn't scare me, Billy," Josephine said. "I wasn't *ever* scared of them, just mad—and just sorry to tears for Aunt Sally. The only time I got scared was when the boys carried you in last night and told us what happened. All the while I was getting you cleaned up and all, I was so afraid you'd die. All I could think to do was talk to you. I talked and talked about every fool thing to come in my head. I thought if I just kept talking to you, you wouldn't quit breathing. After a while, though, I had to pee real bad and I hadn't brought a pot in here, so I quick went to my room, and when I got back, there you were, looking at me. I guess my gabbing kept you too bored to wake up."

Her eyes shone. He lay the breakfast tray aside and put his fingers to her face. She caught his hand in both of hers and kissed it and then held it tight between her breasts and smiled at him like he was the first sunrise she'd seen in weeks.

*   *   *

That afternoon she changed the dressings on his head and arm and both wounds looked like they would heal well. "You'll have a scar on your head but your hair'll hide it," she said. "Nobody but me will know it's there." She applied herself to a careful razoring of his cheeks and neck, then trimmed his mustache and goatee, which she liked very much. She combed his hair back with her fingers and grinned at him as if he were a profoundly simple solution to some complex riddle.

"*What?*" he said when he saw how she was staring at him. Her smile widened and she shook her head and went off to attend her chores. He napped for a time and when he woke she was lying beside him and studying his face with a look as mysterious to him as womanhood itself. She kissed his nose and snuggled to him.

He refused to take another meal in bed, so that evening she helped him get dressed to go downstairs for supper. He insisted his leg was just fine now, it hurt only when he pressed on the bruise, but she anyway held him around the waist as they went down the staircase. Mary and Jenny and the Vaughn girls applauded when he entered the dining room and he beamed and made a small bow.

They dined on chicken stew, baked yams, sweet corn and rhubarb pie. In the course of the supper conversation he learned that the fiddle music he'd heard on waking up the evening before had been played by Hazel Vaughn. When they were finished with their pie, he asked if she would play a tune, so they went into the parlor and she took the instrument off the wall and asked if he had a request. "Molly Brooks," he said, and she smiled and started sawing.

He proved the haleness of his leg by tugging Josephine out on the open floor and swinging her into a dance by his one good arm. She grudgingly allowed Annette to cut in for a turn and then each of her sisters before reclaiming him for her own. By then, however, he had gone light in the head and had to sit down. Josie was furious with herself for letting him overexert and she would not permit him any more dancing, not that evening. He protested that he'd be fine in a minute, but the other girls agreed that he needed to rest, and Hazel retired the fiddle to its wall peg.

Josephine helped him back upstairs and into his nightshirt and into bed and then left the room for a time. When she returned she was in her nightdress and carrying her clothes which she placed on a chair. She shut the door and went to the lamp to extinguish it and he had a moment's clear view of her leanly naked silhouette under the thin nightdress. She crossed to the bed by the light of the moon and slid in beside him. They lay face to face as vague shadows and he felt her warm breath.

"Listen, Joey, I really don't believe I need any more round-the-clock looking after," he said.

"I believe you do," she said, and wriggled more snugly against him. "And if you say the first word about what Annette and Hazel might think, I swear I'll take a chamber pot to your skull. I'll *give* you a head wound to brag about."

Their hands found their way under each other's nightclothes. After a time he whispered, "If there's really a hell, I'm for sure going to it."

"Me too," she said, chuckling low and stroking him lightly. "I'll be right there beside you shoveling that old brimstone."

"No," he said. "You're a child and can be forgiven but—*hey!* Dammit girl!"

She'd given him a mean squeeze. "I'm *not* a child," she hissed.

"*Quit!* All right, then. I just meant you're young enough yet to be forgiven. But I'm old enough I'm supposed to know better."

"Well, I'm glad you don't," she said. And kissed him on the ear, her low laughter full of happy mischief.

She checked his head wound again the next morning and said it was scabbing up nice. Hazel gave him an old hat of her father's which she'd cut the band on so it would fit over his bandages. His arm felt so much better he refused the sling. After lunch he said he wanted to go out to the stable and see how Edgar Allan was faring, and she said she'd go with him.

The sky was thickening with tall gray clouds and the trees wavered in a light wind. As they were crossing the grounds, Josephine stopped short and said, "Oh Lord, Billy, it's the damn dogs!" Coming at a run from the other side of the property were three large hounds, coming fast and without barking. They belonged to Jimmy Vaughn but had lost all discipline since he'd gone away. The Vaughn girls told Bill they were always at rooting up the gardens and digging under the henhouse fence to kill chickens for sport and eat the eggs. Two weeks ago a foolish tramp had trespassed onto the property and the dogs came around the house and ran him down before he could get back to the gate. They rent him variously and bloody and might have killed him if Black Josh hadn't come running and beaten them away with a hoe. They were superior watchdogs, Annette Vaughn said, but they were too wild anymore, and she thought she would have to tell Finley to shoot them.

Bill Anderson stood his ground and watched them come as Josephine hastily armed herself with a stick. The dogs were almost on them, all snarls and bared teeth, and then they saw Bill's eyes and drew up so short they nearly went tumbling. They were even larger than they'd seemed at a distance, the biggest looked to outweigh Josephine—but now they whimpered and turned in tight circles, then sat with their heads hanging and rolled their eyes up for quick glances at Bill but could not hold his stare.

"Sweet baby Jesus," Josephine said, and couldn't help but laugh.

"Look at me," Bill said softly. The dogs whimpered again but looked up. For a moment his gaze was hard, and the dogs' ears seemed to droop even lower. And then Bill abruptly grinned and said, "All right, then," and the dogs heaved up on all fours and wagged their tails in a blur and grinned back at him.

"What in the world did you tell them?" Josie said.

"Nothing but the truth," Bill said. "If they don't quit acting like worthless eggsuckers, they're done for. I guess they'll do better from now on." The dogs flapped their tails and smiled.

"By the way," Bill said, "that big one's Boo, and that's Foot, and that's Ned. You can ask the Vaughns if you don't believe me."

She shook her head and tossed aside the stick and said she didn't need to ask anydamnbody. She hugged him at the waist and they went on toward the stable, the big dogs jauntily following.

He had always been fast to heal and in a few days more he was shed of his bandages. The arm was still sore but working well, and though it was yet a snug fit, he could wear his own hat. Now he and Josephine were going for long walks in the morning and then again in the afternoon. They fished with handlines for catfish and perch in a creek in the deeper woods, then contested at skipping stones on the water. They gathered raspberries off the bushes, shook walnuts off the trees. They played hide-and-seek in the underbrush, and Josephine couldn't understand how Bill was always able to find her so easily, no matter how well she'd hidden herself—and then finally realized he was using the dogs to track her and then telling them to get out of sight so she wouldn't know. When she accused him of cheating, he tried to deny it and to look offended, but he couldn't keep a straight face and finally confessed.

They hiked nearly two miles through the forest to a clearing Finley told them about, a perfect place for target shooting. Josephine had been enthralled by the Navy Colt since the first time she slipped one of them from Bill's holsters hanging on the bedside chair and couldn't believe its lightness, its smaller grip that so much better fit her hand than the monstrous Walker. When she fired the Navy for the first time and discovered its greater accuracy and easier kick, nothing would do but that she have one for herself.

"Let me have one, Billy. You got *two*!"

He affected uncertainty. "Well . . . I don't know if I can do that, girl. These guns are awful special to me."

"So am *I* awful special to you. *Please,* Billy? Let me have one?"

"They're hard to come by, you know, and worth an awful lot."

"They worth as much as a sweet sister who loves you better than anything in the whole wide world?" She hugged herself to him, fairly purring, pressing her lean belly against him and stroking his neck, rising on her toes and pulling his head down to blow softly at his ear. Her ludicrous simulation of a Kansas City siren—as she'd heard the type described—made him laugh out loud.

But when they returned to the house she had a Navy Colt to put under her pillow and she returned the big Walker to him.

During his recuperation at the Vaughn place he learned that Hazel and Annette were in their own way serving Quantrill as valuably as was their brother. Each time the girls went to Kansas City for certain staples and other supplies, they also bought sizable quantities of ball ammunition and boxes of percussion caps, tins of black powder and packets of cartridge paper—bought it all with pursefuls of bushwhacker money. They knew which dealers were Quantrill associates or, just as well, had no allegiance except to profit and would sell the girls whatever they wanted, no questions asked. They knew which days of the week and which hours of the day were the busiest and therefore the best for smuggling their contraband through the heart of the city streets and down the Westport Road to home, there to stockpile the munitions components in a cellar storeroom.

The Vaughn house also served as the weekly meetingplace for the Westport Sewing Circle, a dozen or so women who all had a son, brother, husband or sweetheart riding with Quantrill. When the women came together on meeting days, they went down to the storeroom and sat themselves at several long tables and spent the day making cartridges. The Anderson girls had been admitted to the club the day after their arrival and all three had swiftly proved expert at fashioning ready charges.

The first time Bill went to the cellar with his sisters he was amazed by the high stacks of powder cans, the dozens of boxes of caps and balls. The room was illuminated by a pair of oil lanterns at every table, each lantern screwed down solidly to the tabletop and covered with a securely latched wire cage over the lampglass to protect against accidental upset. Not a person in the room was unaware of what would happen if even a few grains of powder were ignited, and they were as careful of the lamps as of rattlesnakes.

While some of the women made cartridges and stored them in ammunition pouches, others were charging spare cylinders for the bushwhackers' revolvers. All revolvers of the day were cap-and-ball models, and the standard method of loading one was a lengthy process of charging the cylinder's six chambers in turn—measuring an amount of powder into the chamber, then placing a ball in it, then seating the ball snugly with the loading lever pinned under the gun barrel, then fitting the chamber with a percussion cap. The process was of course faster with ready-made cartridges containing both bullet and powder—and far faster still when a revolver's emptied cylinder could simply be replaced with a fully charged one.

Josephine sat on a bench at a table and patted the place beside her for Bill to sit. The table held open cans of black powder, boxes of .36- and .44-caliber balls, a tin of grease, packets of cartridge paper, mounds of thread, a supply of smooth sticks called formers—each six inches long and with a diameter equal to a particular caliber—

and a scattering of small thimbles of varying sizes, each size equivalent to the measure of powder for a specific cartridge.

"First off," Josie said, "we form a case and choke it." She took up a former marked "36" and rolled a patch of paper around it, shaping it into a casing and leaving a slight overlap at the end of the stick. She twisted the overlap and sealed it with a piece of thread. She slid the choked case off the stick and picked up a .36-caliber ball, greased it lightly and dropped it into the casing, then secured the ball in place with another strip of thread. Now she dipped a thimble marked "36" into a can of black powder, shook away the excess until the thimbleload was level, expertly poured the charge into the casing, and then neatly twisted and crimped the end of the paper to seal the cartridge. She handed it to Bill and said, "For your Navy Colt, sir."

CHARLEY HART

One morning the Vaughns invited the Anderson girls to accompany them to Kansas City to get supplies and they excitedly accepted. Not until they'd gone did it occur to Bill that the Vaughns might intend to instruct his sisters in the arts of smuggling. He thought about catching up to their wagon and safeguarding them through the day, but when he shared the idea with Finley, the man smiled and shook his head.

"I used to argue with them girls they ought have a man along," Finley said, "but they won't hear of an escort. They say a man only attracts the wrong kind of Yank attention to them. I reckon they're right. They anyhow seem to know what they're doing, don't they? I'll wager there's nobody, woman *or* man, has snuck more powder and ball out of K.C. than them."

Finley's assurance did not fully ease Bill's misgiving but he decided against going after them. To occupy himself he saddled Edgar Allan and rode with the dogs out to the woodland clearing to practice with the Navy. The sun was high and hot and a thin haze of yellow dust hung over the grass. Honeybees hovered at the wildflowers.

He'd been shooting for half an hour when the dogs suddenly jumped to their feet where they'd been lying under an oak. Their napes roached and they growled deep and stared hard into the dense woods on the far side of the clearing. A rider emerged from the trees, putting his roan horse forward at a walk. Bill had just reloaded the Colt and held it loosely by his leg. Not until the man came into the brighter light away from the high trees did Bill see he was wearing Federal blue.

The dogs were growling and pacing from side to side—and then the big Boo dog went streaking out toward the approaching horseman. The other dogs stood fast. The rider reined up as Boo closed in, barking and harrying the horse from one side and then the other. The horse stood under tight rein and seemed altogether indifferent. The rider regarded Boo as if considering his degree of nuisance. Then the reins abruptly slackened and the horse struck like a snake—clamping its teeth in the dog's hide and snatching him up and slinging him through the air. The Boo dog lit in a yelping tumble and scrabbled to his feet, legs splayed. He shook his head—perhaps to clear it, perhaps to rid it of any foolish notion to try another attack—and then made his limping way back to Bill.

The fur on Boo's back was dark with blood where he had been bitten and his eyes were largely white. The other dogs smelled his blood and fear and whimpered lowly. "I don't blame you all," Bill said. "That's a killer."

The bluecoat had put the horse forward again and the dogs growled and drew back as he closed to within a few yards of Bill.

"I should have hallooed you and told you to keep those curs off Charley," the bluecoat said. "The last dog that tried to bite him got his head kicked open. I'd say yours is lucky he can still walk."

"I'd say he's probably not feeling all that lucky," Bill said.

The big roan had a crooked yellow blaze on its face. The animal blew hard and stamped the ground and regarded Bill with fierce amber eyes. Bill had never known a horse to snatch up a dog and throw it. The bluecoat carried a holstered Army Colt and a smaller Navy tucked into his belt. He wore a black Kossuth hat with one side of the brim pinned up and a bright U.S. Cavalry badge of crossed swords fixed to the front of the crown. His shoulder straps showed captain's bars. He was lean and youthful, cleanshaven but for a sparse mustache. Lank brown hair hung from under his hat.

Bill Anderson did not for a moment suspect that the Yankee was alone. "I'm surprised that horse ain't killed you and ate you," he said. "Hope you didn't pay a whole lot for him." He was squinting so the Fed might not see his eyes scouting the woods beyond for sign of the other soldiers.

"Oh, the price was right," the captain said. He patted the animal's neck. "Got him from a man in Independence who'd been bit by him once too often and was ready to shoot him for stewmeat. He's pretty good with me, though." His eyes cut over to Edgar Allan where the black grazed under the hickory he was tethered to. "I used to have a black myself. Real pretty mare. Only had one eye but she could run like a scalded dog and she was brave as a lion."

"Why'd you get rid of her?" Bill said. He could think of no reason for Yankee cavalry to be in this part of the woods except they suspected the Vaughn property for a guerrilla station.

"Somebody shot her," the captain said. He seemed amused with this game of showing himself alone while his men hid in the trees.

"Name's Hart," the bluecoat said. "Captain Charley Hart. May I inquire after yours, sir?"

"Anderson," Bill said. "William T. Gave your horse your own name, hey?"

The bluecoat smiled. "Vanity. Damnable fault."

"Don't often see anybody this far off the main road," Bill said. He was glad for the ready Colt in his hand.

"Guess you don't," Hart said. "But then if you go seeking after bushwhackers, you have to go where the bushwhackers are said to be." He cast a slow look around. "You wouldn't happen to know of any bushwhackers hiding out nearabouts, would you?"

Bill shook his head. "Surely don't."

Hart appraised him from hat to boot toes. "I've been hunting guerrillas the best part of a year and I've come to have a sense about them. I can tell a bushwhacker just by looking at him." He leaned out from the saddle and spat. Then fixed Bill with a direct look. "And I have to say . . . my sense tells me you're not one."

Bill affected an amused chuckle, releasing a held breath. "Well, you got a good sense there, because I ain't."

"When I heard shooting over here I thought it might be bushwhackers waylaying innocents."

"Nope—just me waylaying knotholes."

Hart looked at the tree twenty yards away whose several knots had been serving as Bill's targets. One of the knots was big as a dinner plate, the others about the size of saucers—and all of them now battered to pulpy splintery depressions in the tree trunk. "It would appear you're a marksman, William T."

"I sometimes hit what I aim at," Bill said.

Hart smiled. "I wonder now, would you be interested in some quick sport before I take my leave?" He pointed at a persimmon tree a few yards to the side of the oak. "A dollar, even odds, says you miss one before I do." He drew the Navy and held it uncocked on his thigh. "Six shots to a turn. What say you?" The man's mien was entirely amiable.

Bill turned to regard the persimmon tree and give himself a moment to consider things. If he agreed to the match, he'd soon enough be standing there with an empty gun. If he refused, he'd rouse the Yank's suspicions. Then he realized the folly of his reasoning. If they wanted to kill him they could have done it already. Marksmen in the trees surely had their sights on him this minute and were just waiting for the captain's signal. But the captain hadn't given it. Most likely the man simply fancied himself a deadeye and wanted to show off for his hidden troopers.

"Silver dollar," Bill said, turning back to the Yankee. "No paper."

"It's a bet," Hart said, and grinned wide. He gestured for Bill to shoot first.

Bill squared himself and cocked the Navy. The orange persimmons were easy enough to see but much smaller targets than the oak knots. A persimmon vanished off the tree with each of his first five shots, the flat reports absorbing into the dense woods and the high indifferent sky. But his sixth round left a visible portion of fruit on the stem. Bill looked at Hart and asked if it was a hit or a miss. Hart asked what he wanted to call it. "Half a hit," Bill said, and the bluecoat laughed and said that was all right with him.

Hart didn't even dismount. He leveled the Navy and fired six rounds just as fast as he could cock and shoot and six persimmons vanished from their stems entirely. He smiled down on Bill from under the rising pall of gunsmoke and said, "That's one silver dollar somebody owes me."

Bill dug out a dollar and handed it up to him. Hart slipped the coin into his jacket and tucked the emptied Navy back in his belt.

Bill flicked the burnt primer from the Navy's chambers and blew out the residue ash of the cartridge paper. He took several cartridges from his coat pocket and was about to begin reloading when he heard the double-cock of a revolver hammer. He looked up to see the Army Colt pointed squarely at his face and Hart glowering behind it.

"Thought you had me fooled, didn't you, bushwhacker?" Eyes, voice, everything of Hart now exuding malice.

"Hey Captain, I already said, I ain't no guerrilla."

"*Liar!*" Hart said. "God abhors a liar and so do I. I knew you for a bushwhacker the minute I laid eyes on you."

A sudden tightness in his belly, a furious need to piss. "I swear to you I'm not," he said.

"You *swear,*" Hart said sardonically. "You'll die with the lie on your lips, damn your soul. Suck your last breath, bushwhacker."

He gaped into the black pistolmouth and raised his hands as if he would fend the bullet.

The Colt flinched. *"Bang!"*

He staggered backward, so fully expecting to be shot that for an instant he was sure he had been.

Hart was swaying in the saddle with laughter. He waved the Colt over his head and horsemen materialized from the shadowed woods and hupped their mounts forward at a lope, a dozen of them, some in Federal blue and the others wearing the unmistakable guerrilla shirt, all of them laughing, and he saw that among them were his brother and the Berry boys.

Jim Anderson swung down off his mount and slapped him on the shoulder, grinning under his thick mustache. He raised a hand toward Hart and said, "Well Billy, I guess you've met Captain Quantrill."

A SURGERY

The Yankee uniforms had come from prisoners taken two weeks ago at Independence. They'd proved a fine means for uncovering false southern sympathizers among the citizenry. Some of the local farmers who professed to be secessionist would gladden at the sight of bluejackets and immediately proffer food and information. The bushwhackers delighted in the look on a man's face in the moment he realized he was confessing his perfidy to the very men he would betray. Minutes later the traitor would be hanging from a tree branch and done forever with duplicity.

Bill learned these things as they rode to the Vaughn place. His brother introduced him to Jimmy Vaughn, brother to Annette and Hazel, and Bill took a fast liking to him. The dogs trotted close by Edgar Allan, familiar with most of these men from past acquaintance but still growling nervously whenever the distance narrowed between them and Quantrill's fearsome horse. Bill himself was still chagrined over the joke Quantrill played on him at the clearing. He'd been trying not to let it show, but his brother had detected his pique and whispered to him not to be blackassed, that these men were always pulling tricks on each other, and anybody who chafed too much at being the butt of a joke today would surely be the butt of another one tomorrow.

Among the men of this small party was seventeen-year-old Tyler Burdette, whose elbow had been shattered by a Fed rifle ball during a skirmish ten days ago. His comrades had done what they could for the wound, but it was a bad one and had worsened in the following days. The nearest doctor to them was in Westport, so Quantrill had set out to take the boy there, leaving the company under George Todd's command. The boy's elbow was now black and bloated bigger than a knee. It smelled of rot and Burdette was afire with fever and every man knew there was nothing for it but amputation. Quantrill had decided on the Vaughn place for doing it. They had been feeding the boy on whiskey all morning and he was now stupendously drunk. He rode with his head lolling, softly singing "Barbara Allen."

Finley and Black Josh greeted them with backslaps and japes. They helped to ease Burdette off his horse but the whiskey had made rubber of the boy's legs and they had to carry him into the stable. Quantrill asked after the girls and Black Josh said they had not yet come back from Kansas City and likely wouldn't until late afternoon.

Finley set an iron poker in the fire and bellowed up the heat. Burdette still singing in a slur as they laid him on the floor and placed a flat oak slab under his arm and stripped the wound of its filthy bandage. Black Josh produced a broadax sharpened to a shining edge. Quantrill was prepared to do the job himself, but Dave Pool—a big-shouldered man whose mouth was wholly obscured in the wild black growth of his beard and who'd been a hewer for a time—said he was better practiced for the task, and Quantrill deferred to him.

As Pool rolled up his sleeves he carefully examined Burdette's arm and agreed with Quantrill that the infection had spread so much that no portion of the limb could be saved. The detachment would have to be made as near to the shoulder as possible. When Finley said the iron was ready, a beefy redhaired man named Coleman Younger, cleanshaved but for chinwhiskers, tightened his grip on the doomed arm stretched across the oak slab. Butch Berry held fast to Tyler's head, Jimmy Vaughn sat his full weight on the boy's legs, and a moonfaced man named Will Haller held down his good arm. Pool set his feet and spat into his palms and hefted the ax amid the smells of stock droppings and mansweat and Burdette's necrotic wound, amid the sounds of Tyler's drunken singing and horse snortings and the huff of the firebellows where Finley stood watching and ready with a rag-wrapped grip on the poker.

The axhead described a smooth overhead arc and *whunked* into the board and Tyler Burdette screamed as his arm came off in Cole Younger's hands. Quick bright blood snaked from the sudden stump and Finley swooped with the blazing poker and slapped it to the wound with a great smoking hiss that reeked of searing flesh and sealed off the arteries. Burdette passed out in mid-shriek.

They coated the raw stump with grease and carefully bandaged it and then several men carried Burdette off to the house to put him in an upstairs bedroom. Quantrill clapped Pool on the back for a job well done. Cole Younger combed his chinwhiskers with his fingers, said it damn sure was a good job. He said he'd once known a man to amputate a friend's mangled arm with an ax, but he was so nervous about doing it that for every drink he gave his friend to get him ready he took a drink himself. "Man got so drunk," Younger said, "that when he finally went to chop the arm off he chopped off a good part of the shoulder too. His friend just laid there cussing him for the half-minute it took him to bleed to death. It wasn't the handiest show of doctorfying I ever saw."

He passed the severed arm to Black Josh and told him to get rid of it. Joshua said he'd bury it in the garden. "It help the flowers grow pretty on its own grave," he said.

TALES OF INDEPENDENCE

The guerrillas built cookfires behind the stable, killed and dressed a dozen chickens and roasted them on spits, baked yams in a covered pit of coals. Bill and Jim Anderson and the Berry boys were joined by Jimmy Vaughn as they sat to their dinner in the shade of a tree. Jim and the Berrys were avid to tell Bill of their adventures with the bushwhackers these past weeks.

They'd gone with Todd and Gregg to join Quantrill near Independence where a Confederate cavalry company had enlisted the guerrillas' help to assault the Federals occupying the town. The main Yankee camp was just outside the town, but the Fed headquarters was in a bank building on the main square and Quantrill's company was assigned to take it.

"We hit the town before sunup," Butch Berry said. "Went galloping down the street shooting at everydamnthing and howling to raise hell."

"This whitehair bucko is a God-gifted rebel yeller, I mean to tell you," Jimmy Vaughn said to Bill, pointing his thumb at Ike. "I was riding next to him and his yells almost made me dirty my pants. I thought some wild Indian had snuck up beside me."

Ike Berry grinned proudly. "Raised some neck hairs, didn't I? Gregg says there ain't a Yankee been born who can do a right rebel yell. Says it has to raise from a southern soul."

The Yankees in the bank knew they were trapped, but the building was a solid fortress and for a time they made a fight of it.

"We must of fired a thousand rounds into that damn bank," Ike said. "The powdersmoke in the streets was thick as fog. The Yanks were on the second floor and shooting with muzzleloaders. They could only get off about one round for every dozen of ours, and they couldn't take any aim at all, we were pouring so much fire at them.

But they were tucked in that building like a turtle in its shell and all we were doing was tapping on it."

Quantrill got frustrated by the waste of ammunition, by the need to dismount and take cover. "He doesn't like it when we have to get off the horses," Jimmy Vaughn said. "The captain's way is to fall on the enemy fast and hard and then make away into the wildwood just as quick."

Quantrill finally called out to the Fed commander to surrender or he'd burn the building and every man in it. "The Yanks waved a white flag from a window and hollered out that they didn't want to burn but they didn't want to surrender to us either," Ike said. "Quantrill looked around at us like he couldn't believe his ears. So he hollers up at the Fed, 'Well then, I guess all that's left is *we* surrender to *you*? How would *that* be?' "

The Yanks were willing to surrender, Jimmy Vaughn explained, but only to an officer of the regular army. They were afraid Quantrill would shoot them if they gave up to him. Back in spring the Feds had declared a no-quarter war and had been executing most of the guerrillas who fell into their hands, so they naturally expected Quantrill to do to them in kind.

"*Would* he have killed them?" Bill said.

Jimmy Vaughn shrugged. "Sometimes he does and sometimes he doesn't. When his blood's up he'll quick enough fly the black flag, but sometimes he takes prisoners to try to trade for some of our boys the Feds are holding."

On this occasion Quantrill wasn't of a mind to argue terms of surrender with a bunch of trapped Yankees. He told them they had two minutes to come out with their hands high or he'd put torches to the place. Then a Confederate colonel named Thompson showed up and promised the Yanks they wouldn't be shot, so they gave up to him and were marched off to a holding pen.

Not so lucky was the Yankee officer who'd tried to hide in a hotel down the street. Butch Berry and Jimmy Vaughn were crossing to the hotel when they heard somebody yell "Look out below!" and a body landed two feet in front of them. "It was a damned Federal captain," Butch said. "Some of the boys were searching the place to see what they might find worth taking and they found him. His throat been cut and both his ears gone and the most part of his belly was missing.

"The men who'd flung him from the upstairs window were looking down and laughing and drinking from whiskey jugs. A graybeard named Larkin Skaggs—the company elder—was at their center. He bellowed, 'And the great Jehovah shall maketh it to rain dead Federals on the land!'" The men around him laughed like Jehovah Himself had told a joke.

"Skaggs is one more of them old-time preachers so crazy for blood nowadays," Jimmy Vaughn said. "He goes back to the first troubles in Kansas. Fought with a gang of ruffians under Atchison and claims he personally cut the throat of one of John Brown's nephews. He's got a big German carbine fires a ball the size of a lemon. What he does, he cuts a bunch of deep crosses into every ball. Says he does it to convey the touch of Jesus, but what those cuts do is make the ball bust apart like a little bomb when it hits. He calls that old piece Armageddon and the damage it'll do a man is something to see."

"That's so," Butch Berry said. "I saw the hole in that Yank's belly."

The Confederates counted three dozen Yankee dead and took more than one hundred and fifty prisoners, half of them wounded. They were all morning at burning and looting, and the guerrillas joined them at it. They put the torch to buildings belonging to Unionists but spared those owned by secessionist folk. The regulars rustled every good horse in town and loaded a train of twenty wagons with Federal weapons and quartermaster stores. The rest of the booty—furniture, tools, tack, dry goods, all the wagons and teams the army didn't take—went to Quantrill as reward for his help. Just before the Confederates departed, Colonel Thompson paroled the captured Feds.

The only horse none of the Confederates laid claim to was a meantempered yellow-blazed roan corraled by itself and pacing around with its ears laid back, snapping at any of the rebs who got too close to the rails. A Yankee corporal who'd served as the company wrangler told his captors he'd found the horse tied to the corral one morning about two weeks ago and had no idea who'd left it there, but it was soon clear enough why its owner got rid of it. The corporal boasted of being the best broncbuster in the regiment but this horse threw him every time—and every time tried to stomp him as he scrabbled out of the corral. Then the animal wouldn't even let him mount up. It would kick at him and snap at him and one time bit him so bad on the shoulder he couldn't raise his arm for days after. He'd long since quit trying to break it and said he dearly hoped somebody would steal it or shoot it and he didn't care which.

The rebs at the corral were daring each other to try to ride the beast when Quantrill showed up. "The minute that horse saw him, its ears perked and it wouldn't look at nobody else," Jim Anderson said. Quantrill climbed into the corral and went up to the animal and stroked its muzzle. He whispered something in its ear and blew soft on its nose and the horse rubbed its yellow blaze against his chest like a cat.

"Not a man there could believe it," Jim Anderson said. "It was like that damned thing had been waiting for Quantrill to show up and claim it for his own."

"I believe you know the horse your brother's talking about," Jimmy Vaughn said, grinning at Bill.

"That I do," Bill said. "One of the dogs made its acquaintance and got the bite marks to prove it."

The guerrillas bore their plunder from Independence to the farm of a supporter named Ingraham. Some of the booty would go to guerrilla kinfolk or to families who regularly helped the bushwhackers, but most would be sold to agents of various Kansas City and Saint Louis businessmen whose only interest was in profits and never mind which side in the war provided them on a given day.

Some days later a Confederate colonel arrived at Ingraham's and with the authority of the Richmond government officially mustered Quantrill's company into rebel service as partisan rangers. The men held an election of officers and Quantrill was chosen as captain, Will Haller as first lieutenant, George Todd and W. J. Gregg as second lieutenants.

"Todd wanted to be first lieutenant but lost it by two votes," Jimmy Vaughn said. He looked around to be sure they were not being overheard. "George was mad enough to spit bullets. There's never been love lost between him and Haller. He calls Haller punkinhead. Haller hates him but he's scared of him. I think some who voted for Haller thought it's what Quantrill wanted because Will's been with him the longest. Thing is, Quantrill and Haller ain't all that close, and I do believe the captain himself would've preferred Todd for first lieutenant. Todd thought so too, and he called for another vote, but Quantrill said no. He said if they took a new vote every time somebody didn't like the outcome of the last one there'd be no end to it."

Jimmy Vaughn took another quick glance around. "Truth to tell, I don't believe George has got over it. He's real unhappy the captain didn't back him for a new vote. And the looks he keeps giving Haller, I'd have to say the results of the election might not be all that final, not just yet."

OF TRUTH AND QUANTRILL

W. J. Gregg and his scouting party of six arrived in midafternoon. He and Quantrill moved off toward the woods to talk while the scouts fed on what chicken and yams remained on the fires. Jim Anderson and the Berrys introduced Bill to each of the new arrivals. The scouts had brought newspapers with them and jugs of busthead whiskey and it was no contest which commodity was in greater demand by their fellows.

After a time Bill went to the vegetable garden and pulled several large carrots and took them to the stable to feed to Edgar Allan, whom he had not properly tended since the morning's adventures. Cole Younger's gray mare and several of the Vaughn horses were installed there too, all of them made nervous by Quantrill's horse, even though it was standing quietly in a barred stall and paying heed to none of them.

Charley's stall was opposite Edgar Allan's, and Bill stood with his back to the big roan as he fed the carrots to the black. But the Charley horse caught scent of them and began snorting and stamping, bobbing his big head. His sudden agitation unnerved the other horses, and they whickered and stepped about in their stalls. Edgar Allan rolled his eyes and bolted the last of the carrots as if fearful the roan might break free of its stall and come lunging for them.

Bill patted the black and spoke soothingly to him, told him to pay no attention to the creature across the way. "You're just smelling the meanness off that thing," he said softly. "Meanness and craziness. But *you* now—you're a noble genius is what you are. Why, I bet if you could hold a pen you'd write a poem so grand it would break the heart of every mare to hear it read. I bet you could do arithmetic. That crazy thing behind me can't tell you two letters of the alphabet is how damn dumb it is. But I'll bet if you—"

"You shouldn't fault Charley so freely, William T. You might hurt his feelings."

Bill turned to see Quantrill leaning on Charley's stall, arms crossed, hat pushed back on his head. He had shed the Federal jacket and wore a guerrilla shirt and a black slouch hat. A Navy was holstered on each hip, another under his arm, a fourth tucked in his belt. "You know how to talk to a horse, though," he said. "Horse likes a low voice. It's what makes him a naturalborn guerrilla. You have to talk low in the bush."

"You're some quiet yourself with them cat feet," Bill said. "Can't but wonder if you're part Indian—no offense."

"Wouldn't bother me a bit if I were," Quantrill said. His eyes were half-closed, making him look sleepy, but Bill Anderson knew the look was deceptive. The man's eyes missed nothing. "I lived with Indians for a time. An Indian saved my life once."

"I heard that story," Bill said. "About your big brother being murdered by jayhawks and the Indian saving you and you joining the Montgomery men and one by one killing all of them who'd killed your brother."

Quantrill smiled.

"I've always wondered is it true."

The smile faded. "That's a brave thing to ask, William T."

"Well, I didn't hear the story from you, so it's not like I'm questioning anything *you* said to me."

Quantrill regarded him closely. "That's almost an admirable argument. Perhaps your true calling is in the law. The legal profession thrives on such nimble turns of reason."

"If you mean some men are good at dressing up a lie to look like the truth, I agree with you there," Bill said.

Every man in the company had heard the story of Quantrill's brother from somebody other than Quantrill. Only a few, Cole Younger among them, claimed also to have heard it from the man himself. Butch Berry had asked Younger if he thought it was a true story, and Cole laughed and said, "Sure it is—even if it ain't." The answer had not puzzled Bill as much as it did Butch.

"It works the other way too," Quantrill said. "Sometimes a lie only looks like a lie. Sometimes it's, well, 'the truth in masquerade.' A poet named Byron said that."

"I know he did," Bill said. "But when it comes to sayings about the truth, I always liked 'tell the truth and shame the devil.' "

"The glorious Bard!" Quantrill said, suddenly beaming. "Wise about truth and all else under the sun. I am impressed, William T. I hadn't taken you for a littérateur. *My* favorite saw about the truth is that it shall make us free."

"Good old Bible," Bill said. "It's just full of notions about truth, ain't it?" He raised his arms and intoned portentously: " 'Great— *great*—is the truth . . .' "

" ' . . . and mighty above all things,' " Quantrill concluded.

They grinned at each other.

"Do you believe it?" Quantrill said. "That the truth will set you free?"

"The truth perhaps will set *you* free," Bill said, "but *I'd* prefer the jailhouse key." He and his brother had fashioned the couplet in their boyhood—and then had to dodge swipes of their mother's broom as she bewailed their shameful irreverence.

"My preference as well," Quantrill said. "Tell me, William, what's the T for?"

"The T? Why, Truth, of course—T for Truth."

Quantrill laughed. "Now I have to wonder if *that's* the truth."

"Sure it is," Bill said. "Even if it's not."

They heard halloos from the direction of the house, the happy voices of young women, the rougher ones of men.

"The ladies," Quantrill said. "Returned from their urban adventure." They went to the stable door and saw the wagons parked alongside the house, the girls being helped to step down. Bushwhackers were unloading the contraband cargo and carrying it to the cellar. "Let us make our salutations," Quantrill said.

"Salutations indeed," Bill said. And they laughed.

As they headed for the house, Bill determined that it did not matter a damn whether the story of Quantrill's brother was true or false.

The man was the elected leader of the most feared band of hardcases in Missouri, a chieftain to men who could not be fooled about courage or conviction, men to whom he'd proved his boldness—and his loyalty—beyond question. In the earlier afternoon, he had heard story after story of Quantrill's coolness under fire, of hairsbreadth escapes effected by his quick thinking and readiness to risk his own skin, of his refusal to desert a wounded comrade. His men said of him that he did not know how to be afraid. Against these testaments of what he was, what matter anything he'd been?

He'd been born in Ohio and not in Maryland as he'd claimed after he went west, and he'd had no older brother ever. He'd been a pensive and solitary boy who from his earliest years hated those who would dictate to others and especially to him. He'd been an avid student of many subjects and his favorites were Latin and literature. He'd been a teacher in various places from the age of sixteen and was by all accounts a good one. He'd been a farmer and a rancher and detested both vocations. He'd been a drifter for a time and gone west at age nineteen and settled for a time in Kansas. He'd been a laborer and worked at unloading timber from freight cars. He'd been accused of murdering a freightyard worker but claimed self-defense and was exonerated. Under the name of Charley Hart—a name he'd taken for reasons known to no one but himself—he'd been a teamster for the U.S. Army and gone on a military expedition to Utah. He'd been a gambler and a fancy dresser partial to white linen suits and a planters hat and diamondback boots, but he'd had a tendency to push his luck and he lost as often and as spectacularly as he won. He'd been a gold prospector in Colorado and was beset by Indians and a brutal winter and of the nineteen men in the party only five survived, and the gold he brought back to Kansas fetched him thirty-five dollars. He'd been close to his mother and in his early years out west wrote frequent letters to her and told her he'd been spared in Colorado because he was destined for greater things, and then his letters ceased and she never heard from him again. He'd been a resident among the Delaware Indians. As Bill Clark in Lawrence, Kansas, he'd been locked a month in jail for dealing in stolen goods—convicted more on suspicion of being Missourian than on any criminal evidence—and had been warned on his release never to return to that town if he knew what was good for him. He'd for a brief time been an admirer of Jim Lane and then saw him as an evil charlatan and came to hate him above all men on earth. He'd been a bandit and again called himself Charley Hart. He'd been a thief of small goods, a rustler of cattle and horses, a catcher of runaway slaves. He'd been in a gang of Missouri ruffians and soon gained its leadership and the band had grown to his present company of notorious raiders. He'd always been adept with the ladies and had known many women but had never been married or even in love until a few months ago when he'd met a Blue Springs girl ten years his junior named Katherine King.

These things and others he'd been and some he still was. And in this summer of 1862 he was just turned twenty-five years old.

A TIME TO BE JOYOUS AND A TIME TO MOURN

Except for a detail of four guards posted about the property, the only ones not at the supper table that evening were Tyler Burdette, who lay upstairs stewing in the rank sweat of his agony, and Mary Anderson, who sat at his lamplit bedside and mopped his face and held his burning hand and whispered endearments which under better circumstance she would have blushed to give voice to.

Everyone else was in the dining hall, seated at the long table of polished oak on which were platters of roast pork, large bowls of biscuits, of boiled greens and potatoes and blackeyed peas, smaller ones of different gravies, a dozen tin plates of pies—cherry and rhubarb and apple. There were jugs of cool water and steaming pots of coffee. The Vaughns would permit Quantrill to sit nowhere but at the head of the table and he beamed on the assembly like a well-pleased manor lord.

The room was boisterous with sundry conversations and the telling of various tales all at once, with joking and laughter. Jenny Anderson was the bushwhackers' twelve-year-old darling. Some of them had been bandaged by her at the Parchman farm and all of them were as protective of her as their own little sister. She herself had a special fondness for a burly blackbeard named Socrates Johnson, who at age thirty was the second oldest man in the company. He was called Sock by his fellows but she always addressed him as

Socrates, and he hailed her as "Lightfoot," in reference to her quick and boundless energy.

The Vaughn sisters sat to either side of their brother and doted on him, petting him and brushing his hair with their fingers, spooning his plate high with huge helpings of everything, elated to have him home and unharmed. Josephine had ensured that Bill sat beside her, and when she saw him watching the way Annette and Hazel were fawning over Jimmy, she nudged him with an elbow and gave him an arched-brow look that said "You see?" Bill smiled and winked at her and she stroked his leg under the table. He whispered for her to behave herself. She showed a sweet smile and pinched him.

Butch Berry had seated himself on Josephine's other side, but he might as well not have been at the table, so utterly did she ignore him. She sometimes looked away from Bill to enjoy somebody's joke or listen to a cross-table exchange, but never to look at Butch. He could not bring himself to speak to her. He was afraid she would fix him with one of her stares, like she didn't quite recognize him and didn't really care to. Or worse, make one of her faces of open vexation. Or worse still, make some loud remark to embarrass him before the room. So conscious of her nearness, he could give mind to nothing else—could only feign interest in the surrounding conversations, could only pretend to know what the joke was when he joined in the table's sudden swells of laughter. He thought he could feel the heat of her skin on his face.

When the meal was done the party repaired to the salon. Whiskey jugs came uncorked and the furniture was shoved back to the walls. A bushwhacker named Lionel Ward borrowed Hazel Vaughn's fiddle and Jim Anderson took out his mouth organ. A Jew's harp was produced, and a hornpipe. Jimmy Vaughn said it was a shame none among them could play the harpsichord in the corner of the room and never mind that it wasn't an instrument for whirla-round dancing.

They cavorted into the late hours, stamping the floorboards and swirling their tangled shadows over the high parlor walls, the men taking turns with the girls, the girls beaming with sweat and exhilaration in the light of so much lusty male attention. Upstairs, Mary Anderson held unconscious Tyler Burdette's hand and said, "You *hear* the fun they're having down there? The quicker you heal up, the quicker we can do some dancing too. Aren't you the lucky one any-way, losing an arm instead of a leg? Nobody needs two arms to dance. Did I tell you I had an uncle with only one arm? Well, I did, and that man was just a dancing *fool*. . . ."

Quantrill proved a sprightly dancer, Cole Younger a jovial one who liked to sing along to the music as he trod the boards, W. J. Gregg a nimblefoot given to dancing by himself whenever he lacked a partner. Dave Pool's blackbearded aspect was serious as a church-man's even as his feet went mad to the liveliest numbers. Hazel Vaughn laughed at Ike Berry's spirited clumsiness and then hugged him in apology and Ike's breath was arrested in the sensation of her wonderful bosom against him. Except for young Jenny, who was a dervish no man could long keep pace with, Annette was their favored partner. She danced so well she made them all feel graceful as birds in their turn with her.

Josephine persisted in having every other dance with Bill, but she was at last approached by a hesitant Butch Berry, who gestured timidly in invitation to a turn. She made a quick face of annoyance—then put her arms out and said, "Well don't just stand there gawking, boy, if it's dancing you want!"

His grin felt the size of a keyboard and his heart was lodged in his throat the whole time he swung her around the floor. He reveled in the bright gaiety of her eyes, the heated girl-smell of her, the way the wet ends of her hair clung to her cheeks and neck. Then their dance was done and she scooted back to Bill. But Butch's grin stayed with him, and his pulse thumped in his head like a victory drum.

She was dozing in the bedside chair and still holding to Tyler's hand when his grasp tightened and woke her. She put a palm to his sweaty brow, his hot cheek, asked if he'd like a drink of water. The bedroom window was gray with dawnlight. His cheeks shone with tears, his eyes were darkly hollowed but bright as embers under a sudden wind. He rasped: "I can't even hug you proper." She held his face between her hands and kissed his parched lips.

When Josephine came into the room at sunrise with a tray of tea and porridge, Mary was kneeling by the bed and holding Tyler Bur-dette in her arms and rocking him as a mother comforting a child.

The boy's open eyes held no light at all. Josie put down the tray and went to the bed and gently drew Mary free of him, then folded his arm on his chest and closed his eyes. Mary hugged Josephine's hips and wept softly against her belly. Josie stroked her sister's hair and ached for the girl's battered heart.

They buried him in the woods at the rear of the property. Quantrill read from the Bible. Mary placed flowers at the gravehead and whispered words over them that none did hear save perhaps the stilled lover in the ground.

BEFORE GOD AND THE DEVIL

The morning after Burdette's funeral, they were sitting around the breakfast table and leafing through newspapers when W. J. Gregg said, "Oh hell, Captain, you better read this." He folded the paper so that the article was at the forefront and passed it to Quantrill.

The report was more than a week old and pertained to Perry Hoy, who'd been among the first to join Quantrill and was one of his closest friends. He'd been captured by the Yankees in early spring and imprisoned in Fort Leavenworth. Because the Union had officially declared guerrillas to be outlaws, Perry Hoy's participation in skirmishes in which Federal soldiers had been killed was regarded not as military duty but as complicity in murder. He'd been tried and convicted and sentenced to death. All the while, Quantrill had been trying to secure his freedom through an exchange of prisoners. Only two weeks ago, he had offered three captive Union officers in trade for Perry, but the Yanks had made no response. Until now.

On a morning described as brightly sunny, on a well-tended parade ground at Fort Leavenworth, before a crowd of two hundred spectators said to be in festive spirit, Perry Hoy had been made to kneel before an army firing squad and was then shot dead.

Quantrill put aside the newspaper and took a small notepad from his pocket and scribbled in it, tore off the sheet and folded it and handed it to Gregg. "Take this to Todd," he said. "Tell him the company meets at the Red Creek camp tomorrow night. Go."

W. J. would later tell Bill Anderson the note said, "Shoot the three—*now*. Q."

Quantrill turned to Bill. "Have you ever made visit to Olathe, William T.?"

"Once."

"Care much for the place?"

He remembered the gunfight in Olathe barely two months ago. "Can't say I did. Might've been pleasant except for some son of a bitch named Porter and a sheriff he owns like a dog."

"Well, I've been meaning to visit," Quantrill said. "Redlegs have been brokering horses there, and I've got new boys in need of good mounts."

"It's a prosperous town," Cole Younger said. His grin was larcenous. "Got lots of everything."

Quantrill looked around at the others, then back at Bill. "You and your boys can ride with us if such is your ambition."

Your boys. Bill looked at his brother and at the Berrys and none seemed to have objection to Quantrill's view of them as Bill Anderson's boys.

"Gregg and Todd have both put in for you," Quantrill said. "Younger and Haller have spoken for you too."

Cole Younger grinned at Bill.

"But mark me," Quantrill said, raising a finger in the manner of a teacher emphasizing a point. "We have a law in this company, a law hard as stone. We don't inform. An informer is a traitor of the worst stripe. We will kill an informer and every man in his family. If any of you cannot swear by that law, then you may take your leave and good luck to you." He leaned forward. "Gentlemen, I'll know your answer."

Bill looked at his brother. Jim said, "I'm for it."

He turned to the Berry boys. "Me and Butch already talked about it," Ike said. "We're with you, Bill—if you're in, we're in." Butch Berry nodded.

"Well then," Quantrill said. He got to his feet and they all stood too. "Do you swear," he said, "swear before God and the devil, before the power of heaven to grant eternal salvation and the power of hell to punish for time without end, do you *swear* to live by the law of this company unto death? If so, say, 'I do so swear.' "

And swear they all four did.

THE LIST

An hour after they departed the Vaughn place they arrived at a farm off the Mission Road. The sun was not yet ascended above the trees. Most of their party remained hidden in the bush as Jimmy Vaughn and Cole Younger sneaked around to the back of the house to guard against escape through a rear window. Socrates Johnson and Ike Berry rode up and hallooed the house, both of them with their pistols hidden under their partly buttoned dusters. Sock Johnson wore a collapsible stovepipe hat he carried in his saddle wallet for just such occasion as this. The door opened and from the inner darkness the man's voice said, "Who are you? What you want?"

"Name's Reaper," Sock Johnson said. "The Reverend Jedediah Reaper, of the Church of Holy Divine. Me and my boy have lost our way and we wonder if ye might help us to get our proper bearings."

The door opened just wide enough for a man to step out onto the porch. He held a lone-barrel shotgun of goodly bore, the hammer cocked, and stood warily, ready to shoot and leap back into the house at a hostile gesture. He looked all about, then kept his narrow gaze shifting between Johnson and Butch Berry. "A preacher, ye say?"

"That is correct, sir," Johnson said. "A poor but dedicated servant of the Lord. And your name, if I may inquire?"

"Never mind my name. How do I know you're who ye say?"

"Well now, sir, I don't fault you for your caution, what with the countryside crawling with brigands of every stripe in these sad days and so many of them traveling under false colors. How's a man to know if the fella saying he's a preacher really is one and not just some outlaw lying in the face of God? Believe me, sir, I take no offense at your suspicion. Such wariness is wisdom—and it is the very reason I carry proof of who I am. I have in my pocket a diploma of graduation from the Holy Divine Seminary. Permit me to show it to you."

Johnson's hand went into the pocket of his duster and through the hole cut in it to give him easy access to the pistols on his belt. He cocked the revolver as he flicked aside the duster flap and the Colt blasted and the farmer flung back against the wall and his shotgun clattered to the porch planks. The man sat down hard with the look of someone recalling an important chore left undone.

A scream sounded in the house and Ike Berry now brandished a pistol too. Johnson reined his horse half-about for a clearer view of the sitting man and then shot him again and the man's head flung blood on the wall and he fell on his side. One foot waggled a few times and went still.

Another scream—and a woman rushed out and dropped to her knees and cradled the bloody head and raised a high keening. A pair of children, a boy and a girl, stood at the door and looked from their parents to the two men sitting their horses—and then past them to the other riders coming out of the woods and toward the house.

Quantrill asked the woman her dead husband's name but she ignored him in her loud grief. He was about to ask again when the older child, the girl, said, "My daddy is Morton Winstead." Her little brother hit her with his elbow and glared at her, then turned his fierce stare back to the men fronting the house.

On his thigh Quantrill held his notebook open to a page containing the names of farmers and townsmen and merchants and men of law against whom the guerrillas had personal briefs, or whom southern loyalists had identified as informers to the Federals. He drew a line through "Winstead." The list was constantly under revision, names crossed off, new names added. The Federals had their own list, the militia had theirs, the redlegs theirs. In this part of the country, the war was this personal and had been from the start.

"It's not solely that your husband was a Unionist, Mrs. Winstead," Quantrill said in a voice raised high enough to be heard over her lamentations. "What killed him was his unwise decision to inform on secessionist neighbors, telling the Federals of their kindness to us. He was responsible for three families losing their father to a Union noose and seeing their farms burned. Tell your friends this is what they can expect to reap if they sow as your husband did."

He paused as if he would give her the opportunity to address him if she wished, but she only continued in her loud grief over her husband's body.

Quantrill looked at the children. "You tell them."

The girl nodded, but the boy just stared in hate.

*   *   *

They came to the farm of another Unionist who'd been warned of their approach. They soon enough found him hiding in a cornfield and there left him lifeless, his blood seeping into the black earth and nurturing a crop he would never bring in. They did no damage to the farm itself. A soft breeze carried the calls of crows passing the news to each other, the high cries of another family bereaved—lorn remnants of a kind of calamity as natural to the world as wildfire and flood and windstorm, as old as the sons of Adam.

On their list too were the names of three men who lived together with a Choctaw woman in a cabin about a mile off the main road. The men professed to be ruffians dedicated to the theft of Kansas horses, but many complaints had reached Quantrill that these men thieved from Missourians as well.

When the guerrillas reined up in front of the cabin and hallooed, the squaw was sent out to see what they wanted. Quantrill told her to get away from the house and she scampered into the trees and out of sight. The three men then came out without further solicitation, calling out effusive greetings and showing stiff grins, explaining to Quantrill that a body couldn't be too careful anymore about greeting strangers with open arms. They apologized for not having recognized him sooner, but they were sure glad to see him because it so happened they had a fresh bunch of good horses they wanted to give him as a present, and, no sir, don't even think about offering to pay for them, his money was no good with them. They were still blathering in this fashion when Quantrill gave a signal and a fusillade of revolver rounds hushed them for once and all.

They found eight horses corralled in a clearing behind the cabin, only two worth taking. The others they left for the Indian woman. And left too—hanging by their heels from the lower limbs of an oak, arms and hair adangle, coattails bunched at their armpits, their dripping blood blackening the ground beneath them—the three dead men, one of them with a note affixed to his shirt: "Behold the wages of thievery."

A DISCOURSE

As they rode through the gold light of late afternoon, a guerrilla pointed to a huge and leafless oak tree and said it was the tree on which some years ago had been hanged the notorious killer Bedford Wills. "It's why that tree's gone dead," he said. "A tree a murderer's hung from will die inside five years."

Some agreed with this belief but others jeered it as an old wives' tale. Some said they knew of hanging trees that had been in use for years and years and they hadn't died yet—but several of them argued that some trees died slower than others, just like some men, and a tree could be dying on the inside for a long time before it gave any sign of it on the outside.

Sock Johnson said the whole thing was bullshit, the same as believing that the way to end a drought was to kill a snake and drape it belly-up over a fencepost. This opinion raised several loud assurances that the snake cure for a dry spell was a true fact and had more times been witnessed to prove true than Sock Johnson had hairs on his face.

They argued whether sunny days could be counted on if you spied a rabbit a long way from its hole, and whether a pig with a stick in its mouth meant a bad storm coming—a portent which Ike Berry said he had never known to fail. Was it really a sure sign of death in the family if a bird flew into the house, as many of them did believe, or good luck if a redbird made its nest nearby? They snickered lewdly as schoolboys in debating Cole Younger's claim that a woman could snare a man to her will by seasoning his food with her intimate female secretions—and Dave Pool raised a loud laugh all around by exclaiming, "Sweet Jesus, so *that's* how that Greene County bitch got me to play the fool!"

They argued about countless supposed sources of bad luck, but when Will Haller claimed that a cross-eyed person was bad luck, especially if encountered at an intersection of roads, Cole Younger nudged him and nodded at Butch Berry. Haller hastened to assure Butch that he didn't mean him, because after all, he wasn't really cross-eyed, just off-eyed, which was a whole different thing and only affected one eye anyway, not both, like cross-eyed did. The others all agreed with this distinction and said so. Butch looked around at their serious miens, then grinned and shook his head and said, "I got to say, that's a heavy burden off my mind"—and they all broke out laughing.

At the head of the column, Quantrill smiled.

A REUNION AND A FRACAS

The company numbered eighty men when it came together that night at the Red Creek camp—a meadow engirt by heavy forest and hard by the Blue River. Their various fires swirled and wavered in a fitful breeze. In the dark distance a lobo called high and keen under a low amber moon and the high spangle of stars, under paledust clouds of constellations already ancient beyond reckoning at the advent of men and their stone-ax antagonisms.

Every fire held a circle of men and there were rounds of visitation from one fire to another. Introductions were made and old friends greeted, rumors passed on, whiskey jugs shared, new clothes and weapons displayed. Larkin Skaggs exceeded all descriptions Bill Anderson had heard: the old man looked like a mad-eyed prophet wandered in from a wildland unknown to any history or map. Andy Blunt seemed wary on meeting the Andersons, expecting them perhaps to be seeking redress for his offense against Josephine. But Bill simply asked if he'd learned any recent lessons in the proper use of his hands. Blunt smiled wryly and rubbed the eye Josie had clouted and said, "Damn right I have."

Dick Yeager was hearty and friendly, his yellow teeth often bared in laughter through a drooping muleskinner mustache. The Andersons would come to know that his family had owned a prosperous wagon business in Kansas until jayhawkers raided one day while Dick was gone to Santa Fe. They took every wagon and mule on the place, burned everything they didn't steal, killed Dick's little brother and crippled his father, distracted his younger sister near to madness. Even in his loudest laughter, Dick Yeager's eyes seemed to Bill as coldly isolate as a winter field.

Fletcher Taylor had been with John Jarrette's small band of guerrillas when it joined with Quantrill. Short and near to handsome in his close-trimmed copper goatee, Taylor was a thoughtful and practical-minded man given to the frequent observation that if a frog had wings it wouldn't bump its ass so much. For his part, Jarrette was now one of Quantrill's best officers. A lean man of high cheekbones and pointed black imperial and eyes blue as sulfur fire. This devilish aspect all the more pronounced by his black guerrilla shirt and its strange yellow stitchings—crescent moons and stars, triangles, mystical symbols whose meanings he admitted not to understand, but his sister, he said with a grin, swore they would protect him in battle.

The Anderson brothers too were now garbed in guerrilla shirts. Josephine had presented Bill with a dark blue shirt bedecked with flowerwork in red and silver, the ammunition pockets lined with soft leather. Jenny surprised Jim with a guerrilla shirt too—gray, with black-and-brown embroidery—and it would have been hard to say which brother received the handsomer garment. Annette and Hazel promised to have shirts ready for the Berry boys on their return.

Jarrette was now showing off his latest prize, a weapon he'd found in an Englishman's hotel room in Independence—a Maynard smoothbore doublebarrel which, in addition to the Colts he carried on hips and belly, he wore in a sling holster across his chest. The barrels were aligned one under the other and each was five inches long and both of cavernous .64-caliber. He charged one barrel with a solid ball and the other with scrap metal and small coins, and either load could remove most of a man's head. He called this gun his Widowmaker.

Others too gave names to certain of their firearms. Andy Blunt's cutdown shotgun was Alice Malice. Cole Younger's Army Colt was Chopper. Dave Pool's monstrous LeMat pistol, chambered for nine .44 rounds from its top barrel and a .60-caliber ball or shotcharge from the underslung, carried the name Hellgate. Dick Yeager addressed his Sharps carbine as Mr. Graves. Some in the company would give no appellation to a gun, but every man's knife had a name. Most of them carried bowies—some the size of small swords—but popular too was the tapered poniard known as the Arkansas toothpick. There were Green River knives and clasp knives and skinners, fighting knives of all sorts. And because killing with a knife entailed closing with your foe so that you smelled him and saw his wild eyes and heard his breath and felt his blood spatter you even as you sometimes stained him with your own, because a knife, in brief, was a far more intimate weapon than a gun, it was generally regarded as female. They called their cutters by the names of wives and sweethearts—Sally, Molly Jean, Annie, Rachel, Maggie May— and of women they knew as deadly legend: Jezebel and Delilah and Bloody Mary, Salome and Lady Macbeth.

At the fire where Bill Anderson now sat, a bushwhacker named Lionel Ward was telling of the marriage he'd been forced into at the points of various long guns after the woman's father caught them in the act in the barn. "She wasn't no spring chicken, you see," Lionel Ward said, "twenty-five if she was a day, and like as not was getting fearful of the fates. I suspicion she had a hand in planning with her da and brothers for that little surprise in the barn. Truth to tell, I didn't mind, for she'd mostly been such a sweet thing to me. But once we'd been stood in front of that preacher, oh Lord, didn't that woman reveal herself for the queen of fishwives! Had a temper she'd kept from me, you see, but now it was off the leash." He stood it for three months, he said, and one night couldn't stand it anymore. He sneaked out and saddled his horse and rode off without a look back. "Took naught but me good Dan and me rifle and the scars on me poor heart."

"Could say you seceded from *that* union too, hey Lionel?" somebody called out, and everybody laughed.

Now came a sudden outbreak of yelling and hollers of "Fight! Fight!" from a group at another fire, and they all ran to witness the scrap.

George Todd and Will Haller were locked together on the ground, grappling in a firebright haze of dust, snarling and punching and each trying to get a chokehold on the other. The bushwhackers formed a wide circle about them, clamoring like harrying hounds, shouting bets one to the other, exhorting the fighters to do their worst.

Todd was the stronger man and now had Haller in a headlock with one arm and was punching him repeatedly with his free fist. Haller's face distorting under the blows, smearing with blood, then he managed to lock his teeth into Todd's forearm and Todd cursed and punched him faster but the bite loosened his hold and Haller slipped free.

Both men on their feet now and gasping, hair askew, eyes in red rage—and then abruptly locking together again and pulling each other down. They rolled to the edge of the fire and the back of Todd's shirt began smoking and he yelped and rolled them hard away from the flames. Haller kept trying to ram his knee into Todd's crotch and now Todd was biting hard on his ear and the top part of it came away in his teeth. Haller howled and bucked wildly and shook loose and they both scrambled to their feet again. Todd still had the portion of Haller's ear in his mouth and he turned and spat it into the fire. Haller steadily and lowly cursing. Then they were clenched again and Todd wrestled Haller to the ground and finally managed to straddle his chest and pin Haller's arms down with his knees. The back of Todd's shirt was scorched from the fire and the taut fabric was embossed with the outline of the sheathed bowie he wore back there on a sling around his neck. He reached back under his collar and drew the weapon forth.

Both men were variously armed but neither had reached for a weapon till now. Some might have thought it understood between them that the fight was one of brute strength and not weapons, but of all men anywhere, none knew better than this bunch the fallacy of fighting by rules. Not even Quantrill, looking on with his arms crossed, said anything in protest of Todd's introduction of the knife.

The bowie's blade was a foot long and three inches wide in its upper portion and its curving saber point was honed top and bottom so it could cut both upward and down. Todd put the tip to Haller's throat and a bulb of blood formed at the indention and then rolled in a thin line around his neck.

"I'm gonna . . . get off you, punkinhead," Todd said in a gasping breath. "You can pull your knife or your gun . . . either one. Or you can . . . get yourself gone."

Todd rose quickly and stepped away from Haller, one hand brandishing the bowie, the other gripped on a holstered pistol. Haller got up slowly and warily. He spat blood. He stood facing Todd, his battered face working with tics, then looked around at the others, some of them solemn-faced, some agrin, all of them quieted now and waiting to see what he would do. He muttered, then spat again, then limped off to where the horses were picketed.

The following morning Todd was elected the company's new first lieutenant. The rest of the day the men were at cleaning their weapons and seeing to their horses, at telling tales and jokes, passing the time until the sun was fled below the horizon and dusk rolled up out of the east like a purple tide. As the last pink streaks faded from the western sky Quantrill called them to mount up and then led the way over the border and into enemy country.

REBEL YELLS

They rode ahead of their raised dust like specters at roam on the dark land. The pale half-moon was in the west when the town's lights came in view. A mile from town, scouts were waiting to report the presence of a hundred Kansas militiamen, though the unit was composed almost entirely of green recruits. "The spies say not a man of them's heard a shot in battle," a scout said. "Say the name of Quantrill puts a goodly white in their eye."

Quantrill conferred with his officers, then sent Gregg with twenty men to deploy around the town and cut off any messenger the Yanks might try to send out.

The town blazing with lamplight this Saturday night as they trotted down the street in a double column, looking ghostly in the haze of dust, raising no sound but the clumping of hooves and the jingling of ringbits and armaments. They had of course been spotted as they closed on the town, and the militiamen were formed up in two ranks on the far side of the central square, the front line down on one knee and both ranks with muzzleloaders ready. The street clear of civilians but there were spectators at every window.

"Stay easy, boys," Quantrill said softly to the men nearest him. "If they wanted a fight, they'd have started it by now."

At the square, the column split off to right and left to form a line facing the soldiers some thirty yards across the way. The officer in command was a goateed major standing slightly to the fore of the ranks with a saber in his hand. A beardless lieutenant was close beside him. They stood like farmers gauging a dark storm in the distance.

Bill Anderson heard Quantrill whisper to Todd, "Look at them. They'd rather be anywhere but here. Would they were all this easy." He raised his hand and every guerrilla brought up a pistol in each fist and the cocking of more than a hundred revolvers at once was a sound to prickle Bill's neck hairs.

"Halloo the commander!" Quantrill called out.

The militia officers were agape—and then the major stepped forward and said, "I am Major Wilbur Halltree, commanding the—"

"Your choice, sir," Quantrill cut in, "is to live or die. Lay down your weapons and I promise parole to every last man."

"Ah now, Captain Quantrill, they don't want no parole!" Cole Younger called loudly. "They want to die for Old Abe Lincoln, so let's oblige them to the last man!"

Quantrill smiled and Younger grinned at the men nearest him. Bill Anderson recognized Cole's outcry for a ploy to let the Feds know who they were dealing with. The militiamen stirred uneasily and exchanged nervous looks and whispers. The lieutenant ordered them to be silent and stand fast.

"*You* are Quantrill?" the major said.

"*Captain* Quantrill, sir, and his partisan rangers of the Confederacy," Quantrill said. "I'll have your answer quick or choose it for you."

The major looked around as if searching for someone he could charge with making the choice. He stared back at Quantrill and said, "But what assurance . . ." and gestured vaguely.

"If I were bent on killing you, sir," Quantrill said, "you would already be over the river and all of your men with you. Now choose."

The major looked at the lieutenant, then at his men, many of whom were nodding like men with palsy. He turned back to Quantrill and said, "Oh hell, man . . . we surrender."

They herded the soldiers into a corral and ordered them to strip off their uniforms and toss them in a wagon, and they relieved some of their boots as well. They then set about seizing all the teams and wagons in town, all the horses and mules, their rebel yells keening through the streets. They ransacked the saloons and liveries and shops. They loaded the wagons with barrels of whiskey, with weapons and powder and balls, with foodstuffs and tools, tack, dry goods, pausing in their labors now and again to take a drink or two, to shoot to shards everything of glass along the streetfronts. Their howling and gunfire sent most of the town's dogs into hiding, but a few rough curs set themselves with napes roached and teeth bared and were shot dead where they stood. It pained Bill Anderson to see dogs killed for their bravery, but he would not warn them away from holding to their natures.

The Berry boys asked after the sheriff and were pointed to a man with bloodied head who sat crosslegged in the square, disarmed and looking addled. He was not the lawman who'd accosted them on their previous visit to Olathe. They asked who'd been sheriff back in June and were told his name was Worrell, but he'd been badly wounded in a scrap with some passing strangers and would nevermore walk without crutches and had gone to live with his married daughter in Lawrence. They asked about Harrison Porter and received directions to his ranch a few miles from town. They told Quantrill what they wanted to do and he said to take five men with them, settle their brief, and bring back all the good horses they found.

No house or hotel room escaped searching. They kicked open locked doors, broke into trunks and chests and closets, rooted out cash and gold and jewelry. Where they found nothing of sufficient value they smashed furniture in their pique. The men were rounded up in the courthouse square and robbed of their weapons, money, watches, whatever ornaments of gold they wore. Some tried to abscond into the outer darkness, into the nearest brush or ravine, but were intercepted by Gregg's perimeter guards. Some sought to hide in outhouses, in haylofts, in wagonbeds, under tomato vines in their garden, and some of them were discovered and some not.

Wives took to the square to plead for their men's safety, but they would have done better to stay at home. Where the raiders found only women in a house their rapacity was checked. Andy Blunt was set to take a small gilt handmirror he fancied for his sweetheart, but the missus of the house beseeched him for it, saying it had belonged to her daughter who'd drowned a year ago. Blunt gave it back and tendered a condolence.

Not so fortunate was the man who tried to hide a bay pony in a small corn patch behind his house. Cole Younger heard the animal nicker and went outside and found it. The owner rushed out and snatched the reins away and said, "I'll die before I'll give up this horse." Cole Younger was full of whiskey and in no temper to be opposed. "Then die it is," he said, and discharged a bullet into the fool's brain. But the flaring pistolblast spooked the pony and it bolted away. Cole chased after it, cursing and threatening to shoot it, but the horse vanished in the darkness and he did not see it again.

So it went through the rest of the night. The town's two newspaper offices were demolished, their printing presses dismantled with sledgehammers, their stores of ink poured over the supplies of newsprint, over the furniture, over the heads of the editors. When the owner of the *Olathe Herald* saw his cache of thirteen thousand dollars, the savings of his life, discovered by a bushwhacker and handed to George Todd, he broke into tears and cried, "Oh God, I am *ruined*!" George Todd told him he shouldn't take it so hard, he should count his blessings, because things could always be worse. To the amusement of his comrades, he proved his point by shooting the man in the foot.

The Berrys reappeared with sixteen finebred horses they galloped through the street and added to the herd of stolen stock. Ike's pale hair hung from under a flatbrimmed hat of Californio fashion. The hat had belonged to one Harrison Porter, whose last words had been, "I don't know *what* gray horse you're talking about and I sure as hell don't know you boys."

By dawn the company had acquired a train of loot fourteen wagons long. The wagons they didn't use they set afire in the street. Quantrill's mood was ebullient. He dispatched the plunder train and the rustled herd toward Missouri with half the company as escort and George Todd in command. He released the captive townsmen from the square and they hurried into the arms of their waiting women and clung to them as they shambled home.

The risen red sun cast lean shadows through the streets. Not a horse or mule was left to the town, not a wagon left uncharred nor a windowpane unshattered. Shop doors hung askew and the sidewalks were littered with glass and broken furniture. But only three men had been killed and the town had been spared the torch. As George Todd might have advised the Olathans, it could have been worse. For other towns to either side of the border, it yet would be.

The bushwhackers mounted up and Quantrill called for the prisoners to be brought forth in a column of twos. None of the soldiers wore more than hat and underwear and boots and some wore less than that. Some stepped gingerly in their stockinged feet as the guerrillas led them out to eastward.

"Where are you taking us?" the major called to Quantrill. "You promised parole!"

George Maddox told him to shut up or he'd shoot him where he stood.

The town fell away behind them. Two miles farther on, Quantrill called a halt. Some of the prisoners now fell to weeping and some to prayer. One boy clutched Andy Blunt's stirrup and said, "*Please* don't shoot me—I got a mother, I got a baby sister."

Blunt was at once embarrassed and outraged. He kicked the boy away and said, "Quit it, for God's sake!" Cole Younger made a sound of disgust and spat.

"Listen to me!" Quantrill said. "I promised parole and parole you now have. Be men of your word and stay out of the ranks."

He hupped the Charley horse forward and the point riders hastened out ahead of him and the rest of the company fell in behind, some chuckling and others grumbling over bets won and lost on the question of whether he would execute the prisoners.

The militiamen watched them go, every man of them feeling gratitude and relief—and rising fear of a terrible joke to be sprung on them at any moment when the bushwhackers turned back to reveal their grins and kill them all. They watched the guerrillas until they were out of sight before they started back to town, and even then they kept looking over their shoulders.

Bill Anderson's prize spoil of the night was a fine gold bracelet he'd envisioned on Josephine's wrist the moment he saw it. "I'll have that if you please," he'd said to the fairfaced woman wearing it. She handed it to him with the accusation, "You are a shameless brigand." To which he said, "I expect you're right, mam" and kissed her hand—and smiled at the rosiness raised to her cheeks by both dander and delight. He'd also come to possess a pair of fobbed watches of excellent manufacture, a match cylinder of pure silver, a man's ruby ring, and cash money that bulged his every pocket. His brother and the Berrys too had enriched themselves with cash, had reaped pocket pistols and watches, jewelry true and false, fancy shirts and boots, gimcrackery of every sort. All in all, it had been a night of such license as none of them had ever thought to possess save in dreams. They could not stop grinning at each other and at the passing world.

*   *   *

The plunder train was slow and ponderous and they caught up to it before it made the border. Todd had sent Fletch Taylor and a crew ahead with the stock, and the herd's dust bloomed low on the forward sky. Quantrill posted lookouts well back of the company to keep a sharp eye for pursuers, but there was still no sign of anyone coming behind them when they crossed the border that afternoon. They were well into Jackson County when they put down for the night. Fletch Taylor had pastured the herd a mile forward of their camp.

They passed a celebrant evening drinking and joking and raising their rebel yells, telling and retelling anecdotes of the raid. Quantrill took Bill Anderson aside and said he'd heard that he and his boys had goodly experience in wrangling horse herds. Bill asked where he'd heard that. Quantrill said it was one of those things you hear and he was just wondering if it was true. Bill smiled. Quantrill said, "I thought so."

He charged Bill and his boys, including Jimmy Vaughn, with delivering the Olathe horses to the Cass County ranch of a man named Dropo, who'd long done business with the guerrillas. They were to take the payment to Annette Vaughn to use toward the purchase of powder and ball in Kansas City. "I'll send word to you at the Vaughn place," Quantrill said, "when I'm ready to bring the company together again."

Shortly before daybreak, Bill's bunch relieved Fletch Taylor's crew of the herd and got it moving south. The rest of the company pushed eastward with the plunder train, headed for neighboring Johnson County where an entrepreneur of Quantrill's acquaintance would pay in gold coin for their load of loot.

A BATHING INCIDENT

Some days later Bill's bunch was back at the Vaughn place and stepping down from their horses and into the girls' hugs and kisses. In the flurry of happy greetings, Josephine embraced Butch Berry in his turn and pecked him on the cheek. For an instant Butch felt like he'd been hit on the head—then tried to hold her to him and kiss her back, but she ducked out of his grasp and flung herself on Bill once more. Mary

Anderson gave them each a welcome hug too, but they could see that her spirit was still sore with the memory of Tyler Burdette.

"Whooo, lordy!" Annette Vaughn loudly declared. "These boys smell like something crawled into their clothes and died. Let's get some tubs filled."

A short time later the five of them were soaking in sudsy wooden tubs clustered in a ragged circle in the stable, scrubbing the trail grime out of their pores, joking and laughing, recounting the Olathe raid to Finley and Black Josh, passing around jugs of the busthead whiskey Josh brewed out in the woods. They'd been at these pleasures the better part of an hour when Annette and Josephine came into the stable with armfuls of fresh towels and clean clothes and prompted outcries of indignation.

"Sweet Jesus, Annie!" Jimmy Vaughn hollered. "It's nekkid men taking baths here!"

Annette made a face of mock shock and handed the clothes and towels to Josh. "As if any of you got something we never saw before," she said.

Finley sniggered. Bill gave Josephine a scolding look and she smiled with exaggerated sweetness.

"Get out of here—both you!" Jim Anderson said. He slung a handful of water at them.

"They sure seem awful ashamed of whatever it is they think we might see, don't they?" Annette said to Josie. "Look at them all scrunched down in those tubs like turtles in their shells."

"Dammit to hell!" Ike Berry shouted. He sat up so abruptly that water sloshed over the sides of his tub. He was rose-eyed with drink and his white hair was plastered to his skull. "Putting on like you're so bold!" He looked around at his fellows and said, "What say we stand up and let em have a good gawk? See how bold they are *then*?"

"I dare you," Annette said. "Doubledog dare you."

"Yeah, doubledog dare you!" Josephine said. She laughed and sidestepped the sopping washrag Bill threw at her.

"I'm with Ike," Jim Anderson said. He took another pull of whiskey and set the jug beside his tub. "Let's just see how bold they are. On the count of three. Ready, boys?"

"One . . ." Jimmy Vaughn said. He braced himself on the sides of the tub in readiness to stand.

"Two . . ." Bill Anderson said, his beard dripping, himself positioned to push up to his feet.

"*Three!*" Ike Berry bellowed—and he stood up in a cascade of gray soapy water, throwing his arms out wide like some stage celebrity in the spotlight, his torso and legs shining white. And in the next horrifying instant realized he was the only one who'd risen.

The other men broke out laughing and the girls squealed and blushed behind their hands and Annette pointed at Ike but Josephine was already looking where she pointed and both girls were bent with laughter. Ike looked down and saw his privates shriveled into their nest of pale hair and jerked his hands over himself and sat down fast. The girls now cackling so hard they had to hold to each other, the men guffawing. Black Josh showed an expanse of yellow teeth.

"You low sons of bitches," Ike muttered, glaring around at the other men in a furious blush. Even his brother in the tub beside him was grinning.

"Think it's funny, do you?" Ike said. He leaned out and grabbed the edge of Butch's tub with both hands and pushed hard and the tub tilted and then crashed over on its side, depositing Butch on the floor in a rush of water and a chorus of cheers, sprawling him on his back, arms flailing and legs flung wide—and for an instant the stable fell mute as every watching eye seized on his stark erection. Then the men were yowling with harder laughter yet and the girls were fleeing for the house in redfaced shrieks of hilarity.

Butch scrambled to his feet and snatched a towel from Josh and whipped it around himself, grabbed up his clean clothes and stalked into one of the horse stalls to get dressed—all the while cursing everybody for no-account bastards, his ears flaming.

The men were choking on their laughter, weeping with it. "Now he's gone all *shy* on us," Jim Anderson managed to say.

"Yeah," Bill Anderson said, wiping at his eyes, gasping, "but say now, don't that boy know how to deal with a doubledog dare!"

"You *see* them girls go flying?" Jimmy Vaughn said.

"Hellfire," Finley said with a skewed grin, "when I saw that ugly thing standing up like that and looking like it didn't care what it went after, *I* about ran away!"

Another swell of guffawing and hooting.

Ike looked over at his brother, whose face seemed carved of strawberry stone. "Damn, boy, the *things* going on in your head."

REPORT OF A CHASE

Word of the company came to Finley by way of some secret informant and he passed it on to Bill and the boys. A force of Federals had tracked Quantrill and the plunder train out of Olathe and over the border and caught up to them a mile into Johnson County. The company made a run for it but they were slowed by the loot wagons. The guerrillas fought a constant rear action as they went, but every time they stopped to fight before running again, they had to abandon a wagon or two. The Federals kept after them for ten days and didn't quit their pursuit until the guerrillas made it into the rugged Sni-a-bar region of Jackson County, just south of the Missouri River. This was the bushwhackers' home country—densely forested and cut with deep ravines, the hills rugged and covered with thickets, the bluffs near the river pocked with caves and sliced through with narrow passes. Quantrill's boys knew every deer trace and hog trail in the region and could move through it like creatures of the wild. To the Feds the Sni-a-bar was a terra damnata; no detachment of Yankees ever entered that wildwood and came out again with as many men as it took in—and now they rarely ventured there at all.

According to Finley's informant, only a single bushwhacker had been killed in the ten-day running fight, and only a few had been wounded. But by the time they made it to the Sni-a-bar, they'd given up every wagon of their loot to the Yanks.

DANCERS

While they waited for word from Quantrill they tended to their horses and gear and helped Finley and Josh with some of the rougher chores around the place. They hewed dead trees at the edge of the forest and trimmed them and with horses and ropes dragged the trunks up near the firewood cribs and axed and stored cords for the coming winter—which some of the local farmers were predicting would be early in arriving and colder than usual. They were into

October and the meadow grasses and pasturelands already going purple and brown, the leaves coloring like fire and some already falling.

Every night, after the house had fallen silent and all the bedroom doors were shut, Josephine tiptoed barefoot down the hall, silent as a secret, and slipped into Bill's room. Sometimes he was fast asleep and wouldn't know she was with him until he woke in the deeper night to her breath on his neck and her arms around him. And, as had become her practice, she would wake in the last dark hour before dawn, kiss his sleeping face, and slip back to her own bed.

One Saturday evening they ventured into Westport for supper and the weekly dance, the ten of them together. Each man carried a pocket revolver under his suit coat, and Josephine thrilled to the feel of the gun against her elbow when she clutched to Bill's arm. She wore the bracelet he'd brought her from Olathe, and she couldn't keep from admiring its rich glimmer on her wrist, nor from kissing him on the cheek every now and again.

After supper they repaired to the auction hall to dance to the music of a fine string band. Mary did not want to join in the dancing at first, saying she'd prefer to sit and watch. But Jimmy Vaughn had lately begun to show a warm interest in her and to ply her with gentle attentions, and he soon had her out on the floor, whirling and smiling in earnest for the first time since Tyler's death. Through the evening, Jim and Hazel became inseparable partners as well, having suddenly perceived each other as keenly attractive.

Butch was less timorous that evening about approaching Josie for a turn, and she accepted each of his invitations without cutting remark or a look of being imposed upon. But they didn't speak or even hold each other's eyes as they whirled about the floor, and she was each time quick to get back to Bill as soon as the number was done. Still, Butch couldn't help but believe he was making gains on her heart.

He'd just finished a vigorous turn with Jenny when he went for a mug of beer to recruit himself, and with no other partner available at the moment, tireless Jenny sat with him. As he drank the beer and watched Josephine waltzing with Bill, Jenny said, "He makes the whole world go round for her, you know. Mary and Jim say he always has, ever since she was a baby."

Butch turned to her but she was watching the dancers as she spoke. "I think she's crazy and I've told her so. Mary too. You can't have your brother for a beau! Not a for-real beau. You can't *marry* him or, you know, *anything,* so what's the use? But all she says is, '*I don't care.*' "

She giggled at her mimicry and turned to Butch and her smile wavered at the look on his face. But he recovered handily, draining the rest of his beer at a gulp and belching hugely to restore her grin. "What say, Jenny Lightfoot?" he said. "Got it in you for another turn?" The words were barely out of his mouth before she was tugging him by the arm to hurry along back to the dancefloor.

For nights thereafter, Butch would long lie awake before falling asleep. He could shape no thought to ease the hollow ache in his chest. He tried not to think at all, but he could not quit accusing himself for a fool. How had he been so *blind*? The moment Jenny told him about Josie, he had seen the truth of things. He stared into the darkness and saw her with Bill, saw them dancing, saw her hugging him, clinging to his arm, petting him, kissing his ear. *Fool!* To have believed he might someday receive such affections from her.

Would any man besides Bill? The question hissed in his head like a snake. He lay sleepless into the night with suspicions so dreadful he didn't know what to think. He could not have said if the impulse he felt at his core was to weep in pity or howl in rage at this base and unfair world.

A LEAVE-TAKING

On a chilly dusk a few days after their Westport visit, they heard Finley and Josh calling halloos behind the house and they looked out to see W. J. Gregg and a dozen guerrillas reining up at the stable. Socrates Johnson was among them and as he came toward the house Jenny ran out and into his arms with a happy shrill and he swung her around like a favored daughter. There was much backslapping and corks were pulled and everybody was talking at once except for Butch Berry, who'd been closemouthed the past few days.

The girls laid out a large fine supper, and the talk at the table was mostly about the ten-day chase the company had led the Federals before making it to the Sni-a-bar. The men then took jugs out to the spacious front porch and pulled chairs in a close circle and conversed in low voices as the misty night chirped and hooted around them.

Gregg said the company was camped at the south end of Jackson County, a couple of miles below the Santa Fe. Quantrill was in a lingering fury about losing the Olathe spoils.

"He's always talked about making a raid into Kansas that nobody'll ever forget," Gregg said, "but now he's talking about it a lot more. He wants a raid that'll scare the bejesus out of every goddam Yankee and abolitionist for the rest of time. *And* one that'll even a lot of scores."

"*And* one that'll get us more loot than Olathe ever saw," Andy Blunt added.

"That's a lot to ask of one damn raid," Bill Anderson said. "Where's he got in mind?"

Gregg took his time about firing his pipe, puffing blue billows into the dim light issuing from the front room windows. He looked around at the Berry boys and Jimmy Vaughn and the brothers Andersons. "Lawrence," he said.

Bill Anderson grinned like he'd been told a mild joke. "Bullshit," he said.

Gregg shook his head and puffed his pipe. Bill looked to John Jarrette, to Socrates Johnson, and neither man disputed Gregg.

"Lawrence is forty miles into Kansas and too much of it open country and there's a thousand Federals in between," Jim Anderson said. "No bunch of raiders can make it *halfway* to Lawrence."

"Going ten miles over the border to Olathe is one thing," Jimmy Vaughn said. "Going to Lawrence is something other."

"Why don't you wise men tell me something I don't know," Gregg said. "I'm just saying what the man's been talking about. Wants to do it come the spring. Cole Younger about laughed in his face, but Todd thinks it maybe can be done."

"Todd would think so," Bill Anderson said.

"It's anyway nothing to debate on for a while," Gregg said. "A hard winter's coming on and we've got to clear out before we lose the leaf cover. We're going to Arkansas and camp with Jo Shelby's outfit. A few of the boys are staying in Missouri and laying low—Cole Younger, for one. What about you fellas?"

"My sisters are here and I intend to watch over them," Bill said. "We'll be waiting for you boys when the wildwood greens up again."

"Well, truth to tell, me and Butch are for Arkansas with the captain," Ike said.

This was news to Bill. He looked at Ike, who shrugged and cut his eyes at his brother to let Bill know it was Butch's idea to go south. Bill knew at once the reason was Josie, and saw at a glance that Jim knew it too. He guessed the boy had had enough of her indifference and had decided to put distance between himself and the cause of his heartache, at least for a time. He felt sympathetic but also suspected Butch might be feeling a touch sorry for himself. You don't know the half of it, he thought, staring at Butch, who would not meet his eyes. Try feeling that way with your sister. See how much distance you can put between you and *that*.

"Well," Bill said, "the company's better off for you boys being with them. You send word on how you're keeping, you hear?"

"We'll do that," Ike said. "And you boys take good care of the girls."

And at daybreak the bunch of them were gone.

III

The Captains

1 8 6 2 – 1 8 6 3

WINTER MOONS

The moon grew plump and pale as a peeled apple, waned into the passing nights, then showed itself again as a thin silver crescent in the twilit western sky. The shed of leaves became a cascade of red and gold and after a time the trees stood skeletal against a sky of weathered tin. The land lay bled of its colors. The nights lengthened, went darker, brightened in their clustered stars. The chilled air smelled of woodsmoke, of distances and passing time. Frost glimmered on the morning fields. Crows called across the pewter afternoons. The first hard freeze cast the countryside in ice and trees split open with sounds like whipcracks. Came a snow flurry one night and then a heavy falling the next day, and that evening the land lay white and still under a high ivory moon.

They hiked deep into the barelimbed woods to targetshoot, lumbering in their heavy coats, their breath pluming white, the men wearing their newest boots to break them in. They worked their horses and curried them. They practiced rope tricks. They played penny poker and finally capitulated to the girls' entreaties and let them sit in and were chagrined when Hazel Vaughn proved the sharp of the party. Snow fell steadily for several days and they went out and romped in it and shaped comic snowmen and constructed bulwarks and waged a snowball war. Evenings they would gather in the parlor with harmonicas and fiddles and Jew's harps and sing and dance in the light of a crackling fire.

The Vaughn library was admirably stocked, and one night they held poetry recitations. Taking turns reading from Poe, Bill and Jim both provoked laughter and catcalls with their histrionic deliveries of such as "The Raven," "Annabel Lee," and "Ulalume." They teamed up on the jangling monotony of "The Bells," alternating the lines between them for maximum effect, and Jimmy Vaughn threw a boot and Jenny shouted "Get the hook!" But then Jim recited "Jenny Kissed Me" from memory, and Jenny did indeed jump from her chair and kiss him for it, and promised never to call for the hook on him again.

Annette was partial to Cavalier verse and moved herself to tears with Lovelace's "To Lucasta," but Hazel's penchant ran to spooky Romanticism, and her presentation of "La Belle Dame Sans Merci" held the room enthralled. Jimmy Vaughn liked Pope, who'd been his father's favorite, and his witty readings of the "Epistle to Dr. Arbuthnot" got loud applause, and so too did Mary's rendition of Shelley's "To a Skylark."

Then Jenny provoked the men to lascivious laughter—and Mary and Annette to blushing chides—when she read "A Sweet Disorder in the Dress." Mary shook a finger at Josie and said, "You put her up to that, I know you did. You are *corrupting* this child, Josephine Anderson." Josie laughed and winked at Jenny, then added weight to Mary's accusation by reading with much passionate inflection another Herrick verse—"Upon Julia's Clothes." At the poem's conclusion the men clapped and whistled and stomped their feet like they were at a Kansas City coochie show, and Josephine took bows like an actress at a curtain call.

Some frosty evenings they sat bundled on the porch steps and regarded the glittering sky and watched for shooting stars. Hazel and Jim would perch on the bottom step with their arms around each other, their whisperings and gigglings rising as blue mist against the moonlight. They enjoyed each other's touch, had in fact become lovers, but they were agreed that their sexual affection did not describe the true love they each expected to find someday. They made no secret to the others of their intimacy, yet none of them, not even young Jenny, was troubled by this unconventional friendship which would have roused brimstone condemnation in the larger world beyond the Vaughn place.

True love had, however, again found Mary Anderson. She sat one porch step below Jimmy Vaughn and leaned back into his embrace. The others were pleased by her recovery of heart and renewed delight in the world. Annette sometimes sat beside them and brushed Mary's hair and once remarked that it was like brushing the moonlight itself.

On those cold front-porch evenings, Josephine would cuddle up to Bill and sometimes slip her hand under his heavy coat and secretly make bold with his person and then laugh softly when he'd growl low in her ear to quit, dammit, there were people around. But she would comport herself properly whenever Jenny joined them and snuggled on Bill's other side.

One day they went to Kansas City, the men taking turns at the reins while the rest of the party huddled together for warmth in the wagonbed. The countryside was layered with snow that day, the sky bright with sunshine and so deeply blue it made them dizzy to stare up into it. The city's frozen streets rang under the horses' shoes. The air was hazed with coalsmoke. The town was thick with Yankee soldiers, but in this season of respite from the guerrillas the feeling of the place was much relaxed, and the only attention their party drew were looks of admiration for the girls.

The girls delighted in the chance to show off their pretty dresses once they were out of the cold and shed of their coats, and the men cut dashing figures in their fine suits. They attended a performance of John Howard Payne's "Home Sweet Home," then went to a minstrel show, then a puppet show, and finally to a sideshow where they marveled at a swordswallower and a boy with skin like a lizard's and a woman with a long black chinbeard that they were permitted to tug on to see that it was real.

They had dinner in a fancy restaurant and dared each other to be the first to eat an oyster off the half-shell. Bill did it and said he loved it and vowed he would henceforth have oysters with every meal he took in Kansas City. Jenny picked up a shelled oyster and examined it closely, then made a face of repugnance and said "Eee-*yew*!" and put it back on the tray of crushed ice. Except for Josephine, the others also refused to put such a thing in their mouths. Annette said she couldn't stand to even look one in the eye, wherever its eye might be. But Josephine followed Bill's example and slurped one off the shell. She rolled it around in her mouth and nodded and murmured "Umm, *gooood*." But even Bill had to laugh at the obvious strain of her smile—and she suddenly spat the mouthful into her napkin and said, "Lord Jesus, Billy, how can you *swallow* that!"

They browsed the stores of the city. The women bought dresses and hats and rings and hairbrushes. The men bought smoking pipes and honing stones and fobs for their watches. In one place, Bill spied a black silk ribbon a yard long and not a half-inch wide, and that evening at supper he gave it to Josephine as a present. She kissed him on the cheek, then folded the ribbon and did something with it in her hair, then dropped her hands and showed him, and the vision of her with the ribbon looped in the spilling gleam of her hair was the most beautiful he'd ever beheld.

"I love it," she said. "I'll treasure it till the day I die."

But even in these isolate months when the world seemed to spin more slowly and to curl into itself against the encompassing cold, the borderland war went on. The Westport Sewing Circle had suspended its meetings until spring, so the Vaughn place was without the women's weekly provision of news and hearsay and rumor, but each time Finley went into Westport for supplies he also brought back newspapers and reports from neighbors and stories he'd heard in liveries and barbershops and saloons. In the bushwhackers' absence from the region, Kansas redlegs and the Missouri militia were settling old scores with secessionist enemies of long standing and wreaking hard times on those they suspected of being guerrilla allies.

The only Missouri newspapers still in business were pro-Union, and they avidly endorsed the aggressive policy of seeking out and punishing bushwhacker supporters. The meanest details of that policy were in the stories Finley brought back from town. Redlegs had this winter burned a dozen farms along the border from Jackson County to the Osage River. In several instances they played a favorite game of putting a rope around their victim's neck and hoisting him off the ground again and again while his wife and children looked on and pled for his life. They'd finally hang the man for once and all, then fire the house and outbuildings before riding away and leaving the family without shelter in the freezing cold.

The militia was not without its own breed of malice. They burned farms and killed stock and now and then cut off a thumb as a reminder not to give helping hand to the wildwood boys again. When they severed a thumb from Milt Charles down in Bates County, he cursed them for sorry sons of bitches even as his wife worked to stem the bleeding and begged him to shut up. He said he couldn't wait to tell Quantrill who'd done this to him. "Well, let's see you tell him who did *this*," the militia officer said, and shot him where he stood.

They hanged Raleigh Watts in the woods about a half-mile from his farm in Jackson County, hanged him from a high oak branch and put a sign around his neck warning that they would kill anyone who took down the body. Nobody dared do it. Winter preserved him against decomposition but not against the crows, and every day his widow wept to see them feeding on his face. Not until spring would the blackened thing that had been her husband at last come down at the break of the weathered rope, and she would gather into a burlap sack the jumble of rotted clothes and flesh and disjointed bones and carry it home for burial.

There was no end of the terrible stories. Linus Weatherford was roped and dragged to death behind a redleg's galloping horse. Boland Jones was tied to the tail of a mule and kicked to death when the animal tried to free itself of him. Jordan McCollum was shoved into his well and large rocks were dropped on him until he was crushed or drowned and nobody knew which. . . . There was no end of the terrible stories.

In the final weeks of that winter, after the snow had gone for good, Cole Younger came to visit. He'd been hiding out in a small cabin in Cass County, near Harrisonville—where his rich father had once been mayor before he was murdered by Yankees, and near where, this selfsame winter, the militia had driven his mother and sisters out of their house and forced her to set it on fire herself. The soldiers watched the house burn until the roof fell through and then rode off.

The women then walked eight miles through darkness and blowing snow to reach Harrisonville and refuge with relatives.

Cole looked to have grown even beefier in his winter idleness. He'd had various visitors these past months, including some of the men who'd gone to Arkansas with Quantrill and then chosen to return early, and so he had plenty of news to share as he sipped at a steaming mug of cider sweetened with whiskey. He said the guerrillas served as Jo Shelby's scouts in Arkansas and acquitted themselves well in hard winter fighting. But Quantrill had not been with them. No sooner had they arrived in Arkansas than he'd left for Richmond, taking Andy Blunt with him and leaving George Todd in command of the company. The way Cole heard it, Quantrill had asked the Confederate secretary of war for a commissioned rank of colonel, but the secretary said no, not unless he put himself and his men under the authority of the regular army.

"He musta been keen disappointed not to get that commission," Cole said, "but he sure as hell wasn't going to join the company to the regulars. Hell, he doesn't want to be under army regulations any more than the rest of us, and he don't give a damn about them cotton-king sons of bitches either. It's why we became bushwhackers in the first place—to fight for Missouri without answering to a bunch of Virginians with brass buttons."

Quantrill hung on in Richmond for weeks before he finally returned to Arkansas and found W. J. Gregg in charge of the company. Todd had quickly got his fill of army rules and gone back to Missouri with a dozen men. They'd been sheltering in an abandoned half-burned mansion a few miles from Cole's cabin.

Jim Anderson asked if he'd had any word of the Berry boys.

"Oh my, yes," Cole said. "Everybody says those two been a pair of devils in the fighting. But hey, listen to this story Gregg told me about . . ." He paused and glanced at the girls, then gave Bill an arched look. Bill told the girls to leave the room. They whined and grumbled but got up and went out and closed the door behind them.

"This was in Springfield," Cole said, "where things got so hot they was fighting house to house. What happened was, the off-eyed boy, Butch, he goes busting into a house with Gregg right behind him and there in the parlor stands this woman wearing nothing but a smile and a little shimmy. Trouble was, she was *real* skinny, no more than skin and bone under a big hank of hair is the way Gregg describes her. No tits to tell of, ass like a board. Well sir, she looks at them boys and says, 'Ravish me if you will, I won't resist nor raise a cry.' Gregg *swears* that's exactly what she said. He'd never seen a woman wanted it so bad, but not only was she terrible skinny, she had this *smell*, like it'd been a goodly while between baths. W. J. said that all in all he just couldn't raise the enthusiasm for it. He was trying to think of how to turn her down polite-like, when that Butch boy says: 'Truth to tell, mam, I wouldn't go poking in there with a borrowed dick.' "

There was laughter all around. Then they heard the smothered giggling at the door and Bill rushed to it and jerked it open and the girls shrieked and fled like spooked birds, still cackling over Cole's story.

But Cole had some sad news too. After Todd drove him out of the company, Will Haller had joined with a band of guerrillas up in Gentry County, then shortly afterward was wounded and captured by Federals. They stood him against a barn wall and shot him dead, then hanged his noseless and earless remains from a tree alongside a main-traveled road as a warning to all other bushwhackers in northwest Missouri.

"It's a mean war, boys," Cole Younger said, "and it'll get meaner yet, you mark me."

YEAGER'S RAID

The days warmed. The early morning hills were hung with blue mist. The rains came briefly every afternoon and the air smelled of the newly ripening earth. The first grasses broke ground. Buds sprouted, fattened, opened to leafery. Bloodroot unfurled its white flower in the meadows and oozed its deadly sap. . . .

They were now going to the woods every day to shoot their pistols. They worked their horses hard, the animals as high-strung as their riders with winter's pent energy. They sometimes recounted to each other the raid on Olathe, remembering the exhilarations of that night, and they saw in each other's faces an eagerness for more.

Finley brought rumors from town that Quantrill and the company were on their way back from Arkansas, traveling in small bands, that some had already arrived and were encamped in various regions of Jackson and Lafayette Counties. But still no word from Quantrill himself.

They watched the greening world around them and waited. As she hugged to Bill in the night, Josephine could feel his readiness to go.

One morning at breakfast they heard Josh shout, "Riders coming!" They rushed to the window to see a band of horsemen loping out of the woods, nine of them, every man wearing a slouch hat and bush shirt and hung with various revolvers and knives.

They ran out to greet them like children set free of the schoolhouse. At the head of the column, Dick Yeager grinned broadly through his muleskinner mustache. "We're bound for Kansas," he said. "You boys care to come?"

"Quantrill's making a *Kansas* raid?" Bill said.

"This got nothing to do with him," Yeager said, "and I ain't got time to jabber. You coming or not?"

They rode through the forest in a column of twos, a boy named Buster Parr far ahead on point. Word had come to Yeager that the jayhawkers who'd stolen his family's wagons and teams had sold them all to a stationmaster in Diamond Springs, a man named Howell, who'd known Dick's father and surely recognized the property as belonging to him.

"He ought have refused to buy Daddy's goods from thieves who killed my brother and nearly did for Daddy too," Yeager said. "I guess he couldn't pass up a jayhawker bargain price. Now he'll know the real price of it."

When Yeager told them he was going to Diamond Springs, the Andersons looked at each other and knew they were thinking the same thing. "There's a ranch a small ways from there," Bill told Yeager. "Belongs to a man named Segur. We'd surely like to pay him a quick visit. Be worth *your* while too—he's got some fine horses."

"Well then, we'll just swing by there," Yeager said. "You can give the man your regards and maybe he'll see fit to let us have a horse or two as a gesture of good fellowship." They all grinned.

They made camp that night near the border and within sight of the Santa Fe. Before dawn Yeager began sending the men into Kansas in twos and threes, spacing them at least a half-hour apart so they would not attract undue attention. They were to rendezvous on Neosho Creek, in the woods at the outskirt of Council Grove.

Three afternoons later the band had come together again. Their scout reported no sign of Federals in the vicinity, and the locals seemed completely unaware of the guerrillas' proximity. But Yeager had a torturous toothache. The molar had been bothering him off and on for months, and then two days ago it had flared up again and thereafter steadily worsened. By the time he arrived at the meeting place, his jaw was so swollen it looked like he had a chaw in his cheek, and his eyes were cherried with pain. There was nothing for it but to see a dentist, and he knew one in Council Grove.

The sun was halfway down a western sky reefed with red clouds when the bushwhackers reined up at the edge of town. "If we ain't back out in a half-hour," Yeager said to Lionel Ward, "ride in there and kill every manjack you see and burn the place to the last stick."

Bill Anderson rode in with him. The band had been spotted by now and word of their presence had spread. Half the town was on the sidewalks and watching the pair of them in an eerie silence broken only by their horses' steady hooffalls. Yeager reined up in front of a door bearing the words, J. H. BRADFORD, D.D., and a painting of a large white molar directly below them.

The doctor had seen them through the window and now came to the door and said, "Dick Yeager! I *thought* it was you!" He had serviced Yeager teeth before, in the days of the family's wagon train business when Dick and his brother and daddy had often came through Council Grove.

"Got a tooth needs rooting out, Doc," Yeager said. He walked in and sat in the patient's chair. Bill took a seat by the window so he could keep an eye on things outside.

Dr. Bradford remained standing at the open door. He looked from Yeager to the townsmen gathered across the street and watching his office, then back at Yeager. "If I do it, Dick, will you spare the town?"

Yeager arched an eyebrow.

"Oh, I'll pull it anyway," the dentist said. "I'm not brave enough to say no. But I'd take it as a professional courtesy if you'd spare the town in exchange for my service."

Yeager turned to Bill Anderson. "You ever been asked for a professional courtesy?"

Bill smiled and shook his head.

The grin Yeager showed the dentist was lopsided for the swollen state of his jaw. "Let's get to it," he said.

Fifteen minutes later, they were mounted up again and headed back down the street, Yeager's jaw now minus a tooth and still swollen, but his pain sweetly blunted by the cherry-flavored opiate solution Dr. Bradford had provided in a small bottle. As they trotted past the gawking townsfolk, Yeager said loudly, "You sons of bitches ought to make that man your mayor for saving your sorry asses."

The band rode away to eastward until they were beyond sight of town, then turned downcountry into the high grass and rode for more than a mile before again navigating west and passing well below Council Grove.

Splashings and suckings of hooves in a night black as a grave, chill with drizzling rain, smelling of mud. The guerrillas reined up and studied the lightless form of the Diamond Springs station. Their sloping hatbrims ran with rainwater. Whickerings came from the corral behind the station and there was an agitation of stamping and darting as the horses there caught the scent of the guerrillas' mounts. Some of the bushwhackers rode around to the rear of the stationhouse as Dick Yeager and the Anderson brothers dismounted and went to the front door and Yeager began a steady hammering on it with the heel of his fist.

Finally the front window went bright with lamplight and a man's face, hair disheveled, showed itself behind the glass, eyes asquint, trying to make out the visitors. "Who's there?" he called.

"Federal cavalry bound for Leavenworth," Bill Anderson said loudly. "Sorry to raise you from your bed, mister, but one of our mounts has taken lame and we need to buy a horse from you right now. Open up."

The face left the window and they heard the scraping of the doorbolt being removed from its holders. The door opened and the man Yeager had come seeking stood there with his nightshirt half tucked into his pants and his suspenders dangling off his hips. He raised the lantern and saw Dick Yeager's wolfish grin. "Howdy there, Howells," Yeager said.

Howells backed up into the store and Yeager stepped in after him and the Andersons came behind, all of them with Colts in their hands. Howells' wife had been standing at an inner doorway, and when she saw the guns she rushed to get between her husband and Yeager, hugging hard to the stationmaster and saying, "No, no, no!"

Yeager tried to pull her away with his free hand so he might have a clear shot at Howells, who held tight to her and cried, "Don't hurt her, Dick, don't hurt her!"

They turned round and round like an intimate threesome at a lewd and clumsy dance as Yeager tried to detach the woman, but the couple clung to each like they were in a fearsome windstorm, the woman whimpering, keeping herself between the men.

"Dammit!" Yeager shouted. He stepped back and aimed carefully and the woman screamed and put both hands over her husband's head and tried to swell herself to cover as much of him as possible. The gunblast shook the room and the round hit Howells in the side and he cried out and sagged in his wife's embrace, the woman shrieking with fear and rage. The next bullet passed through both her hand and her husband's head and sprayed bloody hair and bone bits over a shelf of canned goods. The sudden dead weight was too much for her to hold one-handed and the body slipped through her arms, smearing her with blood. She knelt with it, hugging her husband's head to her breast, wailing like a lost child.

"Sorry about the hand, mam," Yeager said. "It was an accident. I appreciate you were doing your best to protect him."

If the woman heard she gave no indication. Yeager looked at Bill and Jim and said, "Fire it."

As the Andersons flung lamp oil over the floor and walls, Yeager recharged his revolver, then said to the woman, "I suggest you leave him lay and get on outside." Then he went out.

Bill Anderson put his hand on her shoulder and said, "Come along, mam."

She remained as she was, crying, holding to her husband. Jim Anderson struck a match and dropped it and flames jumped up the walls. He hurried to the door and called back, "Hey, Billy!"

Bill grabbed the woman under the arms and tried to drag her away, but she struggled fiercely to get loose and back to her husband. Jim ran over and grabbed Bill's arm and yelled, "*Come on,* dammit!"

"She's not staying in here!" Bill said. The woman was screeching and twisting hard in his embrace, kicking and flailing wildly, trying to gouge his eyes over her shoulder. His face was spattered with blood off her mutilated hand. "Damn you, woman, let's *go!*"

Jim cursed and crouched to pin the woman's legs and they lifted her bodily and carried her out as the fire coursed across the room.

When the bushwhackers rode away, she was standing in the firelight and staring at her ended world, her ruined hand dripping blood into the Kansas soil.

Several Federal outposts received vague reports of the raiders' visit to Council Grove, but the only one that mentioned the direction they'd taken said they'd gone east, presumably back to Missouri, and so the cavalry patrols concentrated themselves all along the Santa Fe between Council Grove and the border. After several hours of roaming that stretch without a sign of the miscreants, the patrols returned to their posts, certain that Missouri guerrillas could never have gotten this deep into Kansas anyway and that the raiders in Council Grove had likely been a gang of local outlaws.

The rain ceased. The clouds broke apart and fell away. The sky was brilliant with stars. A narrow cut of yellow moon showed low in the western sky. They rode westward on the Santa Fe so that the Howells woman would give that direction to any who came seeking after them—then they swung south at the Cottonwood Creek and a mile farther on made their camp for the night. At dawn, they set off to eastward, the Andersons directing the way to John Segur's ranch.

They rode onto Segur rangeland just after midday under a bright and sparsely clouded sky. A pair of herd guards were sitting their horses beside each other and talking about the girls they hoped to see at the next Saturday night dance in Americus. They never caught sight of the band of riders reining up on a low rise a hundred yards away, nor heard the cracking of the half-dozen Sharps that took them off their mounts in the same instant, one man's slung brains preceding him to the ground, the other's heart seized around the two bullets so abruptly entered in it. Yeager left two men with the herd to cut out the best horses, and then the band rode over the next rise and toward the ranch buildings.

A man at the bunkhouse door saw them coming and turned to say something to someone inside. A dozen or so men came outside to look, some shirtless, a few with pistols tucked in their pants. The guerrillas heeled their mounts into a gallop and unloosed their unearthly rebel yells. The ranchmen stood fast, mouths ajar, gaping at the dreadful vision of their deaths thundering toward them. Before any of them thought to draw his gun, the guerrillas were shooting them down—the ranchmen crying out, spinning, staggering, leaving their feet as the bullets found them, dying instantly and not so quickly, clutching at their heads, their bellies. Not a man of them was standing and few were still alive as the bushwhackers rode over them.

The guerrillas reined around and came back at a trot and here and there one or another leaned down to shoot in the head any ranchman who looked to be still breathing. Bill recognized one of the open-eyed dead as the man who'd thrown a rock at their wagon on the day they were exiled from their home with their father's body.

They loped up to the main house where an old man with a shot-gun stood on the porch, shielding a woman in the door who clutched an infant to her bosom. A quartet of large dogs came snarling toward the riders, their napes roached, and Yeager drew his pistol, but Bill Anderson said, "Don't." He gave a sharp whistle that stopped the dogs short. "Get gone," he said, and they whirled and fled around the side of the house. Yeager grinned at him like he'd pulled a card trick.

They reined up in a line before the porch. The woman was young and pretty, auburnhaired, and though she was clearly frightened, Bill thought her aspect also bespoke familiarity with the world's mean-ness. The old man took a step forward and raised the shotgun to his chest and moved the muzzle from side to side like he was deciding which of them to shoot first. He looked Mexican and seemed unafraid, and Bill would have bet that the old man had known some of life's meaner side himself.

"Tell him put the gun down," Yeager said to the woman. She spoke in soft Spanish and the old man took a step back and lowered the shotgun to his hip but kept it pointed their way.

She identified herself as the widow Mrs. Clara Segur Baker, daughter to John Segur, who owned this property. The Anderson brothers exchanged a look, only now realizing she was the woman Arthur Baker had chosen to wed instead of their sister. She scanned the distant litter of her father's hired men where they lay slain in the sun, but whatever thoughts she had about the slaughter, she did not voice them.

Yeager told her they were seeking after her father. If he was hiding in the house, it would be best if he came out now. Clara Baker said her father was in Emporia on business. "Why do you wish to harm him?" she said.

Yeager sighed and looked at Bill. "We ain't got time for jabber. If the sonofabitch is in there, I know how to make him come out quick. Buster, Lyle, Deacon—get in there and fire the place."

The three guerrillas dismounted and started up the steps. Bill said, "Oh hell, Dick, the woman's already a widow and her child an orphan. Let's not burn her house too."

"Damn, Anderson, it ain't like we got all day to look for him."

At the name of Anderson, Clara Baker fixed a sharp look on Bill. But now the three bushwhackers were on the porch and the old Mexican raised the shotgun to warn them back and the one called Deacon slapped the barrel aside and said, "Get that thing out of my face, Pancho." The Mexican swung the muzzle back again and yanked the trigger and the charge carried Deacon off the porch and into the horse behind him and the animal was stung by some of the buckshot too and reared with a shriek and the spooked horses to either side nearly unseated their riders.

The woman whirled into the house and Buster Parr grabbed the shotgun and tried to wrest it away but the old man's hold was iron. Buster rammed him against a porch post and the Mexican lost his grip and fell to his knees and Buster leaped out of the way as a half-dozen men opened fire. They shot the old man more than thirty times in the next five seconds and reduced him to bloody wreckage.

In the lingering blackpowder haze, Yeager calmed his horse and leaned from the saddle to peer down at Deacon's rude remains. "Well shit," he muttered. Then glared up at Buster and said, "Get that bitch out here if you got to drag her by the hair and set that fucken house afire *now*!"

He ordered Deacon's body to be laid out in the house. They had no time to give it proper burial and cremation would have to suffice.

The searchers followed the sound of the baby's crying down the hallway to a bedroom and found Clara Baker hunkered in a wardrobe closet. She was escorted to a safe distance from the house and there sat on the ground with the child in her arms. The house now crackling with flames. Some of the bushwhackers were turning the cows out of the barn and setting it on fire too. Over by the bunkhouse the crows were already at their feed. Clara rocked the baby and regarded her home's destruction and wept without sound in the shadow of the rising smoke.

They sat their horses and waited to see if John Segur would come out of the burning building. When the roof timbers began collapsing in great sparking crashes, Yeager turned to Bill and said, "Guess the bastard's in Emporia like she said. Let's ride."

They rode back toward the border at a steady canter, taking with them twenty head of Segur's best stock and switching to fresh mounts whenever the horses under them foundered. They rode through the night, resting briefly at various creeks. In the morning they came to the Rock Springs depot where they stopped to water and found a single passenger waiting for the stage—a Federal sergeant. The soldier knew instantly who they were and jumped to his feet with his hands up. Yeager laughed and shot him. The stationmaster nearly smothered his wife under his hand in muting her terrified cries lest she annoy the bushwhackers sufficiently to murder them as well.

They rode on, driving the horses before them, using outriders to keep a sharp eye for anyone closing on them from any direction. But their luck held well. They'd seen no sign of military or civilian posse as they came to the station at Black Jack, where the stage had arrived only minutes ahead of them and carrying several prosperous passengers. From one man they took $1,500 and a diamond stickpin. This man's wife was the only woman among the passengers and she was apologetically robbed of her gold necklace, diamond wedding ring, and small music box.

Jimmy Vaughn was the one to relieve her of the music box, and when he opened the lid and heard the opening notes of "Für Elise," he knew it was a gift for Mary Anderson. But a halfwit bushwhacker named Roach wanted the music box too, and tried to grab it from him. There was a cursing scuffle and the lid was accidentally wrenched off and the music mechanism ruined. Jimmy Vaughn put his hand to his pistol but Yeager stepped between them and said he wouldn't stand for men of his band killing each other over gimcrack loot. Jimmy picked up the broken music box and turned it over and saw that the bottom was stamped: "Throckmorton Novelties, City of Kansas."

It was nearly midnight when they fell on Gardner, less than twenty miles now from Missouri. They robbed the express office and rousted the guests in the hotel and herded them into the lobby and took all money and jewelry they found on their persons or in their rooms. One of the women was exceptionally pretty, and Bill Anderson offered to return all of her husband's property—nearly $400, a fine watch, and a heavy gold ring—in exchange for one kiss from her. Dick Yeager laughed and told Bill he was crazy, no kiss was worth that much. The woman recoiled and said she would never permit a lawless brute to touch her. Bill thought she was even prettier in her indignation. "What about it?" he asked the man.

The woman was appalled when her husband agreed to the bargain. The ring had belonged to his granddaddy, the man plaintively explained to her. Couldn't she please be reasonable? It was only a kiss the man wanted.

"Then *you* kiss him!" she said—and slapped him so hard she left the pink imprint of her fingers on his cheek. The wildwood boys whooped and one of them yelled, "Damn right, girl!" She put her face in her hands and cried.

Bill Anderson looked at the man and said, "You're a fool, mister." He turned to go but the woman said, "Wait!" She wiped angrily at her tears and stepped up to him and said he could have the kiss on one condition—that he wouldn't give anything of her husband's back to him.

"An easy bargain," Bill said with a smile. The husband started to protest, but Buster Parr put a pistol to the back of his neck and he fell mute.

The wife was anyway paying no attention to him. She took Bill's face between her hands and he bent to meet her upturned face. He would never know she had not put her tongue in a man's mouth before, not even her husband's, but it was evident to every man watching that her tongue was in Bill's mouth now, and his in hers, and both tongues sporting lively, and the bushwhackers whistled and clapped. The kiss lingered for a long half-minute, and when they broke from it they were both flushed and breathless.

"Mam," Bill said, "that's a prize worth every gold ring in Kansas," and she reddened even more. He held out the gold wedding band he'd taken from her but she shook her head and said, "Keep it." She glared at her husband, then retired to a chair in the corner and sat and stared at her folded hands on her lap. The husband looked ill. As the bushwhackers went out to their horses, Bill said to him, "You for damn sure ain't worth her."

Not an hour later they were back in Missouri and heading for their camp in the Sni-a-bar country. All of them except Jimmy Vaughn, who'd gone to Kansas City in search of Throckmorton Novelties.

Rendezvous and rumors

Already at the Sni-a-bar camp were nearly sixty other guerrillas, including Cole Younger and Socrates Johnson. Some of them had just returned from Arkansas, some of them were new recruits. Even though it was late when the Yeager bunch arrived, Cole and Sock and a few others roused from their blankets to admire by torchlight the horses they'd brought with them. Then they gathered round the cookfire to drink whiskeyed coffee and hear Yeager's account of the raid into Kansas. Cole was much impressed and said, "You boys done a damn wonder."

Sock Johnson introduced various of the new men among them. One was a gangly fellow with a prominent nose and a jaded manner. He'd been a Confederate regular and had fought under Old Pap Price at the battle of Wilson's Creek and was captured by the Yanks in Springfield six months later. He'd been paroled home to Clay County but couldn't endure the restrictions of a parolee's life and found himself in constant trouble with the Federals. When he could take no more, he'd gone in search of Coleman Younger, who was

said to be recruiting for Quantrill. Sock introduced him as Frank
James and said he was born to bushwhack.

With so many new recruits, the company had grown too big to
keep riding as one bunch. Quantrill had broken it up into smaller
bands and named Todd, Pool, Blunt, Yeager, Gregg, and Cole as
their captains, although he remained chieftain of them all. The bands
would operate independently except when some of them might come
together for a larger raid than one bunch could undertake by itself.

Yeager thought it was a smart move. More and smaller bands
meant they could move faster and more easily disappear in the wildwood. The Federals would have to disperse their own forces to try to
hunt them all, and the smaller Yank parties would be easier to
ambush. He drank to Quantrill's cleverness.

They'd been trading gossip and news around the fire for a while
when someone mentioned that Todd's bunch was camped with
Quantrill's near Blue Springs. The remark raised snickers, and somebody said, "Fletch Taylor's bunch, you mean"—and there was more
low and knowing laughter. The Yeager men wanted to know what
was so funny, and Sock Johnson said, "Tell them, Cole."

Well, Cole said, truth to tell, Fletch Taylor was usually in charge
of the Quantrill and Todd bunches because neither man was spending much time in the camp. As soon he got back to Missouri,
Quantrill had gone to live with his lady love, Kate, in a cabin in the
deeper woods near Blue Springs. By some accounts, they'd recently
married in opposition to Kate's father, who thought she was too
young yet, but no one knew if the rumor was true. What everybody
did know for a fact was that a cousin of Kate's named Frances Fry
was living at the cabin with them—everybody knew it because
Quantrill had invited Todd to come meet her. "And it would appear,"
Cole said, "that Todd and Miss Frances took a real shine to each
other, because now George is living out there too."

"The hell you say!" said a hulking boy named Hi Guess. His grin
was utter lewdness. *"Whooo!"*

"I was up to the Blue Springs camp just a few days ago," Sock
said, "and you ought to *hear* some of the suspicionings about what's
going on at that cabin."

"I don't need to hear any such," Buster Parr said, "I got enough
sinful notions about it smoking up my head as it is."

"Well, whatever they're doing," Bill Anderson said with a smile, "I'll wager they're having uncommon great fun at it."

The comment drew sniggers from some, looks of righteous Christian disgust from others.

AN ARREST AND AN OFFER

Some days later, under a daybreak sky that looked carved of quartz, they were having breakfast when a messenger arrived with the news that Jimmy Vaughn had been arrested in Kansas City. He'd been wearing a Missouri militia jacket while he shopped in a novelty store, but he was recognized by a Federal informant who'd known the Vaughns before the war and knew that Jimmy was riding with Quantrill. From the store, Jimmy went to a barbershop. He was leaned back in the chair with his eyes closed to receive a shave and a haircut when four soldiers entered and pointed carbines at him and asked the name of his Missouri outfit. A minute later, his face still lathered, he was in manacles and being led on a chain to a prison wagon for transport to Fort Leavenworth.

"He's been identified by some people from Shawneetown as one of the raiders who burned the place," the messenger said. "The Feds mean to hang him for it. They aim to prove to everybody just how serious they are about dealing with bushwhackers from now on."

A courier had taken the news of Vaughn's arrest to Quantrill and Todd at the cabin. They hastened back to the Blue Springs camp and rounded up some men and the next day ambushed a Federal patrol, killing four Yanks and capturing five. One of the prisoners died shortly after, but Quantrill had offered the Federals at Leavenworth his other four prisoners in exchange for Jimmy Vaughn and was waiting on the Yankees' answer.

BLUNT CHOICE

I HAVE INSTRUCTED THE OFFICERS IN COMMAND OF TROOPS IN THE BORDER COUNTRY OF MISSOURI THAT EVERY REBEL, OR REBEL SYMPATHIZER, WHO GIVES AID, DIRECTLY OR INDI-RECTLY, SHALL BE DESTROYED OR EXPELLED FROM THE MIL-

ITARY DISTRICT. THESE INSTRUCTIONS WILL NOT EXEMPT
FEMALES FROM THE RULE. EXPERIENCE HAS TAUGHT THAT
THE BITE OF A SHE ADDER IS AS POISONOUS AND PRODUC-
TIVE OF MISCHIEF AS THE BITE OF ANY OTHER VENOMOUS
REPTILE. THEREFORE, ALL PERSONS KNOWN TO BE IN ARMS
AGAINST THE FEDERAL AUTHORITIES OF THIS DISTRICT,
WILL BE SUMMARILY PUT TO DEATH WHEN CAPTURED. THE
ONLY CONSTITUTIONAL RIGHT THAT WILL BE GRANTED THEM,
WILL BE THE RIGHT TO MAKE CHOICE OF THE QUALITY OF
ROPE WITH WHICH THEY WILL BE HUNG.

MAJ. GEN. JAMES G. BLUNT,
COMMANDING DISTRICT OF THE FRONTIER

Cole Younger read the proclamation aloud from the newspaper, then looked around at the others and said, "I'd have to say the man is a 360-degree son of a bitch."

"Yep," Frank James said. "Any way you look at him."

DEPARTING THE VAUGHNS

Every day brought darker rumors to the guerrilla camps. The Federals claimed to know that in addition to giving them food and shelter and medical care, the bushwhackers' women were serving as spies and smugglers of ammunition. The Union meant to put a stop to it. They were said to be shaping a plan for arresting every woman in Jackson County related to any known bushwhacker by blood or marriage. The Yankees hoped to achieve two ends at once—to deprive the guerrillas of the women's help, and to hold hostages against further bushwhacker depredations in Jackson County. They had dozens of spies making up a list of the guerrillas' female kin, and rumor had it that they were about to start making arrests.

Some of the wildwood boys thought the rumor itself was a Yankee trick. "They want us to believe it so we'll take the girls off somewhere and hide them," Fletch Taylor said during a visit to the Sni-a-bar camp. "We'd be doing the damn Yanks a favor, wouldn't we—cutting off our main help, our best supply of ball and powder and information? Hell, they're just bluffing."

"What if they're not?" a young recruit named Nestor Gates said. His only living kin in the world was a younger sister residing with an aunt and uncle in Sibley.

"What *if?*" Fletch Taylor echoed. "Well, what if a frog had wings? Then he wouldn't bump his ass so much, would he?"

This argument failed to impress Nestor Gates, and a short time later he was riding hard for Sibley with the intention of putting his sister on a riverboat to Saint Louis. His comrades would not see him again. Just outside of Independence he would encounter a company of state militia cavalry and be challenged for proof of his loyalty to the Union. He would kill one soldier and wound another before falling under a dozen musket balls. They would cut off his ears and hang him by the neck from an elm, and a note on his chest would read: "Crow Cafe."

Bill Anderson was also unconvinced that the Feds were bluffing. "Think about it," he said to his brother. "As much help as the women been to Quantrill, wouldn't *you* put an end to it if you were the Feds?" They told Yeager what they had in mind to do and then departed the camp that afternoon.

They made their careful way through the woodland traces to Westport and it was near midnight when they sneaked up the back trail to the Vaughn place. They weren't even out of the woods yet before the dogs appeared from the darkness, jumping and whining low all around Edgar Allan, and Bill whispered, "Happy to see you boys too." They emerged from the trees and saw Finley and Black Josh standing in shirttails in the shadows outside the stable with rifles in their hands. "Reckoned it was you," Finley said to Bill, "when them hounds wouldn't bark."

Their sisters were elated to see them, had been worried witless since they'd left with Yeager for Kansas. They couldn't let off from hugging them and kissing them, and they made them sit in the kitchen and tell them everything while they went about preparing a big supper.

The Vaughn girls kept asking Bill and Jim what they thought the Yanks were going to do to their brother. Would they really hang him, like everyone was saying? Was there any chance they might just put him in prison till after the war? Couldn't Quantrill *do* something?

"Quantrill's trying to make a trade for him," Bill Anderson said. He hoped they did not remember Perry Hoy. Mary Anderson said little, but her eyes were shouting her fear for Jimmy Vaughn.

The supper laid before them was the most sumptuous they had eaten in weeks—pork stew, corn on the cob, greens in ham fat, black-eyed peas, cornbread. As they wolfed it down, they told the girls they wanted to move them all out to the Parchman farm where they would be safer than in Westport. "Finley and Josh can stay and take care of this place," Bill told the Vaughns, "but you two best come with us."

The girls had heard the rumor of a Yankee plan to arrest the guerrillas' women, but they said they wouldn't leave their home, and anyway they didn't think they had reason to worry. "They've got Jimmy under arrest, for heaven's sake," Annette said. "They have no reason to come for us. They don't need us as hostages against him."

"You all been smuggling powder and ball out of K.C. for more than a year," Bill said. "You got an ammunition factory in the cellar. I'd say that's plenty of good reason for them to come visit."

"They don't know anything about that," Hazel said. "If they knew about it, they would've come for us before now."

"They got more spies now," Jim Anderson said. "They threaten people with jail, with burning their house if they don't tell who's helping us." He took Hazel's hand. "You're coming with us and that's an end on it."

Hazel snatched her hand away. "Says *who*? Listen, Jim Anderson, just because I allow you certain pleasant liberties with my person does not give you authority over me."

Jim's face went pink and grins showed around the table. "I want you safe is all," he said softly.

Hazel's look gentled and she stroked his arm. "I know you do. Just make sure your sisters are safe and don't fret about us. The Yankees have always let us alone and still will, you'll see."

"We won't go to K.C. for a while," Annette said. "If the Feds are keeping an eye on the place, they'll see we're just a couple of helpless girls with only a cripple and an old darky for protection. As soon as they let off hawkeyeing us, we'll be right back at making cartridges for Captain Quantrill, and you be sure and tell him that."

* * *

Next morning, Bill rose well before dawn and studied the dark sky from the window. It had drizzled through the night and the smell of wet earth was heavy on the air, but the clouds had since cleared and he could tell it would be a pretty day. Josephine was still packing her grip when he stepped into the dim hallway and saw Jim Anderson coming out of Hazel's room, stuffing his shirt into his pants, his gunbelts draped over his shoulders. Hazel came to the door in a short cotton shimmy that exposed her long wonderful legs and showed the rest of her in stark silhouette against the lamplight. Jim drew her close and they kissed deeply, then he patted her bottom and she went back in the room to get dressed. He turned and saw Bill staring, and they exchanged gentlemanly nods. And then wide grins.

They took no breakfast but coffee, wanting to be on their way before sunup. Finley had saddled the girls' horses and Black Josh tied their grips to the cantles. There were hugs and kisses all around and Jim gave Hazel's rump a parting fondle. Then they were mounted and hupping their horses into the woods and gone, Bill in the lead, Josephine right behind him.

Forty minutes later the eastern sky was showing long low streaks the color of raw meat when a Federal cavalry patrol came through the front gate in a clatter of hooves and armament and headed up the wagon track toward the house. Annette peered through the front window curtains and said, "Oh Lord, honey, they're here."

Hazel put down her teacup and went to the window to look. "I guess somebody in the sewing club wasn't all that stalwart," she said. "Jim would say he told us so." She looked around the room as if rushing to memorize it.

The dogs raced out from under the porch, snarling, napes roached, and met with a crackling salvo of pistolfire that knocked them asprawl, writhing and yelping. The patrol lieutenant leaned from the saddle as he rode up on the Boo dog struggling to rise on a shattered leg and with a swipe of his saber took the muzzle off him. Then the dogs were under the trampling hooves and done with.

Finley ran out of the stable with a rifle in hand and was shot twice and sent sprawling. A sergeant veered off the column and rode

up to him and saw that his eyes yet fluttered and gave him a coup
bullet in the head.

Black Josh came out of the stable with his hands up high, wag-
gling his arms like a man at a revival, saying, "I'se sure glad to see
you, Cap'n, I'se shorely is." But the Federals had been informed
about him too, and the sergeant shot him in his false grin.

They stomped into the house and found the girls sitting in the
parlor with their hands in their laps. Annette stared pointedly at the
lieutenant's muddy boots tracking the carpet and sighed.

"You're both under arrest for conspiring against the government
of the United States," the lieutenant said.

He knew just where to go, demanding of Annette that she lead
the way to the cellar. One of the soldiers held a lantern. Finding the
storeroom door padlocked, the lieutenant held out his hand and
said, "Key!"

"Why, I ate that for breakfast this morning," Annette said with a
smile.

The officer backhanded her across the face and she swayed but
kept her feet.

"You goddamned *bully*!" Hazel shouted and hit the lieutenant
on the back with the heel of her fist. He whirled and slapped her
harder than he'd hit her sister, buckling her knees—and then she
lunged and tried to claw his eyes and he cursed and punched her in
the breast. She slumped back against the wall, holding herself as if
she'd been shot, mouth open but mute with pain, tears streaming.

The officer drew his pistol and put the muzzle to the lock and
fired. The room flashed with the discharge and the lock blew apart
and the bullet ricocheted and Annette felt it pass through her hair
and it hit a soldier on the stairway. The man yelped and dropped his
rifle and sat down hard, clutching his shin. The soldier with the
lantern went to illuminate his wound.

"God *damn* it!" the lieutenant said, glaring at the fallen soldier.
Then pulled the broken lock off the ring and opened the door and
stood peering into the darkness. He grabbed Hazel by the arm and
pushed her inside and demanded, "Lamp!"

She had a box of lucifers in her apron and her hand went to it.
She saw Annette standing behind the officer but couldn't see her

expression clearly. Annie put her fingers to her mouth, whether to stem the bleeding of her cut lip or in realization of her intention, Hazel would never know.

If she had given it a moment's thought she might have seen the act as one of utter folly, perhaps even madness, and refrained. But her only thought—if thought it might be called—was to even things with this bastard who'd hurt her and her sister.

She struck the lucifer to reveal in the sudden sulfurous flare the tables and bolted lanterns with the small wire cages over them, the boxes of lead balls, the cans of black powder stacked to the ceiling, the open cans on the table, the dark spills around them. . . .

She held the burning match over the table and laughed at the look on the lieutenant's face. And let the match fall.

A PARCHMAN VISIT

"They say it busted windows all the way up in Westport. There were portions of the house fifty yards in every direction. Part of the roof was blocking the road till a mule team pulled it out the way. One fella who lives close by said it sounded like several explosions all at once and shook his house so bad he thought it was Confederate shells. He heard a thump on his roof and went up there and found a man's bare leg with an army boot still on it. The crows showed them where to collect the pieces of bodies."

"Lord Jesus," Mary Anderson said softly. She pushed away her full supper plate and sighed and put her face in her hands.

They were at the table in the Parchman house, nearly a week after the explosion, which the Andersons had not known about until today. Socrates Johnson and Frank James and Riley Crawford had been out scouting for George Todd and stopped by to get a feed and tell them the news.

"Those poor girls," Sock said. "So young and pretty—and both of them damn able. There was nobody better at smuggling powder and ball out of K.C. Quantrill sent Lionel Ward to Fort Leavenworth dressed like a preacher to say he was Jimmy Vaughn's cousin with some bad family news. Lionel said Jimmy cried when he told him about his sisters."

"That must've been *some* bang," Riley Crawford said through a mouthful of greens, his face avid, as if the talk had been of a wagon-show entertainment they'd missed seeing. Josephine glowered at him, and Frank James frowned and nudged him with an elbow. Riley looked at them in puzzlement, his child's nature untuned to the force of the Anderson girls' grief.

"It's a mystery how that powder store got touched off," Sock Johnson said, "but I figure some fool Yank got careless." Jenny came around the table with a steaming pot and spooned more beans onto his plate. He smiled at her and patted her lean girl's haunch.

"I guess nobody'll ever know exactly how it was," Bill Anderson said. He cut his eyes to his brother and thought he could read in Jim's face his own selfsame suspicion: The Vaughn girls had done it and only they could have said why. The brothers would later talk about it and arrive at no conclusion except that, whyever the girls did it, they'd been brave to the bone and had killed more Yankees in that moment than many a bushwhacker ever would.

They ate and drank in silence for a time before the talk turned to the company. Sock said Quantrill and Todd had returned to their women at the cabin to wait on the Yanks' answer to a trade for Jimmy Vaughn. But just two days later Todd came back to camp in a blackass temper. A story went around that he and Frances Fry had got in a drunken fight and she'd tried to put a knife in him and he'd broken her arm in defending himself. Kate was so mad she ran him off the place. There was no telling how true the story was, or who'd even been the first to tell it, and nobody dared to ask Todd. Quantrill was anyhow still at the cabin with Kate—and with Frances Fry too, most likely—and Todd was in charge of both their bunches at Blue Springs.

"Speaking of Todd," Frank James said, "he's been wondering when you boys might be riding with us again."

"I'm not leaving my sisters alone," Bill said. "Not with the Feds rounding up every woman with bushwhacker kin."

"They might not know the first thing about your sisters," Sock said. He winked at Jenny, who winked back and smiled. "Hell, they might not know the first thing about you and Jim. They don't know *all* of us."

"Or they might know plenty," Bill said. "I ain't chancing it. I've got to find the girls somewhere safe to stay."

"There's no such a place in Missouri," Frank James said.

"I know," Bill said. "I'm thinking of going to Arkansas, to Texas maybe. I don't know yet." He restrained a sigh. In truth he was restless and not at all sure he wanted to leave Missouri. He often found himself wondering what the company was doing. He'd been delighted when these three showed up and hallooed the house. "What-all else you boys been up to?"

They'd been giving the Yanks fits all up and down the border, robbing mail shipments, bushwhacking whatever militia patrols they fell on, burning railroad bridges, harrying steamboats from the trees along the banks. They'd been taking horses too, like always.

"Problem is," Sock said, "there's more mustangs showing up lately, and them unbroke jugheads don't fetch near as good a price."

"Well hell," Jim said, "why don't you all break them before selling?"

"*Who* all?" Sock said. "There's not a man in the company can't ride like an Indian, but there ain't a true broncbuster in the bunch neither. Buster Parr said he could break any horse alive, said that's why he's called Buster. The first one he got on about threw him over the trees and near busted his head and everybody said *that's* why he's called Buster. He ain't got on another one, I'll tell you that."

"Bring the jugheads to us," Bill said. "We'll bust them. Hell, I could use the work."

Jim was avid for the idea too and said there was a big clearing about a quarter-mile into the timber that was perfect for the pair of corrals they'd need to put up.

"The captain'll be obliged," Sock said.

Jim asked about the Berry boys. Frank James said they rode mainly with Gregg but sometimes went with Dave Pool too. They'd both proved ready and fearless fighters, but Butch was making a name for himself as having extra-hard bark. "He started him an ear collection," Frank said. "Says he'll have a longer one than Riley's."

"*He'll never,*" Riley Crawford said. His fingers went to his chest where the necklace usually hung and he gave a start to find it gone— then remembered that Mary Anderson had told him she wouldn't stand for having that filthy awful thing at the supper table and made him leave it outside the house.

A CEREMONY OF HEMP

Fort Leavenworth. A warm and sunbright morning of pale blue. At the request of the chaplain, the band plays "We Shall Gather at the River," plays it lustily to be heard over the babble and laughter and clamoring of the nearly one thousand spectators, all of them bright-faced and eager for the proceeding to get under way. Children sit on their fathers' shoulders to have a better view, women work their fans against the rising heat. The rooftops lined with onlookers. Dogs yapping, chasing after each other through the crowd, excited by the celebrant air. Hawkers plying their trade, selling boiled potatoes, bags of salted cracklings, sugar candies. The air carries the smell of these treats and of unwashed men and perfumed women, of the ripe prairie grass beyond the town, of the new-sawn lumber used to replace certain worn portions of the Leavenworth gallows.

An open, two-seat wagon bears Jimmy Vaughn from the guardhouse to his instrument of execution. He sits beside the driver, and a pair of armed guards sit behind him. He looks out at the newrisen sun and the thin range of redstreaked clouds above it, at the gentle roll of green hills, and says to the driver that it sure is pretty. The driver glances eastward and nods.

The crowd raises a great cheer at the sight of the condemned. The wagon arrives at the foot of the gallows steps, and Jimmy Vaughn, his hands manacled behind him, hops out and boldly ascends the steps and turns to stare without expression on the audience of his death—most of them cursing and mocking him, calling for his soul to rot in hell, asking how damn tough he feels now. But some few are shouting encouragement, to trust in God and be brave. Many of them quietly admit to each other that they're impressed with his fearless aspect.

The officer in charge of the execution party asks Jimmy Vaughn if he would care to address the assembly, and Jimmy says he would. The officer raises his hands to quiet the crowd, and it complies. Most of the members of this gathering have heard a number of gallows valedictions in the past year, and following Jimmy's execution, there will be debate in taverns and liveries and general stores about the quality of this one. Every man is interested in the last words of another, for every man wonders, sometime in the course of his days, what his own might be.

He tells them his name is James Jefferson Vaughn and that he is a devout believer in Jesus Christ and southern rights. His only regrets on leaving this world are that he will not again see his beloved Mary nor fight for brave Bill Quantrill—whose name incites the crowd to a clamor of jeering and catcalls.

"I ask you to tell the truth about my death," he says, "to say I died bravely, a rebel to the backbone. And I ask of my executioners the courtesy of a Christian burial." He pauses and scans the crowd as if he would take with him the clear memory of every face. "Know this," he says: "Not hell nor King Henry will prevent my comrades from avenging me. My life will be paid for by two dozen or more. Take it for a promise." He hawks and spits on the planks at his feet, at once expressing contempt and proving that his mouth is undried by fear. "Now do your damned worst."

Some hard jeering follows, but a scattering of applause as well, of nodding respect for his courage. The officer in charge guides him to a spot directly in the center of the trapdoor. As the executioner places a black hood over his head Jimmy Vaughn catches the scent of pipe smoke on the man's fingers. The hangman snugs the noose around his neck and someone presses a glove into one of his manacled hands and whispers for him to release it when he's ready. He hears the hanging party shuffle back from the trap. He thinks of his good parents and his beautiful sisters, imagines them smiling and waiting at heaven's gate. He thinks of Mary's lovely face and remembers the feel of her last fine kiss. He drops the glove.

A blistering noonday three weeks later.

A Federal cavalry column of a hundred men makes its slow way back to its post in Kansas City, now but two more miles to northward. From the high branches of the cedar woods to either side of the road ahead come the risible callings of crows.

The days have been long and sultry and every man of them rides slumped and haggard, exhausted by lack of sleep and the constant tension of watching for ambush. Now, drawn so close to Kansas City, they put aside their fears and snug their carbines into their saddle scabbards and give themselves over to reveries of the good times to come later this night in the bagnios and saloons.

The guerrillas burst out of the cedars like the very avatar of nightmare, shivering the air with a rising chorus of rebel yells, shattering the afternoon with a rage of revolverfire. The Yankee horses plunge and veer, their riders slinging blood, pitching from saddles. Most of the Federals panic, lash their mounts to a gallop in the other direction with no purpose in this world save escape, deaf to the shrill commands of their captain to stand and fight.

The captain sees a beardless bushwhacker bearing on him with his reins in his teeth and revolvers in each hand—and then feels the world tip sideways and goes facedown into the dirt without knowing it or anything else evermore.

An hour later a Federal force from Kansas City will find forty-three of their fellows littering this portion of prairie, many of them already made eyeless by the crows. In the captain's mouth they find a note: "Todd did this. Remember Jim Vaughn."

CAPTIVES

"I'm glad you're here, Billy."

"I know it, Joey. You only tell me three times a day."

"Is that all? I think it a lot more times a day than that."

"Sometimes you think too damn much is what *I* think."

"I know you'd rather be off bushwhacking and I don't blame you. I'd rather be off bushwhacking too, if I was you."

He slapped her lightly on the behind. "You think you know everything."

"Billy?"

"What?"

"You know I love you? I mean, you *really* know it?"

He turned on his side and stared at her dark form, felt her breath warm on his face. "Oh, I guess."

She giggled softly and stroked his beard and kissed him.

"You love *me*?"

"Course I do—except when I feel like wringing your neck. Now let's go to sleep."

"I mean do you *really*?"

"Go to *sleep,* dammit."

"I know you *do*."

"Joey, will you *hush up*."

He could sense the grin on her. "Me you too," she said. "I'll love you for always and always. I don't care we can't . . . you know."

They fell asleep holding each other, though they could not, could never, hold each other close enough.

As it happened, the several members of the Westport Sewing Circle who'd succumbed to Federal threats of imprisonment and told the Yankees about the Vaughn girls had also revealed the names of other members of the club, including those of the Anderson sisters. When asked where the Anderson girls might be, the informers said they didn't know. All they knew about them was that they had once lived with relatives called Parchman on a farm by Brushy Creek just off the Blue River.

They were in the kitchen and readying dinner, Jenny fetching water from the creek. Mary was still darkeyed from hard weeping for Jimmy Vaughn, and Josephine was trying to cheer her with funny rhymes she'd heard Bill and Jim tell. Mary managed a small smile at the first innocuous few, but when Josie began intoning, "There was a bad girl from the city, who on a poor farm boy took pity; so for only a dime and a bit of her time, she let him have fun with—" She broke in, "Josie—don't you dare!" but was grinning in spite of herself.

Then from out in front of the house Jenny screamed.

Josephine streaked across the room and grabbed up her Navy from a chair and raced for the front door, Mary already there and Jenny now hollering, "Let go! Let me *gooo*!"

She ran onto the porch and smack into Mary and the Federal soldier who'd seized her. She raised the pistol to shoot him but someone snatched her arm upward and the round discharged through the porch roof. The gun was wrested from her by a large corporal with a potent smell of spoiled onions. She tried to kick him and he slammed her against the wall so hard she went breathless and her legs quit and she fell on her rump, mouth ajar and trying to draw air. She saw Jenny kicking wildly in the arms of a Yankee carrying her toward the road and the army horses there. Saw Mary crying in pain and fury, pinioned from behind, being dragged away by a grinning soldier clutching her breasts.

The corporal yanked her to her feet and pulled her down the porch steps, her legs flaccid, her strides awkward, and still she could not breathe. Other soldiers now hurrying from the barn and from behind the house and all of them converging on the horses. Then her lungs abruptly inflated and she joined her sisters in howling for their brothers.

Bill and Jim were breaking horses at the corrals, the bushwhackers who'd brought the mustangs—Lionel Ward, Hi Guess, Frank James and Buster Parr—sitting on the rail and watching, when the pistol-shot sounded from the house. Bill dropped the hackamore he'd been about to put on a dappled gray Jim was holding steady, and the brothers vaulted the corral rail and ran to their horses. The six of them set off for the house at a gallop with revolvers in hand, following the narrow serpentine trail, branches and shrubs slapping at them as they went, the horses' hooves throwing clods.

They pounded into the farmyard and spotted the mounted Federals making their way along the fence-bordered lane leading to the main trail. There were six of them, and three rode double behind an Anderson girl. The Yanks saw them coming and reined around with pistols drawn. Those holding the girls as shields formed up across the narrow lane in front of their comrades and the guerrillas drew up a dozen yards from them. A sergeant was clutching Jenny to his chest, and she shrilled, *"Billy!"*

"Stand fast!" the sergeant shouted. "You shoot and they die!"

"Let them loose!" Bill Anderson said. "Do it *now*!" The flanking fences prevented them from getting around the Yankees.

The big corporal held Josephine, and a soldier sat hunched behind Mary with his arm hard around her, and both men held pistols to the girls' sides. Josephine was trying to claw the corporal over her shoulder and it was all he could do to keep his eyes from her fingers. "Quit, dammit!" he said, grappling with her. "*Quit,* I said!"

"Shoot him, Billy!" Josephine yelled. She tried to hit the corporal's face with the back of her head. "*Shoot* him!" The corporal got his forearm around her throat and her eyes widened and she tried to dislodge his arm with both hands.

"*You're throttling her, goddam you!*" Bill shouted, frantic in his helpless rage.

The corporal eased his hold and Josie drew audible breath as he shifted his grip to pin her arms at her sides and press the muzzle of his pistol under her chin.

"You . . . *bastard,*" Josephine gasped.

The other Feds in the party had been slowly backing their horses and were a good twenty yards down the lane, and now one of them yelled, "Here's the company!" He waved his hat at comrades still out of sight around the bend but they all heard the rumble of the coming horses.

"*Shit!*" Buster Parr said. "We got to slide, Bill!"

"*Go,* Billy!" Josephine said, disheveled, breathless.

"They won't be harmed, I swear it!" the sergeant said.

The lead riders in the Federal column came around into view.

"They're on us, Bill," Lionel Ward said.

"*DAMMIT!*" He yanked Edgar Allan around and they all lit out.

They were chased until they were into the deeper wildwood and then the Feds turned back. But the Yanks found the broncos in the rude corrals and took them too.

Captain Bill

When they returned to the Parchman farm they found it untorched, so eager had the Yankees been to make away with the girls. While the others swiftly gathered the remaining stores of food and packed them into their saddle wallets, Bill went to his sisters' loft and looked on their beds and trinkets and clothes and he nearly howled in his outrage. He spied Josie's black silk ribbon on the rude plank dressing table. He put it in his pocket and left everything else where it lay.

The others were remounted and waiting.

He stood on the porch and looked all around and marveled that he had once applied his labor to improving this place and making it what it was meant to be. Then said: "Boys, they took my sisters and

I couldn't stop them. The shame is my own and no one else's. Maybe they'll do like they said and exile them. I pray they do. Then I'll collect them and they'll not be removed from me again, take it for a vow." He spat. "But only a fool puts trust in a Union promise. My intention is to offer Yankee prisoners in exchange for my sisters. Could be they'll agree to it."

"Could be they might, Bill," Frank James said, "if you make a fair offer of three Yanks for each girl."

There were grins all around.

"Any man of you who cares to join me in catching Yanks is welcome," Bill said.

"Before I answer you on that, Bill," said Lionel Ward, "I got two questions."

"Ask them."

"Well sir, I've rode with Jarrette and Todd and Yeager, all three, but I always knew the band was still part of one company and Bill Quantrill was the captain of it. What I want to know is, would you still be part of Captain Quantrill's company?"

"I would, Lionel," Bill said. "What is your other question?"

Lionel Ward shifted the chaw in his jaw and spat and wiped his mouth with his sleeve. "Hell," he said, "I disremember."

"What say the rest of you boys?" Bill said.

"Count me in," Hi Guess said, and Buster Parr said, "I ride with you, Captain Bill."

It sounded so natural that it took a moment for him to realize he'd heard it. He saw by Jim's smile that he had caught it too. And Lionel. All of them now grinning at Captain Bill.

"Well, I'd say *nobody's* gonna ride with you, *Captain*," Frank James said, "if we don't quit all this yammering and *get* to riding."

Bill laughed with them and went lightfooted down the steps and swung up onto Edgar Allan and they made away into the wildwood.

Two days later they added another pair to their band—Dock and Johnny Rupe—brothers met over a dinner table where they'd been invited to sit down by a family of secessionists known to Buster Parr. Buster had not seen the Rupes in eight months, and in that time the brothers, sixteen and seventeen, had gained their growth. Their mother knew she could keep them from the war no longer. But the boys would have to ride double on the family's old mare until they could get proper mounts.

The following afternoon they ambushed a militia patrol of seven men on the Blue River road west of Raytown. But the Unionists fought desperately, and the guerrillas were obliged to kill them all.

"That's gonna be the problem with getting prisoners," Frank James said. "They figure we'll kill them anyway, so why surrender?"

They stripped the militiamen of their uniforms and put them on, and the Rupe brothers selected the two best of the soldiers' horses. Then they rode on.

They spied various Federal patrols over the following two weeks but all of them too large to engage, and then came a span of five days in which their luck was excellent. They came on three Federal patrols on the open range along the borderline and not more than ten men in any of them. In each instance they rode right up to the Yanks, raising their hand in greeting, and then shooting them at point-blank range before the Feds kenned to them as bushwhackers. In the three attacks they took a total of six prisoners—though two of them fell dead off their horses over the next two days.

They were crossing the Blue River near Little Santa Fe, all of them wearing Federal blue, when they were almost ambushed by Dick Yeager's bunch. Dick recognized the Andersons just in time to check his boys, then came out of the trees and hallooed them. It took Bill and Jim a moment to recognize him too—most of the right side of his mustache was gone and the bared portion of lip showed a raw scar. He told them it had been shot off a few weeks earlier in a fight with redlegs in Cass County. "Closest shave I ever had," he said, showing big yellow teeth.

When Bill explained his plan to trade prisoners for his sisters, Yeager offered to help him, and the two bands, thirty men strong, set out to hunt for Yankees.

They fell on a camp of militia scouts just west of the Little Blue, killing two and capturing three. The following day they sat their horses in the silent shadows of a willow thicket hard by a rippling creek and watched a militia patrol coming down the road. When the soldiers drew abreast of them, they charged out of the trees, rebel-yelling and shooting, and they had to laugh at the looks on the militiamen's faces. Most of the soldiers fled for their lives, and the others went down—except for a handful who threw up their hands and surrendered, but in their excitement the bushwhackers killed some of them too. They dispatched the militia wounded, took the uniforms off the dead, tied the six new prisoners to their saddles and hastened away with them, leaving behind a few wounded horses and a dozen naked dead men staring blindly at the descending crows under a pale and unpitying sun.

They camped that night in the heavy shelter of the White Oak breaks, near the Little Blue. Of Bill's thirteen prisoners, two had tried to escape and been killed for their folly, their bodies left to the crows. He would offer the remaining eleven for his sisters.

He and Yeager were sitting at one of the fires, a jug passing around, Yeager talking about the joys of steamboat robbery, when a courier rode in. Quantrill was at the Blue Springs camp and calling his officers together for a council there tomorrow night. Riders were spreading the word to the other wildwood camps.

"He said to tell you he wants you there too, Captain Anderson," the courier said. "He said for each captain not to bring more than one or two men. He wants to keep the meeting small and anyhow only wants to talk with the captains." He went to fetch himself supper.

There again—*Captain* Anderson. And from one of Quantrill's own messengers. Well, why not? Quantrill himself had called them "your boys" since before they hit Olathe. It was all Bill could do to keep from laughing outright with the pleasure of it, with the grand feeling of its *rightness,* with the ticklish certainty of having come upon his true calling.

Yeager was grinning too. "Some of my boys said today they'd like to ride with you if you'll have them, did you know that? Some cousins of Lionel Ward and a couple of Clay County neighbors of the James fella. I'd take it kindly, Captain Anderson, if you don't poach *all* my damn men."

They laughed and went to retrieve plates of beans and cornbread. When they resettled themselves by the fire, Yeager said, "I bet I know what the meeting's about."

"Me too," Bill said.

They had spoken about Quantrill's determination to raid Lawrence, but neither man was decided if he was for or against it.

They yearned to turn Lawrence to ashes, of course, but they knew too that such a raid could prove folly of the worst sort.

Bill chose his brother and Buster Parr to go with him to the council. He would leave his prisoners with the rest of the bunch. He wrote a note to the Federal commander in Kansas City, presenting his offer of eleven Union captives in exchange for his sisters. He promised to move the girls out of the state if they were released. The general could send his answer through the same courier who delivered Bill's note.

THE PRISON ON GRAND AVENUE

There were eleven of them—all bloodkin to known guerrillas and two of them wives of wildwood boys as well—the eldest of them twenty years old. They were held in Kansas City, quartered on the second floor of a dilapidated three-story commercial building in the middle of Grand Avenue. The top floor was rented to a business that used the space for storing furniture. The ground floor was taken up by a liquor store.

Their floor was without partitioning except for a corner that had been fitted with flimsy walls of thin board to enclose it into a sort of privy containing several slop jars. Bunks were set along the walls in dormitory fashion. The windows of the rear wall were small and offered nothing to see but weedy vacant lots, but the front windows were tall and admitted plenty of sunlight and afforded good view of the street. A trio of guards was always on duty at the entrance to the building, another guard placed at the foot of the stairway, and yet two more posted on the second-floor landing.

The landing guards brought the girls their meals every morning, noon and evening, but refused to carry out their slops. They told them to fling them through a rear window into the lot below. The neighborhood hogs liked to root in the shaded earth behind the building and would make short work of the waste.

They got along well enough with a few of the guards, but most of their keepers were Kansans to the core and made no secret of their enmity toward all things Missourian. Josephine more than once got into a strident exchange of insults with them and each time had to be restrained by the other girls before she provoked the Feds further.

*   *   *

They passed their days observing the doings along Grand Avenue, pointing out to each other the handsomest and best-dressed and silliest-looking people to go by on the streets and sidewalks and making up stories about them. There had been an outbreak of rabies that summer and citizens had permission to shoot any dog seen loose on the streets, so the girls occasionally heard gunshots, sometimes followed by yelping until another report put an end to it. The dead-dog wagon came clattering down the street every afternoon, heaped with carcasses and swarming with flies, and Josephine could not help thinking how much the sight would pain Bill.

They gave their evenings over to harmonizing on favorite songs, to practicing their oral imitations of musical instruments. Jenny Anderson could mimic a fiddle, and she laughed with the others when they teased her that she was in need of a tuning. Charity McCorkle Kerr, sister to one bushwhacker and wife to another, could fairly well sound like a piano, which instrument she had been playing since age six. Among these prisoners were a pair of Cole Younger's cousins, and one of them, Amanda Selvey, could put her hands over her mouth and twang like a Jew's harp or trill like a harmonica. The other cousin, Sue Vandiver, was a small brass band all her own, expertly oom-pah-pahing like a tuba or tootling like a coronet or French horn. An otherwise reticent girl named Juliette Wilson, whose brother rode with Dick Yeager, could raise guitar strumming with her tongue and palate, and Josephine could plunk so like a banjo that the others said she sounded better than the real thing.

Before long the girls were dancing nightly to their own music, waltzing to piano and horns and violins, reeling or stepdancing to stringband tunes. People passing on the sidewalks heard them and believed they were playing real instruments up on the second floor. And many were the outraged complaints to the officer of the guard every evening when the girls concluded their musical entertainments with a rousing and harmonious rendition of "The Call of Quantrill" that carried out their windows and down the block:

Arise, my brave boys, the moon's in the west,
the Federal hounds are seeking our nest.

We'll be in the saddle at breaking of day,
and the Quantrill they hunt will be far on his way.

They chase and they hunt us ever in vain,
no matter they search all the brush and the plain.
We ride like the wind, like ghosts in the night,
we are bold wolves in battle and swift hawks in flight.

Few shall escape us, fewer be spared,
our deadly pistols in vengeance are bared.
For none are so brave, so sure in their might,
as men of Missouri defending her right.

In this sultry summer the city smelled of horseshit and of human waste baking in the alleyway jakes, of woodsmoke and cooking, of dust blown in off the prairie, of thousands of people in close urban quarter. The girls grew familiar with the sounds of the city—the clattering and clopping of passing street traffic, the iron-crashings and whistle shrieks from the railyard, the cries of streetcorner news hawks and calls of wagon vendors, the sharp-bark commands of army units on the drill field down the street.

They heard other things too. The building was old and dry in its joints, and sometimes, in the late hours of the night, they'd hear a slight creaking in the walls or a low groan from the floor, and in the morning they'd make jokes about the place being haunted. There was another late-night sound as well—the faint laughter of men and women which seemed to come up through the walls, though the liquor store had closed hours earlier. They thought it was a trick of acoustics, that the building was somehow redirecting the sounds from some neighboring tavern.

In fact, the laughter was coming from the cellar, which they did not know was being used as a temporary jail for prostitutes known to be diseased. The building next door was serving as an army guardhouse, and some of the soldiers, in violation of orders not to fraternize with the cyprians, had hacked holes through the common cellar wall so they could visit the whores and trade whiskey and food for their favors, the medical dangers be damned. They snugged supporting beams into the rude passageway, but the structure was makeshift, and in the liquor store above, sober men would feel a slight list as they traversed the floor. One day a bottle fell and broke, and the proprietor and a patron watched in uncertain amusement as the whiskey rivulets flowed like snakes to form a trough at the base of the wall. The patron said it might be a right idea to shore the wall beam. The whiskeyseller said it wasn't his building, so to hell with it.

The girls would never know either the source of the laughter or that the reason it ceased in their third week of imprisonment was that the guardhouse commander learned of the shenanigans and ordered the whores removed to more secure confinement.

The only vestiges in the cellar of the last good time to take place there were the litter of abandoned underclothes and the empty whiskey bottles and the various scattered carcasses of half-eaten roast chickens. Over the following days the smell of the chicken remains carried out through the cellar window to the snorting hogs that prowled for slops along the rear of the building. But the window was too small to admit them, so the swine burrowed beneath it and then through the rotted rear wall of the cellar. And who can say whether, as they made their way inside, they paid any hog mind at all to the groans of wrenching girders and joists torsioning to the breaking point.

COUNCIL OF CHIEFTAINS

They were recognized by the pickets and allowed to pass along the trail and into a clearing in this dense portion of wildwood. Quantrill's camp was a quarter-mile away and close by Blue Springs, but here was where the council would meet. They gave their horses to a young bushwhacker who tethered them with the others at safe remove from Quantrill's horse. Charley had already bitten two of the other animals, the horsehandler said, and ruined a thumb on one of Andy Blunt's men, some brash youngster who claimed he knew a horse's mind and reached a hand out to stroke Charley's muzzle, saying, "Ho now, boy, you ain't gonna bite nobody, are you?"

A fire burned low in the center of the clearing, and torches stood at intervals around the perimeter, casting an eerie wavering light on the underbranches of the trees. Each of the captains had brought a couple of men with him and there were nearly twenty men assembled near the fire, some few others tending to the horses or posted as videttes. Bill had not seen some of these men, including Quantrill himself, since the previous autumn. There was much shoulder-slapping and sharing of jugs. Then Quantrill called them to gather around him.

He paced slowly inside the circle as he spoke, passing before every man so he could directly address each in turn. He said the Union newspapers were crowing about Gettysburg and claiming the war was all but won. He didn't know what the Richmond high-hats thought about that, but he believed it was time to show the Federals just how far from finished the war was. And the best place to show them was in Kansas—the home to killers who had been murdering Missourians since before it even became a state.

His voice rose steadily as he recounted the devastation wrought upon innocent Missourians by Jim Lane's brute jayhawkers. He retold the atrocities Lane's Brigade had visited on Osceola. He asked his audience to think on the barbarities beyond number that Jennison and Hoyt and their bastard redlegs had committed in Missouri—the farmers hanged, the young boys killed, the women widowed and crops destroyed and homes put to the torch.

Bill felt the anger in the men around him like a rising heat, heard their low cursings of accord. Quantrill heard them too, and moved deeper into his theme.

The black heart of Kansas, he said, was Lawrence—the favored home of abolitionists since territorial days. It had served as the capital of the Free State movement, its streets were named after New England, the town *itself* was named after a damned abolitionist. The place had long been a headquarters for the murdering jayhawks. It was where the thieving redlegs sold most of the plunder they took out of Missouri. *And* it was home to Jim Lane—the Grim Chieftain, the King Jayhawk himself. The man had built a mansion in Lawrence and paid for it with the blood money he got in receipt of Missouri loot.

"Lawrence—it is in *Lawrence*," Quantrill said, his delivery now evangelical, "that we can have our greatest revenge. *And* reap our greatest reward!"

"Let's go *kill* the sonsofbitches!" John Jarrette hollered—and the exhortation provoked cheers.

"Easy to say, John," Cole Younger said, "but there's a thousand soldiers between here and there."

"That's right—they got new posts all along the damn border to watch out for us," Andy Blunt said.

"Those posts are *thirteen* miles apart," George Todd said. "How much bigger hole you need?"

"And look there at Dick Yeager," Quantrill said. "He went *a hundred miles* into Kansas to settle a score and he lost not a man in the doing. Lawrence is not half so far over the border."

"That's true, Bill," Yeager said, "but I went with a dozen men. How many would we be to Lawrence? Three hundred? That's a lot of riders to sneak forty miles into Kansas."

"Even if we *got* there," Gregg said, "we'd pay hell getting back."

There was agreement with this point—and disdain of it as unduly fearful. "We can slide past anydamnbody," Dave Pool said. "We're ghost riders—*hooooooo!*"

Quantrill said they could get past the outposts on a moonless night, and once they were into the unguarded open country they could move fast enough to reach Lawrence before sunrise. The town was so sure of its safety it still had not installed a telegraph, and its local garrison had been reduced to fewer than a hundred soldiers.

"I have considered every objection to the raid, every obstacle," Quantrill said, "and I admit that there are many. But he who never risks can never hope to gain. I, for one, am ready to assume the risk required to gain my greatest ambition—to bring Jim Lane back to Missouri and burn him at the stake within sight of Kansas City."

This avowal raised cheers and renewed cries for vengeance, but again there were remonstrations. Of the captains, Todd and Pool and Jarrette were strong for the raid, while Younger and Gregg and Blunt were reluctant. Bill looked at Yeager and saw him grinning. He figured Dick would choose to go.

Quantrill raised his hands and the bickering fell off. "Think on it," he said. "Consider what you have heard tonight. Examine it every way you will. And I'll have your answer, every man, at sundown tomorrow."

"You ain't got to wait for my answer, Bill," Todd said. "I say we sack the damn town and burn it to black dirt."

"No!" Quantrill said, cutting off the renewing arguments. "I want no answers now. You have until end of day tomorrow to decide. Tomorrow give your answer, each and all, before your comrades."

*   *   *

They debated into the night, Quantrill remaining apart from all discussion, then every man got some sleep and rose again before daybreak to resume the argument over breakfast. Opinions remained strong on both sides. They broke for dinner, and afterward sat apart to reflect.

Jim sat beside Bill in the shade of a maple and uncorked a bottle. They passed the whiskey back and forth in silence for a time, then Jim said most of the captains looked to be leaning toward the raid. "Yeager's decided for it. Appears Blunt might too. W. J. still thinks it's a fool notion. What say, Billy—which way you inclining?"

"I won't be going," Bill said. "I've been thinking hard, but no matter how I look at it, I see I can't go. Not with our sisters in a Yank prison. Not while I'm waiting on an answer about getting them out of there. What if the Feds want to make the trade while you and me are away in Kansas? Hell, what if neither of us gets back from Kansas? How long would the girls stay locked up then?"

Crows were chittering in the lower branches of a neighboring tree. He felt that their bright eyes were on him, their aspect amused and curious.

"But any of the boys in the bunch who want to go can go," he said, turning back to Jim. "So can you. I have to stay."

"Well hell, Bill," Jim said, "then I have to stay too."

There came a cry of "Rider coming in!"

A horseman with an eyepatch loped into the clearing and reined up, his mount lathered with hard use. He was arrived from Kansas City, and the tidings he carried were grim.

KANSAS CITY FATES

One of the guards was a blond boy from Indiana who fancied himself a charmer of women, and from the day the girls had arrived nearly a month ago, he had been making overtures to Mary Anderson. But the girls all agreed that there was something of the toad about him, and they didn't fault her lack of interest. At first, she had been polite in her rebuffs, and then she had tried to ignore him, but the Hoosier persisted in his attentions. Yesterday, when he and another guard had come in to collect the breakfast pails, he'd made bold to run a finger through her hair and remark on its prettiness. She had simply walked away, shaking out her hair with her hands as if to cleanse it of his touch, and left him smiling awkwardly and red-faced. But when he did it again this morning—this time stroking a full handful of her yellow locks—she whirled and slapped his face sharply and told him to keep his hands to himself.

In the face of the other girls' laughter, the Hoosier was embarrassed to a rage. "You puke Missouri whore!" he said. He snatched her to him and roughly groped her rump with one hand and squeezed her breast with the other. She yelped and flailed at him and there was a flurry of female shrieking and cursing as the girls leaped to her defense. The other guard grabbed the furious Hoosier boy from behind and pulled him away from them—and as he did, Josephine hiked her skirtfront and executed a hard and perfect kick to the Hoosier's crotch. His eyes bugged and his mouth fell open and his comrade let him drop to his knees. The Hoosier cupped himself with his hands, bent forward and retched hugely.

"Now who's the *puke,* you ignorant bully!" Josie said. She was set to kick him again but the other guard pushed her away as more guards came stomping up the stairs.

The sergeant in charge demanded to know what in purple hell all the hullabaloo was about and everybody but the Hoosier started talking at once. When the sergeant at last came to understand what happened, he gave quick orders to shackle a twelve-pound ball to Josephine Anderson's right ankle.

As communal punishment they are to be denied dinner but they don't care. They tell Josephine again and again how proud they are of her, and they laugh at each other's repeated descriptions of the Hoosier as he went down on hands and knees and puked like he'd been poisoned. They've cleaned up the mess and dropped the dirtied rags out a rear window and heard a hog below snortling loudly over the treat fallen to it from above.

Josie sits on her bunk, Mary beside her and petting her and every few minutes asking if there is anything she can do for her. Jenny stands out in the middle of the floor and demonstrates again and again the kick her sister used to bring the soldier down. "Lordy! It was just so *grand,* Jo!" she says. "Billy and Jim are gonna be proud of you!"

Josephine grins.

"I can't believe they locked this awful thing on you," says Charity McCorkle Kerr. She fingers the chain attaching the heavy ball to the iron clasp on Josie's ankle.

"Truth to tell, it makes me feel like a desperado," Josie says. She affects a wicked leer and pretends to twirl the ends of a long mustache in the manner of a stage villain.

"All they've really done is give me a weapon," she says. "Look." She cradles the cannonball in both hands and stands up, its chain swinging. "Next time a keeper gets improper with one of us, I'll just go up to him and take a bead on his foot like this"—she holds the cannonball out—"then . . ." She lets the ball drop. It bangs on the floor resoundingly and makes an indentation.

"Wouldn't *that* set the bastard to howling and hopping on one foot?" Josie says with a wide grin.

The floor quivers under their feet for a moment and ceases.

The girls look at each other. "What in the *world* . . ." Sue Vandiver starts to say—and the floor groans and renews its reverberations. The bunks rattle. The walls shudder and give off dust.

"Oh my God," Amanda Selvey whispers.

The doorlock clatters and the door flies open and a guard yells, *"Come on!"* and they hear his boots thumping down the stairs.

The building jars sharply and every girl falls down shrieking. Timbers and joists pop like gunshots and the walls break open with tremendous cracklings and plaster falls and the air enfogs with powder and dust. The floor moans and tilts on its moorings and bunks go sliding across the room.

Mary and Jenny help Josie to stand up with the iron ball hugged to her chest as the other girls scramble for the door, some of them on hands and knees. Holding to each other, the Andersons stagger after them, coughing and choking in the haze. Just as the first girls lurch out on the landing, it tears free of the wall and plunges in a monstrous crashing and terrified chorus of screams.

"*Windows*—we'll jump!" Josie shouts.

They veer toward the front windows, leaning against the slope of the floor, but it suddenly dips to their right and Jenny loses her grip and tumbles away, shrieking *"Josieeee!"*

Josie and Mary turn to go after her but then the ceiling rips apart and furniture comes smashing down and the floor buckles and the whole world gives way.

The pall of dust over the collapsed building was so dense that rescuers could barely see each other at a distance of two yards. They were guided by the pitiful cries of the survivors. It was an hour before the first victim was extricated, and it took the rest of the morning and half of the afternoon to find and remove the others. The street was jammed with onlookers shouting questions and conjectures about what had happened, avid to know if anyone had been killed.

The first ones brought out were Jenny Anderson and Juliette Wilson. Jenny's legs were mangled and her face badly torn. She would carry the scars and require a cane the rest of her life. Juliette was alive when found, but her ribs had been stove and had punctured both lungs, and a few minutes after she was borne from the ruins she was dead, drowned in her own blood. They found four girls together, two of them maimed of limb but destined to live, and two with only cuts and bruises who would forever regard themselves as favorites of God. Sue Vandiver, Amanda Selvey, and Charity McCorkle Kerr were each one found crushed dead.

As the girls, dead and alive, were carried from the wreckage, many of the women looking on were moved to tears and some even to anger, and several were heard to shout *"Murderers!"* at their own soldiers.

Mary and Josephine Anderson were the last to be uncovered, the elder girl lying atop her sister. When the rescuers lifted Mary out of the rubble, she screamed with the pain of various broken bones. Her spine was fractured, her legs partially paralyzed forevermore.

Josephine was pinned down by a heavy beam across her chest. Except for a bloody nose, her face and head appeared uninjured, and though her eyes were bloodshot, she was not crying. As the rescuers worked to loosen the beam, a man with an eyepatch smiled down at her and said, "Don't you worry, honeygirl, we'll have you out right quick." Her bare legs were exposed on the other side of the beam, and he reached down and tugged her skirt hem to her knees. Her feet were shoeless, and there was a dark swelling of bonebreak above the manacle on her ankle. Then the beam was free and several of the men took hold of one end of it and heaved together to raise it and lay it aside.

And now they saw the iron ball embedded in her chest, a portion of its chain impressed with it. Saw the bloodsoaked dressfront and the blood pulsing from all around the edge of the ball. It was a wonder she could still be living, that her eyes yet held such ferocity as they did. She coughed softly and blood showed on her lips and the light in her eyes seemed to waver. In a voice she could not have raised above its rasping whisper but which every man of them heard as clearly as if she'd spoken it at his ear, she said: "You'll be sorry. . . ."

VERDICTS

The early rumor was that if their guerrilla kin did not themselves come to claim their bodies, the girls would be buried in Leavenworth cemetery. Once the war was over, any family that wanted to claim the remains and remove them for burial somewhere else would be permitted to do so. The maimed and injured girls were being cared for in a special ward of the army hospital at Fort Leavenworth until they were fit to travel. Then they would be exiled from Missouri as decreed.

There was talk all over town that the Federals had deliberately undermined the building to make it fall, that they had hoped to kill *all* the women in it. The Yanks were of course denying the accusation as a base and outrageous lie, insisting they did not make war on women beyond arresting and exiling those of them related to bushwhackers. But the talk was that they'd done it to show the guerrillas the high price of bushwhacking from now on.

This information came to them by way of the man with the eyepatch who but a few hours earlier had smiled on Josephine and called her honeygirl. He was known in Kansas City as Jack Andrews, a supplier to wagon train companies, but his true name was Leonard Richardson and he was a spy for Quantrill, one of the many who worked for him in Kansas City and Leavenworth.

When Richardson told them which of the girls had been killed, Quantrill sent a rider to retrieve John McCorkle and Nathan Kerr. Both of them rode in his bunch, so he would have no one but himself tell them of the death of Charity, sister to one and wife to the other. Dick Yeager sent a man back to the White Oak camp to give John Wilson the news of his sister Juliette.

Cole Younger was pacing hard, cursing, spitting repeatedly. The two cousins killed had also been favorites, and his family's experiences in this war made it easy to believe the Federals had arranged to bring the building down.

"It's how they do, the bastards," he said. "They kill old men from ambush, they make women to fire their own homes, and now . . . *now* they kill girls by bringing a building down on them. *God damn it,* I can stand no more!"

Quantrill held silent, leaning on a tree and smoking a thin cigar and watching Cole with narrow eyes as he paced in the dying light of the late afternoon. He observed too the shadowy faces of the other captains as they listened to Cole's fulminations. All these men had lost kin to the Unionists, lost friends and neighbors who had committed no crime but to feed them and bind their wounds and give them a place to sleep for a night. News of Federal meanness was hardly news at all anymore, but neither was it something a man got used to. Every new instance of Federal brutality only added to the pain of every previous one. But the news had never before been so awful as this, the killing of young women, of *girls*. Quantrill sensed that the heart of every man he looked on was echoing Cole Younger's cry that he could stand no more. Every face he looked on was set in murderous fury.

When Richardson had named Josephine Anderson among the perished and told of the ball shackled to her leg, Bill's only surprise had been at his lack of surprise. Of course she would have been the one to be shackled. Of course she would have refused to show them her tears. Of course she would have said the last words she did. While she'd been imprisoned, he had been near to howling with his frustration. Had been frantic in his wait for the Yankees' answer to his offer of a trade for her and her sisters. Now he was done with dread and consternation.

He had not protected her as he should have, and so she'd been arrested. And so she'd been killed. But even the crushing weight of his guilt was as nothing beside his rage. It was beyond utterance. It defied every form of language from poetry to madhouse scream. He could but feel it, coiled and ready in the cold and deepened darkness of his soul.

He regarded his brother's grief-hung face and the fury in his eyes. He saw the other chiefs nodding at Cole's rantings, heard their muttered blood oaths. And then met Quantrill's thin glinting gaze. They held each other's eyes and it seemed to him Quantrill was telling him something and that he understood it, though he could not have said what it was.

Cole Younger was shouting now that he didn't care about the fucken odds, he was for going to Lawrence.

Quantrill tossed aside the cigar and stepped in front of the assembly and for a moment studied the sun, still a small distance above the trees. Then looked at them and said, "It is not yet sundown, but if all of you are ready . . ." There was a clamor of ayes. "Then I'll hear each man in turn. What say you . . . Todd?"

"You know my choice—we make an ashpit of the place!"

"Younger?"

"We loot the town to its last dollar and take it off the map."

"Yeager?"

"Lawrence and the torch!"

"Pool?"

"Lawrence! If not a man of us gets back, so be it, but Lawrence pays for the girls, for everything!"

"Blunt?"

"Lawrence. And make of it what Lane made of Osceola."

"Jarrette?"

"Lawrence. And kill every male big enough to hold a gun."

"Gregg?"

"I guess there's no selection anymore. Lawrence it is."

Quantrill's eyes glittered into Bill's. "Anderson?"

"Lawrence."

When they got back to the White Oak camp, Dick Yeager called the men together to tell them the plan. Bill and Jim Anderson headed directly for the other side of the camp, where Bill's prisoners were under guard in a makeshift pen of tree limbs.

The Berry boys fell in beside them and nodded their greetings. Jim grinned and clapped them on the shoulder. As they strode across the campground, Ike said that as soon as they'd heard what happened, he and Butch had left Pool's camp and come to the White Oak breaks. "They were like our sisters too," Ike said. "If you'll have us back, we'd be proud to ride with you."

"You boys never have to ask," Bill said.

Ike's white hair had grown to his shoulder blades and he was now cleanshaved. Butch's mustache had thickened. His off eye looked further skewed and his good one seemed much aged. His necklace of ears had grown heavier, and the driest, lowest ones clicked against his belt buckle. His cheekbone showed a fresh scar which Bill and Jim would come to learn was made by a Federal rifleball. They would learn too that his Joey horse had been killed from under him a month ago and he was now riding a paint, which he believed hid better in the bush and which he had not given a name nor would.

The prisoners saw them coming and those who'd been sitting rose quickly to their feet. As the pairs of brothers drew closer, the captives read their faces and shrank from the front of the pen. Some began pleading for mercy, swearing they'd never harmed anybody in Missouri, that they'd been forced to wear the Yankee blue against their will, that they would never take up a gun against the South again. The guards moved out of the way just as each of the brothers pulled a pair of Colts and started shooting.

In ten seconds the eight revolvers were emptied and all the prisoners down and done with screaming. But a few still twitched or groaned. Bill and Butch put up their empty guns and filled their hands with loaded ones and went into the pen and delivered one more shot to each of them, square in the head.

Butch then set about cutting an ear from each of the men he'd killed. Bill watched for a moment and then calculated that he himself had done for five of the prisoners, then took from his jacket pocket Josephine's long ribbon of black silk and into it tied five tight knots.

DIES IRAE

Regard the town. Its clean wide streets and neat sidewalks deserted at this gray hour before daybreak. Everywhere is evidence of a thriving community. Consider the newly cleared lots, the commercial buildings under construction, the rising frameworks of new houses. Imagine the day-long clatterings of hammers and raspings of saws in their workaday anthem of civic expansion and prosperity on the increase. Behold the hill of Mount Oread and the splendid homes along its shady base, a neighborhood of leading citizens, including the state's first governor, including Senator Jim Lane. Pay notice to Ridenhour & Baker's, the largest grocery store in the state. Admire the Eldridge House, four stories high and luxuriously appointed, the grandest hotel, it is said, west of the Mississippi. Look on the many shops and restaurants, the handsome office buildings, the stately courthouse and its immaculate square. Attend the shadowy arboreal beauty of South Park where Massachusetts Street runs through it. See there the tents of the twenty Negro soldiers of the Second Kansas Colored Regiment, and two blocks to the east observe the camp of the Fourteenth Regiment of Kansas Volunteers, presently manned by twenty-two white recruits. Remark the easy passage of the Kaw River under its layer of light morning mist. A few windows and livery doors now showing yellow lamplight as the town comes slowly awake. But none of these early risers will prove correct in his expectations of the day, except as concerns the weather. It has been a sweltering summer, and as the eastern sky shows its first thin streaks of red, the air is still and already warm, presaging another day of scorching heat.

They sat their horses on a brushy rise and looked on the town in gray dawnlight. Quantrill sent W. J. Gregg with two men into town to find out if it was really as unaware of their presence as it seemed.

The company stood impressed by its own achievement. Few among them had truly expected to arrive at Lawrence. They would be intercepted by Federal forces, there would be a ferocious fight, and they would retreat to Missouri before Yankee reinforcements showed up—such had been the general anticipation. Yet here they now were, nearly four hundred strong, the town unwarned and Federal regulars nowhere about except for the small local garrison. They'd been two days on the move, with videttes a mile out to every direction and reporting to Quantrill every hour. They'd come into Kansas just south of Aubrey, the moonless night as dark as ink, and slipped past the local outpost in a long lean quiet column of twos. Quantrill then broke up the company into various bunches and dispatched them in different westward directions so anyone who tried to track them would not know which trails to hold to. Miles farther on, the bunches came together again. But the darkness was so nearly absolute they had finally not been sure where they were, and they'd been obliged to impress one guide after another at gunpoint as they went from farm to farm. And here they now were—redeyed and haggard. And grinning like wolves.

As the town began to clarify in the light of the rising day, Bill Anderson heard Larkin Skaggs intone in a low rasp: " 'Thou mighty city, in one hour hast thy mighty judgment come, and the light of a single lamp shall shine in thee no more.' "

Skaggs had asked to ride with Bill after hearing of his execution of the Yankees at White Oak. He was one of an increasing number in the company who objected to Quantrill's occasional taking of prisoners in hope of trading them for captive guerrillas. Everyone knew the Yanks rarely made deals—when they caught a bushwhacker they killed him on the spot or took him to Leavenworth for hanging. Most of the wildwood boys expected no less if they should fall into Union hands, and so believed in a black flag war—no quarter given, none ever asked. Jim had objected to Skaggs as a lunatic, but Bill said lunatic or no, the man was a capable killer of Federals, and accepted him into the bunch.

Now Gregg and the scouts returned and reported that all was well. "They got no notion at all we're here," W. J. said.

Quantrill turned to his officers and said, "Remember: I will not have a woman harmed. The man who injures a woman today will answer directly to me. Be sure your boys bear it in mind."

He stood in his stirrups and looked back along the column and raised his right fist high, his brown guerrilla shirt adorned with the beautiful blood-red stitchwork of young Kate King. "For justice and Missouri!" he bellowed. "Aut vincere aut mori!"

And they fell on Lawrence like a biblical wrath.

They came howling down Massachusetts Street, shooting to left and right, shooting every man fool enough to come outside to see what was happening, to show his face at a window or an open door. There were cries of "Remember Osceola!" and "Remember the girls!"

Quantrill had neatly laid out his plan and his captains executed it exactly. Andy Blunt's men went to block the west end of town while W. J. Gregg's bunch swung away to cut off escape from the east. Dave Pool took a dozen men directly to the top of Mount Oread to watch for Federal cavalry. In minutes they had the town closed off.

Bill Anderson turned his men off Massachusetts and onto a side street and bore toward the camp of the Fourteenth Kansas Volunteers. The white recruits heard the pandemonium and came scrambling out of their tents in their underwear. Their mouths fell slack at the apocalyptic vision of wildhaired guerrillas galloping at them on mad-eyed horses showing huge teeth. The frontmost Yankee raised his hands in surrender and Bill Anderson's bullet struck him above the eye and slung him out dead. Some of the soldiers were too frightened to come out of their tents and so were trampled when the raiders rode over them. Half the boys were killed on the guerrillas' first pass, and then the bushwhackers came around and set to dispatching the wounded and to looting the meager camp.

A recruit with a bloody hip was on his knees, hands clasped and stretched up to Bill Anderson, pleading for his life as Bill walked Edgar Allan up to him. The boy could not have been more than sixteen years old. "When you enlisted for the blue," Bill said, "you gave up every claim on mercy." And shot him. He reckoned his tally at five, withdrew the black ribbon and tied the new knots. They're paying, Joey, he thought, they're paying.

Twenty yards beyond the camp, a barechested recruit was running hard for the woods, but Butch Berry loped his horse after him. When he came even with the boy he laughed down at him. The recruit looked up as he ran and Butch shot him and the boy's legs quit altogether. Butch reined up and dismounted and unsheathed his shortblade.

Larkin Skaggs ripped down the Union banner from its pole in the center of the camp, tied the flag to the end of his horse's tail, then rode about the camp whooping and trailing the Stars and Stripes in the dust, his horse shredding it under its rear hooves.

While the Anderson bunch was at killing the white soldiers, the Negro troops bivouacked to the west were taking flight into the surrounding woods. They'd heard the gunfire and the screams and knew a bad reckoning was at hand. By the time the guerrillas arrived at the colored camp, it stood deserted.

Bill at last regrouped his bunch and they went trotting back out to Massachusetts Street. The town clattered with gunfire and quivered with rebel yells, rang with the cries of wounded and dying men, the keening of witnessing women. The air was misting with woodsmoke and assuming a scent of blackpowder. The streets were littered with bloodstained men at awkward sprawl. Wherever a fallen townsman was trying to regain his feet or crawl away to some imagined haven, a guerrilla rode his horse over him and then shot him again. Bill saw two dogs lying dead but no sign of others anywhere.

The government and newspaper offices were the first targets put to the torch. Now the guerrillas were at looting the banks and stores and business offices, bearing away money, jewelry, whatever of monetary worth they came upon, then setting afire each ransacked place. The entire business district was ablaze, the dark smoke rising straight as pillars into the windless sky. Many of the wildwood boys wore new boots, new hats, new clothes with the price tags still dangling from them. Bill spied George Todd galloping across the intersection ahead, bedecked in a handsome new suit and hat.

Some of the raiders carried lists of the names and addresses of the town's politicians and lawmen, its newspaper editors, its traffickers with jayhawks and redlegs—death lists compiled by Quantrill's spies—and they were hunting these men all over town. As Bill and his men made their slow way down the street, their attention was pulled in every direction by sudden concentrations of gunfire and shrieks and death screams. Everywhere stood houses in flame, and more being fired. Women were trying to save what possessions they could, shoving furniture out into the yard, flinging clothes from the windows, and some were assisted by the same men who'd set the fires. At the addresses on the death lists, guerrillas sat their horses in front of the burning house and waited for the people within to come running out, coughing and crying, and then shot the men among them and every boy too who looked old enough to use a gun.

Mortal dramas were playing out on every street. Women interposing themselves between their men and the men who would kill them, pleading with the guerrillas, arguing, trying to bargain, even cajoling them in their efforts to save their men's lives. In some few cases they would succeed, in most not.

They came to a street where three guerrillas were crowfooting around a shrilling woman trying desperately to protect a man from them with her body, holding him tightly to her as a mother hugs a frightened child, whirling with him this way and that in her efforts to keep her back to all their guns at once.

"*Please,*" she begged, "have pity!"

The bushwhackers laughed. "We are fiends from hell, woman," one said. "There is no pity today."

Bill rode past them and seconds later heard the gunshots behind him and the woman's wail of grief rising to mingle with so many others. And in that moment was aware of the ache in his jaws, so tightly were they clenched.

The saloons were the first places many of them had hied. They'd cleared off the shelves and then rolled whiskey barrels out to the sidewalks and stood them in upright rows and smashed away the tops so a man could dip himself a schoonerful without even having to dismount.

Larkin Skaggs galloped ahead of the bunch in his haste to get at the nearest row of sidewalk liquor, the shredded Union flag still dragging behind his horse. He was already on his second mugful of whiskey when Bill and the others reined up and stepped down from their horses. Mugs were passed to them and they each dipped a drink. The surrounding din was incessant—the gunfire and rebel yells and bushwhacker laughter, the screams of fear and pain and sorrow.

"Sweet baby Jesus," Ike Berry said, glancing up and down the street. "I never even dreamt the like." His look was troubled.

Bill Anderson was surprised by his sudden irritation at Ike's remark. Then he saw the look on his brother's face and snapped, "What are *you* so hangdog about?"

"I ain't," he said. Then shrugged. "It's just, I don't know. I guess . . . I wish there was more *soldiers* to fight, I don't know." He looked off across the street.

"If at least these people were Dutchmen," Ike said. "Daddy used to say the damned Dutch always got it coming, no matter they fight back or not."

Butch Berry stood apart from them, his necklace of ears holding three raw additions he'd taken at the Federal camp. He was watching a drunken bushwhacker trying to make his horse stomp on a hatless man with a bloody head who was struggling to drag himself off the street. He spat.

Bill stalked into the saloon and snatched a nearly full bottle from a bushwhacker so drunk he didn't even object, then commandeered a table at the back of the room. A minute later Jim and the Berrys came in with refilled mugs and sat with him. They drank in silence and none looked into the eyes of another.

He knew now what was chafing him. He'd heard its timbre in Ike's remark and seen its shadow in his brother's face. He'd been quick to volunteer his men for the attack on the army camps in town because he was set on killing Federals, and if the only ones to be found here were recruits, so be it. Recruits were anyway the seeds of seasoned veterans. But the men of this town had proved to be cowards who would not fight and looked to their women to protect them. Men so despicably weak as that were unworthy of such effort of destruction as this. The scale of hate being visited on this craven town felt to him so excessive it was itself a show of weakness. Give him men of war to kill, not such contemptibles as these. Give him redlegs who hanged farmers . . . militiamen who burned the homes of widows . . . Federals who murdered girls. . . .

Frank James came in from the sidewalk and asked Bill what he wanted the bunch to do. "Tell them suit themselves," Bill said. Frank shrugged and went outside.

They drank without talking, the din from the streets relentless, the smoky air now carrying into the saloon the distinct odor of burning flesh. Their fellows came and went, hollering brags of how many

Unionist sons of bitches they'd killed so far this day and how much loot they'd reaped. Larkin Skaggs came in, listing with drink, and grabbed up an unattended bottle. He bellowed that the Great Jehovah was this day cleansing the sinful stain of Lawrence from the earth—then lunged back out into the maelstrom.

Quantrill entered and grinned at the cheers that met him. He spied Bill's group and came over to the table to sit with them. He said he'd been to Jim Lane's house with a dozen men but found only his wife and daughter at home. The woman claimed the senator was in Saint Louis and would not return home for several weeks more. Quantrill expressed his disappointment and informed her that the senator would have no home to return to. He had some of the boys help her remove the preserved foods from the house so she and the girl would not go hungry, then set the place afire and took pleasure in watching it burn.

He didn't believe Lane was in Saint Louis, Quantrill said, but his men had not turned up a sign of him anywhere in town. The mayor too had eluded them. But the entire business district was aflame and much of the rest of the town was now burning and most of the men on the death lists were even now swinging their picks in hell, so the day was not without its consolations. "The Yankee nation will long remember it," he said.

He paused to light a thin cigar and only now seemed to notice the table's subdued mood. He sighed and stared at the open doorway admitting the cacophony of destruction without. "I know," he said. "It does not gladden a man's spirit to meet with such cowards. The women of this town are brave and plucky to the last one, but the men are less than rabbits."

He turned back to Bill and said, "But then, who thought we'd even *get* here? Who knew for certain there wouldn't be a thousand Yankee soldiers waiting for us this side of the border? They have their spies too, after all." He turned up his hands in a gesture of mystification with fortune's turns. "Yet here we are. And *not* here are a thousand Yankee soldiers. Should we have turned back for the lack of them? Should we have refused to kill these vermin because there were no soldiers to fight for them? Because they will not fight for themselves?"

"They're not worth all this," Bill said, gesturing toward the door.

"Most of the boys don't share that opinion," Quantrill said. "Sufficient unto them that they are killing men of the same Yankee persuasion that has brought grief to their families. They are exacting their portion of what Sir Bacon calls 'a wild justice.' It's a madness, William T., and I must say I wasn't sure you didn't have it too. Since the tragedy at Kansas City, I mean."

Bill stiffened. "I'll avenge my sister, Bill—against the fucken Federals. They killed her and I'll kill them all day long and every day. I *yearn* to. And I mean their informers too. I'll hang an informer—burn his damn house, widow his wife, orphan his pups. But *this* . . ." Again a gesture at the door.

"I know," Quantrill said.

"You *know*? Then why . . . ?" He wasn't sure what he would ask of him.

"Because the madness is also my own," Quantrill said. His smile was near to serene. "I've not unholstered a pistol today. I've not struck a single matchstick. But I'll not deny, today or any day to come, that my hand is on every death and every lick of fire. Some will call me a coward for this day but they will be lying."

He quit his smile and leaned on the table toward Bill. "Mark me, William T. The mass of men know that their hearts are a riot of lusts and base desires, but they fear the risks of acceding to those wants. They desire to do violence to their enemies but they are too fearful of provoking violence unto themselves. They fear *consequences,* you see, and such fear is the rankest sort of cowardice. They cannot bear this truth and so they cleave to the lie of morality, that sum of shams, to defend themselves against it, and thus do they lay a second kind of cowardice atop the first. They warrant no pity." He pointed at the door. "I desired to kill them and I was willing to risk any odds set against me, prepared to suffer any consequence. They can call me a monster for this day, but not a coward."

He sat back and resumed his tranquil smile and contentedly puffed his cigar.

Bill stared at him. "I don't know if that's an admirable argument or the rankest load of bullshit I ever heard," he said. "But I guess it's worth a shot in the neck." He pushed the bottle over to him and Quantrill picked it up, raised it in a toast to Bill, and took a deep drink. They grinned hard at each other.

Then one of Pool's lookouts came rushing into the saloon to report the dust of a distant column of riders bearing for the town. "It's Federals for sure, Captain," the scout said.

Quantrill stood up. "Gentlemen," he said, "the ball is over."

Ten minutes later the guerrillas were ahorse and heading back to their Missouri hideaways with their wagonloads of loot, some of them so drunk they swayed in the saddle as they rode away, rebel yells trailing behind them. Quantrill led them in a southward swing to get by the advancing Feds.

Not until days later would they come to know that Jim Lane had escaped them by bare minutes. When he'd been wakened by the shooting and the warning cries, he'd run downstairs and snatched the nameplate off his front door, then raced back through the house and past his gaping wife and child and out the back way, still boot-less and in his nightshirt. He ran into the nearest cornfield and raced between the cornrows and did not stop running until he reached a deep ravine nearly two miles out of town and there he collapsed, breathless with fear and exhaustion, his feet bloody. Yet he survived.

Not so lucky was the town's mayor, who'd hid himself in a waterwell in the shed beside his house. When the bushwhackers set both buildings on fire, the smoke was drawn into the well and suffo-cated him.

A RECKONING

Lawrence lies in smoldering ruin. The spires of smoke cast far shad-ows over the eastern countryside. The business district is entirely razed and more than a hundred homes are now charred rubble. Of the houses still standing, few have escaped looting. The hazed air holds a horrid stench. There are bodies on every street and some are mistaken for Negroes until recognized as burnt white men. Young boys are impressed into service to keep the crows away from the dead. Women wander the streets in search of husbands and sons, and every anguished cry of discovery adds to the unceasing chorus of grief. The town will be finding and burying bodies for a week, and some will go into private graves and some into graves together. No accurate count of the dead will be made. The records will show that at least 150 men and boys were interred in the days following the raid, but the true count is certainly closer to 200. For a fact, not a woman has been killed. Not a woman has been deliberately harmed in any way beyond the devastations to her heart and soul. . . .

Yet Larkin Skaggs is still at pillaging. Raging drunk, shooting anyone he comes upon who does not give him cash or jewelry on his demand. He reels in the saddle as he trots his horse through the smoky streets, drawing a growing attention as he goes, for the word is spreading that the guerrillas have gone, all but this drunk and laggard graybeard.

Despite his besotted state, Skaggs abruptly arrives at the same awareness and thinks to make away. He heels his horse to a canter but heads in the wrong direction and comes upon a large crowd of citizens and all of them bearing arms. He yanks his mount around as the men open fire. Bent low over the horse, he kicks it hard and goes galloping back through town, a hue and cry rising behind him.

A fifteen-year-old boy whose two brothers were killed this day sees him coming and braces his ancient musket against a hitching post and shoots him in the side as he comes by. Skaggs yelps and tumbles off the horse. He struggles to his feet as a party of Delaware Indian army scouts comes riding around the corner. The boy yells, "That's one of them!" and points at Skaggs, who staggers toward he knows not where, completely bewildered by this turn of fortune. He sees a scout riding toward him and sees the Indian's carbine come up and sees its muzzle flash and in that instant his days are done.

Thus did Larkin Milton Skaggs of Kentucky—who in better times did preach the Gospels and the merciful ways of Jesus—become the only guerrilla casualty in Lawrence, Kansas, on the 21st of August in 1863.

The Delaware scalped him. Then the pursuing townsmen came running up and they shot the dead man a dozen times more and then clubbed him with their gun butts until his teeth were broken out and his eyes crushed, until his bearded visage was but hairy pulp. Some of the men wept in their fury as they battered him. They tied a rope around his neck and dragged his body through the town, calling to neighbors as they went, laughing to see women smiting the corpse with horse apples, to see little boys urinating on Larkin Skaggs whose indifference to it all was absolute.

They hanged him by his feet from a tree branch and ripped away the last of his clothes and shot him several times more. Later in the day some Negroes cut him down and pulled him through the streets behind their wagon as they sang "Kingdom Coming." They finally flung the debased body into a ravine beyond the town limits, and there the crows descended to it.

Over time, the wracked remains of Larkin Skaggs would rot and deliquesce to the bones. Portions of the skeleton would be disjointed and carried away by dogs. A gang of boys would discover the skull, toothless and variously perforated and fractured, and it rattled with rifle balls when they took it for use in their club's rituals. Months later the clubhouse would burn down and the skull come apart in the fire. In time even the last of its shards would reduce to powder under the wear of the world's turning and mingle with the dust and be blown out to the trackless regions of open prairie and then to the deserts beyond.

REPERCUSSIONS

From the New York *Daily Times:*

> Quantrill's massacre at Lawrence is almost enough to curdle the blood with horror. In the history of the war thus far, full as it has been of dreadful scenes, there has been no such diabolical work as this indiscriminate slaughter of peaceful villagers. Even the rebel authorities in Richmond, steeped in wickedness as they are, cannot yet be so dead to all human feelings as to sanction such monstrous outrages. We find it impossible to believe that men who have ever borne the name of American can have been transformed into such fiends incarnate. It is a calamity of the most heartrending kind—an atrocity of unspeakable character.

From a message directed to Federal authorities by the governor of Kansas:

> I must hold Missouri responsible for this fearful, fiendish raid. No body of men large as that commanded by Quantrill

could have been gathered together without the people residing in Western Missouri knowing everything about it. Such
people cannot be considered loyal, and should not be treated
as loyal citizens; for while they conceal the movements of
desperadoes like Quantrill and his followers, they are, in the
worst sense of the word, their aiders and abettors, and
should be held equally guilty.

From General Order #11, August 25, 1863:

> All persons living in Jackson, Cass, and Bates Counties,
> Missouri, and in that part of Vernon included in this
> District . . . are hereby ordered to remove from their present
> places of residence within fifteen days of the date hereof. . . .
> Officers commanding companies and detachments serving in
> the counties named, will see that this [order] is promptly
> obeyed.

Now would this war even more earnestly afflict everyone caught
in it—soldier, guerrilla, civilian, each and all. If there had been any
doubt that the massacre at Lawrence presaged still harder days
ahead, General Order 11 did dismiss it.

The order pertained to an area of the border from the Missouri
River south to the Little Osage and encompassing nearly three thousand square miles. Its intention was to rid the border of those who
had long been providing the wildwood boys with shelter, horses,
food and information. Except for the very few who could prove their
loyalty to the Union, all residents in the region were forced to abandon everything they owned except what they could bear away, which
in most cases was very little. Most of them had already been robbed
of all money, all worthwhile stock, all good wagons, and had to
make do for conveyance with whatever worn mule or ill-used ox
they still possessed, with whatever rude cart or makeshift wagon. Or
they had to leave on foot and take only what they could carry on
their persons.

The enforcement of the order was charged to redlegs and militia
units and they attended to the duty with high zeal. They torched
every farm they came to, and where the families had not yet departed

they robbed them of everything of value and then burned the rest together with the farm. He who objected was shot dead where he stood—or hanged, if the enforcers were militia in a mood for sport, or dragged to death behind a horse as a redleg entertainment.

In the span of two weeks twenty thousand people were dispossessed. Columns of refugees crowded the dusty roads and wagon traces. Some of the pilgrims were set upon by bandits nearly as ragged as themselves and robbed of their last small portion of shabby goods. The countryside grew hazed with the smoke of their burning properties and nothing would remain standing of them but the blackened chimneys. For decades to come, this woebegone region of Missouri would be known as the "burnt district."

Some lucky few had kin in other parts of Missouri where they could take refuge, and some had people in the deeper Southland. But most of the banished had nowhere to go. What kin they had were likely to be alongside them. Some navigated for Texas, some to the western wildlands, some to the northern plains. But most set out with no clear notion of where they were going except that it was away from a home no longer standing, a place gone to ash and smoke.

LITTLE ARCHIE

They sat their horses in the shadows at the edge of a wood near the north line of Vernon County and watched a militia patrol closing up fast behind a southbound refugee train. The exiles were more than a week past the Order 11 deadline for clearing out of the region. Six wagons lumbering along the borderland road under the newly risen sun, all of them listing on unevenly-sized wheels, all of them lugged by worn mules with ribs stark against the hides. The only man among them was a one-legged scarecrow of a figure who rode with the piled furniture in one of the wagons. The only other males were boys, the eldest about thirteen. They were looking back at the soldiers, and even from this distance, watching them through field glasses, Bill Anderson could sense the refugees' fear. He passed the glasses to his brother and yawned.

The train halted and the militia closed up around them. Jim Anderson said he counted fifteen soldiers. They were making the party unload the wagons. The women pitching out cookware, armfuls of clothes, shoving furniture off the wagonbeds to crash on the ground. "Looking for hid money," Jim said. Bill nodded. He was studying a pair of crows perched on a lower branch of an elm.

A pair of soldiers dragged the one-legged man out of the wagon and another Fed flung his crutch into the roadside brush. More soldiers were off their horses now and rummaging through the spill of furniture and clothing. A few yet sat their mounts and seemed to be enjoying the show.

"I believe those Union stalwarts are in need of counseling toward a more Christian outlook," Bill Anderson said. Arch Clement laughed behind him, and he turned and grinned at him.

"Christian outlook," Archie said. "That's what they're in need of, all right." He was seventeen years old and still so fair of skin his attempt at a mustache was but a line of fine blond wisps. He was short and hardmuscled, with thick wrists and large hands admirably adept with most tools and every sort of weapon. He'd been with the bunch only a month but had already proved himself utterly. . . .

He had come to them from the horde of orphans and runaways wandering the desolate border country since the advent of Order 11. As refugee families streamed out of the region, many of the boys among them, some as young as fifteen, broke away to go join the guerrillas. Grown men too were still finding their way to the bushwhacker bands—deserters from the regular army, fugitives from the law, hardcases of every stripe. Despite Order 11's vast dispossessions on the border, the guerrillas suffered no shortage of recruits.

Arch Clement had found the Anderson band's camp and sneaked past the pickets to present himself at the main campfire before anyone even realized there was a stranger in their midst. When the boy said he was looking for Bill Anderson, Frank James was suddenly at his side and holding a cocked pistol to his head. Arch cut his eyes at him and said he better shoot or take it away. Frank laughed at his audacity and likely would have killed him where he stood except that Bill stepped out of the shadows and told him to put up the gun. Bill was impressed with the boy's achievement in getting by the pickets and his bold indifference to Frank's gun at his ear. "Say your piece, then," he said.

Arch told them his name and that he was from Johnson County, that his momma and younger brother had died when he was a child. His daddy had been hanged by redlegs and his two older brothers shot by the Feds, and his only sister had run off a few weeks ago and he had no notion of where to. All he desired to do anymore was kill Union men. He made claim to have killed three men already but didn't care to say who except for a Kingsville liveryboy who'd been private with his sister and thereafter ignored her as you would a common whore. He'd lain for that one in the shadows outside the livery one night and when the fellow headed for home he'd stepped up to him and brained him with a brick and then brained him a few more times to make sure he was well departed to his Maker. He thought his sister would be properly grateful to know what he'd done, but she only wept when he told her about it and a few days later she was gone.

"I figure if that was all the sense she had, then to hell with her," Arch Clement said. He wanted to join Bill's company above all other guerrilla bands because he'd heard it was the only one that always and truly flew the black flag.

Bill smiled at the boy's smooth cherubic features and short stature so out of keeping with the big Army Colt on one hip and the huge bowie sheathed on his lower leg. Riley Crawford was no taller and was skinny besides, but Riley showed broken front teeth and a variety of scars to belie any notion of him as an untried innocent. This Clement manikin looked like a bedraggled choirboy, never mind his tattered hatbrim and variously ripped shirt and his boots held together with wire. But the visible portion of his revolver shone in its worn holster and Bill knew the bowie's blade would gleam as well and hold a razor edge.

A big wildbearded man sitting by the fire said, "You best just run along back to your momma's teat, babyboy." His name was Holland Peck. He grinned around at the smiles of his fellows and took another pull off his jug.

Arch Clement showed a smile the company would come to know well—small and privately amused, under blue eyes cool and unyielding as marble. "I already got my fill from your momma's teat," he said.

Holland Peck stood two inches over six feet and weighed above 220 pounds. He gawked at five-foot-five Archie Clement for a moment before realizing the runt was serious. "You little shit," he said. He put his jug aside and stood up, reached into his bushwhacker shirt and produced a foot-long Arkansas toothpick. "I'll cut you for crowbait."

Arch Clement slipped the bowie from its leg sheath.

"*Bladefight!*" The call rang through the camp and the company quickly converged in a wide circle around the combatants.

The shouted betting begged for wagers on the boy. Archie was backing up with the bowie held at his thigh, Peck advancing on him in a crouch, his dagger low and forward. Then Archie feinted to right and left and Peck was awkward in keeping with him and Archie ducked forward and slashed the big man's knee and sprang clear of his counterstroke. Peck took a step after him but the ruined knee gave way and he went down hard. Archie jumped past him, dodging his wild flail, and backhanded the bowie through his nape and neckbone.

Holland Peck, paralyzed, toppled onto his back, his clove neck gushing blood. He made an effort to speak, his aspect suggesting sudden possession of a profound secret he would share, but his moving lips made no sound and then he was dead.

Arch Clement bent and wiped his blade on Peck's pantleg and then reset it in its sheath.

It was the quickest mortal knifefight any of them had witnessed, and none was unimpressed. Knife duels to the death were rarely fast affairs. Every man of them had seen some that endured the better part of a hour and claimed both principals. It was commonly held that the winner in a knifefight was the second man to fall dead. And here Arch Clement stood without a nick.

Some new recruits were assigned to bear away and bury the body, and Arch Clement was welcomed to the company with nods and smiles and a few cautious pats on the shoulder. Because the late Holland Peck had no outstanding debts to anyone in the company, Bill Anderson let Arch have the man's horse and armament and possibles. Arch also laid claim to Peck's hat, which had fallen off in the fight and proved only a little large. Among Peck's possessions he found a guerrilla shirt, which of course was hugely baggy on him, but no matter. He regretted that Peck did not have smaller feet so he might have acquired better boots as well.

The following day they were twenty miles to the north, taking a dinner of roast corn and potatoes in the barn of a secessionist farmer. Their talk was mostly of Larkin Skaggs, whose fate at Lawrence they had learned of only a few days ago, and they were still in a fury about it.

"Those sorry Kansans didn't have the sand to fight when we were there in a bunch," Sock Johnson said. "Couldn't do a thing but hide behind their women's skirts. But when it was only one drunk man left in town—oh, they were some brave souls then! Especially after he was dead."

"Then the damn Feds go and *scalp* him," Ike Berry said. "We never did nothing like *that* to them."

"This war can't get mean enough for them bastards," Hi Guess said. "It's always something to learn from the Feds about meanness. *Scalping*. Sweet baby Jesus."

"Well hell," Arch Clement said. "We ought to do them in kind, don't you all think?"

"Not that easy," Bill Anderson said. He nodded at Riley Crawford. "That sprout tried to take a scalp a few days ago. Show him, boy."

Riley Crawford blushed and took from his pocket something dark and withered and about half the size of his palm, with a few strands of brown hair attached to it.

"Took him a quarter-hour to get that much," Bill said. "By then that sorry head looked like somebody's been working it with a hoe."

"We need us a damn Indian in this bunch, what we need," Frank James said. "The Feds got Indians."

"Well, so happens I had an uncle rode with Jim Kirker down in Mexico," Arch Clement said, "and he showed me just exactly how they lifted the hair off those red niggers." The remark drew their full attention. They had all heard tales of the famous Irish scalphunter who for a time lived in Missouri.

"Well then," Bill Anderson said, grinning back at him. "I guess you can show us."

"My pleasure, Captain," Arch Clement said.

Most among them would take no scalps ever. Some thought the act unchristian—the Good Lord didn't have objection to shooting a man who had it coming, but He drew the line at going at him like some heathen after he was dead. Others didn't care for the mess of it, which so stank up a man's clothes he could hardly stand the smell of himself. Some, like Riley Crawford, never got the proper knack of it and settled for taking easier trophies if they took any at all. Ears were quick and neat, noses, triggerfingers. But even among those who would take a scalp now and again, sometimes there simply wasn't time for it. . . .

As they watched the militiamen bullying the small train of border country refugees out on the prairie this red-sun early morning, there dangled from Arch Clement's saddle ties a quartet of scalps, one of them not two days old. The crows on the elm branches were eyeing this fresher morsel, and one still drying on Butch Berry's saddlehorn. Here and there were other, older scalps—hanging from Dock Rupe's belt, flapping from each of Buster Parr's boottops, dangling from Edgar Allan's bridle. Now Bill Anderson hupped Edgar Allan out of the trees and the men fell in behind him in a proper cavalry column and they set off at a lope for the refugee train.

The militia lieutenant sat his horse and watched them come, taking them for the Federals whose uniforms they wore. As the cavalrymen drew closer he saw that the lead rider was a field officer and he effected a smart salute. His fingers were at his hatbrim when Bill Anderson's bullet passed through his eye and the back of his head spattered the horse behind him. Both horses reared in fright and the lieutenant's foot was snagged in the stirrup as he fell and his panicked horse bolted away with him bouncing and twirling alongside, his arms flapping overhead as if he were in some religious ecstasy.

Pistols popping and issuing pale billows, the guerrillas rode through them and most of the militiamen fell where they stood, some still clutching whatever refugee possession they'd had in mind to thieve. The bushwhackers then dismounted and shot them all in head or heart to dispatch alike the wounded and the feigning. Then set to taking trophies. Arch Clement rode out to where the lieutenant had come free of his horse and lay with arms and legs splayed at odd angles, and when he rode back a fresh scalp hung on his saddle.

At the first gunshot the refugees had flung themselves under the wagons. Now they were slowly showing themselves again, fearful and uncertain. The women clutched to each other and some held close the youngest children. One of them had fetched the crippled man his crutch and Ike Berry helped him get upright. The oldest boy stood apart and studied the men in Federal blue as some stripped the dead men of their ammunition and searched their pockets and some examined the militia horses and singled out a few to take with them. Then he cried out, "You ain't Feds!"

As he went through a militiaman's effects, Frank James gave the boy a crooked smile. "You complaining, son? You ruther we were?"

"You're bushwhackers!" The boy beamed. "Lookit you-all's hair! Lookit your Colts!"

"Captain Billy's wildwood boys," Ike Berry said as he replaced the emptied cylinders of his revolvers with loaded ones. He looked at the women and the crippled man, all of them agawk. "You all be sure and tell it right. It was Bill Anderson's company saved your Christian souls today."

Lionel Ward stepped up to a wounded militia horse and shot it pointblank in the head and jumped aside as the animal dropped like its legs had been yanked away. A pair of guerrillas set to skinning the hide off its flanks and haunches and then cut out thick steaks and wrapped them in shirts taken off the dead militiamen. Fresh meat had lately been hard to come by. Bill told the refugees to help themselves to all the meat they could cut off the carcass but be quick about it and get back on their way south.

RED SEPTEMBER

By the calendar it is still a few days before the start of autumn, but in this latter part of September the wildwood greenery is paling fast, some of the trees already gone purple, amber, bright blood red. Duck flocks daily arrowhead to southward. The nights carry a chill. The old folk say it's the fires. All those Yankee burnings have put too much smoke in the air for too long, they say, over too big a region. The weather's turned strange with it. The skies have the look of unseasonable frost coming on, the air has the feel of it. But then the earth could use an early winter. The world needs to slow for a time, rest itself, heal up some. Next spring will be here soon enough—and the bush war back with it.

They'd come racing back to Missouri with every Federal in Kansas on their heels. Quantrill ordered them to split up into their smaller bands and hide deep in the wildwood. Bill and his bunch had gone with Yeager's to a hideaway hard by Miami Creek in Bates County, but a few days later Yeager took his men farther east, away from the border country and its hordes of Yank hunting parties. Bill's bunch stayed in Bates, and a dozen of Yeager's boys chose to stay with them.

Although Order 11 cleared thousands of southern families from the borderland counties, there were still plenty of supporters in neighboring counties to provide food and respite for the guerrillas. Even in the borderland itself, a few seceshers had fooled the Feds into believing they were Yankee loyalists, but they were still helping the bushwhackers all they could. Union patrols continued to scour the countryside, however, and most of the guerrilla bands were staying well hid. Quantrill was keeping to Kate King's company in the Blue Springs cabin hideout and making plans for the winter move south. And once again living with them, rumor held, were the reconciled George Todd and Frances Fry.

In these last weeks of the summer of '63, only Bill Anderson's band went hunting after those who were hunting them. They followed no clear plan from one day to another but were guided by hunches, by rumors heard from pilgrims met on the trails, by information gained from the few farmers still about. Sometimes Bill let Edgar Allan go whichever way he inclined, and as the horse chose was the heading they followed. Such waywardness was not without advantage: if they themselves didn't know where they would be tomorrow, neither did the Yankees. It was a war of chance encounters and they became the masters of it. When they wanted to travel fast and far they rode at night, for no Union outfit would venture into the bush after sundown. The darkness belonged to the wildwood boys.

They roamed from Jackson County down to Vernon, ranging all of the territory evacuated by Order 11, and some days they found quarry and some days not. And some days found themselves confronted by superior numbers and having to retreat into the deeper forest. They perfected the trick of sending a handful of men into the open to be seen by a passing Union party and gulling it into giving chase to where the rest of the company lay in ambush. They now wore Federal blue more often than not, and time and again rode right up to a force of unsuspecting Yanks who would not know the truth until it was killing them.

So it went, through the end of summer and into the first fall days of that red September. And in that time Bill Anderson's company grew to forty men hard and true. His silk ribbon now held twenty knots, and stories of his exploits were told throughout the borderland.

And the stories all called him Bloody Bill.

Among them was a man named Oz Swisby, a skilled banjo-picker and singer and composer of songs which could never be sung in polite society. He'd reworked an oldtime ditty into a song about their company, and it caught the men's fancy and became a favorite.

> We're Bloody Billy's wildwood boys,
> we're riders of the night.
> We're mean-ass sons of bitches,
> and we love to fuck and fight.

Only in the deep reaches of the night did he sometimes permit himself to dwell on her. He slept but fitfully anymore, yet he never felt physically tired. He'd waken under the midnight stars and regard the immense dark mystery above him and wish that he could know if it was there by accident or design. This was the hour when he'd think of Josephine and the fierce spirit in her eyes. He would each time wonder if such a spirit, freed of the flesh, flew up like a spark off a campfire to die as ash in the blackness—or if somehow the spark burned forever in the void. He wondered if the stars themselves might not be the spirits of the dead and if comets might not be the most restless of them, the least reconciled to their fate. Was the essence of Josephine even then streaking through the endless dark of the universe? The notion was the loneliest he had ever had. Thereafter, every shooting star he saw filled him with a hollow sensation for which he owned no name.

Came a courier from Quantrill with word that he intended to start south for the winter within the week. Their brush cover was already too much reduced by the Yankee fires and the early leaf fall, and Union patrols in the region were more numerous than ever. Quantrill wanted all the bands to make the move together for the greater safety to be had in numbers. He called for a rendezvous at Perdee's farm on the Blackwater River on the last night of September. They would leave for Texas on the following dawn.

SOUTHWARD BOUND

The conjoined bands numbered three hundred men as they made their way south in a double column through the largely deserted borderland. Most of them wore Federal blue. Dave Pool was in charge of the forward scouts, and Gregg and Yeager commanded the two outrider parties that kept watch for Union patrols far out to either flank.

Bill's bunch was now well familiar with the hardships of the country they were passing through, but most of the larger company was seeing for the first time the destruction visited by Order 11. Hardly a mile of road lay unlittered with broken-wheeled wagons, smashed furniture, staved barrels and sundered trunks, scattered and tattered clothing of all description. Here and there the rotting carcasses of horses and mules, cows and pigs and dogs. Here and there a hasty human grave, most of them made too shallow and since excavated by coyotes or feral dogs, the remains devoured to ragged and disjointed skeletons. A carrion stench weighted the air, and mingled with it was the odor of ashes. Crows everywhere tittering contentedly at the glut of good pickings.

The men cursed bitterly on seeing the charred ruins of homesteads where they'd taken supper and a night's rest, where they'd entertained themselves and their hosts with music and song and stories of vengeance against redlegs and Feds. Now nothing stood of these places but blackened stone chimneys at either end of ashpits. Except for the squalling of the crows, the only daylight sound was of their own low cursings, the horses' hooffalls, the chinking of bridle rings. There were no other birds but the crows. It was strange to traverse so much sunlit country without hearing birdsong, without the sound of roosters, livestock, dogs.

"When a region goes dogless," Cole Younger said, "you know it's done for." He had decided to go south with the company this year. Of Quantrill's captains, only Andy Blunt had chosen to stay back for the winter.

There were still some dogs around, Bill Anderson said, but they kept themselves hidden in the daytime and only came out at night. He said he'd come on a pack of them at twilight just a few days ago. But he did not tell of his dismay to find he could understand nothing of what was in any dog's head, nor convey to the dogs what was in his own. He'd concluded that they must have been mad. He could think of no other explanation.

"So many of them been shot trying to protect their home," he said, "the ones left don't like to show themselves in daylight anymore."

Quantrill chuckled. "About halfway sounds like us."

George Todd was riding directly behind Quantrill and said, "Speak for yourself, Bill. *I* ain't scared of showing myself to any Fed party anytime, anywhere."

Todd had been highly mutable in his moods since the company began the ride south. The rumor was of another fight with Frances Fry at the cabin, worse than the one before, and this time Quantrill was pulled into it. A pair of Todd's boys posted near the cabin as lookouts claimed to have witnessed the whole thing. They said they heard a shriek and then the Fry woman (a right fine looker, they said) ran out into the open dogtrot with Todd directly behind her and cursing her for a goddam whore, his hair steaming and wetly plastered to his head with what looked to be coffee. She tried to kick him and he slapped her off her feet just as Kate and Quantrill came out. Kate was in a fury and demanded that Quantrill kill him, but Quantrill said killing seemed a little excessive. Kate said if he didn't do it, she would. Todd took umbrage and asked Quantrill if he was going to let the crazy bitch threaten him like that. Quantrill took offense at Todd's calling Kate a bitch and told him he'd better just mount up and go. The lookouts said the hollering scared the birds off the trees, said it must've carried for fifty yards around. Todd finally stomped off and got his horse and rode back with his men to the Sni-a-bar camp.

George had been in short temper for days afterward, but he seemed pretty much over it by the time Quantrill showed up and called all the bunches together at Perdee's. They greeted each other cordially and seemed easy enough as they sat together at the supper-fire. When they discussed the winter plan with the other captains, nobody detected any show of hard feelings between them.

But once the company set out for Texas, Todd's attitude had begun to turn contentious. He argued with Quantrill's every choice of campsite. He sniggered at his remarks on the beauty of the day-break sky or the lonely look of the ravaged countryside. Quantrill had ignored his attempts to nettle him, but it was obvious to the others that George was not entirely shed of his soreness over the cabin incident. Some believed his resentment went back to Will Haller's election over him as the company's first lieutenant and Quantrill's refusal to hold another vote.

In any case, Quantrill had clearly had enough, because this time he didn't let Todd's taunt go unremarked. He looked back at him and said, "I didn't say I was scared, George. Do *you* think I'm scared?"

Their eyes held for a moment—then Todd grinned wryly and said, "Oh hell no, Bill. I wouldn't be riding with you if I did."

"That's fine then, George. You ever think I'm scared of anything or anybody—of *any* man at all—you be sure and speak up."

"I'll do that, Bill."

Quantrill turned to Bill Anderson and winked, and Bill had to grin at the man's coolness. Still, he liked and admired both men and hoped the bristlings between them would quit.

A BANEFUL NOON

They forded the Spring River and crossed into Kansas about fifteen miles from the Indian Territory on a late spring morning under a pale yellow sun and thinly clouded sky. Dave Pool and his scouts were waiting in the shade of a stand of dusty cottonwoods on the far bank. They reported a Federal wagon train a few miles north and bearing this way along the main road. A troop of one hundred cavalrymen escorting eight supply wagons, a civilian carriage, and one wagon carrying a damn musical band.

"Must be somebody important," Dave Pool said, "having his own musicians with him and all." If they cut through the woods, Pool said, they could intercept the Yank train just west of Baxter Springs.

They debouched from the forest into a wide stretch of brown prairie cut through by a main wagon road. Quantrill directed the larger portion of the company to keep to the trees and out of sight. The sun was straight up and there was no lean at all to the shadows.

Trailing a low cloud of fine dust, the Yankee train was a quarter-mile up the road and coming at a walk, each of the wagons behind a six-mule team, the cavalry escort flanking it to either side. Bill Anderson fixed his field glass on them and saw that one of the wagons had been modified to accommodate a colorfully uniformed band of musicians. The bandsmen were laboring with their instruments and the notes of "Hail Columbia" began faintly to clarify themselves.

"Who in purple hell *are* they?" Cole Younger said.

"Listen!" Fletch Taylor said, just now catching the sound of the music. He grinned and swung his arms in the manner of a conductor.

The other wagons looked to Bill Anderson to be bearing supplies. There were several civilians in the entourage. An officer came loping up to the fore of the column and gestured toward them as he spoke with the point riders. He rode a fine gray stallion, and even at this distance his uniform was dazzling in its riot of gold braiding and polished brass, its rakish white hat plume. It was the most splendid Yankee uniform Bill Anderson had ever seen.

"There's the son of a bitch in charge," he said.

Quantrill took a look through his own glasses and said, "Oh my, he is a regal vision, isn't he?"

The Fed pointmen started toward the guerrillas at a canter.

"Coming to say howdy to their fellow bluebellies," Bill said, affecting to straighten the lapels of his Federal jacket in the manner of a fastidious officer. Quantrill laughed. The band was into a rendition of "John Brown's Body," the notes carrying more clearly as the train slowly came on.

The pointmen slowed as they drew closer. Bill could see their faces now and saw their sudden suspicion as they caught sight of the irregularities in their Union outfits, their long hair and the clutch of revolvers every man carried. The two Yanks reined up fifteen yards away.

"Howdy, boys," Quantrill called. He beckoned them forward. "Come on up."

"Oh shit," one Yank said. He turned a mournful look on his fellow, a gray-mustached sergeant who leaned out and spat a streak of tobacco, wiped his mouth with the back of his hand, and said, "Yep. And we have stepped square in it." He hupped his mount ahead another few yards and the other Yank came up beside him.

"Hello, bushwhackers," the sergeant said. He smiled sadly at his dark turn of luck.

"Partisan rangers of the Confederate nation," Quantrill said in the tone of a correcting schoolteacher. "Who's your commander?"

"General Jim Blunt," the sergeant said. "On his way to Fort Gibson. He's going to be sore disappointed about this. He thought you boys were a welcome party sent out to escort us the rest of the way."

"Blunt?" Quantrill said. *"James G.* Blunt?"

"Listen, boys," the sergeant said, "I hope you're of a mind to take prisoners because I surrender."

Bill Anderson grinned at him. "The selfsame Blunt who put in a newspaper that the only choice he'd ever give a guerrilla was the kind of rope to be hanged with?"

The sergeant made a rueful face and nodded. The younger Yank looked near to tears.

"Well now," Quantrill said. His elation was manifest. He signaled for the rest of the men to come out of the trees and form a double battle line to either side of him.

In the distance, the fancy Federal officer threw up his hand to halt the train. The band had just struck up "Tenting on the Old Campground" but then abruptly fell mute. The fancy officer peered through his binoculars and then hurriedly ordered the cavalry column into a battle line of their own. A civilian couple in a buggy drove up to speak to the officer and a moment later turned the buggy around and hastened back to the rear of the wagons.

"I'd say they're on to us, Bill," Bill Anderson said.

"*Bill?*" the young Yankee said, gaping at Quantrill. "Lord Jesus—you ain't *Bloody* Bill?" It was more plea than question.

Quantrill scowled. "Hell no, I'm too handsome to be him." He nodded at Bill and said, "That's your man right there."

Bill's Navy was already in his hand. The young Federal threw up his hands and babbled something no one understood or cared to. The sergeant went for his own sidearm in a futile but necessary try. Bill Anderson's revolver cracked twice and the Fed horses spooked and bolted as their riders tumbled.

Quantrill raised his Colt high and bellowed, "No prisoners!"

In fifteen minutes it was done with. Ninety-one Yankees lay scattered over the prairie in a dust-and-gunsmoke haze. Bill Anderson tied eight new knots in Josephine's ribbon. The company lost one man. Lionel Ward, liked by everyone, had been shot dead by a trooper who then tried to get away with the bandsmen on their wagon. John Jarrette led a dozen men in pursuit for half-a-mile before the wagon lost a wheel and overturned, scattering men and musical instruments and yanking the entire shrieking team of mules down too. The guerrillas killed every broken man of them and so many times shot the trooper who'd killed Ward that the man was rendered faceless. They set the wrecked wagon afire and flung the Yankee bodies into the flames and the air was soon steeped with the smell of their roasting.

Among the few who escaped were the couple in civilian dress. The man and woman had scrambled from the buggy and mounted on horses and galloped off side by side. The guerrillas didn't want to risk shooting the woman in trying to bring down the man and so both of them had got away.

Butch Berry shot down the horse of the fancily uniformed officer, who staggered to his feet and offered up his pistol in surrender. Butch laughed and pointed his pistol in his face and said, "Tell the devil Butch Berry says hello, General." The man's look in that instant struck him as so comical he laughed harder. "Wait! Not me! I'm—" and Butch shot him dead. Then took his scalp. Then rode over the battleground, waving the dripping trophy above his head and shouting that he'd killed General Blunt and receiving his fellows' cheers for it.

They turned out every Yankee pocket and made quick inspection of their horses and rejected them all. They found a wagonload of tinned rations and sat to a gluttonous feast of beef hash and lima beans, sardines and stewed tomatoes, peaches and spiced apples. Someone made the gladsome discovery that the Fed canteen he'd confiscated contained whiskey. Within minutes every canteen on the field had been tested and more than half were found to be holding spirits too.

"These goddam Yanks!" Buster Parr said with a wild whiskey grin. "I love them so!"

A full gallon demijohn of brandy was found in the abandoned buggy and the men presented it to Quantrill as a gift. He thanked them and poured drinks for his gathered officers. They drank toast after toast as they fed on the fine Yankee rations, and in short order not a man of them was sober.

"We did it, boys," Quantrill said. "We whipped Blunt. The regulars never whipped him, but we did, by God—we did!" It occurred to Bill Anderson that he had never seen Quantrill even mildly drunk before.

"I deserve some damn credit," Quantrill said. "A promotion! I deserve to be a major."

"Hell, why not a colonel?" Bill Anderson said.

John Jarrette thought a colonelcy was a damn right notion and raised his whiskey cup in toast of it. Cole Younger said he wouldn't follow another order from Quantrill if he was anything *less* than a colonel.

Quantrill was beaming. "Well hell, Coleman—then colonel it is!"

Every man in the party cheered the self-awarded promotion and took another drink to celebrate it.

Drunken Riley Crawford, a canteen of whiskey in one hand and a Yankee saber in the other, was slashing and thrusting at the air all about him, bellowing that he was Captain Kidd. the meanest pirate on the Seven Seas. Several bushwhackers sat nearby, eating and drinking and taking mild entertainment from Riley's besotted play. Now Crawford was backing up, swordfighting with several opponents at once and cursing them for Spanish dogs, and he stumbled on a Yankee corpse and nearly fell. He glowered at the dead man and said, "Sneak up on me from behind, will ye? Take this!" And thrust the saber into his chest.

His audience applauded, and one man called out, "You got him good, Riley!"

Crawford whirled about and narrowed his eyes at another Federal sprawled nearby and cautiously stalked toward him, saying, "And *you!* Trying to slip up on me flank, hey?" He slapped the Yankee across the shoulders with the flat of his blade. "Get up, you son of a bitch! Get up and take it like a man!"

And up the Yankee rose in a terrified scramble, thinking the boy had seen through his ruse of pretending to be dead. The blood of a head wound had run down and encircled his eyes so that he appeared to be wearing scarlet spectacles, and whether he or Riley was the more terrified would have been hard to say. The onlooking bushwhackers burst out laughing and one said, "Lookit! Young Crawford's raised the dead!"

Riley flung aside the saber and drew his Navy Colt and shot the man in the chest and knocked him supine again. Then stepped up and shot him five times more.

His audience was gasping with laughter. "Say, Riley," Hi Guess said, "are you *sure* he's done for?"

"Poor fella come back from the grave just so Riley could put him right back in it," Dave Pool said.

"Ain't it the drizzling shits, though?" Archie Clement said. "I remember shooting that rascal myself. Thought sure I killed him."

Riley Crawford, sobered to some degree by the harrowing experience, glared at Arch and said, "Well, you sureshit didn't kill him *enough*, did you?"

As always, among the effects they found on the dead Yankees were letters from home, and as they sat on the ground, gorging on Federal rations and toping on Federal drink, they scanned the missives to see if any might be worth reading aloud. By now most letters sounded the same, especially those from mothers, which too often reminded them of their own mothers and made them homesick and so they no longer cared to read mother-letters, never mind hear them aloud. Most sweetheart letters were also largely forged of sentiments so conventional it was hard to distinguish one from another—yet they sometimes contained salacious detail and so were always worth a quick scan. A company favorite was the letter Cole Younger took off a dead Yank in early summer and had since read aloud many times and still carried in his shirt, stained and creased to tatters. It contained an Illinois girl's wonderfully graphic reminiscence of the farewell fellatio she'd granted her doomed soldier boy under a walnut tree in the evening shadows while her unsuspecting parents kept to the house. It still put Cole's listeners in a hormonal agitation whenever they heard it. And there was the one John Jarrette carried, a Boston lassie's letter telling the cavalryman whose brains Jarrette splattered onto an elderberry bush that she couldn't wait to be naked with him again and be attended by The Captain, the name she'd bestowed on his member. Every time Jarrette read the passage expressing her delight in her beau's lapping attention to the "cherries" on her "milk puddings," the men yowled and bayed like hounds.

Blunt's troops, however, seemed to be sorely lacking for intrepid ladyloves. Their letters were quickly run through and discarded as yawning bores. Only Ike Berry made an interesting find, but he revealed it to no one other than his brother and the Andersons. He took them aside and showed them a small oval photograph he'd found in the jacket of a Federal corporal, a likeness of a young blonde beauty with brave dark eyes and full lips, wearing a black choker around her neck. Jim let a low whistle and Bill said she sure enough looked like something to fight a war for. There'd been no letter nor anything else in the corporal's effects to say who she might be, but the back of the picture bore an ink drawing of an artist's easel with the canvas showing an eyeball, and underneath the drawing the stamped information: NATHANIEL SOBELSKI, PHOTOGRAPHIST—HARRISONVILLE, MISSOURI.

"A Missour girl sweet on a Yank," Butch Berry said. "It's enough to make me spit."

"Butch has a point," Bill said. "She's not without serious fault."

"Nobody's perfect," Ike said. "I could get her to see the error of her misplaced loyalty."

The Andersons grinned wide and Butch snorted and spat.

But even to them Ike did not reveal the whole of his discovery.

He did not show them the small gilded locket and neckchain he'd taken off the dead man. When he'd opened the locket and seen the small tangle of dusky yellow curls nestled within, he'd stared at it for a time before accepting that it was a lock of her private hair. He'd felt of its springiness between his fingers, put it to his nose and believed he detected a faint scent of female essence. He imagined her as she applied the scissors and his chest went tight.

He was enthralled by this blonde beauty who had made her soldier boy so bold a gift. He thought of her as Rachel, a name he had always admired. He would henceforth compose nightly letters to her in his head, would praise her beauty and her daring heart, would tell her everything of himself and his deepest yearnings, would inquire after her opinions on the whirling world. He would envision her as she read his letters on a porch swing in the soft gold light of late afternoon. In nights to come he would imagine a time when the war had ceased to be, imagine himself seeking her out, wooing her, gaining her favor, declaring himself, promising to provide for her and to protect her better than the corporal ever could (the corporal unable, after all, to protect even himself). He would imagine them married and with a home and children, living on a fine tract of bottom he knew of in Ray County, making their way in this life with no need of anyone but each other and their sons and daughters. It was a life so right his eyes would go hot every time he dwelt on it.

On all of his remaining nights, just before he went to sleep, he would open the locket and touch the special hair. And if her true name was not Rachel, that was all right. He would love her, did already love her, whatever it was.

They buried Lionel Ward under a purpling maple, adding to the wide earth's mass of interred bones and bonedust, to its store of dead beyond number. The ninety-one Yankee dead they left to rot under the passing sky—two dozen of them scalped and blood-crowned, many more of them docked an ear, absent a nose, minus an index finger. The crows were already at feed on them, and the wind would carry the swelling stink with its news of the waiting feast and draw more scavengers yet. Let the damn Feds find their fellows in such state and take warning from it.

IV

The Camps

❧

1863–1864

MINERAL CREEK

They ferried across the Red River into Grayson County, Texas, on a cool October afternoon of cloudless sky and bright tangerine sun. A flock of blue herons as tall as schoolchildren rose off the upriver bank with a smooth working of wide slow wings. Bill Anderson regarded their flight and rued his lack of art to capture the beauty of it. He wondered what Poe might write about those gangly birds with their snake necks and dagger beaks and fierce mad eyes.

The ferryman spat a streak of tobacco at a watersnake wriggling near the pushpole. He told Quantrill he was smart not to try to ford the river, that there were quicksand bogs all along the Red of such size they'd been known to swallow entire wagons and their teams with them. "There's more human bones rotting under the Red than in all the cemeteries twixt here and Fort Worth," the ferryman said, showing a black grin through his stained beard.

Bill Anderson heard him and smiled. And thought the Red was a Poe river, all right.

Scouts had gone across three days ago to search out a campsite and they were waiting on the south bank to report to Quantrill. They'd found a good spot on Mineral Creek, and Quantrill said to lead the way. They rode along a trail winding through yellow grass to their stirrups, through shinnery and groves of cottonwoods squalling with crows. Just before sunset they reined up at a wide shortgrass meadow bordering the creek. Quantrill studied it carefully and then nodded. "This is it, boys. Our winter home."

There was plenty of forage for the horses, and the creek was thick with turtles, with catfish and trout. The surrounding woodlands abounded with deer and wild pig. They formed into work parties and set to hewing trees and trimming timber and constructing a cookshed and rude quarters against the coming cold. They built large stone firepits and dug slit trenches in the woods. A family of hardfaced moonshiners emerged cautiously from the trees one day to sell them excellent spirits at better prices than they'd get in town, and the guerrillas made a deal with them for two wagonloads of whiskey every week. All else they would need by way of supplies they could get at the town of Sherman, some fifteen miles to the southeast, and Quantrill and his officers established rosters for supply runs.

A courier came to them from General Henry McCulloch, C.S.A., commander of the District of North Texas, whose headquarters was in Bonham, some twenty-five miles east of Sherman. He conveyed his regards and congratulations to Quantrill and his men on their splendid victory over General Blunt at Baxter Springs. He'd heard the news from General Sterling Price himself, who was encamped in Arkansas and to whom Quantrill had sent a report about the engagement. He said he might call on Quantrill to assist in various military objectives in the Red River region. Quantrill responded with his own compliments and said he and his men stood ready to serve the general in any capacity.

At first they were content to spend most of their time in camp, making trips to town only as part of a supply detail or to visit the pleasure houses. Having lived in constant wariness for so long, they were slow to let down their guard, to believe fully that they were at safe remove from Yankee territory and its relentless hunting patrols. They passed their first weeks preparing for winter and tending to other requisite matters. They hunted and fished, smoked and jerked meat to lay by. They reshod their horses, made pistol cartridges, mended their clothes with needle and thread.

For recreation they drank and played music and sang. They had shooting contests and Quantrill usually came out the winner, although Bill Anderson won sometimes and so too did Todd. Nobody else ever won except Cole Younger and Butch Berry, who each won once. They held horse races, but Quantrill's Charley couldn't be beaten, and after a time nobody would bet against him anymore, so Quantrill proudly retired the horse from the competitions.

They got up a wrestling tournament and every man was required to ante two dollars to enter it, whether he wished to wrestle or not, and the champion would receive the full kitty. The matches in each elimination round were determined by lot and without regard to differences in size. They took place in the late afternoons with most of the company in attendance and clamoring with cheers and sidebets. Not a man refused to wrestle in his turn, not even little Riley Crawford, who within seconds of entering the ring against Dave Pool was slammed unconscious and didn't come to for twenty minutes.

Disqualification was common in the early rounds. Arch Clement had to forfeit after losing his temper in a match with Valentine Baker and kicking him so hard in the balls that Baker couldn't walk properly for a day. Buster Parr was ejected for biting off a portion of Dick West's ear when it looked like Dick was about to pin him and others had to intervene to keep Dick from getting a gun and shooting Buster.

Both of the Berrys reached the third round and then Butch lost to Cole Younger and Ike lost to George Todd. Quantrill surprised most of the men by making it to the fourth round, then came up against Todd, who repeatedly and enthusiastically threw him and seemed to prolong the match deliberately before at last pinning him down. Bill Anderson did not lose until he went up against Oz Swisby in the fifth round, and Jim made it to the late rounds before losing to big Hi Guess.

When Hi defeated Oz, and Todd at last defeated Cole Younger in an epic two-hour tussle, they were matched for the championship. Their contest lasted nearly three hours before Todd finally forced Hi's shoulders to the ground. Both of them had to be helped to their feet. Quantrill presented Todd with the prize of eight hundred dollars, and Todd raised the poke over his head with both hands and grinned at the cheers—which went even louder when he announced his intention to buy every man of the company a turn with a Sherman whore. Some of them put him on their shoulders and paraded him around the camp with others following behind and all of them singing:

> "Hurrah, hurrah! For southern rights hurrah!
> Hurrah for the bonnie blue flag that bears the single star!"

Jim Anderson nudged Bill and nodded toward Quantrill, who stood looking after the celebrant Todd and his crowd of admirers with the mien of a man watching a funeral train.

Some days later came a notice from General McCulloch's headquarters that General James G. Blunt, United States Army, was alive and well and ensconced at Fort Leavenworth, Kansas. According to accounts in the Kansas City newspapers, he had escaped the guerrillas at Baxter Springs in civilian clothes and in the company of a woman. There was no more to the message, and Quantrill asked Cole Younger and Bill Anderson if they sensed a frostiness to it.

"Got a cool tone, all right," Cole said. "Probably thinks we were lying. Hell, we didn't *know*."

"The man's disappointed is all," Bill said.

"That's no reason to call us a liar," Cole said. "He's no more disappointed than I am."

No one was more disappointed than Butch Berry. When he learned the man he'd killed was not General Blunt but only Major Somebody with a penchant for ornate uniforms, he took the man's scalp off his horse's bridle and flung it in the fire.

Toward the end of their second month in Texas the men began to get restless. They more often rode into town to take their pleasures in the cathouses and saloons. The local merchants welcomed them like heroes and saw their profits soar.

Quantrill rarely went to Sherman with his men. He preferred long solitary rides on Charley, and where he went no one knew. He spent much time at reading, in writing daily letters to Kate. She was living with her father in Blue Springs while the guerrillas were away.

He sent a rider to Missouri every week with his accumulated letters, and the courier would return with her letters to him.

But now he began to receive complaints about his men's conduct in town—reports of raw profanities bellowed within earshot of women and children, of loutish public drunkenness, of firearms discharged inside the city limits. When a sheriff's deputy tried to arrest a pair of bushwhackers who were fistfighting in an alley while some of their fellows stood by and made bets, the brawlers turned on the lawman and plunged him into a water trough and might have drowned him if W. J. Gregg hadn't come along and made them stop.

By the end of November, Sherman was lacking deputies and the sheriff rarely showed himself on the streets. While there was no denying the prosperity the guerrillas brought to Sherman, some of its citizens were having second thoughts about these wildwood boys with their rough manners and dangerous shifts in mood.

Quantrill went into town and had a talk with the mayor, then with the newspaper editor, who relayed in print his assurances to the townfolk that his men would henceforth comport themselves in better fashion. Back in camp, he called the company together and warned them against harassing the citizens. Some of the men looked sidewise at each other and arched their brows. George Todd smiled around at them and yawned behind his hand.

At first, Bill more often chose to keep to the camp than to go larking in town. Evenings he sat by a lantern with his books, days he went for walks in the woods and passed the hours along the upstream creek with no company but the chittering crows. One day he idly began to scale stones over the creek surface and the exercise suddenly put him in such vivid mind of Josephine he felt his breath seize in his chest. She had always excelled at this game and he remembered the beautiful grin she'd give him whenever she made a good throw. The memory made him feel so achingly hollow he did not return to the creek again, and started going to town with the others.

IN THE PURPLE MOON

A cold and windless December night of unseasonable rain a few days before Christmas. The small room was on the second floor of the

Purple Moon Emporium and was dimly lighted by a candle on a corner shelf. The room's plank floor only partly muted the din from the saloon downstairs—the ceaseless piano plunking and lusty singing, the laughter and bellowed conversations, the sporadic smash of glass and intermittent rebel yells. The guerrillas had bought the whole place for themselves on this night and none of the locals dared to intrude on their fun. The proprietors were a married couple named Preston, but only the missus was mingling with patrons this rowdy eve, exhorting the boys to have fun but please don't break the furniture, making sure the Negro maids kept the girls supplied with fresh towels. The rulesman—whose duty it was to ensure a proper decorum in the guests—had been granted the night off. The mister had shut himself in his office and sat listening to the guerrillas at their frolic, hoping they would not burn the place down nor maim any of the girls who were making him rich.

The room's only furniture consisted of a bed, two ladderback chairs on which hung the woman's dress and Bill's clothes and gunbelt, and two small tables, one holding a washbasin and some folded towels, the other an oil lamp with the burning wick turned down low so that the room was cast in dim amber light. The girl Bill had bought for the night was named Amanda. She was plumper than he preferred and she talked too much, but she had a pretty face and a pleasant disposition and he liked her well enough. She didn't like to be in a completely enclosed room and had asked if she might leave the window sash slightly open despite the cold weather. He'd said all right and was glad he did. He liked hearing the rainwater spattering on the ground below the window, liked the cold earth smell mingling with the warm scents of camphor and the girl's perfume. The blanket slid off his shoulders as he joined himself to her, and the chill air on his back was not unpleasant as they rocked together in the ancient rhythm.

They afterward sat propped against the pillowed headrail with the blankets pulled up to their chests and Bill smoked a thin cigar and shared his bottle with her. Except when she'd pause to take a drink, she kept up a steady patter about various subjects of little interest to him. She lived on the premises—only a few of the girls did not—and as usual she was complaining about the greedy Prestons and the high room rent they charged on top of the thirty percent they took from each girl's nightly income.

The rain was falling with a harder clatter now and when there came a rapping on the door they barely heard it for the rain and the raucousness downstairs.

"Who's there?" Amanda called. The door partly opened to admit a narrow cast of brighter light from the hallway and show a portion of silhouetted woman in a shimmy who said, "It's me, Mandy." She slipped inside and shut the door.

Amanda got out of bed and went to her. "Honey, what is it?"

The woman stood against the far wall, and palely naked Amanda put an arm around her shoulders and held her close. Bill could not clearly make out her features in the dim lamplight. She said a big drunk jasper might be coming after her. The fella had been too drunk to get it up, and after about fifteen minutes of trying to help him out, she'd told him that was enough, there were other fellas waiting to come up and he'd have to leave now. But the fella wouldn't go, and when she insisted, he shoved her back on the bed and climbed on top of her, holding her down with one hand and trying to put his limp thing in her with the other. She reached down beside the bed and got hold of the chamber pot and swung it up against the side of his head.

"You should've *heard* it," she said. Her voice was slightly raspy but Bill heard no fear in it. She knocked him clean off the bed, and when he rose up on his knees she let him have it again, harder, on the same ear, and down he went. She jumped over him and snatched up her shimmy and ran out into the hall and couldn't think what to do but come in here to hide.

"You did right, honey," Amanda said—then heard Bill laughing low and both women looked his way. He could not see their expressions in the dim light. "It ain't funny," Amanda said. "He might've hurt her."

"I'd say he's lucky she didn't beat him to death," Bill said—and grinned wide when he heard the girl chuckle.

Now a man in the hallway was shouting, "Where you at, bitch?" There was laughter and somebody yelled, "Quit that damn hollering and go down and get another one!" There was a succession of banging doors and various voices swearing at the intrusions. Bill slipped a hand under the pillow and gripped his Navy.

Their door abruptly swung inward and hit hard against the wall and the doorway showed the silhouette of a large man holding his pants up with one hand and gripping a pistol in the other.

"You little cunt!" the man said. He pointed the gun at the woman and cocked it and Amanda jumped aside.

The room shook with the flaring blast of Bill's Colt and the man lurched sideways against the door jamb and his knees almost buckled but he held upright. He turned toward the bed and started to bring his gun up again and Bill shot him again and the man fell out of view into the hall and his pistol clattered on the floor.

Bill flung the blanket off the bed, swirling the gunsmoke haze, and got up and went to the door and saw the man sitting spraddle-legged with his back against the hallway wall, his palms turned up at his sides, his chin on his chest. There was little blood, only a thin streak from a hole in his side and a thicker one from the wound over his heart. Bill stepped into the hall and pulled the man's head up by the hair to look at his face in the light of the hallway lamps. He recognized him but didn't know his name. A recent recruit to Todd's bunch. His eyes were half-closed as if he were puzzling over some difficult question. His left ear looked like a flattened plum. Bill let go the man's hair and his head dropped forward and he slid over onto his side.

Men and women in various states of undress had come rushing our of their rooms all along the hall and bunched up around Bill and the dead man, all of them talking at once and wanting to know who it was and asking Bill what happened. Some of the girls to the rear of the crowd were saying let me see, let me see, and others were saying quit shoving, goddammit. One girl said, "I like your outfit, Bill." All the men were holding guns and most wearing only pants and boots and all of them pale-skinned as ghosts. The hallway air was woven with cloying perfumes and a rankness of sweat and sex. Amanda had put on her shimmy and pulled a sheet off the bed and now helped Bill to secure it around his nakedness.

The clamor of the revelry downstairs was undiminished. Bill thought it unlikely the gunshots had even been heard down there.

His brother eased up beside him and whispered, "You hit?" Bill shook his head.

He heard George Todd say, "Make way," and the crowd hushed a little and opened up to let him pass. Quantrill had as usual not come to town, and Todd was in charge of the reveling bunch. He was in his undershirt and had a revolver tucked in the front of his pants. He stood beside Bill and looked on the upturned face of the dead man.

"Mick McCourt," Todd said. "Deserter from the regulars. Showed up in camp two weeks ago and seemed to have sufficient sand, so I took him on. What happened?"

Bill told him. Todd nodded and said, "Well, he had it coming."

He told two of the recent recruits to bear the dead man to the undertaker's. As the body was lugged away, the others started back to their various rooms, the women chittering excitedly, the men once more giving them their full attention, fondling their asses, every man and woman of them feeling more pleasurably alive for Mick McCourt's reminder of how abruptly life might take its leave.

Todd started away too, then looked back at Bill and the sheet he was wearing. He grinned and said, "Hail, Caesar."

Bill had to grin back. "The hail with you too, George."

Amanda tugged on Bill's arm and said, "Come on, sugarboy."

They went back in the room and closed the door. The chilly air smelled of gunsmoke. The other girl was standing by the window and looking out at the falling rain. "Say, girl," Amanda said as she went to the oil lamp to raise the wick. "You know who this is just saved your pretty ass?"

The other girl turned from the window just as the room brightened with yellow light, and Bill saw her clearly for the first time.

Imagine Josephine Anderson as she might have appeared had she lived another three years. True, the eyes are green rather than violet, and the hair is so much lighter it is almost blonde. But Josie might well have grown these three inches or so taller, and might well have rounded thus in the hips and gone this much fuller of breast. Might have somewhere acquired the white scar indenting her lower lip. But see how the cast of mouth is hardly unchanged, is poised as always to smile or go wry in displeasure, to make sharp mock or to laugh in delight, to give or receive a kiss. And see the familiar intensity and fearlessness of her gaze. Just so—granting the impossible difference in eye color—might she have come to look in face and form had she lived to age nineteen.

Just so did Bill behold this girl. He felt the beat of his heart in his throat. Her own eyes widened at the way he was looking at her, but she did not seem uneasy, only curious about what might be in his head and what might come next.

Amanda finally got the wick just where she wanted it, and now turned to the woman and said, "This here, I'll have you know, is none other than Bloody Bill Anderson." Then she saw how they were looking at each other. "Say . . . you two met already?"

The girl smiled at Bill and his chest went tight in a way it had not since he'd last looked on Josephine's smile.

"I can't speak for the captain," the girl said, her eyes moving quick and bright in the way Josie's did when she was mischief-bent, "but maybe we have. What do you think, Captain?"

"Hey, girl!" Amanda said. "You can just quit making those eyes. Matter of fact, you can just get your ass back to your own room."

"Amanda, honey," Bill said, "I want you to go over to my poke and take another ten from it and go someplace and have yourself a time."

"Aw, Bill," Amanda said. "We were having a good time."

"Do it now, Amanda."

"Aw, Billy . . . *damn*." She went to the chair where Bill's clothes lay and dug into his poke and extracted ten dollars. Then folded her dress over her arm and went to the door and looked back at them. "Say, Bill, how about the *both* of us?"

"Good night, Amanda," Bill said. He and the other girl had not stopped looking at each other.

"You can use my room if you want, Mandy," the girl said.

"Goddamn you, Bush Smith!" Amanda said. "I wish the son of a bitch shot you!" She slammed the door so hard behind her the lamplight wavered on the walls.

"*Bush Smith?*" Bill said.

"That would be me," she said.

"Nor a real likely name, if you don't mind my saying so."

"Is that so? Maybe I ought to change it to something more likely—to *Bloody Bill,* maybe."

"Maybe you should take off that shimmy."

"Maybe you should take off that silly-looking sheet."

They both did as they should. Then stood looking at each other for a long moment. Then were in each other's arms and could not kiss deeply enough as they staggered toward the bed and fell into it.

They made love through the night, pausing now and then to sit up crosslegged on the bed and puff Bill's pipe and have a sip or two of whiskey and sometimes they talked and laughed softly and sometimes they simply stared hard at each other before again joining together. Now the window was showing the first gray hint of dawnlight and the room was cold enough to show their breath and the Purple Moon had at last fallen quiet. They were moving together very slowly and tenderly, both of them worn and sore but in no way that called for complaint, and when they climaxed this time, it was with soft sighs and the gentlest archings and flexions.

His weight rose off her and she opened her eyes and saw him braced on his arms and staring down at her. He was crying without sound, tears running down his face, dripping from his beard.

"Oh honey, *what?*" she said. And pulled him down to her and rocked him and crooned to him as he clung and clung to her and surrendered to all his pent grief.

After a time he was done with it and they lay facing each other and he told her of his sisters. Told of Mary and Jenny who were yet prisoners in a Yankee hospital at Fort Leavenworth and both crippled and both to be exiled from Missouri. Then told of Josephine. Killed because of his failure to protect her. Told of the bad dreams that woke him every night feeling like he could not breathe for the hot tightness in his throat. He told everything. About the special closeness he and Joey had shared since her babyhood, about the ways they'd touched each other from the time she'd grown to be a girl, about the becrazing circumstance of being unable to love each other as fully as they wanted to. And about her black silk ribbon and the three dozen knots he had so far put in it.

She listened with no hint on her face of what she might be thinking, not until he remarked on the resemblance she bore to Joey, and then he saw her eyes go uncertain. He put a hand to her face and said, "Hey girl, I'm not crazy. You're not her and I know it as sure as I know she's dead. It's just that, when I saw you, I saw her too—for just a second. Then I knew I wasn't looking at her but at somebody just as special in a lot of the same ways."

"What was she like?"

He saw her in a hundred different moments in the span of a few heartbeats. "She had a way of carrying herself. A way of looking at things, of *seeing* things. She had a gentle heart but she was tough as a chain. She never shied at a damn thing the world showed her. The way she'd look at me made me feel . . . I don't know . . . like she was seeing me for who I really am. Like she knew me even better than I do."

Her gaze searched every region of his. "That's just exactly how *I* felt when you looked at *me*," she said. "You think I'm crazy or I'm lying, but it's true. And I'll tell you right now, mister, I—"

The last thing he would have thought to do just then was break out laughing—but that's what he did.

She raised up on an elbow and stared at him in astonishment. "You think I'm *lying?*"

He thought she might be set to hit him and he waved his hand in dismissal of her notion. And managed at last to tell her he wasn't laughing because he didn't believe her, but because he did.

She made a mock scowl and tugged at his beard in chastisement—then grinned hugely as he put his face to her breasts, still laughing hard, and then she was laughing too. She pulled his face up and kissed him, and the clumsiness of kissing while laughing made them laugh the harder. They laughed until their bellies cramped.

"Hey, girl," Bill said, "let's get out of here."

"Let's," she said. "And I never will come back, I promise you."

"I know it. Let's go to the hotel."

"No," she said. "Let's go to my house."

BUSH SMITH'S TALE

They ride out in her buggy, Edgar Allan trailing on a lead rope. The rain has stopped and the air is clear and cold and the horses' exhalations plume like smoke. The lower eastern sky is streaked in hues of fire above the imminent sun. Two miles north of town they turn onto a narrow lane cutting through the trees and ascending a gradual rise into the deeper wood. A quarter-mile farther, the trail debouches into a small clearing and there her place is, a one-room cabin with a porch and a small dooryard enclosed by a rail fence. There is a stable as well, next to a swift creek rimed with frost at its banks. The property will not really be hers, she tells him, until she meets the four remaining mortgage payments. He unsaddles Edgar Allan and frees Bush's horse of the traces and tethers both animals on long leads from the stable so they can drink at the creek. Then goes inside and sits at the little table near the hearth while she prepares breakfast for them and tells him who she is.

Two years ago she'd run away from her family's farm in Bates County, Missouri, along the north bottom of the Marais des Cygnes, her mother dead four years by then, her bad-tempered father a worsening drunkard. As her body had begun to assume a woman's swells and hollows, her daddy had more and more looked at her in ways a daddy ought not look at a daughter. She hated to abandon her brother Ned, two years her junior, but she figured she'd best run off before her father acted on the notions he'd been getting. She stole his horse and journeyed north to Doniphan County, Kansas, to live with a good friend named Lena Jeffers, whose family had moved up there a few months earlier. The Jeffers were impressed that she'd made the 120-mile journey by herself. They were kind and sympathetic people, and glad to take her in, knowing the sort of man her father was.

By the end of her first year with the Jeffers she was being courted by Tommy Colehammer, whose small family was their nearest neighbor. In the spring he asked her to marry him and she said yes. He gave her a small but exquisite diamond ring that had belonged to his grandmother, and they set the date for latter July. She didn't really love him—she looked Bill in the eyes when she said this—but she liked him well enough, and he was sweet and truly did love her, and he would give her what she wanted above all else in this life, a home to call her own. Tommy's daddy was going to deed them two hundred acres a little south of Wathena. They planned to build a house large enough for all the children they would have.

Since moving to Kansas she had regularly written to her brother

Ned, who rarely wrote back. Nearly illegible in their semiliterate scrawl, his periodic letters were always brief but full of complaint, mainly about their daddy, who worked him too hard. He said she was smart to have gone away and he was about ready to run off too. The only reason he hadn't done it yet was his fear of the army press-gangs roaming the countryside. He said he'd rather be a bush-whacker than get put into a uniform and made to take orders all day and get marched out to some battlefield to be blown apart by a can-nonball. She ignored his bushwhacker talk as childish fancy and wrote to him of her engagement and asked him to come live with her and Tommy, but she had not received a response. Tommy assured her that as soon as they were married he would arrange for Ned to join them.

The only guests at the wedding were the Jeffers family, who lived but a mile from the Colehammer place, and Tommy's three uncles, who shared in the ownership and operation of a hotel and adjoining livery stable in Saint Joseph, Missouri, just across the river, where Tommy himself had been born. Two of the uncles were married but childless and were accompanied by their wives. Bush would never forget the look and feel of that midsummer forenoon in the Cole-hammer farmyard, the clear sky and soft sunlight, the smell of fresh grass and the aroma of beefsides turning on spits. Puncheon tables stood laden with platters and bowls and jugs. Lena's Uncle Roland sawed on a fiddle and Tommy's bachelor Uncle Emmett plunked a banjo, and the duo sent the strains of ancient Appalachian ditties out over the Kansas plain. The preacher had just arrived and was taking a drink with the men when someone harked everyone's attention to a low dust cloud beyond the cottonwoods on Hooper's Creek and closing toward the farm from the wagon road. Conversations fell off. The music quit.

A company of riders came into view around the bend in the road, forty or so, coming at a lope and turning off the road and trampling through the Colehammer fields of wheat and corn. Their dust rolled ahead of them to fall over the farmyard as they reined up before the wedding party. The leader sat his horse in the midst of them, a man with a close blue beard and eyes that shone as if he were in fever. Every man of them wore red leggings.

Bush had never seen so many guns nor breathed such a smell as these men carried, an effluvium beyond rank flesh and tainted clothes, a malodor that seemed to rise out of something deep within them and long since gone to rot. An instinct she hadn't known she possessed prompted her to slip the diamond off her finger and hide it in her bodice.

The redleg captain accused both the Kansas and the Missouri Colehammers of giving information on Union troop movements to Joe Hart's guerrillas, who'd long been raising hell across the river in Andrew County. The Colehammers admitted to being southerners but swore they'd never given help to Hart or any other guerrillas or ever would. They produced their parole documents and showed them to the redleg captain as proof of their Union fealty. But the captain hardly glanced at the papers. The redlegs were studying the blooded horses in the corral, the good mules and excellent wagons, the well-kept barn and the large fine house.

"When I saw how they were looking around at everything, I knew what was going to happen," Bush says. She sets two plates of bacon and cornbread on the table, then refills Bill's cup and pours a cup for herself and sits down. "I was scared, of course, but I think I was mostly sad. I knew everything was just about to change, that nothing was going to be the way I had thought it would be."

One of the redlegs had been walking his horse slowly around the wedding party's wagons, then suddenly reached down into a buggy and brought up an old Mississippi rifle. "They got guns, Captain!" he shouted. Bonded southerners were prohibited from bearing arms, and there was not another gun among the wedding party.

The preacher strode quickly toward the redleg captain, shaking a finger at him and saying, "You men just hold on. That's *my* rifle and not—" But the captain drew his pistol as he shouted, "Hostile action, boys! Defend yourselves!" And shot the preacher through his top teeth.

There followed a blurred sequence of rapid action, of blasting gunfire and the screaming of men and women. Bush would never have clear memory of what she did in that time, but she vaguely recalled holding tight to one of the tables and waiting to be killed. She saw men running, being trampled by horses, saw blood jump from heads, saw men spin and fall. Little Tector Jeffers, Lena's twelve-year-old brother, was standing two feet from Bush when he was shotgunned off his feet and into an awkward sprawl of carnage and bloody bits of him spattered her white dress. She saw Tommy Colehammer running toward her and couldn't imagine what he had in mind to do. Had the poor boy been thinking to *protect* her? He was almost to her when a red spray burst from his chest and he fell dead at her feet in his handsome wedding suit.

The whole thing did not take two minutes. A mist of gunsmoke drifted over the yard. There had been eight adult men in the party and five boys grown beyond childhood and none was left alive. The only males spared were the Jeffers' youngest boys—one seven years old and another not yet four. None of the women had been harmed but for Lena's sister, who'd been nicked in the hand by a stray bullet, and Tommy's mother, who'd been knocked down by a redleg horse and her leg stepped on by another. The leg wasn't broken, but the pain had her breathing through her teeth. Bush was the only other female casualty—her lower lip had been split deeply and blood ran off her chin to add to the red stains on her dress, and how it happened she didn't know or ever would.

The raiders rounded up the livestock, loaded the wagons with the sides of beef and other foods, with plunder from the house and barn. They went from one woman to the next and took from each whatever jewelry she wore—rings, necklaces, lockets, brooches. They were laughing like they were having the best time possible, laughing right through the women's keenings.

"I cried too," Bush tells Bill. "Partly for all those good people killed—for poor Tommy. But the truth is, I was mostly crying for myself. After a bit I felt so weak and foolish for doing it that I quit."

While the redlegs were at their looting, another bunch of their fellows came riding from the south, driving before them a small herd of horses which the Jeffers women recognized. They saw now the distant smoke and knew it was rising off their own homestead. An hour later the Colehammer house and all outbuildings and cribs were burning too and the fields were afire. The redlegs at last rode off in whooping jubilation, taking with them all the horses and stock, all the wagons, and their parting dust mingled with the rising smoke.

Some of the women had needle and thread in their purses and Lena's aunt stitched Bush's lip while others cleaned and sewed and bound the arm wound on Lena's sister. Then they turned to putting away the dead. By sundown they had buried the men in graves all in a row, working with no tools but tree limbs and charred pieces of board and their bare hands. The graves were too shallow to keep off the coyotes and other scavengers that would come in the night and the women all knew it and some of them wept with this knowledge—but none said anything of it because the graves were the best they could fashion and there was nothing else to be done for it. They'd spoken little as they worked, every woman and girl of them keeping to her own reeling thoughts as she dug, as she helped drag man and boy to his grave—fathers and husbands, brothers and sons. The Jeffers women then took leave and started back to their farm with the two boys to see if they might find anything worthy of salvage. They departed into the gathering twilight, bereft refugees scruffing down the road.

"Even though the wedding never did happen," Bush tells Bill, "the Colehammers made me feel like I was part of their family just the same. What was left of the family, I should say. It was only Tommy's momma Caroline and his twelve-year-old halfwit sister Florence and his uncles' two widows. The widows said we could live with them in their hotel in Saint Joseph, so that's where we headed."

Bill listens without interruption. Their breakfast plates are still untouched.

They walked five miles to the river and then went north another two miles to the ferry crossing. The women plucked pennyroyal and crushed it with their fingers and rubbed its pungent sap on their faces and arms to keep off the mosquitoes. As they walked through the night, Bush took inexplicable solace from the low quarter moon and the countless stars that had endured since God's shaping of them who could say how long ago—and strange comfort too from the river's utter indifference to the events of that day or any other.

They had not a dime among them but the ferryman took pity and carried them over for free. When they arrived on the street where the hotel stood, the eastern sky was red as an open wound. A few people about at that early hour saw them shambling past and could only gape at their spectral aspects.

She was shown to a room and there slept the rest of the day, sweating and twitching with bad dreams. When she woke to a shaft of sunlight slanting through the window, her first thought was that she would not stay with this brood of new widows. After bathing, she put on the clean dress the aunts had provided, then joined them all for supper and ate two helpings of everything, despite the red pain of her bloated lip.

That night, when everyone else was asleep, she eased down the hall to the room where Emmett Colehammer, the bachelor uncle, had lived, and put on an outfit of his clothes. She turned up the pant-leg bottoms to her ankles, belted the pinched waistband with a rolled bandanna, folded the shirtsleeves to her wrists, stuffed her hair into a gray slouch hat to achieve a slightly better fit as well as the male disguise she was after. His boots were large for her, of course, but Uncle Emmett had not been a big-footed man, and a double pair of thick stockings took up much of the looseness of their fit—with still enough room in the toe to hide her ring. She was glad for the absence of wall mirrors.

She went downstairs and into the kitchen, found a sharp knife and slipped it into her bandanna belt, then filled a sack with cold bis-cuits and several tins of food without even looking to see what kind it was. Then she went out and across the sideyard to the hotel livery. She'd prepared an elaborate lie to tell the stableboy but no one was in there, though a lantern was burning bright on a shelf. She spied a cowhide jacket on a wall peg and took it, thinking it would do a bet-ter job of concealing her breasts than did the baggy shirt alone. She saddled a strong-looking mare and tied her food sack to the saddle-horn, then stepped up onto the horse and hupped away. By sunup she was twenty miles to the south and still going.

Her notion was to return to her father's farm (she refused to call it home), collect Ned and move on, though she had no idea where they might go. Her brother was almost sixteen now and she under-stood his fear of being forced into an army uniform. She thought that if they disguised him as a woman they might fool any pressgangs they ran into—but then again, they might attract even more notice from every man they encountered.

Such were her thoughts as she bore south, ferried over the Big Muddy, skirted Kansas City, and held to the lesser trails down through the border country. She slaked her thirst at water crossings, fed on biscuit and peaches or hash or beans, whatever canned good she drew from the sack. Each time she met with horsemen or wagon travelers going in the other direction, she'd tug her hatbrim lower and simply raise a hand if the other party hallooed as they passed. She had thought her outsized costume might raise curiosity, but found it was in keeping with the motley dress of these met pilgrims. She made her nightcamps in the woods, well off the trail, but made no fire that might attract passersby.

"I was a woman alone in bad country," she says. "I didn't even have a gun. I'm not without sand, Bill, but maybe you understand my caution."

Bill reaches across the table and holds her hand.

The bad country she spoke of had suffered so greatly in the wake of Order 11 she hardly recognized it. "I'd heard how terrible things had been," she says, "but I never imagined. So *many* places burnt to the ground. Everywhere you looked there was nothing standing but black chimneys."

"I know," Bill says.

She was three days getting to her daddy's place and found there nothing but charred ruins which looked to have been that way for some time. At the weedy edge of the woods behind where the barn had stood, she found no new gravemound beside her mother's. She walked slowly through the ashy remains of house and barn and found no bones that looked human, only a cow skull and ribcradle. Her urge to cry was mostly self-pity—she'd never felt so alone in the world—and she did not yield to it.

She rode to Red Hill, a hamlet where her family had regularly bought supplies. It too had been razed. Of the original dozen buildings, only one still stood, the old general store, though its shelves had long been barren. The remnants of two families were living there, and the only men among them were a few young boys, a very old man, and a pair of twenty-year-old cripples—one legless and the other blind. But the old man remembered her daddy, and some of the women now recognized her and asked her to step down for a cup of hickory tea. When she asked what had happened to the town, they looked around as if to see what she might mean. Then someone said, "Yankees—what else?"

One of the women gestured at Bush's lip and said, "You seen a recent hard time yourself, sister girl." Then looked closely on the lip and said it looked sufficiently sealed for the thread to come out. "You'll have a scar to the grave," the woman said, "but the sooner the stitches come out, the less of a sight it's like to be." So Bush let her snip and pluck. When the job was done, the lip felt bulbous. She looked at it in a hand mirror and saw that it was still grossly swollen and the cut still looked raw. "Too bad," the woman said. "Pretty thing like you."

They were sorry to say they had no idea what had become of her daddy, but there were rumors about the boy Ned. One story was that he'd joined a band of bushwhackers in the early spring and was killed shortly after, though no one knew where or even if any part of that story was true. The old man said he'd heard Ned Smith went to Texas, to Fort Worth, but he didn't remember where he heard it.

Bush refused to believe he was dead, but there was no way to know if he'd truly joined a guerrilla band, or, if he had, which one it might be. She could think of nothing to do but go to Fort Worth and seek for him, though the women all advised against it. Nothing but ill fortune could come to a woman alone on the trail. She'd been awful lucky so far not to have met with bad trouble, they told her, but if she rode on by herself her luck was sure to run out. She thanked them for their concern but would not be dissuaded. The next day she set out, provisioned with a sack of hoecakes and raw turnips and a few ears of roasted corn.

Her luck held most of the way through the Indian Territory and then finally ran out two days north of the Red River. She was wakened one morning by the barking of a scruffy yellow dog glaring at her from the shadowy brush in gray dawnlight. The mutt would not be run off by the stones she threw at it, but kept barking and barking and dodging the rocks. Pretty soon here came a pair of riders out of the gloomy scrub. She quickly stuffed her hair in her hat and buttoned up her jacket, then stood with legs apart and hands on hips in the way of a man unafraid. The horsemen reined up at the edge of the clearing where she'd picketed the mare, and even in the weak light she could see their grins. One was big and full-bearded, the other only mustached. The mustache was playing out a length of lariat from the coil in his hand.

They spared no breath on amenities. "Know why that dog's barking at you?" the bearded one said.

She gave a shrug and said in a gruff voice, "Don't like strangers, I guess."

"It's trained to sniff out quim," the bearded one said.

She broke for the brush behind her but the lariat noose looped lazily over her head and shoulders and abruptly snugged taut and yanked her down. She tried to get to her feet as they dismounted, but the mustached one gave the rope a hard snatch and down she went again. As they closed on her she kicked out and caught the bearded one on the shin and he yelped and fetched her a kick to the ribs that blew the breath out of her. The mustached one said, "Don't, Wallace," and stepped between them. He knelt beside her and slipped the rope off her. Her vision was blurred by tears of pain and she was still gasping for breath as he eased her over to her bedding, then used her own knife to cut through her bandanna belt and the buttons of her pants, all the while saying, "Easy, easy now," in the tone she'd heard wranglers use on horses they would break. He tugged off her boots and threw them aside, then pulled off her baggy pants and handed them to the bearded one, who searched them for money and cursed and flung them away.

They didn't pluck any flower. She had surrendered her maidenhead to Tommy Colehammer one twilit evening a couple of months earlier in the Jeffers barn, in full agreement with his reasoning that all they were doing was getting a head start on what they'd be doing plenty as man and wife, and they'd done it a bunch more times in the days to follow. But it's a whole different thing when a couple of hardcases figure to just help themselves. She had thought to fight them, then realized she'd suffer the worse for it and they'd still have their way, so she simply lay there and let it happen. They each had a turn with her, and what she chiefly remembered about it was the dog lying on its belly beside her and looking at her as if it wondered what she might be thinking. After spending himself, the bearded one tried to kiss her but she turned her face away, and the mustached one said, "That's all right, Wallace. She ain't got to if she don't want. That lip don't look all that kissable noway."

Bill's grip is now so tight on her hand she winces and says softly,

"Bill." He eases his hold and lets a long breath. *Wallace*, he tells himself. *With a beard.*

"Maybe I shouldn't have told you," she says. "I want you to know everything."

"I'm grateful," Bill says. "You know who they are? Where they went?"

She shakes her head.

"I'd find them, you know. Settle it proper."

She smiles tiredly and pats his hand. "I know you would. That's not why I'm telling you."

"I guess I know that," he says. *Wallace. With a beard.*

Then they were gone, men and dog, and the mare gone with them. The risen sun was hot on her legs when she finally got to her feet, grunting with the pain of her kicked ribs and grimacing at the soreness in her sex. She put on her pants and gathered her boots and the ring was still in the one. She rolled up her bedding and tucked it under her arm and hiked out to the main road and headed on south.

She remembers little of what passed through her mind over the next couple of days except for the awful thought that if she found herself pregnant she wouldn't know whether it was by Tommy or one of those sonsofbitches—a fear that would be relieved a week later with the onset of her menses. She kept a sharp watch for the dust of riders coming from either direction and each time she spied it she took to the trees or shrubs to hide until the horsemen were past. There were streams where she could drink all along this route, but by the afternoon of her second day of walking she was ravenous. At dusk she could smell the river not far ahead, and then suddenly caught a savory smell of cooking that made her moan in hunger.

What she smelled was a rabbit stew simmering on the hearth of the ferrymen's cabin. There were two of them, partners who took turns operating the ferry. When she presented herself on the shadowed porch and asked if she might have something to eat, they stood in the door and gawked at her as if uncertain of what they were looking at. Then one said, "You got money?"

She wasn't about to trade a diamond for a plate of stew. The alternatives were that she could go without eating or she could pay them some other way. In that moment, she knew what she was about to become, but she was too tired and too hungry to argue with herself about it. She stepped forward into the better light and took off her hat and shook her head and her hair tumbled down. The ferrymen's faces came alight. They grinned at each other and then at her. "Well now, darlin," one said, "we might could strike a bargain."

"I thought maybe we could," she said.

There were several lighted oil lamps in the room and she picked one up and asked if they had a candle. The men looked at each other and then one of them went into the other room and came out with a thick short candle fixed to a tin holder. She said it would do just fine and asked him to light it, then took it from him and said she'd be back directly and went into the small sideroom and closed the door. She dropped her pants and squatted, scooped some of the fresh wax drippings off the tin plate with her finger and fashioned a small shallow cup on the end of her thumb, then inserted the cup as far up inside herself as she could. She didn't recall where she'd heard of this method to protect against conception, was not even sure it worked, but she was glad it came to mind. For all she knew she was already pregnant, but if she wasn't she didn't intend to get that way if she could help it. She then opened the door and said she was ready.

After the business was done with, they fed her well and gave her a blanket and permitted her to sleep on the floor in the sideroom. Twice in the night she was awakened by travelers hallooing the ferryhouse for a crossing. She heard men's voices and laughter, horse snortings, hooves clomping on ferry planks, splashings. She was surprised the ferrymen left her undisturbed through the night, but not at their smirking announcement in the morning that for the same price she paid last night they'd give her breakfast and see to it she got a safe ride to Fort Worth in the bargain. On impulse she informed them that the price of the same treat they'd enjoyed last night was a full plate of breakfast, a ride to Fort Worth, and a dollar apiece. She'd said it with a confident smile, though in truth she was afraid they'd get angry and simply take what they wanted.

But all they did was haggle. Seeing as she was getting breakfast *and* a ride too, they said, one dollar ought to cover for both of them. They bargained back and forth and finally settled on a dollar and a half, breakfast and a ride. As she pocketed the money and headed into the sideroom with the first of them, she thought to herself, Well girl, there's no question about it now.

She pauses in her story to stare hard at Bill across the table. "Do you understand?" she says. "I chose it, Bill. Nobody was forcing me. Oh, I was still hungry, but I wasn't starving. And I always did have a diamond ring right there in my boot."

"I'm not judging you on it," Bill says. "Not now nor ever."

"I just want you to know the truth of it," she says.

"I'm knowing it," he said.

"Well then, I'll finish telling it and be done," she said.

After breakfast she went down to the landing with the ferrymen and waited for a wagon which might carry her to Fort Worth. But only horsemen, solo or in bunches, presented themselves for crossing all that morning and into the afternoon. The sun was midway down the sky when there came a wagon driven by a graybeard acquaintance of the ferrymen. He was taking a load of hardware supplies to Sherman and was armed as heavily as a bushwhacker. Sherman was as far as he was going, but he knew some dependable transport men in that town who delivered to Fort Worth and would be glad to take her there. She said all right and climbed aboard.

The old man was glad of her company and didn't mind sharing his food with her if she'd do the cooking that night. She had thought she'd have to strike a special deal with him too, but his only interests in her were as cook and auditor. He chattered happily about his days in Sam Houston's army and the great fight at San Jacinto and didn't seem to mind that she only half-listened and didn't say much herself. At one point he jutted his chin at her, his eyes on her lip, and said, "Met with a mean fella, did you?" She wasn't up to explanations and only shrugged. She studied the Red River country they passed through and she thought she would like to live in it.

At sundown they were still about eight miles from Sherman, and so they put down for the night in a pasture hard by a wide swift creek. She helped the teamster unharness the mules and tether them in the creekside grass, then borrowed a shirt and pants from him and went upstream into the thicker brush and washed her clothes and bathed herself by the light of the early moon. While they ate supper, her clothes dried on a fireside log.

Her sleep that night was restless, troubled by one bad dream after another, all of them of Ned, though she couldn't recall any details each time she'd wake up except that he rode a white horse and his face was unearthly pale. As they set out the next morning, she quite suddenly knew she would not find him in Fort Worth, knew it without knowing how, but knew it in her bones.

They were still a few miles from town when she glimpsed a portion of chimney through the trees on a rise about a quarter-mile into the woods. A short way farther on, nailed to a tree at the head of a narrow lane branching off the road, a hand-painted sign read CABIN FOR SALE—GARP REALTY and had an arrow pointing down the lane. The thought of owning a little house all of her own tightened her chest with longing—and all in a moment she knew what she wanted to do and thought she might know how to do it.

Then they were rolling down the main street of Sherman and she liked what she saw. The old man knew the town and drove directly to the back street warehouse receiving his delivery. He drew up the team and said he'd see about getting her a ride to Fort Worth, but she said never mind, she'd decided to stay in Sherman. The teamster gave her a puzzled look, then shrugged and wished her well.

Her first stop was at the Hastings & Son jewelry store, where she presented the diamond for appraisal. The elder Hastings arched a brow at her outsized getup, but he was impeccably polite. He studied the ring carefully for a minute and then tendered an offer. She didn't know if he was being fair or had sensed her desperation and was playing on it, but it was more money than she'd ever had of her own, and she didn't know what else to do, so she accepted it.

She next went into Regina's Dress Shoppe, and when she emerged she was a vision in a blue dress with hat and parasol to match. She had no trouble finding the office of Garp's Realty. She described the location of the cabin whose chimney she'd spotted from the road, and Mr. Garp said, "Oh yes, that property." The man who'd built it had suddenly taken a notion to go to California, and Garp had bought the place at a bargain price, but freely admitted he was sorry he had. The place had stood unoccupied for the last eight months. It was too small for a family, too far from town for anyone whose trade was in Sherman, too close to Sherman for anyone wanting nothing to do with a town. "Which is why," he said, "you can get it for a real bargain yourself, little lady."

He drove her out to the place in his buggy. She admired its excellent construction, its well-chinked walls and solid plank floor, its stone fireplace with an ample hearth, its few but sufficient pieces of rude furniture. She strolled a portion of the grounds—the entire property covered nearly fifty densely wooded acres and included a portion of creek—and she knew it was the home she'd longed for. He said he was tired of holding on to it and was ready to let it go for hardly more than he'd paid himself. He quoted a price. She countered with an offer of half that amount. He grimaced. He said he would come down fifteen percent. She repeated her offer of half the original price and asked who else would buy the house, considering all the drawbacks he himself had pointed out. He said he'd go down twenty percent, even though he wouldn't make enough on the deal to cover the cost of the ink on the deed. She held to the half. He sighed in huge exasperation and said he would come down by twenty-five percent and that was it, take it or damn well leave it.

They settled on a price thirty percent below his original quote. The money she'd made from the sale of the diamond—excluding what she'd spent on clothes and the portion she'd set aside to buy a horse and buggy—was short by about a third, so when they got back to Garp's office they worked out a one-year mortgage plan to pay off the balance. Then went together to the bank and secured the loan, the property itself serving as collateral, and the deal was done.

"I'd hoped to have enough to buy the place outright," she tells Bill, "but I guess I already knew what I'd have to do if I came up short."

At the livery where she purchased a fair horse and an adequate buggy, she made a discreet inquiry of the liveryboy, who looked a year or two younger than herself but old enough to know the information she sought. After a moment's stunned gawk, he gave her the street directions she wanted—and with a grin said he'd be sure to pay her a visit. She winked at him and felt a blush that was probably as bright as his.

On the next block, a street lined with saloons and gaming halls, she found the Purple Moon, where she asked a thin-eyed bartender if she might have a word with Mrs. Preston. A half-hour later they'd made an arrangement whereby she could use an upstairs room every evening for the cost of two dollars plus thirty percent of her night's take. In addition to the room, she would have the protection of both

Mr. Preston and the Purple Moon's rulesman, a burly fellow whose specific duty was to deal with troublesome customers.

"Not much chance of some fella doing you here like that one did," Mrs. Preston said, gesturing at Bush's lip. She suggested that Bush rent living quarters in the place, but Bush told her she had a home, thank you—and the truth of it filled her with pride. She had anyhow told herself she'd live in a packing crate in an alleyway before she'd live in a whorehouse. To her mind, it was one thing to earn your way as a whore, another to actually live like one, and however narrow that distinction, she was determined not to lose sight of it.

Her four months at the Purple Moon have been more profitable than she'd hoped. She has made double payments on the mortgage from the start, and only a third of the bank loan remains outstanding.

She rises from the table, retrieves the coffeepot and refills their cups. If she's concerned about how she will finish paying the loan, now she has renounced her trade, she makes no mention of it. Bill cannot get enough of looking at her, of breathing her scent. She returns the pot to the hearth, then laughs as he catches her arm and pulls her onto his lap. They cannot keep from grinning even as they kiss and run hands over each other. Bill carries her to the bed and their clothes sail through the room.

She's never stopped fretting about her brother, of course, has not passed a day without wondering where he might be. When she heard that Quantrill's company had made its winter camp at Mineral Creek, her first thought was that maybe Ned was with them. She questioned every bushwhacker she serviced at the Purple Moon. The first few said they'd never heard of Ned Smith, but there were a lot more guerrilla bands other than Quantrill's, they told her, with winter camps all over Arkansas and Texas, and maybe he was with one of them.

Then about two weeks ago a young bushwhacker with a ruined thumb he said had been made that way by Quantrill's horse said sure he knew Ned Smith, a real good fighter for a boy naught but sixteen years old. They'd ridden together with Andy Blunt, one of Quantrill's captains. Blunt had stayed in Missouri this winter to be near his sweetheart and protect her family and neighbors from Unionist raiders, and about half of his boys, including Ned Smith, had chosen to stay with him.

She was greatly relieved to know her brother was alive—but for two weeks now has been frantic to think he might be killed any day by Federals or the militia.

She tells this to Bill in the aftermath of their lovemaking on this first morning together in the cabin. He strokes her hair and says, "Blunt's sweetie lives on the Blackwater, in Johnson County, and he's got camps all around there. Shouldn't be hard to find him. Suppose I send somebody up there to fetch young Ned?"

She hugs his neck so hard he affects to be strangling.

Nuptial notice

That afternoon he rode out to the Mineral Creek camp. Most of the men were gathered around high crackling fires, talking and joking, playing cards on blankets spread on the ground. He was greeted with japery and winks and questions of where he'd been keeping himself and what her name might be. He sat his horse and looked around at them, smiling wryly and nodding at their jibes—and he had a moment's clear realization of how dearly he held these rough comrades. He scanned the camp but did not see Quantrill anywhere. "Muster round, boys," Bill said, "I have a notice for you."

Speaking loudly, wanting to be heard by all the men in camp, not only the closely gathered of his own command, he announced that he and Miss Bush Smith would be getting married in Sherman tomorrow, in the office of the justice of the peace.

The joking and laughter fell off to murmurs and scattered uncertain chucklings. The men were looking at him with ready grins, as if expecting the rest of a half-told joke. Bill smiled around at them and said if anyone was wondering if the Miss Bush Smith he would wed was the same Bush Smith some of them had been entertained by on the second floor of the Purple Moon, the answer was yes. But Miss Smith was now retired from the profession and his gain was their loss.

The assembly had hushed but for the low-voiced questions

snaking through it. He say *marry*? The one with that scar on her mouth, *that* one?

"I'm serious as a preacher, boys," Bill said. "I love the woman and will marry her tomorrow. I'm saying it to every man of you so there's no misunderstanding. So nobody can say he didn't know. So nobody will ever make an unkind remark about it without intending to. I would hate to kill somebody, especially a friend, for an unkind remark about it that he did not intend."

In the sudden silence he saw his brother in the crowd, face ajar, saw Butch Berry looking at him as if he wasn't quite sure who he was, saw Cole Younger leaning against a barrack wall and smiling, pausing in his whittling to tip his hat to him, and Frank James too, smiling wide.

And then Sock Johnson hollered, "Well, goddam, Bill, that's just *grand*!"

"Congratulations, Bill!" Ike Berry shouted. At the outer edge of the encircling company, Dick Yeager raised a fist in salute.

Then somebody was shouting, "Hip, hip, *hooray*!"—and every man in the company joined in: *"Hip, hip HOORAY!"*

Bill raised his hands to quiet them and said the ceremony itself would be a private affair in the JP's office attended by only his brother and the Berry boys, but they were all invited to be at the celebration in the Purple Moon directly following the nuptials, and the drinks were on him. There was a chorus of happy approval and then somebody began bellowing "For He's a Jolly Good Fellow" and the others quickly took up the song.

W. J. Gregg pushed his way through the crowd and yelled, "Unass that horse, Anderson!" Bill slid off Edgar Allan and Gregg clasped him in a hearty bearhug as others pressed around them and slapped Bill's back and shoulders and punched him in the arms and called him a sly sonofabitch and a goddam rascal and a good old boy. Arch Clement, redfaced and beaming, took Bill's hand in both of his and pumped it hard. It was the only time he would ever see Archie look touched by tender emotion, and he grinned at the boy and patted his shoulder in thanks.

Then Jim was gripping his hand and saying, "I'm damn glad for you, Billy."

"Well, I'm damn glad you're damn glad, Jimbo," Bill said.

Jugs began making the rounds and a fiddler struck up "Pretty Polly." A jug came to Bill and he hoisted it high and bellowed, "To all you fine sons of bitches!" Big-bearded Dave Pool held his own jug aloft and shouted, "To *you*, Bloody Bill—and your darling bride!"

Now George Todd was at Bill's side with an arm around his shoulders, offering his own toast: "Here's to a dozen sons brave as their daddy!" Bill asked him where Quantrill was, and Todd shrugged and said, "Off on one of his rides and mooning about the Kate girl, I guess. The only reason he didn't bring her down here, you know, was he would've had to let other fellas bring *their* sweeties, and then what kind of camp would this be?" He showed an enormous grin. "I'd say he's gonna be *real* surprised about this."

"I'd like him to be at the celebration," Bill said. "Tell him when you see him."

"Oh, I will," Todd said.

They drank several healths all around and then Bill said he had to go, he had a matter to tend to. The remark drew laughter and whistles and joking comments about the matter's name being Bush Smith. He made an obscene hand gesture at the jokesters and remounted Edgar Allan and called for them to listen up, he had a couple of other things to say. Because he would be living with his wife, he was putting his brother Jim in command of his bunch here in camp and naming Arch Clement as Jim's lieutenant. The other thing was that two of them wouldn't be at the celebration tomorrow for sure because he needed them to go up to Missouri and find Andy Blunt's company and bring back his bride's brother, a boy named Ned Smith.

Ike Berry and Valentine Baker were the quickest to volunteer and Bill gave them the mission. They both had personal reason for going and he knew it. Valentine Baker's wife was living with her family in Johnson County and not far from Warrensburg, where Blunt's sweetheart lived, and this was a chance for Baker to have a quick visit with her. As for Ike, he had not quit mooning over the blonde girl in the photograph he'd taken off the dead Yank, and Bill had no doubt he intended to go to the Harrisonville studio where it had been made and see if he could find out who she was. As Bill hupped Edgar Allan out of the camp, Ike and Val were already making ready to ride.

* * *

When he got back to the cabin the sky was firestreaked above the fled sun and a chill tide of evening shadow was rising out of the woods. The trees shrilled with roosting crows. He delighted in the sight of the smoking chimney, the front window pale with lamplight. He put Edgar Allan in the stable and came back around to the dooryard gate and saw her waiting for him on the porch, smiling, her hands out to receive him.

They stood on the little porch with their arms around each other in the dying light of day. After a time he said, "Got something for you," and took an envelope from his coat and gave it to her.

It was the deed to the property, paid in full. She stared and stared at it in the twilight and then carefully refolded it and replaced it in the envelope. When she looked at him again her eyes were bright and brimming.

"You would've got it yourself, anyway, sooner or later, " he said. "Turned out sooner. It's your house now, girl."

"*Our* house," she said. She took his hand and pulled him to the door. "Now let's just go in here and seal the bargain, mister."

A REMONSTRATION

They drove to the JP's office in her buggy and arrived just before noon. There was little traffic on the street this cold gray day, few pedestrians on the sidewalks. Icicles were dripping from the eaves of the gallery where Jim and Butch stood waiting for them. Quantrill too. Bill helped Bush alight from the buggy and introduced her first to Jim and Butch, and they both touched their hatbrims. It was Butch's first sight of her and he was staring hard with his good eye. When she smiled at him he reddened and cut his gaze away.

Bill turned her toward Quantrill and said, "Darlin, this is Bill Quantrill—*Colonel* William Clarke Quantrill. Bill, this is Bush."

Quantrill took off his hat and bowed to her in the grand manner of a cavalier, the effect enhanced by the Confederate greatcoat he wore. "Dear lady," he said, replacing his hat, taking her hand and kissing it. "An honor." His eyes were bright and redstreaked, and Bill suspected he'd been drinking at this early hour, something he'd not known him to do before.

"The honor is mine, Colonel," Bush said. She was redcheeked from the cold and wore a lovely yellow dress of her own making under her partly open woolen coat.

Quantrill showed her his best smile and dipped his head modestly. Then asked if she would mind terribly if he took a quick minute of Captain Anderson's time for a private word.

Of course not. She turned to Bill, whose gaze on Quantrill had gone thin, and said she would wait for him in the office, out of the cold breeze. Jim Anderson gave her his arm and they went inside, and Butch followed after.

Quantrill gestured for Bill to come away from the JP's door, then stood with his hands behind his back. "Tell me, William T.," he said, "what are you doing?"

"Getting married, Bill," Bill Anderson said, making no effort to hide his irritation, "as if you didn't know. Now you tell me: what's so important we have to talk about it this minute?"

"I was told you were getting married," Quantrill said. "But I refused to believe it unless I heard it from you."

"Well, now you have," Bill Anderson said, vexed the more by Quantrill's tone of condescension. "What do you want, Bill? I've got a bride waiting."

"All right, then, to the point," Quantrill said. "A married man wants to be with his wife. He wants to have children, he wants to *settle*. It's *why* he gets married. There aren't many bushwhackers with wives, as you well know, and those few are the most miserable among us. There's not a minute they don't miss home, not a day they don't fret about their women. If they have children, their torment is all the greater. You know the ones I speak of, you've seen them. Mopers to a man. Every bushwhacker I've known to quit the war was a married man. So, what I'm wondering is, are you thinking to quit the war, William T.?"

He was surprised by the question—and by his realization that it had come to him yesterday but he had not recognized it. It had come as a vague and shadowy distraction at the edge of his mind the moment he'd asked Bush to marry him and she'd said yes. It had held itself just beyond the shaping reach of thought, but now he realized it had *felt* like a question, and the feeling had lingered with him since. And here Quantrill had set it in front of him as obvious as a wall.

"If you're thinking to quit," Quantrill said, "I hope you'll think about it real well. The whole Yank army this side of the Mississippi knows you and it's not about to forget you just because you leave off fighting and get married and take up raising kids and hogs. They'll hunt you down and kill you whether you're holding a Colt or a plow handle, and they won't give a damn if you got ten children and a wife expecting another. A graveyard parole's the only kind you and me are ever going to get from the Federals, William T. The only way around it is to fight them till we win or lose. That's why no man of us should marry till this war's done with. 'He who hath a wife and children hath given hostages to fortune.' Sir Bacon said it well."

"Whether I marry or not, whether I quit the war or don't," Bill Anderson said, "it's none of your goddam business or Sir Bacon's either."

His anger was with himself as much as with Quantrill's effrontery, and he knew it. It angered him that he had avoided the question until now, that he had kept from it because he was unsure how he might answer it—or worse, be unable to answer it—and the mere possibility of a lack of resolution enraged him.

"Every bunch at the camp has its captain with them but yours," Quantrill said. "You belong with your men, William T. I can't see you behind a plow."

"Go tell it to somebody who cares a damn what you can see," Bill said.

He turned and stalked back to the JP's office, paused at the door to compose himself, then smiled and went inside, saying, "Here comes the groom!"

Following the ceremony, the newlyweds went across the street to a photographist's studio and posed for a marriage picture, Bush seated and smiling prettily, holding a bouquet of paper flowers, Bill standing behind her with his hands proprietary on her shoulders, his aspect seriously matrimonial. Then each sat for an individual portrait for the other to carry. Hers shows a beautiful bright-eyed woman with shining hair and a smile indented by the scar on her mouth. His would be the likeness of him most widely reproduced in all the years to come. By all accounts, he was the handsomest of the Missouri guerrillas, and this picture stands in clear evidence of the claim. He has a hand to his coat lapel in the popular and affected pose of the day, his high-cheekboned face unmarked by blemish or concern, eyes cool with self-possession, beard trimmed close but black mane rampant, dark longcoat buttoned but leaving visible the laced lapels of his guerrilla shirt, hatbrim rakishly upturned and with a pale star stitched to it, a gleaming buckle on a wide belt holding a cartridge case and a holstered revolver on either hip. The only photographs of him that will ever be as widely seen as this one are the pictures that show him dead.

Then to the Purple Moon, where they were greeted by cheers and applause, and the celebration that ensued was a raucous affair. Despite the short notice for the occasion, the girls of the Moon were all present and in their finery, and the guerrillas took turns dancing with them to the lively strains of a string band and the Moon's pianist. There were barrels of whiskey and beer. Sides of beef roasted on spits behind the building. Bill and Bush had the first dance and then his comrades began taking turns with her on the floor. He was congratulated again and again, until his arms ached from comradely punches and his back was sore from glad poundings.

He was aware of Quantrill's absence—and of Butch Berry's. Immediately following the ceremony in the JP's office, as Jim and Arch in turn hugged and kissed the bride, Butch had shaken Bill's hand listlessly and said, "I see why she's so special." His face bespoke a welter of emotions, and Bill knew he was referring to Bush's resemblance to Josephine. "She's special all in her own way, Butch," he said.

"I'm sure," Butch said, and left. And was not here now.

Now Buster Parr was cutting in on George Todd for his turn with Bush. Todd kissed her hand and gave her over to Buster, then came to stand beside Bill. "That's a darlin wife you got yourself, old hoss," he said. "You're a lucky fella."

Bill smiled. "I cannot dispute you, George."

Todd relieved a passing bushwhacker of his jug, raised it high and said, "To love and long life," and took a deep drink. He passed the jug to Bill, who nodded and drank to the toast.

"I don't see the colonel anywhere," Todd said, affecting to search the crowd. "I guess a man with his responsibilities ain't got the time." He looked at Bill and shrugged. "Course now, I can't say he was too awful pleased by the news."

"I can't say so either," Bill said.

"When he told me he thought it was a mistake for a bush-whacker to marry," Todd said, "I said to him, 'You know, there's talk you and Kate got married not so long ago.' And he says, 'Hell, that was only a lie I started myself so nobody would think she was a damn whore—or ever had been.' It was all I could do to keep from saying, 'Well, she's maybe never been a whore, but she's certain sure always been a cunt.' "

He went off to dance with a laughing blonde, his words still sounding in Bill's head.

TEXAS WINTER

On an early afternoon two weeks into the new year, they heard horses blowing out by the dooryard gate and they swiftly slipped out of bed and into their clothes. They had rarely left the house since the day of their wedding, and they made love whenever the inclination moved them, no matter the hour. As Bill stamped his boots into their proper fit, he heard hallooing. He went out on the porch in shirt-sleeves, pistol in hand. A light snow was falling. Some winters here didn't see enough snow to whiten the ground, but the locals were saying this year there'd be plenty of it.

His brother and Butch Berry sat their horses just beyond the dooryard fence. They'd ridden the animals hard most of the way to exercise them, and then walked them the last half-mile, and steam rose off the horses' hides. A few isolate crows trilled in the stark branches against a sky the color of tin.

"We don't want to interrupt nothing important," Jim called to him.

Bill laughed and beckoned them to come on. They dismounted and Jim looped the reins around a fence post and came through the gate and clumped up the porch steps. "Lord amighty, I'm freezing my ass," he said. "I thought it was supposed to be warm down south." His cheeks were raw and his thick mustache lightly frosted. He sniffed the air. "Is that cinnamon cider?"

"Best get you some before Bush drinks it all," Bill said.

Jim went inside and Bill started to follow, but Butch still stood outside the dooryard and holding his horse's reins. Bill turned at the door and gave him a questioning look. Bush called for them to get in or stay out, but shut the door. Bill stepped back out and pulled the door closed.

"I only came to say I'm sorry I didn't show at the celebration," Butch said softly. His good eye held steady on Bill while the off one seemed intent on the crows calling to his left. "And I'm sorry too I run off without congratulating your bride. I don't know why I acted so. It's just, well . . . she reminds me . . ." He made a vague gesture.

"I know," Bill said, and cleared his throat. Apology was not a common exercise among these men. It was Bill Anderson's belief that most apologies were simply fear masquerading as honest regret. But he knew Butch Berry for a true friend and a man afraid of nothing in this world, and his apology had heft.

"It's anyway no excuse for me to've acted low," Butch said. "I thought it over and all I can say is I'm sorry and I wanted you to hear it from me. And now I'll be getting back to camp."

As Butch made to mount up, Bill said, "Hey boy, you'll *really* be sorry if you pass up a hug from Bush and a cup or two of her cinnamon cider. If I was you, I'd get in here and get my share of both."

Butch lowered his foot from the stirrup and stared at Bill a moment—then grinned and said, "Hell, I thought you'd never ask."

They spent the rest of that day together, the four of them, sipping cider and smoking, talking and telling jokes. After a time, they started lacing the cider with Bill's jug and after a while longer dispensed with the cider altogether. Bush began preparing a big kettle of rabbit stew and two large pans of cornbread. The little room was soon thick with savory aromas and Jim and Butch did not have to be argued into staying to supper.

They told Bill and Bush about Christmas Day, when a bunch of guerrillas went into town and got fairly well drunk in their celebration of the Good Lord's birthday. They galloped up and down the streets, howling and shooting the bells in church steeples, shooting rooftop weathercocks into a spin, shooting the knobs off doors. Ben Christian, the owner of the only hotel in town and a friend of Quantrill, hastily sent a rider out to Mineral Springs to fetch Quantrill while he went out to remonstrate with the guerrillas.

The bushwhackers laughed at the innkeeper and said they'd show him what a real disturbance was—then rode their horses into his hotel and scared the living God out of everyone within. The animals knocked over and broke up furniture, tore the carpeting with their hooves, chewed up the potted plants. Women shrieked as the guerrillas shot apart the lamplights and a chandelier, showering the lobby with glass.

The bushwhackers then repaired to a photography studio to have their pictures made. They posed in groups and individually, brandishing pistols and bottles and cigars and fearsome aspects. But then the photographist ran out of plates, and in their anger the bushwhackers who'd not yet had their pictures taken made ruin of the man's studio and equipment.

Then Quantrill arrived, accompanied by George Todd and three dozen men—including Jim Anderson and Butch Berry—and the celebrants were rounded up and driven back to camp, laughing and regaling their sober comrades with the details of their spree, George Todd laughing as hard as any of them, most of them entirely unmindful of Quantrill's disapproving glare. The next day, however, when they'd sobered somewhat, Quantrill took them back to town and ordered them to apologize to Ben Christian and the photographist and to pay for the damages to their establishments.

Even some of the men who hadn't been on the spree thought Quantrill was going too far to make the roisterers pay for the damage. "We been fighting the Yanks so these people can sit home all safe and get rich," Fletch Taylor had said. "And we're making them even richer with all the money we spend in their damn town. But let us do a little whooping and they're quick to complain on us and put their hand out for more money. That don't speak of a proper gratitude, you ask me."

Jim said it surely did look like Quantrill was more concerned with Ben Christian's property than with his own men's right to have a little fun. One of the new boys asked George Todd if *he* would've made the fellas pay and apologize, and Todd just spat and shook his head. The new man turned to a friend and said, "See? I told ye."

Bill said if Quantrill wasn't careful, he might lose his whole company to Todd one of these days. Jim said Quantrill seemed to be thinking the same thing, and that was probably why W. J. Gregg wasn't with the company anymore—which was news to Bill. About a week ago, Jim said, W. J. and Todd had got into a bad argument over some money Gregg said Todd owed him. Todd got so hot about it he told Gregg he'd kill him if he didn't get out of camp before morning and never come back. Gregg's friends saw the quarrel as a personal matter between him and Todd and were keeping out of it, but Todd had a lot of new wildboys in his bunch ready to do anything he said, and Gregg was sure he would put some of them up to killing him. He went to Quantrill and asked him to intervene, but Quantrill said he couldn't. He said it wouldn't do any good to cause splits in the company over a personal difference between two men. His advice was for Gregg to leave the camp. Gregg was saddling up to go when he told all this to Jim. He said he'd never been as disappointed by any man as he was by Quantrill. A dozen friends were leaving with him. He said for Jim to tell Bill so long, and then he was gone, off to join Jo Shelby's regulars.

"W. J.'s a damn good man," Bill said. "I hate to see him gone. He's been with the company as long as anybody, and it's a bad sign for Quantrill not to back him." He had not seen Quantrill since his wedding day. Nor dismissed the insult of his presumptuous counsel against his marriage. Or forgiven his absence from his wedding celebration. Or forgotten the implication of his remark to Todd that Kate had never been a whore.

"Ah hell, enough of this," Bill said. "Who cares a damn about Quantrill's troubles, anyway? Let's kick our heels."

And so they did. Jim Anderson took out his harmonica, and Butch Berry produced his Jew's harp, and they started in on "Drunken Hiccups." Bill and Bush whirled around on the small span of cabin floor. After a while Jim cut in on Bill and handed him the mouth organ, and then Butch too claimed his turn with Bush as Bill filled in with twanging the harp. And though this woman could not but remind Butch Berry of the lost Josephine he'd so hopelessly loved, he did not feel the desperate flailing of his heart he'd felt in dancing with Josie, but only the swirling joy of it.

So it went into the early darkness. Someone passing in view of that cabin in its white landscape under the full winter moon would have seen its chimney smoke rising in a gentle blue column and smelled the redolence of the supper stew, seen the warm yellow glow at the window and heard faintly the music and the laughter—and would surely have envied those within.

Cole Younger was the next to go. He hallooed the house from the dooryard fence one late morning and turned down Bill's invitation to dismount and come inside for coffee. A half-dozen men were with him, all of them outfitted for a long journey. Cole said he was tired of the bushwhacker life and anyway didn't care much for the sort of recruits coming into the company nowadays. Most were half-crazed young boys, naturalborn killers and thieves who'd joined the guerrillas for no reason but the occasion to murder and steal more freely. When he told his men he was leaving, most of them had gone over to Todd's bunch, which had become about the worst collection of hooligans he'd ever seen. He didn't see much difference anymore between a gang like Todd's and any gang of redlegs, and he didn't even want to imagine how much worse the meanness would get come next summer. The war was anyhow lost, and he didn't feature getting killed for a cause without a hope in hell left to it.

Bill said Cole was waving the white flag a little too soon, in his opinion. Cole said he would never in his life wave a white flag but he wouldn't wave a black one anymore either. The way he saw it, once the war was done with, there would be Yankee banks everywhere, and it would practically be his sworn duty as an unsurrendered rebel to rob as many of them as he could. Until then, he believed he would pass the time in California. Bill said he was sorry to see him go. Cole said he was sorry to see him stay. Then he was gone.

Not two weeks after that, Jim brought word that John Jarrette had quit the company too. He'd been promised the rank of captain in the regulars and had gone off with thirty of his men. Of his boys who stayed behind, most of them joined with Todd.

Still another seasoned bushwhacker lost to the company was George Maddox. He'd received word that his wife had been taken seriously ill, and so had returned to Missouri to be with her. But someone peached him to the Federals and he was arrested as one of the bushwhackers who'd been recognized at Lawrence. He would spend the rest of the war behind bars and finally come to trial in Ottawa, Kansas, the only guerrilla ever tried for the Lawrence raid. But as rumor would have it in the years to come, unknown associates of Maddox visited with members of the jury and money changed hands. For a fact the jury would acquit Maddox of all charges and howls of outrage would shake the courtroom as he was hustled out a rear door and onto a horse held by his waiting wife.

The winter deepened. The farmers had been right in their predictions of heavy snow, and the world seemed to slow under the weight of it. When he went out to the stable in the mornings to fork hay for the horses, he would pause in the yard and breathe deep aching lungfuls of the chilly air. His breath rose in blue billows. The trees stood bare. Nothing moved in that gelid landscape but a few curious crows looking like oiled shadows on the naked branches, snickering and whistling.

They went for long walks into the skeletal woodland, holding to each other, giggling at their slips on patches of ice, at their clumsy missteps in the snow. They made running slides on the frozen creek and each hooted at the other when the slide ended in a sprawl. They engaged in snowball skirmishes. They constructed snowmen so ill-formed that Bush felt as sorry for them as cripples. He built a sled and pulled her on it and they'd ride it tandem down the hill, holding tight to each other and whooping all the way, sometimes capsizing in a tangled laughing heap before reaching the bottom.

One late afternoon of long shadows under a rosy sky he brought down a deer at sixty yards with a single pistolshot to the head, a big buck with a wide rack. Bush helped him to lug it home on the sled. They dressed it by firelight on a frame behind the house and for weeks after feasted on venison.

Sometimes he would take out his battered volume of Shakespeare and read to her from the sonnets. His favorite was the one in which the poet tells his lover that even when he is in disgrace with fortune and men's eyes and almost despising himself, the very thought of her makes him feel so rich that he wouldn't trade places with a king. Hers was the one comparing the lover to a summer's day.

He bought a bathtub in town, an oversized clawfoot model, and with the help of Jim and Butch carried it home on a flatwagon they commandeered from the camp. They had to cut the doorway wider to get the tub inside, and they set it next to the hearth. They then added a plank to the door and cut it to fit the expanded doorway and they felt like expert and clever craftsmen when they were done. Jim and Butch stood looking at the tub and then looked at Bill, who grinned and winked. Bush smiled at them and said, "What are all you wicked boys thinking?" Then all of them broke out laughing, and Butch said, "Come on, Jimbo, let's go over to the Moon and pay the girls our respects. What I'm thinking won't allow for a damn thing else till I do that."

The nights were long now and they were glad of it. The wind keened under the eaves and fluted at the edges of the windows and door. Almost every evening, they would boil large kettles of water until the tub was full and steaming. She'd knot her hair up on her head and let him relieve her of her clothes. He'd take his time about it, pausing in the process to kiss portions of her as they came exposed, breasts, belly, buttocks, the backs of her knees. Then she'd undress him as slowly and with as much caress. They'd inhale through their teeth against the bathwater's heat as they gingerly sank themselves in it. They'd take turns bathing each other, one of them now standing, now kneeling, now on all fours, now giggling or sighing, as the other ministered with soapy hands and cloth. They would joke about being the cleanest two people in Missouri. She'd recline against his chest, his arms around her, their knees jutting from the water, and they'd softly sing songs of their own making as the walls around them quivered with firelight and shadow. When the tubwater turned cool they'd step out and dry each other and sit naked on a quilt in front of the fire. He'd unloose her hair and brush it gently as he'd been taught by his sisters until it hung straight and loose and shining. She'd comb his hair free of its knots and sometimes braid it for the pleasure it gave her. She'd trim his beard and his mustache. They'd pause now and again to kiss like they were trying to breathe each other's soul. Then they'd take to the bed and make love, and afterward lie entwined under the blankets and looking through the frost-bordered window at the night sky, some nights seeing the moon or some portion of it and some nights only its glow and some nights a blacker sky clustered with stars. The first time they saw a falling star together, she'd squeezed his hand and whispered, "Momma always said to make a wish." But all he thought was, *Joey*, and he'd hugged Bush more tightly to him and buried his face in her hair.

He rarely dreamt, but when he did, it was often of a crashing building, of falling bricks and rising dust and the mortal screamings of young women. He would come awake without sound to the dim glow of the lowered hearthfire, Bush snugged against him, her easy breath of sleep soft on his neck. He'd lie open-eyed until his heart slowed and the comforting warmth of Bush's skin and the scent of it and of her hair were all he was aware of, and then he'd sleep again. But one late night when he went into the dream, her hand was on his chest and even in her sleep she felt his heart's sudden jumping and she came awake too. She heard his halting breath and knew he was crying and knew why. She put her hand to his face and said softly, "You didn't kill her, Bill. You didn't. I think she'd cuss you like a fishwife if she knew you thought so."

He drew her closer and said it was all right, to go on back to sleep. They lay in silence for a time before he said, "I don't want to leave you."

"I know that," she said.

They lay awake for a long time but said no more, only held each other close and felt the beating of their hearts.

One night she asked if the men he'd sent after Ned shouldn't have returned with him by now. He said the rascals might've made the acquaintance of some affectionate Missouri girls and decided to wait out the winter as near to them as they could. Ike might even have found the girl whose picture he'd fallen in love with, and she might have introduced Ned and Val to friends of hers—although Val likely would have gone back to stay with his wife.

"After all, why spend the winter in a bushwhacker camp—in

Texas or anywhere else—if you could spend it in close company with a girl?" Bill said. "Or even better, with your wife?"

Bush waggled her brow and said, "Like somebody we know?"

Bill made a face of mock innocence and put both hands to his chest in a gesture of "Who, me?"—and she broke out laughing and fell on him with her hands to his throat, affecting to choke him, saying, "I swear I'm going to wring that thoughtless boy's neck just like this!"

Thus did the months of their winter pass by.

BREACHES AND RECOGNITIONS

Through the winter, Jim and Butch made frequent visits, and they always brought tidings and news.

The problems between the guerrillas and the residents of Sherman had grown worse. The bushwhackers resented the townfolk's seeming lack of gratitude for their defense of them against the Yankee nation. They were bitter about the constant protests to Quantrill and General McCulloch, mostly about misdeeds the bushwhackers saw as harmless fun. They were outraged by price gougings for everything from blacksmithing to supplies to restaurant meals to saloon whiskey. When the girls at the Purple Moon tried to raise their prices too, George Todd and Dave Pool said they would tie every one of the bitches to a bed and burn the place down before any of their men would pay a penny more to get laid. The girls had said nothing more of a price increase.

For their part, the good citizens complained of the bushwhackers' increasingly brute misconduct, of their nightly drunken howlings and terrorizing of the town. They had no respect for private property. They held shooting contests and horse races in the streets, and they bullied and sometimes thrashed any man who made objection.

To try to occupy the guerrillas and keep them out of Sherman for a time, General McCulloch had ordered Quantrill to go in hunt of Confederate deserters, whose number had been increasing through the winter. Quantrill had replied that he'd be proud to take on the mission but could not begin right away because most of his men were suffering from the flu. McCulloch was suspicious, but there wasn't much he could say except for Quantrill to get started as soon as possible. When Quantrill told the men about the exchange of messages with McCulloch, they all laughed and affected to have bad coughs.

"He wasn't about to make the company go hunting deserters," Butch Berry said. "He knows the boys don't fault any fella who takes leave of the regular army and all its rules and regulations. Hell, there's a couple of dozen deserters in the company."

Jim said there was more to it than that. Quantrill knew how popular George Todd had become with the men, especially the younger and wilder ones, and he was doing all he could to keep himself in favor with them too.

"True enough," Butch said. "The trouble is, there's lately been more townfolk complaints about robberies and bullyings and such. And Todd's been letting the boys get away with it. If Quantrill puts a stop to it, a lot of the boys'll get blackassed. If he doesn't make them quit, he'll look like he's scared of standing up to Todd."

"*And* McCulloch will really come down hard on him," Jim said.

"He's got a problem is what he's got," Butch said.

"I'm real sorry to hear it," Bill said with a smile.

The sun arced higher every day. The frozen creek cracked open, then broke apart in the forming current. The snow thinned, lingered in patches, then was gone for good. The hard ground commenced giving way to mud. The air softened. The trees put forth their first leaves. Bill regarded the burgeoning greenery and could not help thinking that it would soon enough grow its way up to Missouri.

On a late and chilly afternoon of red sunlight filtering through the new leaves, Jim Anderson and Butch Berry arrived at the cabin with urgent news. Quantrill had arrested one of his own men, Payne Jones, for the murder of a Confederate officer, a major related to Ben Christian, the hotel owner and Quantrill's close friend.

The way Jim and Butch had heard the story, Payne Jones had played in a high-stakes poker game in the hotel one night and the major came out the big winner. Two days after that the officer was found dead on the south bank of the Red River, shot a bunch of times and robbed of his money, his eyes eaten by the crows. Everyone figured river bandits had done him in, but a few days later

Quantrill found a letter under his door from a bushwhacker named Phillips who confessed to helping Payne Jones do the killing. Phillips claimed that when the major left the hotel to go back to his camp, he and Jones had caught up to him at the river and shot him and took his purse. But Jones reneged on his promise to split the money and kept the larger share for himself because the robbery had been his idea. So Phillips wrote the confession and left it for Quantrill and sneaked away in the night. The letter said that the major's purse had a white star stitched on it and one of its points was missing, and if Quantrill searched Payne Jones' possibles he'd likely find it.

Quantrill went to Jones' barrack and told him to lay his possibles out on his bunk. And there the purse was. Jones said he'd never seen it before, that somebody else must have put it there. But John Koger—one of Quantrill's cadre of "old men" who'd been riding with him from the first, and whom nobody had ever known for a liar—told Jones he was sorry, but he had to say he'd seen him with the purse the night before. Oh yeah, Jones said, *now* he remembered—his sister had given him the purse for a present. Quantrill called him a lying and thieving murderer and placed him under arrest. He sent word to McCulloch that he was transferring the major's killer to him for justice. He assigned three men to take Payne to the general's camp in Fannin County and hand him over.

"You say the major was kin to Ben Christian?" Bill Anderson said.

"His father-in-law," Jim said.

"That's the second damn time Quantrill's put Christian ahead of his own men," Bill said.

"True enough," Butch Berry said. "But listen to this. Before the three guards set out with Payne, some of the boys saw Todd talking with them. And guess what? Not Payne nor the guards ever did show up at McCulloch's camp."

"Flat disappeared, the four," Jim said.

Bill smiled. "I'll bet they disappeared to Missouri. And I'll bet the general had a few things to say to Quantrill."

"He thought Quantrill had let them go and was lying to him," Jim said. "Said he was *this close,* by God, to bringing him up on every damn charge he could think of."

"Quantrill must've been a little blackassed himself," Bill said.

His smile widened. "Did he have the balls, I wonder, to ask Todd if he knew anything about those long-gone rascals?"

"Truth to tell, he did," Butch said. "And George said he had no idea what became of those men. Told Quantrill he'd be willing to take a party out in search of them if he wanted, but Quantrill said never mind. They say he was giving George a 'you're a damn liar' look, and George was giving him one back like 'I dare you to say so.' I tell you, it's got real raspy between those two."

"What Quantrill did then," Jim said, "was call the whole company together and give a speech about how any man among us who robbed or killed southern folk or rebel soldiers was no guerrilla but only a damned bandit, and he'd have no bandits in his command. Said he'd no longer stand by any man in the company who committed crimes against the townsfolk or on Confederate soldiers. He said any man who didn't like it could mount up and leave. He was looking right at George Todd when he said it, but Todd just smiled like he was listening to a funny story."

"He said that?" Bill said. "He'll side with townfolk and the regular army over his own men?"

"Nobody left camp, either," Jim said. "Not even Todd."

"Well, somebody's leaving it now," Bill said. He asked Jim to stay with Bush and told Butch to come with him.

The smoke of campfires and barrack stovestacks rose thin and pale blue over the camp. It was the first time he'd been there since the day before his wedding. When his men spied him come loping toward their barrack they raised a terrific cheer that drew the attention of the other guerrillas. Archie Clement stood at the fore of Bill's bunch to greet him, smiling wide. "It's fine to see you, Captain," he said.

"Get the outfit set to ride," Bill said. "We're moving to our own camp."

The Anderson men whooped at the news and hastened to make ready, strapping on gunbelts, gathering bedrolls and saddles, heading loudly for the corrals.

And here came Quantrill out of his hut and strolling toward him. Behind him came George Todd, Dave Pool, and Dick Yeager. Bill and Butch sat their horses and watched them come.

"Well now, William T.," Quantrill said, "I was thinking to ask you into my house for a drink in celebration of this rare honor, but it would appear you're not staying long enough to step down off your horse. Quo vadis?"

"So you won't stand by a man of the company against a damn regular or even a townsman?" Bill said.

"Ah, my address to the men," Quantrill said, giving Butch Berry a quick glance. "More precisely, what I said was I won't have bandits in my command."

Bill swept his hand at the gathered guerrillas and said, "Are these men of your command?"

Quantrill looked around as if to be sure which men Bill meant. "Aye."

"And not a man of them an outlaw?"

Quantrill smiled. "You're a clever disputant, William T., and there's no denying it. However, there is a distinction between outlaw and bandit. A guerrilla who robs and kills Unionists may be declared an outlaw by Unionists, but he is no bandit unless he also robs and kills men of the South. It's a matter of circumstance, you see. No man is a bandit until circumstance proves him so."

"Circumstance be damned," Bill said. "A captain stands by his men."

"You're being willful," Quantrill said. "A wise leader always regards circumstance. A man shouldn't grip so tightly to a principle that he can't unhand it when circumstance voids it of worth. It's like trying to save a sinking ship by holding tighter to the tiller."

"You're full of shit," Bill Anderson said.

Todd looked close to open laughter. Most of the others stood smiling as well.

Arch Clement rode up and said, "The boys are ready, Captain Bill."

"You disappoint me, William T.," Quantrill said.

"Oh damn," Bill said. "I pray Lord Jesus will forgive me." And he led his men away.

He encamped them a quarter-mile into the wildwood flanking the cabin, and he named the company the Kansas First Guerrillas. Kansas had not only been his own home for more than ten years, but also the home of a number of his men, and he regarded the name as a fitting defiance of the notion that the state belonged entirely to Yankees. A courier brought congratulations from General McCulloch for his break with Quantrill.

He stood on the porch that night, Bush's arms around him and her head resting on his shoulder, and could see the light of the company fires far back among the trees. Holding to her in the chilly darkness, breathing the scent of her hair, feeling the warmth of her flank against him, the soft press of her breast on his arm, he knew he would have to leave her.

A captain stands by his men, circumstance be damned.

The instant he'd said it to Quantrill he'd known he believed it above all things on earth. As he stared at the fires burning in the wildwood camp, he reflected that not a man of them had ever questioned if he would be leading them back to Missouri. They'd never had a doubt of who he was.

Even as he held Bush close, he already missed her terribly and felt his loneliness twisting hard in his chest.

She raised her head from his shoulder and kissed his cheek and hugged him more tightly. As if she'd heard his thoughts, she said softly, "Don't feel so low about it, boy. It's what you have to do."

He gawked at her.

"I always figured you'd go back because of Joey," she said. "It grieved me because I didn't see how you can measure revenge for her. How many do you have to kill? For how long? For as long as there's the war? For as long as you live? How can it ever be made even? But what—"

"I don't *know,*" Bill said. "I don't know how long or how many or even if—"

"I wasn't finished," she said. "What I know now is, even if they hadn't ever done a thing to her, you'd *still* go back." She stroked his beard. "One day I just knew it. I suddenly felt it and knew it was true and it damn near made me cry. I thought of every argument I could raise to keep you from going before I finally realized I not only couldn't, I shouldn't even try. I love you, Bill. I love who you are and I'd be the rankest fool to try to argue you into being somebody other."

She smiled and petted his face.

"If I'm anything in this world more than a horse thief, I'm their captain."

"I know."

"If I quit them—" He gestured vaguely.

"Then I might not recognize you anymore," she said. "And *that*, Captain Anderson, would be just terrible."

He touched her smile. She kissed his fingers. "Do you truly understand?" he said.

"Oh, hell no. Do *you*?"

"Not in any way I can say that makes sense."

"*That* I understand," she said.

"I still don't want to leave you."

"I know," she said. "And you know I'll be here waiting for you. Now that's an end on it. Let's not say another word on it. Let's just go on inside and do that thing we do so well."

Two weeks later Butch and Jim reported that McCulloch had summoned Quantrill to his headquarters at Bonham and then tried to arrest him for insubordination. But Quantrill had suspected a trap, and he managed a neat escape, together with the forty men he'd taken to Bonham with him. He made straight for the Red but sent a rider to Mineral Creek to warn Todd and the others and they'd cleared out quickly too. The regulars gave chase but by the time they arrived at the river the bushwhackers were all on the other side, beyond reach of McCulloch's authority. Quantrill stood up in the stirrups and patted his ass at the soldiers in an old gesture of contempt—and then they rode off laughing.

"Funny thing is," Jim said, "McCulloch put out word that the Anderson guerrillas helped in the chase after Quantrill and Todd. Why you reckon he did that, Bill?"

Bill shrugged. "Probably wants to put us in better stead with the locals than Quantrill was. Get them to quit complaining so much to him. That's good. If we don't give the good folk reason to be upset with us, the general will be happy and not press us to work for him like he was pressing Quantrill." He grinned. "Tell the boys watch their manners in town from now on."

* * *

Quantrill and Todd had set up a new camp in the Choctaw Nation, but after two weeks there, Fletch Taylor came back across the river to join Bill's company. He said he couldn't stand the sniping between Todd and Quantrill anymore.

"I swear, I've seen them come *yay* close to pulling guns. The thing is, they're scared of each other. Whoever stops being scared first is the one'll come out top dog."

A WOEFUL ACCOUNT

The new grass leaned in the spring wind, the trees swayed, the first sporadic rains arrived. The company set about smoking and jerking beef and venison to be in good supply all the way back to Missouri.

On a drizzly afternoon, Jim Anderson showed up at the cabin, accompanied by a young bushwhacker he introduced as Jack Henry. The man was wan and gaunt and his right sleeve was folded on the stump of his arm and pinned to his shoulder. As the men clumped into the house, crows looked on from the dooryard fence.

Jack Henry was one of Andy Blunt's boys who'd stayed with him in Missouri over the winter. He was only seventeen but had long been shed of boyhood, and his face showed that he carried hard news. When Bush heard that he'd been with Blunt, she put aside the pan of cornbread she was preparing and came to sit at the table with them.

The cripple had been avoiding her eyes. "My brother's dead, isn't he?" she said.

Now he fixed his gaze on her. "Yes, mam, I'm sorry to say."

She sighed as if she'd been expecting just this news for some time, but she didn't weep nor make any show of grief. She simply looked worn.

"Ike Berry too," Jack Henry said. "And Val Baker."

"Shit," Bill said. He glanced at Jim, who said, "Butch knows. He went off in the woods."

"Tell it," Bill said to Jack Henry. . . .

Blunt's camp was in the snowy hills a few miles from Warrensburg and consisted of a half-dozen scattered and well-hidden dugouts, each one housing three or four men. In January Ike Berry and Val Baker showed up. They'd been visiting with Baker's wife at her parents' place a few miles downriver and were rested and well-fed. After all the backslapping how-do's were done with and a jug was started around, Ike told of his errand to fetch Ned Smith. Blunt said the boy had proved himself as brave and tough as any man in the company and he'd hate to lose him, but if he wanted to go he could go.

Ned was glad to hear his sister was safely in Texas, but he didn't want to leave the company—not until Ike told him that Bush was married to none other than Bill Anderson. The boy was jubilant to learn he was brother-in-law to Bloody Bill, and now was eager to get to Texas and be introduced. Jack Henry asked if he could ride back to Texas with them and they said sure. His parents had been run off their farm by Order 11 and gone to Nacogdoches to live with his uncle, and he wanted to go make sure they were all right.

They set out on a day so cold their spit froze before it hit the ground. It wasn't till Ike Berry led them east off the Blackwater trace and onto the Holden road that Jack and Ned learned of the picture he carried of the blonde girl, and of his hope of finding out who she was from the Harrisonville photographist who'd made the likeness. They all but Ike thought it was a fool's errand. Even if he should learn her name and where she lived, she wasn't likely to be swept off her feet by one of the bushwhackers who killed her beau and scalped him. Maybe not, Ike said, but he had to try.

In Harrisonville they discovered that the studio and several adjoining buildings had been burned down by redlegs more than a year ago. Nobody knew what had become of the old picturetaker who'd owned the place. Ike's disconsolation lingered for days as they made their way south through the ruins of the borderland counties, the region now long deserted and seeming lifeless in the pale dead of winter, its eerie silence broken only by the callings of crows. Valentine Baker had wanted to go around this badland and avoid the risk of running into any Yankee patrols, but Ike argued that there was no need to add all those miles to their journey. He said the Federals weren't likely to do much patrolling in this wasteland anymore, especially not in the winter. And so they pressed due south and made it through the region of Order 11 without incident, and Ike said he told them so. They had just crossed the Marmaton in Vernon County one early afternoon when a militia patrol of some thirty men came riding over a hill and spied them.

They tried to run for it, but as they raced around a bend in the trail, Jack Henry's horse was shot from under him and flung him tumbling down a steep snowy slope. Two of the militiamen rode up to the edge of the rise as he was struggling to get to his feet and one of them shot him in the arm and other in the chest. He would have no memory of being shot yet again, this time in the back, as he lay facedown in the snow.

He woke up in a raging fever, the taste of his own blood in his mouth, swathed in bandages and his own high stink. He was in a narrow bunk in a dimly lighted back room of a house, being watched over by an old man and his crone of a wife. Their name was Pinker, and their farm stood less than a mile from the trail where he'd been shot. They'd heard the gunfire and trudged out through the snow to see what they might find, and what they'd found was him, sopping bright red against the white snow and near to dead. "It was the cold what saved ye," the old man told him. "Slowed the blood from all running out." This couple, whose four sons had all been killed on different occasions by Unionists of one sort or another, had fashioned a rough travois of tree limbs and branches and on it dragged him back to their place. They tended to his wounds and waited to see if he would ever wake again. Six days later he did.

They'd dug the balls out of his back and chest and treated the wounds with oil of turpentine, and they said he was in little danger of dying from either of those wounds. But the bullet that hit his arm had fragmented even as it shattered the elbow, and now the arm was poisoned beyond salvation. Pinker said it would have to come off. "We can do her," his old woman said, "we've had lots of practice." Then he passed out again. The next time he woke the arm was gone.

They gave him the additional hard news that his three comrades had been killed within two miles of where he himself had been shot. The way the Pinkers had heard the story told in town, the guerrillas tried to make a stand in an abandoned barn, but the militia set it afire and drove out two of them—the one left inside was already dead. The pair to come out were shot up so bad they couldn't ride, so they were hung right there next to the burning barn. The militia put a notice on the tree that they would kill anybody who cut them down, and as far as the Pinkers knew, nobody yet had or was likely to.

He was nearly two months in recovering and learning how to do for himself with one arm, and was still skeletally thin when he told them he had to go. He'd had two ten-dollar gold pieces in his pocket on the day he'd been shot, and they were still there. He gave one to the Pinkers in exchange for their old mule, a scrawny beast the Feds hadn't thought worth stealing, and he would not let them refuse the payment for it.

Just before he left, they brought him more bad news. Andy Blunt's boys had been caught in the open by two companies of militia and eleven bushwhackers were killed, including Captain Blunt. The militia was bragging of how they took him back to their camp and hung him from a tree for two days so everybody could have a good look at him, then they stripped his body and threw it in a gully where the crows and wild dogs could feed on it.

"When you see Bloody Bill in Texas," old man Pinker said, "tell him nothing he does to these sonofabitches can ever be mean enough."

Jack Henry plodded off on the old mule and followed the Pinkers' directions to where his two comrades still dangled from the cottonwood close to the razed barn. The weathered warning sign was still on the tree. Jack Henry pulled it off and flung in the bushes. The dead men were but rags and bones anymore, their hides withered stiff and black, their faces long since taken by the crows. But there was no mistaking Ike Berry's white hair nor Val Baker's wild black tangle. He cut the bodies down and took a lock of each man's hair. Then he went to the charred barn and gently kicked through the ashes and soon enough uncovered Ned Smith's blackened bones.

"I'm real sorry I couldn't bury them, Captain," Jack Henry said. He gestured with his arm stump as if such explanation might be necessary. "I'm sorry, mam," he said to Bush. She sat with her hands folded in her lap and nodded.

He was now on his way to Fort Worth, but had wanted to stop here to let them know what happened to their fellows, and to hand over the small portions of them he'd brought back so they might have something to bury.

He withdrew something from his shirt pocket and handed it to Bill. "It's from Ned.'

It looked like a dark stub of a thin cigar. Bill passed it to Bush. She looked at him in question and he held up and waggled his index finger. Her lips parted as she understood, and she held the bone as if it were some rare object of glass.

He had already given Ike's lock of hair to Butch Berry. When he got to Fort Worth, he would give Val Baker's lock to his widow in Johnson County.

Now Jack Henry was gone, Jim too, and Bush asked Bill if he would give her some time alone. The drizzle had abated and he went walking in the misted woods, his thoughts mostly of Ike Berry, dear as a brother, who had died in love with a pretty blonde Union girl he'd never even met. He'd never had the pleasure of dancing with her, kissing her, knowing her scent or the feel of her hair. Bill's fury was like ice in his belly.

When he got back to the cabin she was sitting as before and he could see that she'd been crying. She asked him to sit down and please just listen to her without saying anything until she was finished.

She had been thinking very hard about Ned. At first all she could think was how much she wanted the men who killed him to die terrible deaths. Her desire for revenge felt like a corset snugged so tight around her she could hardly draw a proper breath. She had considered giving him a ribbon of her own to put knots in like he did with Joey's.

"I'll do it," Bill said. "You—"

"Please, Bill," she said. "Just listen."

It was the notion of the ribbon that made her realize she was feeling the same sort of terrible hatred that was always tearing at him, that seemed to be at large over the whole country like a craziness. She recalled the things she'd asked about his desire to avenge Joey, wanting to know if it was even possible to satisfy that desire. Then she remembered somebody she'd known in the days when she was living with the Jeffers family in Kansas, a neighbor widow named Sarah Raulerson, who sometimes came to visit. The Jeffers hated to see her buggy coming toward the house because they knew what they were in for. She was never in the house but a short time nor halfway through with her tea before she began talking of how much she hated the damned Yankees for killing her husband at the first Bull Run and how she prayed every night for the Good Lord to strike dead every Union man, woman and child walking the earth. It was a lament everyone in the surrounding countryside had heard from her many times over, and always, as she proceeded in the telling of it, she became increasingly agitated until she was at once sobbing in her grief and cursing in her hatred.

Today was the first time she had thought of Sarah Raulerson since before she'd left Kansas. And as she'd considered the pitiful memory of Sarah and her bitter anguish, she imagined countless other women all over the country, Southern women and Yankee women both, and all of them telling the same story and all crying their hearts out and all of them cursing countless men and women and children they did not know, yet hating them so bitterly they wished them all dead. She imagined them cursing and crying that way for the rest of their awful lives.

She had been looking at her hands in her lap as she spoke, but now she looked up at him and her aspect was utter resolution.

"I wish you weren't going back to it," she said. "I wish it more than I ever wished for anything. If I thought there was some way to stop you, I'd do it. You'll do what you must, but I want you to know that every minute you're away I'll be hoping that you'll change your mind and quit that damned war and come home to me. I don't care about the war or who wins or who loses or for revenging Ned or for anything else. I care about *you*. But I swear to you, Bill, I *swear* I will not be another Sarah Raulerson. Whatever happens, I will not live the rest of my life with nothing to it but weeping and hating. I will not."

She stood up and came to him and kissed him fully on the mouth.

He wanted to tell her that he understood, but before he could speak she put her fingers to his lips and said, "No, please. It will all go as it goes."

Then she grinned and said, "And where I think it should go right now is directly to the bed over there. What do you think, Captain?"

He laughed and swept her up and to it.

* * *

Two weeks later, Bill's scouts reported that Quantrill had departed the Indian Nations for Missouri, and George Todd and his band had gone with him.

Bill told Jim they'd be moving out themselves in two days, but the day before they were to leave, there came a hard storm and the rain did not let up for five days and the country turned to mud. Bill said there was no need to set out in such dismal weather, they'd wait till things dried out a little. But the rain kept coming, off and on, and the mud remained, and for the next ten days the men were miserably wet and daily more restless, their tempers drawn to such fine edge that every day saw several fistfights. The horses stamped and lunged in the corrals, as tense and agitated as the men, as ready to go.

He spent every hour of the delay in the private company of his wife. They were touching each other constantly, stroking, caressing, holding close. They spoke little for there was little need. He snipped a lock of her hair and bound it with a sturdy thread and kept it in his shirt pocket. He said he would write to her when he could and send the letters by one of his men, but there was no telling how regularly he could do it or if the rider would get through to her—and if he did, whether the carrier would get back to Bill with her letter in turn. She said she would expect no letters from him at all. That way, any she received would come as a grand surprise.

She had attached a clasp to her brother's fingerbone and wore it as a brooch on her breast. Few of those to see it in years to come would realize on sight what the ornament was made of. "Now I have you both close to my heart," she said, one hand fingering the brooch, the other the necklace locket in which she carried Bill's photograph. She had turned the picture upside down in deference to the superstition that such was a way to make sure an absent lover kept you in his thoughts.

Bill asked Jim to pick somebody to stay behind and watch over Bush and help her with the heavier chores, and Jim selected a fifteen-year-old recruit named Lamar Hundley. The boy at first protested, saying he wanted to go to Missouri too, that he could kill Yankees as good as any man. But when Jim said that Captain Anderson had specifically asked for *him* to be his wife's protector in his absence, the boy said oh well, all right then, and could not keep from beaming.

He swore to keep Miss Bush safe from all harm and do her bidding without question.

At last came a sunwashed morning when they embraced on the porch and Bill kissed her and she put her hand to his face in farewell. Then he descended the steps and mounted Edgar Allan and led his men away.

V

The Casualties

1 8 6 4

OF RAIN AND RIVER CROSSINGS

They had four days of fair weather after they crossed the Red, and then the sun once more gave way to a dark and rumbling sky and they did not see sunshine again for three weeks. All through the first week they were beset by daily storms of furious thunderclaps and bright serpent tongues of lightning that sometimes struck trees in shimmering pale blasts and terrorized men and horses and left the trees smoking. The wind heaved hard and cold and slung the rain sideways. The horses cried at its whipping sting in their eyes and the men rode with heads bent against it. Their greatest effort was at keeping the breeches of their firearms dry. They held their hats to their heads and their clothes were plastered to them and their boots were heavy with water.

The storms at last ceded to a steady rain that sometimes came down hard and straight for hours—clattering in the trees and crackling on the risen waters of the bottoms and the swales, drumming on the men's hats and streaming off their brims—and sometimes eased to a misty drizzle. The noon skies looked like churned lead. The horses were spooked by sudden blooms of blue fire at the metal of their harness, by blue streaks on the gun barrels. "Saint Elmo's fire," a bushwhacker named Fulton called it. He'd been an able seaman on a merchant ship and had often witnessed the phenomenon—but after one too many harrowing storms on the high seas, he'd chosen to put as much distance as possible between himself and Mother Ocean and therefore moved to Missouri.

Their pace was plodding through the deep mud. They could not raise a campfire in that sodden world, could only lie rolled in their drenched blankets on the highest ground they could find and sleep fitfully if at all and shiver through the long nights of solid gloom. Bill heard Sock Johnson muttering to no one in particular that he would go back to religion if Lord Jesus would let him at least *remember* what it felt like to be dry.

They forded the Spring River into Missouri in the last days of May, under an afternoon sky the color of old tin that showed but a vague paling where the sun might be. This stonebottom ford was rarely more than a foot deep but now the water was up to the horses' bellies and running fast. They slogged their slow and careful way up into Vernon County and the border district razed by General Order 11. Ike Berry had been killed somewhere this side of the Marmaton River and who knew whether his bones yet lay under the hanging tree where Jack Henry had left them or if they had been scattered by scavengers or perhaps come upon by Christians and properly interred. Butch Berry was riding as the forward scout and out of sight of the rest of the company, but Bill Anderson knew what dark thoughts must be writhing in the boy's head.

The border district had become even more of a wasteland than they had witnessed the previous summer. In this season of relentless rain the gray countryside was as ghostly as the column of riders moving through it like forty-one maledict shades. The ruins and deserted farms looked like relics of a time far more distant than last year. With exception of Jackson County, the war on the border was fairly well done with. There was nothing or no one left here to fight for. The war had moved downriver into the central counties flanking both sides of the Muddy, and toward that new badland did Bill Anderson lead his men.

Every river crossing was more perilous than the one before, the ferries even more dangerous than swimming the horses across, which they did at the Marmaton. Most of the bushwhackers couldn't swim, and so clung wide-eyed and desperate to the saddlehorns. They crossed the same way at the wider and faster Osage, but this time some of the horses panicked badly and one broke loose of its rider midway across the river. The men nearest him caught a quick last glimpse of the boy's white face as the spuming brown current whirled him off and pulled him under and he never made outcry. He was new to the company and none knew anything of him except that his name was Hammett, but whether it was his Christian name or surname was a point of debate. No part of him would ever surface except for his slouch hat, which an old Negro would find caught in the bankside roots of a willow two miles downstream and get good use of for the rest of his days.

The South Grand was booming so fiercely they dared not try to swim the horses and instead rode five miles upriver until they came to a wooden bridge. It was wide enough for a wagon, but the structure was worn to such frailty they could see it trembling with the force of the rushing water. They tested its endurance one rider at a time, every horse white-eyed at the sway and quiver of the planks underfoot. Bill was the last man to go over. By then the bridge was shaking so badly he'd had to keep a tight rein on Edgar Allan and talk to him all the way across.

At last the rain ceased altogether. The clouds broke apart and a glaring afternoon sun reflected so brightly silver on the wet world around that they were forced to squint against it all the rest of that day as they plugged on through the heavy mud and dripping woodlands.

NEW BLOOD

Some days later and just before dawn, Butch Berry reported an outfit of thirty militiamen encamped a few miles to northward. Bill led the company at a lope and in single file along a hog trail through the thickest part of the woods and they came to a brushy rise overlooking the militia camp just as the sun was beginning to redden the trees. Butch sneaked up on foot behind one of the pickets and the dozing man did not have time to be surprised when an arm snaked around his throat and a knifeblade slid through his backribs into his heart. At the same time, Buster Parr was bringing down the other picket on the far side of the camp.

A quarter of an hour later, twenty-four militiamen lay dead under a drifting blackpower haze and only six of their fellows had escaped the sudden storm of wildwood boys. Arch Clement and Butch Berry took three scalps each, and fresh Federal hair hung from Buster Parr's boottops. Riley Crawford began putting together a new ear necklace, but he was chased away from some of the bodies by the bushwhackers who'd killed them and wanted the ears for themselves. Bill formed three new knots in Josie's ribbon. The guerrillas stripped the dead men of their uniforms, complaining of the blood they would have to wash out of them. They left the litter of naked bodies to bloat under the rising sun, then sat to the militia breakfast still warm at the cookfires—coffee and hoecakes and bacon and beans, their first hot meal since Texas.

A sunbright morning of pale sky and thin shreds of rose clouds. Flowering dogwoods draped in white, crabapples in pink. Crows tittering at irate mockingbirds, watchful of a hawk at high spiral. Fields flooded yellow with black-eyed Susan. The scent of dog fennel on the soft wind.

They were navigating eastward, moving at a trot, bridle rings chinking and hooffalls thudding the ripe earth, scouts out right and left, all of them now in Federal blue. Butch Berry far ahead on point.

And then Butch was loping back down the trail to them. "Yanks coming. Fifty."

As the two companies came in sight of each other, Bill raised his hand in greeting, one Yank officer hallooing another from a distance. They closed to within ten yards before the Yank captain's face showed suspicion and he caught sight of Bill's long hair and the scalp on his bridle. He had just enough time remaining to him in this world to look sad before Bill's bullet passed through his neck and sent him sprawling from the saddle. Then all the guerrillas were pouring fire into them and twenty-two Federals littered the ground after the rest had fled the smoky field.

The wounded pled for quarter. Arch Clement stood over one and said, "Ah, Yank, don't beg, it's just too pitiful"—and shot the man at such close range the Federal's hair smoked from the powderblast.

Butch Berry went from one fallen blue to another, seeking any who still breathed, and the three he found might have been entreat-

ing a deaf man for all the heed he paid them before cutting their
throats.

So it went through June and into July. Where they found no Feds to
fight, they did whatever mischief they might to harass Union opera-
tions. They cut telegraph lines, burned bridges on the Yank supply
routes, felled huge trees across army wagon roads. They posted
themselves along the wooded riverbanks and shot up passing steamboats. The Union controlled the Missouri newspapers, of course,
and editorials across the state thundered with outrage at guerrilla
"barbarisms" and lauded every act of Federal "reprisal." The guerrillas were not soldiers, nor even men. They were savages, brute creatures as far removed from Christian notions of honorable warfare as
wild Indians, entirely deserving of extermination, and editorials from
Kansas City to Saint Louis called for Union forces to rid the country
of them by any means necessary.

They mostly stayed south of the Missouri River in those weeks of
early summer, roaming the hills and vales and woodlands of Johnson
and Lafayette and Saline counties. Though they did not know that
territory as well as the border country most of them called home,
they knew it well enough. Nor did they lack for friends in this region
to feed and shelter them, to give them news of other guerrilla companies and information about Federal movements.

Some of the other bushwhacker bands were not faring so well.
Every few days the Anderson men came on yet another woodland
gravesite where a body—sometimes several—had been buried in
such haste that a hand or foot still jutted from the freshly turned
ground. Some of the shallow graves were laid open, the scavengers
having already been there and fed on the carrion, the flies still thick
and droning, the crows heavy in the trees, and the ragged guerrilla
shirts of the moldering remains were sufficient testament to who
they'd been and how they came to be there.

They heard of guerrilla bands annihilated by Yankee ambush, of
captured bushwhackers stood against barn walls and shot, or
hanged in the deeper woods and left to rot till they fell free of the
rope and then decomposed into the earth out of which they'd been
raised. They heard of secessionist folk being forced to attend execu-
tions of guerrillas and to bury the bodies—or, in some cases of

hanged bushwhackers, to keep watch on the dangling dead men and report to the Federals anyone who ignored the warnings and cut them down.

Whichever way the wind did blow, it carried the smell of the war's greater malignity.

"You boys hear what Abe Lincoln said after he come off a five-day drunk?" Sock Johnson poses the question as the column trots along a hog path through the wildwood.

"All right, I'll play the fool," says Fulton the Sailor, riding alongside him. "What'd he say?"

"I freed the *who*?"

Few of them have heard this one before and the men within earshot of Johnson all laugh.

"I'll tell you what," Buster Parr says, "if that bloody-mouthed son of a bitch ever *did* say that, I'd still want to kill him, but I might not take as much pleasure in it."

"And if a frog ever *did* grow a pair of wings," Fletch Taylor says, "he wouldn't bump his ass as much."

At the Saline County farm of a secessionist named Walston, where they took what by then seemed a lavish supper of beans and fatback and warm biscuits, they learned that George Todd had come through only two days before. He was said to be encamped near the mouth of the Sni-a-bar.

The next day they found him, and the two outfits had a festive reunion. Todd was in high spirits, and when Bill saw so many of Quantrill's men among his company, he knew why. His guess was confirmed over a jug and a plate of beans.

"It come to a head a few weeks ago," Todd said. "We were playing seven-up one night and the son of a bitch accused me of cheating. Truth to tell, I was, but I'd anyway had about enough of him, and if it hadn't been the cheating it would've been something else, but the time had come for sure. Bastard always thought he had me buffaloed, but I stood right up and said he could pull his pistol or his knife, whichever way he wanted to have at it—or he could put his ass on that crazy damn horse and get out of *my* camp." He took a drink and grinned.

318   James Carlos Blake

"And so?" Bill said.

"And so he got on his horse and left. Not twenty men went with him."

He said Quantrill was now in Howard County, on the north side of the river, hiding in some deepwoods camp with his meager band. "I heard he had tooth trouble real bad, had to have a couple cut out," Todd said. "Heard he was in some goodly pain. About breaks my heart, don't it yours? They say Kate the Cunt's with him now, playing nursie." He never referred to the woman anymore except as Kate the Cunt.

"Well, she's your company now," Bill said. "Congratulations, Captain Todd."

"Thankee kindly, Captain Anderson."

Dave Pool's boys had been raising hell from Jackson County to Saline, Todd told him, and Dick Yeager and his band were somewhere in Chariton. "We bunch up together every now and again," Todd said, "mainly me and Pool." He'd recently met a bushwhacker captain named Clifton Holtzclaw, whose company of hardcases had made a fearsome name for themselves all through Boone and Howard and Cooper counties. "When I told him I knew you, that's all he wanted to talk about. It's like that everydamnwhere we been for the last three weeks. 'Bloody Bill did this, Bloody Bill did that.' Bloody Bill and his scary-ass scalpers. I could get jealous."

"I've heard plenty about your doings lately too, George."

Todd grinned. "We're promoting a lot of bad Unionist dreams, ain't we? You and me, old son, we're who the bastards are scared of."

"And I say we keep it that way," Bill said, grinning back at him.

There was plenty of busthead whiskey on hand and they celebrated late into the night. They told tales and jokes and japed each other freely around the fires. Sometimes the japing got rough, as when a Todd man named Tuckett said the company was lucky to have him in it because he'd been raised in this region of Missouri and the country was as familiar to him as the feel of his sweetheart's ass. "Well hell," another man said, "by that reckoning, half the company ought to know its way around here real good." And the fight was on.

At one point in the evening, Frank James stopped by the fire where Bill and Todd were sitting with some of the other men and said he wanted Bill to meet a new recruit. He beckoned a young man forward into the firelight.

"I tried my damnedest to warn him off the likes of us but he's a willful pup," Frank said. "All of seventeen years old and reckons he's too grown up to heed his older brother anymore."

The boy was young and lean. He tipped his hat and said, "Captain Anderson, I'm proud to ride with you." His voice was high and thin.

"Another beardless pushhard," Bill said with a smile. He asked the boy his name.

"Jesse, sir."

"There's two rules, Jess. Stand by your fellows and don't ever bring me a Fed prisoner."

LETTERS

Came a morning when Jim brought to Bill's attention an editorial in one of the Lexington newspapers. It exhorted the local citizens of town and country to do all in their power to assist the Union army in overcoming the guerrillas, even to take up arms against them.

"The other Lexington paper did the same thing a few days ago," Jim said. "Bad enough we got fewer friends than ever to spare us a fresh horse or a little food now and then. We sureshit don't need any farmers being gulled into believing it's their patriotic duty to shoot at us when we show up at their door. Some of them are dumb enough to do it."

Bill was incensed. He wrote a lengthy letter and addressed it to the editors of both papers, upbraiding them, saying that their advice to the locals was "only asking them to sign their death warrants." What the people really wanted, Bill said, was protection from thieves and robbers, which his men were not. On the contrary, his guerrillas were the best protection the populace had against such bandits, who were even more afraid of bushwhackers than they were of Federals.

He then addressed the locals directly: "Listen to me, fellow-citizens, do not take up arms if you value your lives and property. If you proclaim to be in arms against the guerrillas I will kill you. I will hunt you down like wolves and murder you. You cannot escape." He smiled at the menacing lines.

Reading over his shoulder, Jim chuckled and said, "That ought to keep the yokels away from their shotguns."

He sought to make the good folk understand his righteous cause and see that he was but another victim of the war, a man driven to his present circumstance by Yankee brutality: "I have chosen guerrilla warfare to revenge myself for wrongs that I could not honorably avenge otherwise. I lived in Kansas when this war commenced. Because I would not fight the people of Missouri, my native state, the Yankees sought my life, but failed to get me. Revenged themselves by murdering my father, destroying all my property, and have since that time murdered one of my sisters and kept the other two in jail twelve months."

On rereading these words, he heard in them the timbre of self-pity, which even as rhetorical device he'd always found disdainful. The perception so vexed him that he reverted to the minatory mood: "Take arms against me and you are Federals. Your doctrine is an absurdity and I will kill you for being fools. Beware, men, before you make this fateful leap. I feel for you. You are in a critical situation. I have no time to say anything more to you. Be careful how you act, for my eyes are upon you."

Boo! he thought. Jim was grinning large.

The letter included an aside to a Colonel McFerran, whom he ridiculed for his grossly exaggerated lies of victory in a pair of skirmishes with Bill's company, and one to General Egbert Brown, Commander of the Central District of Missouri, whom he criticized for the recent jailing of southern women who had assisted guerrillas and tried to help Confederate prisoners escape:

"I do not like the idea of warring with women and children, but if you do not release all the women you have arrested in Lafayette County, I will hold the Union ladies in the country as hostages for them. I will tie them by the neck in the brush and starve them until they are released. General, do not think I am jesting with you. I will resort to abusing your ladies if you do not quit imprisoning ours."

He signed, "W. Anderson, Commanding Kansas First Guerrillas."

"You don't mean it about the women?" Jim said.

"If old Egbert really thinks I'm the devil he says I am, maybe he'll believe me enough to set the southern ladies loose. I don't guess it's real likely." He looked up at Jim. "What do you think?"

"I think if Momma had named me Egbert, I'd still be wondering why she hated me so damn much."

Bill laughed. "If she'd named *me* that, I never would've answered to it. She wanted my attention she would've had to point and say, 'Hey, you.' "

His letters to Bush and hers to him were no different in their lyrics from those of any lovers perforce apart—as heavy with the hoary sentiments and worn banalities of all lovers through the ages, yet no less precious to either of them, as to any lover, for being so.

His were short and intermittent, as he had told her to expect. He reminded her to burn each in its turn as soon as she'd read it, the better to avoid all chance of them ever serving as evidence of her complicity with guerrillas. He always wrote of the most recent Federal abuses in Missouri and rendered pitiful descriptions of the victims, of families bereaved, of their destroyed properties and ruined crops. "The countryside sounds of the weeping of new widows and fatherless babes," he wrote. He entered quick catalogs of the company's latest acts of retribution. He would always close with a reminder of how deeply he loved her and how much he missed her, how he often dreamt of them embraced in their steaming bathtub by the amber glow of the fireside, enclosed in their own small portion of the world and with no need of any of the rest of it. His closing line was ever the same: "I think of you only when I breathe."

Her letters contained descriptions of the property in its splendid summer flowering—the shady creekside bursting with cardinal flowers and creamy morning blooms of rain lilies, the fields thick with bluebells and spiderwort, the meadows alighting each evening with buttercups like little pink lamps. She was grateful for the presence of the Hundley boy, who'd proved a great help in keeping up the place. She always shared with young Lamar whatever news of the company and its victories Bill posted in his letters. She said she missed him more than she could properly express and so would not even try to.

Her closings were an echo of his own: "I think of you only when my heart beats."

Across the Muddy

On an early morning hazed with river fog they swam their horses across the Missouri into Carroll County. Clinging to the saddle-horns, many of the men shivered from cause other than the water's chill, having heard since childhood that river mist was inhabited by the spirits of the drowned. As his horse pulled him sloshing from the water and onto the bank, Riley Crawford looked near to demented with fright. He swore he'd felt a hand trying to grab him by the ankle and pull him under. Some of them laughed at him for a superstitious child, but others nodded with big-eyed belief and couldn't distance themselves from the river fog fast enough.

They made their way to a farm off the main road. Bill kept most of the men back in the trees while Sock Johnson and Oz Swisby went to the house. After a time they returned with a man named Hamer, whose farm it was and who had come along with Sock and Oz thinking he would be aiding a troop of Federals. Then he saw the rest of the company and the sudden sag of his face bespoke his realization.

He led them to the home of a man named Potts, whose name was on a list Bill carried. Provided by spies in Carroll County, the list bore the names of men belonging to the local home guard, an organization that rankled Bill for its overweening notion of itself. "Bunch of farmers wanting to wear Federal blue and play at war, to be guerrilla killers all day and then go home to a warm supper and a ready wife." Fifteen minutes after arriving at the Potts place, the guerrillas were on their way again, Mrs. Potts' wails falling faint behind them.

By midafternoon they had visited eight farms and at each one killed the home guardsman who lived there. The rest of the men on the list resided in neighboring Chariton County, but Hamer said he wasn't very familiar with that region and pleaded to be relieved of his guide duty.

"All right then, Mr. Hamer," Bill Anderson said. He affected to regard his list with hard concentration. "H-A-M-E-R. Is that the correct spelling? Gregory Hamer, of the Sixteenth Missouri Home

Guard that last month burned the home of a Confederate hero who lost a leg at Vicksburg? Whose wife was bad sick at the time you boys fired the house and has since died? Whose children now live in a lean-to?"

Hamer blanched. He half-raised a hand as if he would make a point, but already Butch Berry was dropping a noose around his neck and snugging it tight in the same motion, dallying the rope to his saddlehorn and hupping his horse into a hard sprint, snatching Gregory Hamer of the Sixteenth Missouri Home Guard off his saddle and out from under his hat. The man bounced flailing and scraping over the ground, losing first one boot and then the other. A hundred yards down the road, Butch reined up and cut the rope. As the company trotted past the corpse, they shared amusement at the sight of its grotesquely attenuated neck.

They impressed another guide in Chariton and over the next days they left men of the Sixteenth Home Guard hanging from trees and barn rafters, shot dead in fields and corrals, throatcut in dooryards, on porches.

One late forenoon they reined up before a young farmer repairing a boundary fence. His eyes were an agitation of uncertainty as they cut from man to man and saw a blue coat on every one. Bill asked if he were a Union man, and the man nodded. "Are you certain, now," Bill asked, leaning forward in his saddle. "For sure, you're a champion of Mr. Lincoln?"

The man nodded again, though with less vigor.

"Ah," Bill said tiredly, "how sad for you. We are true sons of Missouri and cannot stand the notion of a Union man breathing our air."

The man's eyes sprang wide. "No, *not* a Union man!" he cried. "Secesh! I am secesh! I thought *you* was Union!"

"Could be this one's telling the truth, Bill," Sock Johnson said.

"He's lying," Arch Clement said.

"No, not lying! Believe me! Please! Bitte!"

"*Bitte?*" Butch Berry said. He leaned from his saddle and spat. Guerrilla eyes narrowed all around.

Sock Johnson shook his head and said, "Oh hell, Dutchy, you done it now."

As he reined his horse back toward the road and the others swung their mounts after him, Bill said, "Persuade that Dutchman to give up his informing ways."

Arch Clement's bowie was already in his hand.

"The devil is loose in Chariton and Carroll counties with scarcely three feet of chain to his neck." Thus spake *The Missouri Statesman* in these deepening summer days.

They ranged east into Randolph and into his one-time home of Huntsville. Former neighbors displayed smiles, professed gladness at the sight of him, but he cursed them for cowards, for not taking arms against the Federals. Accompanied by Jim and Arch and the two James boys, he stalked into the main street bank and when they came out again Jim carried a sack containing more than $40,000. Frank James felt his little brother's elbow in his ribs and heard him whisper, "Hot *dang*, Buck!"

Down into Howard County. They got word that a detachment of Yankees was in Fayette and bragging they would wipe out Bloody Bill's gang and scalp every man of them just as they had been scalping Federals. Bill set up an ambush on the Fayette road and waited for the Feds to come along in the morning. But the informer who had brought word of the Federals to Bill had taken back word of the ambush to the Yanks. The Federals tried to catch the guerrillas by surprise from behind, but a vidette spotted them and gave the alarm.

The fight was short and fierce and the Feds abandoned the field, leaving a handful of dead comrades and one killed guerrilla, a man named Luckett. Riley Crawford lost a little finger to a passing pistol ball and searched the ground for it in vain, distressed by the thought of ants or some crow making supper of it.

Bill himself was shot in the hip but the bullet broke no bone. Jim and Butch would cauterize the wound that night with a heated pistol barrel and grin at Bill's yowls and curses and loudly agreed with each other that he was lucky the round had just missed his ass or it might have done brain damage.

Bill put $35 in Luckett's pocket, together with a note instructing that he be given a proper burial. Then he had the dead man strapped over his horse and the animal was sent loping down the road toward town. The fallen Yankees were left where they lay. When a wagon party came out to collect the bodies, they found them capped with blood. Between the teeth of one was a folded note: "You come to hunt bushwhackers. Now you are skelpt. Clement skelpt you."

This sultry morning they are moving slowly through a region of shadowed bottomland. Crows calling. Frogs clangoring in the river reeds. Dragonflies wavering above the high grass. The air heavy with the smell of mud and verdure. As they ride, the young James boy is lecturing on the hoop snake.

"There's just no getting away from a hoop snake if it takes a mind to go after you," Jesse says. "It'll take its tail in its mouth and make itself into a wheel, and it'll roll faster than any horse can run."

"Lord Jesus," Frank James mutters. He spits and drops farther back along the column, beyond earshot of his brother.

"I'd ride my horse up a steep hill, what I'd do," Hi Guess says, beaming with his cleverness. "See it get me then."

"It'll roll right *up* that hill after you," Jesse says. "Hoop snake can roll uphill, can roll *over water*, can roll right up a danged tree. It can bite you dead right through your boot."

"Is it any way to keep from dying of its bite?" Buster Parr says. "You know, like how you treat a rattler bite?" He'd been the one to bring up the subject—and was sorry he had—after seeing a snake slither across the road ahead of them. The sight had reminded him of his baby sister's claim, years ago, to have seen a hoop snake rolling along the hog path behind their barn. He hadn't believed her, but Jesse said he should have, and had commenced his monologue on the mythical creature.

"There's but one way to cure the bite of a hoop snake," Jesse says. "First, you have to kill it before it gets away, and to do that, you have to shoot it in the heart. Now its heart is *exactly* ten inches below the head. If you don't hit the heart you'll never kill it. You can shoot it a dozen dang times, you can shoot its dang head *off*, but if you don't hit the heart it'll just slither away like a raggedy old rope and grow a new head before sunup. But you hit it in the heart and that's all she wrote. Then what you do is, you cut off a piece of the carcass and wrap it around the bite and leave it in place for twenty-four hours *exactly*, not a minute longer and not a minute less. You do that and you'll be as right as the rain again."

They went into Boone County and reveled in the river town of Rocheport. Most of the residents hailed them as heroes. The bush-whackers paid for their first few rounds of drinks in the various taverns and then simply began helping themselves to the liquor, and no saloonkeeper dared to protest. The women gorged them with home-cooking. Men made presents of good horses to those guerrillas in need of new mounts. They passed to them every scrap of information they had about Federal doings in the region. They cheered and guffawed like spectators at a stageshow comedy while the bushwhackers fired fusillades at a passing steamboat, the bullets whining off the smokestack, gouging the railings and woodwork, humming into the pilothouse and splintering the walls over the heads of the captain and his officers where they hunkered down and prayed they wouldn't run up on a sandbar or tear the hull open on a sawyer.

As he strolled down the main street the next day, Bill spied a young boy of about eight grinning at him. He stopped and winked at the boy and said having his company in town was better than a circus, wasn't it? "Oh, *yes sir*!" the boy said. The day before, Bill had taken a silver pocketwatch off the bank president, and now he presented it to the boy and smiled at his speechless delight.

WOLF DAYS

The company continued to draw recruits, fierce young men and boys eager to ride with Bloody Bill, the scourge of Union Missouri. By the last days of July, the Union command in Missouri elevated him to the top of their wanted list. "Anderson is the worst of the lot," wrote one Yankee general to another. "His brigands are like a pack of wolves who have tasted human blood and henceforth will feed on nothing other. The sole solution to the problem he constitutes is to kill him, for he will surely continue to kill every Union man he can."

From the start, the Federals had sometimes hanged captured guerrillas and left them to rot on the rope, posting signs that warned against removal of the bodies. On rare occasion their Indian scouts had taken a scalp or two. But in this bloodiest summer of the Missouri war, the Yankees had been regularly retaliating in kind—scalping one or two men in every bunch of killed guerrillas, docking ears and noses and fingers.

And now the war grew still more malevolent. . . .

Back in Carroll County, they ambushed Union patrols and cut telegraph lines, then cut them again as soon as they were repaired. They once more terrified steamboat traffic on the river. They camped in the bluffs north of DeWitt and Bill sent a pair of scouts to reconnoiter the oxbow region around Wakenda Creek, where Yank patrols were said to be roaming. By morning the scouts hadn't returned, so he set out with two dozen men to look for them.

They found their heads mounted on adjacent posts of a farm fence within sight of the creek, nettled crows flapping off them and into the trees as the horsemen came cantering. Pale as wax, hair wild, eyes hollowed blackly and lips in ruin, the faces looked like poorly wrought carnival masks swarming with ants. The fence posts beneath them showed blacked streaks of blood. A search was made of the area but neither man's body was found. Butch Berry said they had likely been flung in the creek and carried on the current to the Muddy. "Some downriver farmer's going to have an interesting moment when he goes to water his mules and sees what comes floating by."

Arch Clement had been fighting a grin and now yielded to it. "I'll tell you what," he said. "You can't get your throat cut any worse than that."

While a couple of the men dug holes with their bowies to bury the heads, Jim put his horse up beside Bill's and said, "I can remember a time when this sort of thing might've set me back on my heels a little."

"I can't," Bill said.

"They must've thought to jolt us with this," Butch Berry said.

"Damn fools," Archie said. "We'll show them jolts."

At the beginning of August they got word of the Confederacy's plan to invade Missouri. General Sterling Price, commanding the rebel force, would come across the Arkansas border in September, march up through eastern Missouri, and attack Saint Louis. Once that key city was in Confederate hands, the South could recapture the rest of the state. Old Pap sent a request to all Missouri guerrilla chiefs to do what they could to keep Union forces busy and at a distance from Saint Louis.

They stormed through Clay County, moving fast, burning Unionist farms and laying ambushes for Yankee patrols. Fletch Taylor led a small party of men across the Missouri into Jackson County to cause what consternation they might, but in a skirmish with Federals he had his right arm shattered by a rifleball. The doctor his men impressed to attend him said there was nothing for it but to come off, and so it was done. His men then took him to a trusted Lafayette County family, left him there to recover, and rejoined the company over the river.

East of Richfield they caught a party of twelve Feds out in the open and killed them all. Every man of the Yanks was scalped but their leader, a young lieutenant whose severed and earless head hung dripping from a maple branch where Archie Clement tied it by its own hair.

They headed back for the central counties, their pace varying, their route a meander. They came on farms that had been fled minutes before their arrival, the chimneys churning smoke, the animals in their pens and stalls, dinner plates sometimes still on the table, half-full and warm. They never bothered to search out the families hiding in the woods nor tried to determine if they were of Yankee or rebel allegiance. Bill's rule was that any who fled them were Unionist, and in every case of a deserted farm he ordered his men to gather all the food they could carry off, then shoot the stock and fire the house and outbuildings. By the middle of the month they were being hunted by every Federal and militia unit in central Missouri.

> The very air seems charged with blood and death. East of us, west of us, north of us, south of us, comes the same harrowing story. Pandemonium itself seems to have broken loose, and robbery, murder and rapine, and death run riot over the country.
> —*Journal of Commerce* (Kansas City)

Darling wife—

I defer to no man in my hatred of Federals or my joy in their destruction,—but these newer rituals do sometimes seem less acts of war than antics of madhouse riot. But then, as you well know, I have been quite mad for some time,— from the very instant I met you, I have been mad for YOU. Never doubt that you are in my heart and thoughts every minute. I never shut my eyes at night without first stroking the lock of your hair and then studying your likeness by the light of the fire. . . .

Cherished husband—

You do what you must do, I do not doubt it for an instant, but I do not dwell upon it. I have not used our lovely tub since your departure, nor will I until you return. I bathe at the creek. Were I to sit in that grand tub without you, I would feel adrift at sea. . . .

They met with Clifton Holtzclaw's company in the hills of north Boone County and complimented each other on their good work. They shared a bottle and by the time they had emptied it they'd agreed to join forces, and so the Kansas First Guerrillas now numbered more than eighty men.

But Holtzclaw had sad news as well, which he'd recently heard from George Todd. In late July, Todd and Dick Yeager had teamed to made a good raid on Arrow Rock in Saline County—they drove the Feds out of town and burned their headquarters, rustled a good bunch of horses, and got several wagonloads of goods. But as the Yanks made their retreat, they kept up a steady rear-guard fire, and Yeager took a bad head wound. Todd transported him a few miles upriver to the farm of an old couple named Jorgenson, who had several times given the guerrillas refuge and feedings. George gave them money and left Dick to their tending.

A couple of weeks later, Todd got word that a Yankee patrol had showed up at the Jorgenson farm and gone straight to the barn loft where Yeager was hidden. They dangled him from a tree by his ankles and shot him repeatedly until he looked like a side of raw beef pasted with bloody rags. They tied him behind a horse and dragged him into town and there decapitated him and told the citizens to have a good look at how bushwhackers ended up. They rode off and left his remains in the street for the townfolk to bury.

The word to George was that old Jorgenson had betrayed Dick for a fat reward. When Todd went back to the Jorgenson place, the old man came out of the house with his hands together like he was praying. He swore he hadn't been the one to inform. Todd had the house searched, all the outbuildings, the well. A poke of U.S. money—nearly $200—was uncovered behind a stone in the spring-house. Mrs. Jorgenson tried to shield her husband but Todd flung her aside and clubbed the man with a singletree like he was trying to beat out a fire. He broke his knees, his arms, his skull, then dragged him broken and groaning into the house and set the place aflame. Then sat his horse out front and watched the building burn while the old woman stood by and shrieked like she'd gone crazy.

August wore on. The Kansas First Guerrillas were several times badly bloodied. Two of their members were killed in a fight with militia in lower Boone County, then two more in a scrap with a Federal detachment north of Rocheport. A company scout named Oliphant was captured by the Feds and hanged before a crowd of civilians, then cut down and his body burned by the roadside. For some of the new Yankee recruits the entire episode was so vehemently novel they cast up their breakfast to the great amusement of their seasoned fellows.

Back in Carroll County and encamped on Wakenda Creek, the company was ambushed by a Federal patrol in the middle of a moonless night. Dock Rupe was on picket and cried out the alarm just before he was throatcut by an Indian scout. The fight lasted ten minutes and no man clearly saw another but only caught glimpses by the flaring lights of the gunfire storm. The Yanks at last retreated, nine of their dead left behind, and the guerrillas rode away in the other direction, the dust of their departure settling in the darkness on three of their own killed comrades.

Among the casualties was Bill himself, who'd been hit in the upper arm by a bullet fragment without damage to the bone. Hi Guess took a round in the thigh but would be all right to keep riding with the company. Arch Clement was shot cleanly through the calf. Frank James had been scraped on the side of the head by a passing round and the long welt where the hair had been removed looked more like a burn than a bullet wound.

The worst of the wounded was the younger James, who'd been shot in the chest and two miles down the road fell off his horse. The company halted long enough for comrades to hoist him back onto his saddle and then Sock Johnson lashed the boy's feet together under his horse's belly and tied him snugly to his saddle by the waist. When they reined up at the Rudd farm to tend their wounds at last and take a day's shelter, the James boy was slumped unconscious against his horse's neck and the front of his shirt was weighted with blood. His eyes fluttered as they carried him into the house and put him on a bed. He coughed weakly and blood spilled over his whiskerless chin. His breath rasped. The Rudd woman shooed the men away and set to tending him. Not a man of them believed he would survive the night, but at dawn he yet clung to the spirit.

As the company readied to ride off, he beckoned Bill to the bed-side and whispered hoarsely that he would be ready to rejoin him by the time they returned.

"Sure you will," Bill said, and wished he believed it.

A month after losing his arm, Fletch Taylor was back with the company, his comrades much impressed with the swiftness of his recovery and the skill of his riding and shooting in spite of his crippling. "I don't need but one arm to fight a bunch of damn Yankees," Taylor said. "It's anyhow more of a fair fight this way."

Some days later, they ambushed a militia patrol near Russellville and Taylor was at the forefront of the charge when his remaining arm was hit from behind by a revolver round. Both bones of his lower arm were shattered, but amputation was unnecessary. Still, Fletcher Taylor took it for a sign that his luck was arrived at the rim of the abyss. He told Bill he'd had enough and was quitting the war. Bill gave him no argument. The next morning Fletch said so long to them all and that he hoped they'd meet for a drink some day. As they watched him being led away on his horse by a bushwhacker who would see him home, somebody said softly, "I hope Fletch's wife truly loves him, else it'll be a goodly while before his ass gets wiped again."

INCHOATE LEGENDS

They said this about him, they said that, they said the other. . . .

Everyone knew of his vanity, his adoration of his own handsomeness, his morning habit of inquiring of himself in a handmirror, "Good morning, Captain Anderson. How fare you this morning, sir?" and every time responding, "Why, I fare well, sir, very damn well indeed."

They had all heard of his black silk ribbon, and by some accounts it now held more than a hundred knots. Some said that he'd tied so many knots on top of knots that they couldn't be counted anymore, that the ribbon was drawn up into a single lump of a knot, like a cancer grown big as a fist.

They said he had forever gone mad, that he rode into battle screaming his sister's name as foam flew off his lips, that in the midst of a skirmish he would weep in becrazed fury because he could not kill Federals fast enough. They said he carried a pirate's sword to chop off enemy heads.

They said he could commune with wolves, howling back and forth with them over the miles of open prairie. That he could see in the dark like a bat, could smell any lie. He could know the thoughts of the dead when he stood over their graves. He could hear a human heartbeat at a distance of fifty yards. He never slept. It would not have surprised any who trafficked in such lore to learn he could set fires with a hard stare, could look hard at an overhead hawk and see the country all around as the raptor saw it.

They said he'd been shot upward of three dozen times and had taken wounds that would have killed any other man, said he'd been shot in the belly, in the head, shot where his *heart* should be—and still he lived on. Some said he got his magical protection from his wife, who was an Ozark goomer woman. Some whispered he'd made a bargain with the Devil, though others said that made no sense at all, that the Devil didn't make bargains to gain what was already coming to him. . . .

TUNES OF THIS WAR

They are trotting in a double column through a wide meadow awash in goldenrod and flanked by dense wildwood. Crows observe their progress on this bright morning smelling faintly of woodfires. Riley Crawford is telling a story of a one-eyed dog he used to own when he was just a boy—Riley now all of sixteen—a dog given to poking around the creek in search of adventure who one day was bitten on the nose by a snapping turtle that wouldn't turn loose for love or money.

"I mean to tell you," Riley says, "you never heard such a holler as that poor dog was raising. I had to—"

His hat tilts and jumps from his head with a portion of his skull still in it and his head jerks around as if he would see where it was going—but he is already dead and the rifle report fading as he rolls off his horse and sinks into the tide of yellow flowers and the yelping company goes scattering into the cover of the trees.

They spent the rest of the morning searching the surrounding country for the sniper, for some sign of a unit he might belong to. The videttes reported no hint of Feds in the area. The guerrillas were convinced the shooter was a loner who was still in his nook up in a tree or under a bush and they were enraged that they could not flush him out.

"The son of a bitch is probably looking at us right this minute with a shiteating grin," Frank James said, scanning the wildwood all around. "I almost wish he'd shoot another one of us, just so we could get an idea where he's at."

They retrieved Riley Crawford from the field of flowers. In death the boy looked even smaller than his diminutive living self, seemed even younger, a child in oversized garb playing at war. They lashed him to his horse and rode on.

Two miles down the road they arrived at a small farm where lived a young couple and their three small children. While some of the guerrillas searched the outbuildings and others went through the house, still others made use of the farmer's pick and shovel to bury Riley Crawford in a small clearing in the trees behind the house.

Bill asked the farmer if his allegiance was Union or southern. The man was hesitant, wondering perhaps if he was faced with true Federals or guerrillas in disguise—or Federals pretending to be guerrillas in disguise. Then said he wasn't either one, he just wanted to stay as far out of the war as he could.

Bill spat. "That line's been too long worn away for anybody to stand on it," he said. "You best pick a side, mister. Go ahead, pick—maybe you'll guess right. Or you can just tell the truth and say what you really believe."

"I used to believe Jesus was coming," the man said. "But anymore I believe he's changed his mind."

Bill made a small smile. "My, that is a hopeless outlook."

Butch Berry heard this as he brought his horse up beside Bill's. "He got reason to be hopeless—look here." He handed Bill a Union army cap. "The boys found it in a corner of the barn."

Bill studied the cap, and the look he turned on the farmer was not without disappointment.

"I won't lie to you," the man said. "I can see you're bushwhackers—all them six-shooters, you all's hair. Four days ago a troop of Yanks stopped here and made my wife feed them. They had a bad wounded man with them and they patched him up some in the barn. Must've left his hat. That's the truth of it."

"I'll wager this is the son of a bitch who fed the man who shot Riley," Arch Clement said. He was already at fashioning a proper thirteen-coil noose.

"When you helped a Yank, you chose your side," Bill said. The verdict was rote and he had grown weary with imposing it.

Buster Parr came out of the house with a fiddle and a bow in his hand. He asked the farmer if he could play the instrument, and the man said he played passably.

Arch had the noose ready. "Enough palaver. Let's raise him a little nearer to Jesus. Maybe that'll restore his faith some."

"You know 'The Rose of Alabama'?" Hi Guess asked the farmer. The man said he reckoned he did.

"It was Riley's favorite song," Hi said to Bill. "Be kinda nice to let this fella play it. I mean, we didn't have a preacher to say words over Riley or nothing, why not play a song for him?"

The notion was appealing in its novelty, and Bill gestured for the man to play.

The minute the farmer drew the bow across the strings, most of the bushwhackers broke into grins. By the time he was midway through "Rose of Alabamy," they knew they were in the presence of a master fiddler, and some of the men were singing along to the music:

So fare thee well, Eliza Jane,
and fare thee well, you belles of fame,
for all your charms are put to shame
by the Rose of Alabamy.

He played the tune for a good five minutes before at last stroking the final note and raising his chin off the fiddle, his face losing the shut-eyed smile it had held all through the number that had been his reprieve. But now somebody hollered "Do another!" and he hastened to it, tucking the instrument in place and stroking into a lively rendition of "Old Joe Clarke." When he was done with that one, he didn't wait to be asked but segued directly into "Cripple Creek," and then "The Bully of the Town," and then "The Johnson Boys." He went through one number after another with hardly a break in notes between them for fear that even a moment's respite from the music would snap the spell and the guerrillas would think to get back to the matter at hand. He played for his life, played each number with more fervor than the one before.

Some of the men were stepdancing and some doing dances of their own invention. Buster Parr shyly asked the man's wife if she would take a turn with him and she glanced at her husband and then quickly accepted, though her smile was a stiff mask of desperation.

She spun around with one after another of the bushwhackers as her husband played on. He was careful not to repeat himself, as fearful of repetition as of hesitation between numbers, but more than an hour after he'd begun, he'd exhausted his repertoire of lively tunes, and he segued into a composition of slower pulse.

It was not a tune to dance to, and the guerrilla who held the man's wife in readiness for the next turn now blushed and let go of her and backed away. This tune was so different from the music of the past hour that the bushwhackers only stood and stared. The wife read their unsmiling faces as a bad sign and could think of nothing to do but to sing the song he played:

I wonder as I wander under the sky
how poor baby Jesus was born for to die for
poor wretched sinners like you and like I.
I wonder as I wander out under the sky.

The man sensed the stillness around him and opened his eyes and saw their faces, but he played on, and they let him finish the number. Then he handed the instrument and bow to his wife and kissed her cheek and she began crying without sound.

"A fine valediction," Bill said, and gestured to Arch Clement.

They left him hanging from a branch of the maple tree in his dooryard, the wife and children kneeling at his dangling feet and weeping their prayers to Jesus, whom the man had quit waiting for, but to whom he was now departed.

My darling wife—

The days blur one onto the other in their sameness. The evenings in camp sometimes seem to me as unreal as dreams, the men laughing and singing and telling jokes at the campfires, who only hours before were hard at killing. I confess to you that the pleas and the death cries of Federals and their informers, the wailings of their widows and children, are grown tiresome to me for their monotony. But such "music" remains, after all, the most popular tune of this war. O my sweet girl, I cannot but wonder sometimes at the uncertain nature of my thoughts. . . .

Beloved husband—

My dreams of you are longer and more frequent than ever. I see you standing before me and smiling in your handsome wicked way and I run to your arms and we laugh and do the most wonderfully sinful things!—how I hate to wake from them! The tune I hear most often anymore is the sad refrain in my heart pining for your return. . . .

REPRISALS AND A REVENANT

Into September and the bloodtide rises.

Ambushes and daily skirmish. Scalpings, dockings of ears and noses. The Federals decapitate two guerrillas on the bank of the Chariton and leave the heads on the dead men's chests.

Two days after, Arch Clement flays a Union lieutenant's face, then carefully arranges it on the ground, remarks that the fellow looks a little glum, and places an empty ammunition box over it to keep the crows off until the Yanks have their look. In the nosehole of the flensed skullface, he wedges a wild carrot.

They make the rounds of friendly havens through central Missouri, now taking a meal at this farm, now getting fresh horses at that one, now spending a night on a bed of hay at this other. They engage in several scattered skirmishes with random Federal units, inflicting many more casualties than they take. When they arrive at the familiar Rudd place in Carroll County, a hollow-eyed specter shambles out onto the porch to greet them, his skeletal frame hung with an overlarge Federal uniform and a quartet of revolvers.

"I thought you all would never get back," he says in his thin strained voice. "I thought the war would be ancient history and I'd still be waiting on you."

Frank James beholds his younger brother like something risen from the grave. Bill Anderson grins and says, "Sorry we took so long to come collect you, but we've been somewhat occupied." Then laughs. "Damn boy, I don't believe anything can kill you unless maybe it sneaks up from behind."

QUANTRILL AND A DEBACLE

They joined now with Todd and Pool, and in their combined strength of two hundred men they struck at larger Federal patrols and encampments, inflicted greater casualties, and drew still larger numbers of Yankee troops into the pursuit of them—well serving Sterling Price's strategy as his Army of Missouri began its move up from Arkansas and into eastern Missouri.

In Howard County they made a camp in the red cedars on Bonnefemme Creek a few miles south of Fayette and debated whether to try an assault on the Federal post in that town. They'd been told that the garrison had been reduced to a mere two dozen men, but the Yanks were well fortified in a log blockhouse atop a low rise. Todd was leaning toward the attack, but Bill thought the post might prove impregnable and cost them dearly. Todd took a party of men and went on a wide scouting mission to ensure there were no other Federals in proximity to come to the garrison's aid.

The company was already at breakfast when Todd returned at dawn—and with him was William Clarke Quantrill and a band of two dozen men, all of them in Federal blue. Bill was in the company of his brother and Butch and Arch under an oak atop a low rise, feeding on hardtack and jerky. They watched the arrivals step down from the saddle and turn their mounts over to the horse pickets—except for vicious Charley, whom Quantrill tethered to a tree at a distance from the other horses. There was much loud salutation between men who had not seen each other since late spring. Todd and Quantrill accepted cups of coffee at one of the fires and stood talking together. They both looked to Bill a bit stiff in their posture, and he thought that if they'd put aside their differences they had not put them aside very far.

Todd pointed in Bill's direction and Quantrill came up the low rise and said hello to them all. He looked leaner than when Bill had last seen him, near to gaunt. The violet halfmoons under his eyes bespoke too many sleepless nights. Bill gestured for him to sit down. The others got up and moved off beyond earshot of them.

Quantrill settled himself crosslegged with a tired sigh and smiled wryly. " 'Christ, if my love were in my arms and I in my bed again.' Don't you agree, William T.?"

"I do," Bill said. "But I also agree that if a frog had wings he wouldn't bump his ass so much."

"Ah, but you have a new name, don't you?" Quantrill said. He raised his cup. "Here's to Bloody Bill—the most feared man in Missouri."

"Damn newspapers," Bill said. "They've made me out so fearsome it's a chore to keep from scaring myself."

"Actually, there's another Missourian even more fearsome than yourself," Quantrill said. "Name's Holcomb. Lives in Burton. Knows more about dealing pain than any man I ever met. Had me howling and begging for mercy, I tell you true. The very thought of ever meeting him again makes me all weak in the bladder."

"That dentist I hear you went to?"

"He will instruct you in whole new notions of pain."

"I've never been myself, but I witnessed Yeager in a dentist chair one time. Wasn't pretty."

Quantrill's smile fell away at the mention of Yeager. "I heard about the unpretty things the Yanks did to Dick in Saline."

"George squared things for him with the fellow who sold him out."

"Is that so? Well, I'm sure Dick's glad to know he's all squared."

His tone carried a note of mockery that reminded Bill of the last time they'd spoken—when Quantrill had advised against marriage to Bush—and the memory roused the resentments that attached to it. "What are you doing here?" Bill said.

Quantrill's brow rose slightly at his tone. "Old Pap has called for bushwhackers to distract the Feds while he pushes for Saint Louis," he said. "I thought we should get together and decide how we could use our companies to draw the most Fed troops away from the east and do Old Pap the most good. I took Kate to her daddy's place in Blue Springs and I've been hunting you boys since. Finally ran into Todd last night." He grinned. "We came this close to shooting each other for Yankees in our bluecoats."

"I thought you and George had a parting of the ways."

Quantrill shrugged. "That's done with. Helping Price is more important than any disagreement between us, and George knows it. Actually, it's a good thing I've come along. Last night George said he was thinking of attacking the blockhouse in Fayette—if you can imagine that. That's folly and I told him so."

As they talked, George Todd started up the rise toward them. They watched him come. Quantrill grinned and said, "I was just telling William T. how near to shooting each other we came last night."

Todd's face was tight in the way Bill knew it to get whenever he was spoiling for a fight. He stood over them and stared hard at Quantrill and said he'd decided to attack the Yank post at Fayette this morning.

Quantrill stared up at him. "That's unwise, George."

Todd spat. "If you're too scared," he said, "don't join us in it. I wouldn't ride with a fearful man anyhow."

Quantrill and Bill got to their feet "It's not a matter of being fearful, George," Quantrill said. "It's a question of good sense."

Todd squared himself. "You saying I don't have good sense?"

Quantrill sighed and turned to Bill. "Maybe he'll listen to you."

Todd cut his eyes to Bill, his gaze demanding to know who he sided with.

He thought Quantrill was likely right, no cavalry outfit could breach that highground blockhouse. You only had to look at it to see its invulnerability. Still, everything that had ever nettled him about Quantrill was roused and thumping angrily in his veins—the presumptuousness of the man, his condescension, his subtly mocking manner. He remembered Quantrill's sly nuance to Todd about Bush's past.

"Hell, we outnumber them at least four to one," Bill said. "If we don't fight with odds like that on our side, we ought to just put up our hands and surrender, let them shoot us against a wall."

Todd grinned hugely. Quantrill looked from one to the other, and then turned up his palms in resignation.

It was over in fifteen minutes. Bill and Todd led the first two assaults, but there were twice as many Federals in the fort as they had thought, and the first Yank volley put down a dozen mounts and riders. The guerrillas never saw anything of the Yankees except their rifle muzzles jutting from the loopholes and issuing smoke, heard nothing from them but rifleshots and great rocking cheers each time a handful of horsemen went down in the risen dust and drifting haze of powdersmoke.

Bill circled back to the treeline where Quantrill was supposed to be ready to lead the next charge, but just as he got there, he saw Quantrill and his twenty boys cresting a hill a quarter-mile away at full gallop and then dropping out of sight beyond it. He would not see any of them again.

Quantrill had given a folded note to Sock Johnson for relay to Bill and Todd. Bill had already read it by the time George came riding up—wild-eyed and gasping, only half his men still horsed, the rest coming off the field on foot or lying wounded or dead on it. The note was a single line: "I won't ride with fools."

Todd cursed and balled the paper in his fist. "If that cowardly son of a bitch hadn't run away," he said, "we might've had the day! I'll kill him, by God!" He drew a revolver and called for Bill to ride with him after Quantrill and his bunch.

But Bill was looking at the horseless bushwhackers staggering off the field and into the cover of the trees, most of them wounded, some of them badly, and he knew they couldn't have won the day with even a hundred more men. He heard the cries of dying comrades and animals still out in the open, heard the Yankee rifles as they kept firing on whatever yet moved out there, and he felt the folly of the attack like a weight in his chest, felt himself made small by his own willfulness. *All these men down because you didn't want to say he was right. Well, he was right about that and right about you being a fool.*

He argued against going in pursuit of Quantrill, saying they had too many wounded to gather up and get to someplace safe where they could be tended. Dave Pool and others agreed, and Todd reluctantly capitulated. But he was still in a rage, and even as they dragged their wounded off the field and doubled them up on the horses still serviceable, he pointed at Bill and said, "You're wrong if you think he's your friend. He's nobody's fucken friend! Next time I see him I'll kill him where he stands without a damn hello, and woe to the man who tries to keep me from it."

"Let's go, George," Bill said.

They left fifteen dead at Fayette and carried off forty wounded, and five of these died in the saddle and were hastily buried in the roadside woods. They navigated northward the afternoon long, distributing the most badly wounded at the farms of various Howard County friends, leaving them there to recover or not as they would.

Todd remained in sullen temper through the day, and Bill knew

George was still rankled at him for refusing to chase after Quantrill. When they reached the Randolph County line that evening, he was not surprised by Todd's announcement that he thought they could do a better job of distracting the Feds if they operated as smaller bands, so he was going his own way with his company. Dave Pool shrugged apologetically at Bill and took his bunch with Todd's. Holtzclaw and his boys stayed with Bill.

Marlowe's farm and a higher meanness

Into Monroe County and wide fields of goldenrod, lush meadows of rose mallow, through dense green woodlands showing the first hints of amber. The men remark on the difference between the lingering greenness of these late September days and last year's early leaffall.

At the farm of a family named Marlowe that swore they were secessionist, they took a noon meal of roasted potatoes and gravy, some of the men sitting on the floor of the crowded house, others out in the barn, some few with the horses hidden in a brushy ravine behind the house. The Marlowes' two pubescent daughters were both afflicted with the skin disease called Saint Anthony's fire, their faces so badly ravaged that some of the bushwhackers gaped in open revulsion while others politely averted their eyes.

Oz Swisby was the first to finish eating and went out on the porch to wait on the others. He had earlier taken off his Federal bluecoat and tucked it under his cantle, and the guerrilla shirt he wore was bright red. He took out his pipe and was in the midst of lighting it, humming the tune to "Come All Ye Fair and Tender Ladies," when he was slammed backward by a Yankee rifleball that made instant ruin of his heart even as the gunshot was still on the air.

They flung aside their tin plates and some of them rushed to the door and windows, revolvers drawn. Marlowe had been sufficiently foresightful to put in a rear door when he built the cabin, and Bill led the way through it as rifleballs whacked the front of the house.

The rest of the men were running from the barn and taking outside cover, all of them firing into the treeline some hundred yards distant, where the cloud of riflesmoke positioned the Feds. Now the horseholders came riding up from the ravine, each man of them trailing a half-dozen mounts. Jesse James led the horses that included

Edgar Allan, trailing them by their reins in one hand and firing his pistol with the other and guiding his own mount with his knees.

The Yankee party must have thought them a smaller bunch, because when the full company of more than sixty guerrillas was in view and galloping toward the woods, howling and shooting, the Federals fled. Jim Anderson led two dozen men in chase for a mile or so before reining up and watching them vanish over a distant rise.

Their forward scouts—Sock Johnson and Fulton the Sailor—had sent back no word of lurking Yankee troops, and so Bill had posted only a single vidette at the treeline, a boy named Robinson. They found him throatcut in the underscrub.

They bore his body back to the Marlowe place and were quick about burying him and Oz Swisby in the soft earth behind the house. Bill gave Marlowe money and told him if they ever disturbed the remains buried there or reported them to Union troops he would know it and he would come back and roast the entire family alive. Marlowe and his wife swore they would keep the graves a secret, but the daughters made no show of fear at Bill's threat. He supposed that they had already seen so much of the world's meanness—even in their own faces—to have grown inured to its timbre. Nether one of them had seemed much affected by the sight of a dead man who had politely thanked them for dinner a half-hour earlier.

They found their scouts two miles away where the road passed through a dense tree hollow. The head of Fulton the Sailor rested on a knee-high tree stump at the side of the road and his body hung by its feet from a branch of a nearby elm. Some waggish Yank had inserted a corncob pipe between Fulton's teeth so that he appeared to be grinning around it in spite of the flies trafficking in his mouth and eyes.

But Fulton could not hold their attention against the spectacle of Socrates Johnson. The things they had seen in the course of this war had made quaint the notion of shock, but here the Yankees did succeed in capturing their attention. From four different trees dangled Johnson's quartered portions. The bolder crows had persisted at their clustered feedings on the rent and dripping flesh until Butch Berry fired a shot to disperse them into the higher branches, where they perched and glowered at the intruders and squalled their protests.

"That's how they used to kill people back in the olden days," Frank James said. "When they wanted to make a lasting impression on anybody who might be thinking to follow a wayward path."

"Looks like it makes a pretty lasting impression on the fella who gets it done to him too," Hi Guess said.

Fulton the Sailor had been popular with the company, Sock Johnson fairly venerated. Sock had been Jenny's great favorite, Bill remembered, and had doted on her like a darling daughter. His hands began to pain, and he eased his grip on the saddlehorn.

"That's four good men we lost today and two of them butchered and we've put down not one goddam Fed in return," Butch Berry said. He spat hard and his off eye looked wild. "I say we got a big bill to collect."

They buried the men deep among the trees and then found heavy broken branches to put on the graves to keep off the larger scavengers.

Darling wife—

I am weary with my own rage, from which there is no respite but my dreams of you. How I miss you, my lovely girl! In my dreams the scents of your skin and your hair are so real that I am shocked, on waking, to discover I am not with you. Shocked,—and remanded to my fury. . . .

They crossed down into Boone County, every man of them aching to encounter Federals or any man who did support the Union, but by sundown they had met none. Bill was about to call a halt for the night when Butch and his scouts reported that George Todd and Dave Pool were encamped with their companies on the farm of a man named Singleton a few miles to southward. Butch had taken a drink with them, and they sent word that Bill's company was welcome to put down in their camp.

They sat around the fires under a starbright sky showing a skullwhite shard of moon in the west. Todd had no news of Price's Army of Missouri, but was as curious as Bill about where Pap might be and what he would have the guerrillas do in service of his invasion. He gave no sign of still being disgruntled with Bill, but he made no mention of Quantrill, which Bill took as evidence of his persisting displeasure toward the man. Todd was saddened to learn of the men Bill had lost at Marlowe's farm, and was wroth to hear of their mutilations. Dave Pool had been close friends with Sock Johnson and was almost tearful in his sulfurous cursing of the Yanks. At every fire in the camp, the wildwood boys spoke in hard voices of the barbarities committed on their fellows.

They passed a restless night, tossing in their blankets, cursing low, muttering their maledictions to imagined auditors. Bill slept not at all but stared at the stars all night and felt his heart like some becrazed creature banging on the bars of its cage.

In the morning their mood was still smoldering. Feeling restless and craving to know where Price and his army might be, Bill mounted up with thirty men and asked Todd where the nearest town lay. Todd pointed down the southward trail. "About three miles yonderway. Place called Centralia."

VAE VICTUS

The town stood on a stretch of rolling prairie three miles from the Singleton farm. It was little more than a stageline waystation and a whistle stop on the North Missouri Railroad, a hamlet of some hundred residents, comprising a depot, a freight house, a general store, some two dozen houses, and two hotels. On this late Tuesday morning of bright sun and few clouds, the smell of dust on the air, thirty men of the Kansas First Guerrillas, all of them dressed in Federal blue, trotted their horses down the street.

A dog barked nearby. A rooster crowed. People on the sidewalks paused to watch the horsemen pass. Those in the street hastened out of their way.

Arch Clement glanced around with a scowl and said, "Look at them. I'll wager the war's never touched this place."

Behind him, Jim Anderson said, "They probably think the war's but a rumor."

"Todd says the place is Unionist to a man," Butch said.

Bill reined up in the middle of the street and studied the town. A small group of men was gathered on the porch of the Eldorado

House, the nearest of the two hotels, and all of them were regarding the arrivals in Union blue. One of them stepped up to the porch rail and called out, "What outfit are ye boys with?"

Bill made no answer but only stared at the man until he made an awkward shrug and turned away. Some of the others retreated into the hotel.

"That's all they do, the likes of them, gawk and talk," Bill said. He spat. "I don't see a man of them missing an eye or arm or leg, but I'll wager there's not a pair of balls on that porch." He thought of Sock Johnson suspended from the various trees, of Fulton the Sailor's disembodied head made an object of jest. His anger of the day before had not at all eased in the night, and now, sleepless and raw-eyed, he squinted against the risen sun's tormenting glare off the glass windows and the pale street.

"*Damn them,*" he said. "Sack the place."

Jim and Arch gave quick orders and the morning was shattered with rebel yells. Some of the men dismounted and ran into the freight house while others heeled their horses into a gallop and raced through the town, taking possession of every good horse they came on, shooting in the air and at everything of glass in sight, laughing at the people scattering like spooked chickens, at the shrieks of the women yanking their children to them and fleeing into their houses. Some went straight for the general store and made short work of looting it, smashing out the front windows with flung bolts of cloth, overturning shelves of goods, cutting open tins of peaches and apple sauce, oysters and salmon, slurping the contents on the spot. They stomped into the two hotels and robbed every guest. One man offered to protest and Frank James broke his nose with a pistol barrel and no one else even thought to resist.

Bill Anderson cantered Edgar Allan up and down the street, relishing the feel of a proper meanness toward this town that had the audacity to think itself exempt from the war.

There came gleeful whoopings from the freight house, where the men had discovered an untapped barrel of whiskey. They rolled it out on the platform, set it upright and broke open the top. A carton of tin cups was produced from one of the stores and the bushwhackers were shoving each other aside in their eagerness to dip into the barrel and gulp the whiskey like water. Somebody found a case of new boots and Dave Pool had the clever idea to tie a pair together by the straps and hang them over his saddle and then fill them with whiskey. "Bedamn if that ain't a sage use of bootleg," Buster Parr said. Others were already putting the rest of the boots to the same use.

Now an outcry at the end of the street announced the arrival of the stagecoach from Columbia. As it rolled up to the Boone Hotel, it was surrounded by bushwhackers ordering the passengers to alight. The terrified driver pled not to be shot as a pair of bushwhackers clambered aboard and began rummaging through the topside luggage. The passengers stepped down and were quickly relieved of their pocketbooks. When they learned who was robbing them, one man said, "Why steal from *us*? We're southern men, same as you."

"Bullshit you are," Hi Guess said. "If you were good southern men, you'd be wearing the gray or riding with us."

Even as they went about their plunder, they kept a steady traffic to the whiskey barrel. Bill sat his horse and accepted a cup of spirits handed up by Arch Clement. They were toasting each other when there sounded a high keen whistle from down the track.

Archie's teeth showed hugely. "Bedamn if our luck ain't made of gold!"

It was the noon train from Saint Louis headed for Saint Joe—three passenger coaches and an express and baggage car. As it rounded into view of the depot, the guerrillas had already converged on the track and were heaving heavy wooden ties across the rails. The train came to a shrilling, steaming halt a dozen yards shy of the barrier. The wildwood boys swarmed aboard and kicked off the engineer and brakemen and stormed into the coaches, shooting into the ceilings, demanding everyone's money and jewelry.

Accompanied by Butch and the James brothers, Bill went directly to the express car and ordered the agent to open the safe. It yielded more than three thousand dollars, which Bill handed in a sack to young Jesse for guardianship. Breaking open the baggage in the car, Frank James discovered a suitcase holding more than ten thousand dollars in greenbacks. When Bill and the others looked to see what he was laughing at, they too had to grin.

"Sweet baby Jesus," Jesse said, beaming at the others. "I ain't never had no fun!"

Arch Clement appeared at the car door, showing his peculiar smile. "Captain Bill, you'll want to see this."

Bill followed him past the passengers who'd been forced off the train and stood in fearful clusters in front of the stationhouse. They went up the steps of one of the coaches, and the pair of bushwhackers posted at the door stepped aside for them. Arch swept a hand into the coach like he was presenting a stage act and said, "Behold!"

In the coach were twenty-three Federal soldiers with not a gun among them and every face hanging like a mourner's. Two bushwhackers stood at the far end of the coach, holding Colts in both hands and grinning at Bill.

"These gents are on furlough," Arch told Bill. "They were bold enough to admit they are men of General Sherman. They were with him in Atlanta."

"Houseburners and well poisoners," Bill said. "Killers of mules and dogs and old men. Violators of women. Silverware thieves. That's what I hear about the bummers of crazy Sherman's outfit. The only thing of worth about you sonsofbitches is your uniforms. Get them off."

The Yanks stood up and began to strip.

Watching them jostling each other as they shed their uniforms, Bill Anderson felt a sudden and discomfiting tiredness that had nothing to do with muscle and bone. More a weariness of purpose. A faltering of tenacity. *How many?* Bush had asked. *For how long?* He had a momentary vision of shooting each man of them in the knee and letting it go at that.

And then one of the Federals said, "Dammit, Wallace, watch your elbow!"

A short soldier was rubbing his eye and glaring at the big Yank beside him. A big man with a thick brown beard.

Wallace. With a beard.

"Say now, Wallace," Bill said, "you ever been in the Nations, nearabouts the Red?"

Wallace gawked at him in surprise at being addressed by name. "No sir, I never."

Wallace with a beard. Bill's incipient uncertainty gave way to revived rage.

"Get them outside," he said to Arch. "Over by the store."

Townfolk and passengers watched the Yanks file off the train in their underwear. Arch ordered them to form a double rank alongside the general store.

"We need one for Wyatt," he said, and Bill nodded. One of their comrades, Cave Wyatt, was a Federal prisoner in Columbia, and Bill wanted to trade for him.

Bill mounted Edgar Allan and hupped the horse up in front of the double rank of Federals and asked if there was a sergeant among them. No man spoke up. Bushwhackers had formed up to either side of him, most of them with a pistol in one hand and a cup of whiskey in the other, all of them well drunk now and cursing the prisoners in rankly obscene terms—calling them fuckers of their own mothers, cornholers of their sisters, practiced suckers of pizzles, avid eaters of shit. Mothers covered their children's ears.

"Are you sure none of you is a sergeant?" Bill said.

A Federal stepped forward and gave his name as Sergeant Tom Goodman. "If you're gonna shoot the sergeants, there's only me. So do it and be damned."

Bill smiled. "Brave last words, Sergeant. But save them for another day." He motioned for Jim to take the man aside.

Seeing that Goodman was not going to be harmed the other Federals became more hopeful. Even the locals and the train passengers breathed more easily.

"Wallace, step out!" Bill called, and the bearded man hastened forward, face brightly expectant that he would be put aside with Goodman. "Right here, Captain," he said.

"Here's your parole," Bill said—and drew his Navy and shot him through the eye.

Before the others could even start to beg for their lives, Arch Clement shot one in the heart—and then the other guerrillas opened fire.

Federals spun and staggered and left their feet as they were hit by bullets. They sprawled kicking and writhing. They fell against the building wall and slid to the ground, painting red streaks on the clapboard. Some of the wounded tried to crawl from the scene, though where they might be thinking to go defied all speculation. Whatever dream of life yet clung in their heads was ended at pointblank range.

The prolonged crackling of revolvers raised a great cloud of white gunsmoke to waft on the easy breeze which carried too the screams of the perishing Yankees and the shrieks of women standing witness to their slaughter.

A single Yank was able to get away from the execution ground, breaking through the line of guerrillas and absorbing no fewer than seven bullets as he went. He made it to the depot and scrambled so far under the low crawlspace that the guerrillas could not make him out in its darkness. They took turns hunkering and coaxing at the crawlspace, assuring him that if he came out they would not harm him further. Archie Clement promised they would write to Lincoln himself and say he deserved a damn medal, deserved to be a general. The man made no answer. So they set the building afire and after some minutes he came crawling out, his underwear sagging with blood. They loudly cheered his pluck. And then shot him dead.

They ordered the train crew to pull the ties off the tracks, then torched the coaches and made the engineer get the locomotive rolling and hop off, letting the train go on its own, the smoke of the flaming cars churning high and black to mingle with the smoke of the blazing depot.

And then they departed, laughing and singing, taking with them a small collection of good horses, boots of sloshing whiskey hanging from their saddles, new Federal uniforms rolled behind their cantles, wallets crammed with tins of foodstuff.

They would never make the trade of Goodman for Wyatt. The Yankee sergeant would be their prisoner for ten days, and then, during a crossing of the Missouri River near Boonville, effect his escape. He was the only Federal ever taken prisoner by Bloody Bill Anderson who lived to tell of it, and for years afterward he would rarely have to pay for his own drinks

Two hours later a pall of smoke still hung over Centralia and its litter of executed Federals when Union Major A.V.E. Johnson arrived at the head of his mounted infantry troop. He found residents and stranded travelers alike still gawking on the dead or wandering about like halfwits displaced into an alien geography.

The major was horrified and outraged in equal parts by the slaughter of the Federals. On learning that there had been but thirty men in the guerrilla band and that its leader was Bill Anderson—the very man he was under orders to hunt for in Boone County—he was determined to run them to ground immediately, never mind the warnings of those who'd heard the bushwhackers say there were many more of their fellows in a nearby camp. Johnson left twenty-five men in town and led the rest in the direction the guerrillas had fled.

They'd been back at the Singleton farm less than three hours when scouts brought warning of Yankees coming from Centralia—125 men armed with muzzleloaders and riding plug horses. Even those who'd been sleeping off the whiskey and labors of the morning leapt up at the call to arms despite their throbbing heads and were pistoled and horsed in minutes. Dave Pool was furious in his whiskey haze, cursing the Yanks for giving him no rest. Bill too was still half-drunk, his head howling with pain, as he and Todd quickly shaped a plan.

Arch Clement sat his horse and waited. The late afternoon light aggravated the dull whiskey pain behind his eyes, and the crows in the trees were carrying on with such a clatter he wanted to shoot them all. He wished he had some whiskey left to take the edge off his hangover. The six men of his party were all suffering in like manner and their ill moods carried into their horses, the animals stamping and snorting with malicious urge.

Now the Yankees appeared over a low hill and one of their front men spied the guerrillas and pointed. A cry went up and their officer drew his saber and waved it forward and the Yanks came on at a lumbering gallop.

Arch and his party reined about and retreated—but had to hold their mounts back to keep from putting too much distance between themselves and the pursuing Unionists. Now another rise loomed ahead and as the guerrillas disappeared over it the Yankees were a quarter-mile behind.

When the Yanks achieved the crest, they reined up short at the sight of two hundred guerrillas sitting their horses at the bottom of the hill in wait for them.

Some trooper bellowed "Holy shit!" and might well have been speaking for them all.

Major Johnson hesitated but briefly before ordering his men to dismount, fix bayonets and form a battle line, the standard tactic of the infantry manual. The horseholders—every fourth man—quickly retreated with the mounts to the off side of the hill.

The bushwhackers gawked. "Am I *awake?*" George Todd asked Bill Anderson. "Are those fools intending to fight us on foot?"

"*Now* we'll even some hard scores," Butch Berry said. The wild roll of his off eye heightened his becrazed aspect. Bill thought he could smell the boy's hatred like a sulfurous vapor. His own head felt afire and his blood roared in his ears.

Pistols drawn, they heeled their mounts into a lope, their battle line moving forward in an even row—and then every man of them raised a rebel yell to shiver the sky and kicked his horse into a gallop and they charged up the hill.

"*Readyyyy,*" Major Johnson commanded. "*Fire!*"

Only three guerrillas were unhorsed by the fusillade, most of the musketballs sailing over the line of horsemen for the downward angle of fire. The Yanks had no chance to reload. The sole Federal armed with a revolver, Johnson stood cool and steady in the haze of riflesmoke and fired at the bushwhacker now at the fore of the thundering line and coming straight for him. He missed the guerrilla with three consecutive shots and then the rider was on him and for an instant he saw quite clearly the blue-eyed boy's wildly grinning face before Jesse James' .44 pistol ball blew his brain apart.

The Centralians had thought they'd seen horror in the round when the twenty-two Federals were executed, but this day's second visitation of guerrillas—this time to make short work of the soldiers Johnson had left in town—made them understand just how little they knew of such things. As they watched the bushwhackers taking ears and lifting scalps, they realized how utterly ignorant they'd been about the harsher truths of this war. And still they had not seen the worst—and they would not, not with their own eyes. But they would hear of it from the Federal troops who arrived the next day and went out to the field to collect the great sprawl of their comrades out beyond the low hills of the prairie where they served no army now but the black ranks of the crows. The Yankees buried their dead in a single long grave just outside of town without permitting any of the townsmen to look on the corpses, but the locals later heard the soldiers' saloon talk of decapitated comrades, of heads swapped from one dead man to another in effort of some horrific joke, of heads placed on the muzzles of upright muskets, sans ears and nose and eyes and none unscalped, of heads set facing each other with wide grins and holding pipes or cigars between their teeth. They heard of faces beaten to pulp and bone shards, including that of Major Johnson, who had also been scalped and would never have been identified except he had not been beheaded nor stripped of his uniform. They heard of men impaled on their own bayonets. Of men with their severed sexual parts in their mouth.

The final tally would never be certain, but by the Yankee army's own estimate, 150 Union soldiers—including the furloughed troopers on the train—were killed by bushwhackers in and about Centralia in the course of that dread September day.

That night he takes out Josephine's ribbon. He has not tied a knot in it for many days. His careful count of the knots arrives at fifty-four. He remembers the winter visit to Kansas City when he gave it to her, recalls how she tied her hair with it and how the vision she presented caught his breath.

You told them I'd make them sorry, and I have. But any more, little darling, it'll make me sorry too. I don't guess you'd want that. You know I'll always love you. He rolls the ribbon and puts it back in his jacket and he will not take it out again.

OLD PAP

They decided to split up again, the better to elude the Yankees. "See you when I see you," Todd said, and rode off with his men to southward. Bill took the Kansas First Guerrillas west into Howard County.

They rode by night and made fireless camps in the deeper woods during the day. He posted videttes in every direction and was kept apprised of the massive hunting parties scouring the countryside in search of them. They got sporadic word of Federal reprisals—the burning of Rocheport, where the guerrillas had been so well received, the promiscuous hangings of secessionist farmers, some of whom had helped the bushwhackers, some of whom Bill had never known.

*   *   *

The news of Sterling Price was glum. Halfway to Saint Louis, he had chosen to attack the Yankee garrison at Pilot Knob rather than simply skirt it. The decision was a major blunder. In a two-day battle he lost 1,500 men. His army too weakened and demoralized to make the planned assault on heavily defended Saint Louis, he turned toward Jefferson City, the state capital. But his wagon train was slow and his ranks ridden with men of poor discipline, and by the time he reached Jeff City, it had been so greatly reinforced that to attack it would have been further folly. So he made for Boonville, which he could easily occupy, and sent word to all guerrilla bands that he wished to rendezvous with them there.

Archie Clement had been riding as a forward scout and was waiting for the company when it arrived at the Boonville Road. He sat his horse beside an oak against whose trunk was seated a decapitated German farmer with his hands holding his head in his lap. A stalk of yellow grass hung from a corner of the farmer's mouth and his expression was almost wistful. Arch grinned and waggled his brows at his passing comrades and cut leering glances at the dead man. Some of the newer members of the company chuckled uncertainly at the spectacle as they trotted past it, but such sights had by now lost all novelty for the others and they scarce remarked it. Bill Anderson looked on it and felt a profound sense of fatigue.

When the Kansas First Guerrillas reined up in front of the Boonville hotel serving as Price's headquarters, the men of the Army of Missouri regarded them mutely. Quantrill's band had struck them as a rough breed, but a day later they saw Todd's bunch and were persuaded that guerrillas came no meaner. But even Todd's company had not prepared them for the sight of Bill Anderson's bunch. The general came out to shake Bill's hand and say he was honored to meet him, and Bill was impressed with the tall man's bulk of more than 250 pounds. But Price could not keep from gawking at the wildhaired band before him, most of them still outfitted in filthy Federal blues and smelling of blood and smoke and graves laid open. He regarded with dismay their necklaces of ears and fingers, the scalps dangling from bridles and saddlehorns, from belts and boottops. He had heard that these men took grisly trophies, but he had dismissed such reports as Yankee mendacity or the routine exaggerations of the press. Yet here the truth was, in all its raw stink.

Bill read Price's face and turned to Jim and told him to see that the horses were watered and fed. Jim caught his look and understood and quickly got the company away from there in a clatter of hooves and a raise of dust.

As the bushwhackers rode off down the street, Bill presented Price with a pair of silver-mounted revolvers he had acquired from a Federal wagon train earlier in the summer. The general was appreciative and invited him into his private office for brandy and a cigar. They exchanged a few brief compliments and then Price told of his plan to advance on Kansas City. He needed the guerrillas to disrupt Yankee rail transport and to distract Federals from K.C. He had already given Quantrill and Todd their assignments. He wanted Bill to continue harassing the Federals throughout central Missouri and to inflict all the damage he could to the Northern Missouri rail line. He gave him a copy of a special order that specified exactly that mission. Bill read it and folded it and put it in his jacket. There was an awkward pause; then Price cleared his throat and consulted his pocket watch and said he regretted to cut short their meeting, but . . .

As they left Boonville behind them, somebody joked that Price probably weighed more than twice as much as Arch.

"He maybe weighs twice more than me, but he ain't any more man than me," Archie said. "Looked a little too tender about our prizes, you ask me."

Butch asked Bill what Old Pap had to say.

"Said if he had ten thousand like us he could take Missouri and hold it forever."

"Ten thousand!" Hi Guess said. "Shoot, we had ten thousand like us, Bill would be the general and Price maybe be a sergeant."

Bill had to grin.

"If we had ten thousand like us," Butch said, "we wouldn't need Price nor anybody else to own the whole damn state ourselves. To win the whole damn war!"

"If Fletch Taylor was here," Jim said, "you know what he'd say."

They laughed, and several of them intoned together, "If a frog had wings . . ."

A PLEDGE

Beloved husband—

Poor Lamar sees me talking in agitation to myself and must think I am quite mad. He does not know I am addressing you, pleading my argument that you come home. I can say it no plainer: DAMN the war. Please, Bill, be quit of it. Come home. Think of us in our lovely tub, our own little boat out on the wide sea and away from all this troubled world. . . .

Dearest wife—

I still kill the enemy where he presents himself to me, but oh my love, I am so sick of killing them! I would quit this war on the instant, but I cannot quit my men,—and for all their disappointment in Price, they will not abandon him. Yet only a fool will deny that if Price is defeated in his next engagement he will be finished,—and Missouri finished with him. Therefore have I made a bargain with myself which I present to you as a pledge: I swear to you that on the day Pap is beaten, I will be shed of my duties of captaincy and will come home to you. May resolutions come quickly, so I may fly to your embrace. . . .

RESOLUTIONS

They ambushed Union patrols nearly every day, made Union informers to know the terrible error of their ways. Unloosed storms of gunfire on every steamboat they spotted, shot apart telegraph lines. Ranged over the hills and all along the bottoms of the wildwoods of central Missouri.

In the course of a skirmish with a large militia force in Howard County, Hi Guess received a bullet in the chest and one in the belly.

Frank James cradled him in his arms and others stood and watched Hi's legs weakly kick in the dirt, his eyes wide but seeing none of them as he addressed a woman named Clarissa, telling her he loved her truly and wanted to marry her and to please wait for him. Then he was dead and they made haste in putting him in the earth.

A week later they were traversing an open stretch of country in Chariton County when a Federal cavalry company four times their size loomed over a hill and charged them. The guerrillas raced for the wildwood just beyond a low rise, and once again their superior horses easily outdistanced the Yankee mounts. Most of the company was already on the high ground when Buster Parr's horse was shot from under him. Buster had been bringing up the rear and was still on the prairie and none of them knew he'd gone down until Butch Berry looked back and saw him a hundred yards behind and the Yankees closing on him.

Butch brought his horse about and watched as the Yankees drew up around Buster and some of them dismounted and pulled him to his feet. Buster was favoring a leg and Butch heard his distant scream when one of the Yanks kicked it. The horse was screaming too, lying on its side and kicking awkwardly, and a Federal dispatched it with a bullet.

The other bushwhackers had now seen Butch halted and realized the Yanks had left off the chase. Bill told Arch Clement to stay with the men and be ready to lead them away fast, then he and Jim rode back to where Butch sat his horse at the rim of the rise.

The Feds had formed a battle line to either side of the dismounted soldiers clustered around Buster and holding him upright. Some of the Yanks were spitting on him and punching him. One hit him in the head with a rifle butt.

"Son of a *bitch*!" Butch Berry said.

The Federals were waving to them now, beckoning, pointing at Buster as if daring them to come for their man.

Butch drew his Colt and turned to Bill, his face wild. "Let's *do* something!"

"Do *what*, goddammit!" Jim Anderson said. "You so one-eyed blind you can't see there's two hundred fucken Feds down there? We're not fifty."

"*Bill!*" Butch said.

Bill Anderson looked at him. Then looked back to Buster among the Yankees. "I can't risk the whole company for one man," he said.

The Federal commander moved his horse up behind Buster and drew his saber. He raised it high for the watching guerrillas to see. The blade caught the sun and flashed as the officer brought it down and Buster's head slumped sideways, and even at this distance they saw the bright glint of blood that arced from his severed neck.

The soldiers let him fall and some of them kicked him even as he lay dying or already dead. They tied his feet to the end of a rope attached to a saddle and they waved at the spectating guerrillas once more and rode away, dragging Buster's remains behind them.

"Let's go," Bill said, reining Edgar Allan around.

The man was lost, he tells himself, lying in his blanket that night. There was nothing to be done for it.

You were his captain.

It would have been worse than folly. The circumstance was clear.

Ah, the circumstance. Of course. But tell me, Captain: was it that you did not dare to risk your own life, now you've told the lady you'll return to her on Price's imminent defeat? Tell me true.

The company is my chief charge. I cannot risk the entire company for one man.

Yes, of course. Quantrill always said you were a sly debater. Do you not recall your upbraiding of him for placing circumstance above his man? More to the point, Captain, I ask you this: if not the entire company, how many will you risk for one man? Half the company? Ten men? One? And I ask you, sir: if a man of the company is not worth the risk of at least one of his comrades—and if that one is not you, the captain of them, then what are you captain of? And still more to the point: what are you?

Maybe I never was but a damned horse thief.

He stares at the utterly uninterested stars and berates himself in a howling silence, curses himself for an irresolute weakling and for being the sort of pathetic fool who wishes he could have a moment back again so he might use it properly. *Fool!* A man takes an action or he does not—and then the moment is fled to wherever all moments in relentless succession do irretrievably flee.

*   *   *

The Federals had retreated through Independence street by street, giving way and breaking apart before Jo Shelby's relentless rebels and the guerrillas spearheading for him. In a small clearing in a stand of sycamores at the edge of town, a dozen bloodsmeared Kansas cavalrymen led by redbearded Doc Jennison—once the jayhawking scourge of the borderland and now a Federal colonel—hastily tied off their wounds and cursed the God that ever permitted the notion of Missouri to enter the mind of man.

"Colonel, look there!" A trooper pointed to a ridge about a quarter-mile distant, where a rider sat his horse and surveyed the town below. There were no trees behind him and he made a stark silhouette against the sky.

"The cheek of the bastard!" Jennison said. "Out in the open as bold as you please. Got an angel on his shoulder, don't you know." He turned to one of the men and said, "Hand me that Spence."

The man passed over the Spencer carbine and said, "I'm not real sure, Captain, but looks like he's in blue."

"He's a bushwhacker," Jennison said, levering a .56-caliber round and cocking the hammer and bracing the barrel on a sycamore stump. "I can tell a bushwhacker from a mile off."

"What if he's not?" another man said. "What if he's really one of ours?"

"Then he's got this coming for being such a damned fool," Jennison said.

As Jennison took aim, the horseman stood up in the stirrups for a better view and made an even sharper target of himself. "Good Christ, boy," Jennison said softly. "you might as well whistle for it." He held a breath and squeezed off the round.

"Captain Todd stood up in the stirrups to have a better look, and *bang,* his neck pops open. He never made a sound, he just fell. There was no stopping the blood. He couldn't talk, but his eyes were moving over all of us like he was looking for somebody. Then he gives this big grin like he found him, only it was like he was looking at something the rest of us couldn't see. He died smiling, no telling at what."

Relating this report was Charley Webb, who'd ridden with Todd until two days ago. He'd then sought out Bill Anderson's company in Carroll County to join with them.

"Captain Pool said he wasn't about to bury Captain Todd out in the woods when there was a perfectly good cemetery right there in the town. So we carried him down and got us a couple of shovels from a livery and started digging a hole for him. Next thing we know, here comes this fella in a suit and tie who says his name's Beattie and we're digging in his family plot and he won't stand for some stranger buried there. Said as soon as we were gone he was going to have his man dig up the body and throw it in the river. Captain Pool told him he lived in Kansas City and intended to come to Independence every few weeks to put flowers on his friend's grave, and if he ever heard so much as a rumor that George had been dug up, he would find Beattie and put *him* in a grave and all his family in there with him. Well, that shut up Mr. Beattie fast enough, but just to ease the matter for him, Captain Pool gave him a fistful of money and *that* seemed to improve the fella's disposition a whole lot. By the time we were patting down the dirt on Todd's grave, Mr. Beattie had brought some flowers from somewhere to put on it."

The following day came the news of Price's defeat at Westport. Pap was in retreat with the remnants of his army, heading back to Arkansas. Dave Pool and his guerrillas had gone with him. The word was that Quantrill had departed to Kentucky with his meager band.

Dearest—

Price is finished. Many of the best of us are killed. Quantrill is gone. My war is done. I shall take leave of my forty good men in the morning and follow this notice to you by a day. Then we shall evermore be Texans and sail love's sea in our sturdy tub.

OCTOBER 26, 1864

It has rained in the night and on this chill dawn he wakes rolled in an oilskin under a dripping hilltop maple and in each hand holds a Colt. He has slept more soundly this night than he has in months, and he stretches with great satisfaction. A few feet away Jim sleeps on, nothing of him showing from under the enveloping slicker but the thick tangle of his hair.

He rises and tucks the pistols into his belt, fits himself with the rest of his armament, then picks up his slicker and rolls it up and regards the Ray County countryside. Pools of pale mist linger in the swales and hollows. The trees to the east are afire with the rising sun. A ragged white arrowhead of geese wings to southward in the reddening sky. At his back the distant woods are still steeped in lingering night shadows. He hears the call of a solitary crow. Below the hill the camp is already roused, the men gathering at the cookfires. The air is scented with raw earth and woodsmoke, the rising aromas of coffee and bacon, the smell of moldering leaves. He recognizes Butch Berry as one of the riders heading out to relieve the night pickets.

Jim comes awake and stretches with a groan, then throws off his slicker and gets up. He buckles on his gunbelt and stands by his brother to look down at the camp.

"Let's get down there," Bill says. "I got something to tell the bunch of you."

Jim arches his brow in curiosity, then grabs up his oilskin and hurries after him.

Arch Clement sees them descending the hill and readies a cup of coffee for Bill. At their ropeline tethers, the horses are saddled and stamping, eager to be about the day's business.

At the central cookfire Bill says, "Listen up, boys," and the men converge around him.

But now they hear distant rebel yells of warning and see Butch Berry and Tom Tuckett, one of the night pickets, riding hard out of the northern treeline, about a furlong distant.

"Yanks!" Jim says. "A *bunch* of them, judging by those boys' hollering!"

A half-dozen Missouri militiamen, the advance riders, come galloping out of the woods, all of them with revolvers in hand, trailing Butch and Tuckett by a hundred yards.

"Make for the south wood, boys!" Bill shouts. "Go!"

In seconds the company is ahorse and riding hard up the hill, Bill and Jim and Arch bringing up the rear. Butch and young Tuckett are fifty yards behind them and pulling away from the militia pointmen.

Then Tuckett's horse is hit and goes down. The boy tumbles like a flung doll—but he scrambles to his feet and starts firing at the pointmen and drops a horse and rider.

Butch Berry reins about and starts back for him.

Bill pulls Edgar Allan around at the foot of the hill as the rest of the militia force comes bursting out of the trees three hundred yards away. They look to be thrice the guerrillas' number.

The rest of the company vanishes over the hilltop, but Jim and Arch rein up on the crest and look back and Jim hollers, *"Bill!"*

The militia pointmen are shooting as they close on Tuckett and are forty yards from him when the boy staggers and falls. Butch reins up hard beside him and alights from the saddle and pulls him to his feet and tries to get him onto the horse but the animal shies, then bolts away. Supporting Tuckett with one arm, Butch shoots with the other and two militia horses go down shrieking, their riders flailing over the ground. The other three Yanks go galloping past him, all of them shooting, and Butch brings down another horse just as he is hit and he drops to his knees, still clutching Tuckett to him.

Twenty yards beyond Butch, the pair of remaining militia pointmen rein around and draw spare pistols.

Bill hears Jim shout, "Come on—they're lost!" He sees Butch struggling to his feet and refusing to unhand his comrade. The militia force is coming hard on a rising howl and hardly a hundred yards from him.

He heels Edgar Allan into a sprint and closes up fast behind the pointmen as they fire on Butch, and Butch sits down hard and Tuckett slips from him. Bill shoots one of the Yanks off his horse and the other looks back big-eyed and then ducks low in the saddle and veers away at a hard gallop.

He pulls Edgar Allan up short beside Butch, who is risen to one knee. He yells his name and leans from the saddle and puts his hand down to him as the Union troop thunders toward them in a storm of hooves and gunfire. Edgar Allan flinches and yelps and then is hit again. A rifleball hums a hole in Bill's hatbrim, his right leg jerks and goes numb, a bullet cuts through his jacket and burns his ribs.

Butch looks up, his face streaked with blood, his shirt drenched red. He sees it is Bill and grins wide and white—and reaches up and clasps his hand.

And in that instant—his own grin feeling hugely grand—Bill sees a glorious incandescence and nothing more. . . .

As the larger portion of the militia outfit chased the Kansas First Guerrillas into the wildwood, the jubilant commanding officer and a few others stood gathered around Bill Anderson and looked on the handsome unmarred face, the blue-rimmed hazel eyes. They couldn't believe it was him, but the orders from General Price that they found in his pocket confirmed it. Some of the militiamen unsheathed their knives but the CO said no, not yet, he wanted the body fully recognizable.

They confiscated a wagon from a nearby farm and loaded him onto it, the back of his head soggy with blood where the pistolball smashed his skull. Then they bore him away, singing "Battle Hymn of the Republic" as they went. Butch Berry and Tom Tuckett they had scalped and stripped of their blue uniforms and slashed with sabers and mutilated in their private parts and beaten with rifle butts until none who ever knew them would have recognized their remains, which were left to the ants and crows.

They took him to Richmond, the Ray County seat, and laid him out in the courthouse for everyone to see. Some of the authorities both military and civilian cut locks of his hair for mementos before he was put on public display, stripped of the Union bluecoat, clad in his artful shirt. Also on public view were his six Navy Colts, a scalp taken from his horse's bridle, some letters from his wife, a likeness of her and one of him and her together, a lock of hair presumed to be hers, a poke containing six hundred dollars in greenbacks and specie, a pair of gold pocketwatches. But the article that drew the most prolonged and intense regard was his black silk ribbon with its knots. Many who looked on it made effort at a careful count, and yet no two sums agreed, varying from forty-eight to sixty-one. Some swore for a fact it held more than a hundred.

His horse and one of his Navies were awarded to the officer in command of the hunting party that brought him down. His watches and the rest of the guns went to the other officers. The money was divided among the enlisted men of the force, and some of them would never spend their share but keep it as a souvenir. All other of his articles, including the black ribbon, would disappear before evening and no one would know where they went.

The local photographist was summoned and Bill Anderson was propped up in a chair and pistols placed in his hands and pictures made. A journalist on the scene jokingly asked if the guns were empty—and could not keep from laughing aloud when an officer snatched them from the corpse and removed the cartridges before putting the pistols back in the dead man's hands.

They kept him on exhibit all through the day, then lighted the courthouse with torches and extra lamps and let people look on him into the night as well. As the news of his death had spread, gawkers from every county roundabouts came to join the long line and have their own look. Not until well after midnight had the last of them come and gone, and taken with them a tale to tell again and again.

But the best of the tales would belong to the few locals who went out on the street quite early next morning and spied something odd atop the telegraph pole at the end of the courthouse street. On drawing nearer and looking harder, they saw it was the head of Bloody Bill Anderson. The Yankee commander was notified and he ordered it removed, but he made no effort to know who committed the act, and no one cared that he did not, and all that day militiamen were smiling.

They buried his remains in an unmarked grave but everyone knew which plot it was, because for weeks after, every time a soldier in the vicinity had the need to piss, that was where he'd do it. Even after the army departed Richmond, no grass did grow on that grave thereafter, and some said it was not army piss that had burned the plot barren, but the hellfire from below.

"AND I DON'T WANT NO PARDON . . ."

He rode with the company down to Arkansas where they would make their winter camp and there said goodbye to them and shook hands with Arch Clement, their newly elected captain. Then he rode on to the Red and ferried across it and made his way to her place and found it abandoned.

The yard had gone to high weed and the cabin was missing its oversized door and had been ransacked of all furniture, including the big tub. He went into town and learned that the Purple Moon had changed ownership and was now called the High Hat. Most of the girls who had worked there last winter had moved on, but one who had not was a girl named Amanda. She told him that when the news of Bill's death came to Sherman, several girls who knew her went out to the house to offer condolences, but Bush would not receive them, refused even to answer their halloos. The Hundley boy finally came from around back of the house and told them to go away. He obviously took the news badly too, for that night he came to town and got terribly and belligerently drunk and picked a fight with a pair of teamsters, and when it was over, one teamster lay dead and so did Lamar Hundley. A few days after that she was gone and no one knew where.

He navigated westward, hired on as line rider on a New Mexican ranch through the remainder of the winter, then moved on in the first warm days of spring. He shivered in the high passes and sweltered in the deserts, went weeks without encountering another soul during which he spoke to no one but himself and his horse. What he most often spoke of were the days when he and his brother were at the rustling trade with their father. He recounted to his mount the thrill of those nights when they drove the horses at a gallop under the moon and stars. Sometimes he spoke of his sisters, whom he had not seen since before their crippling in Kansas City. He'd heard that all the women prisoners had now been exiled from the state, but he had no notion at all where the girls might be. He heard the news of Appomattox nearly two months after the fact. And a report that Quantrill had been killed, though none knew where or even if it was true.

He rode after his shortening shadow every morning and played it out behind him in the dying day's last red light. He held to this course until it delivered him to the end of the continent. The sight of the Pacific—brightly blue, undulant and endless—made him lightheaded. He took off his boots and walked barefoot in the wet sand and each time jumped back from the rushing surf as if it might snatch him away.

He took employment as a keeper of the peace in a nameless San Diego bordello and never had to use his pistol except once when a bad actor cut him across the ribs and he shot the fellow's knee to fragments. He lived in a room over a cafe and kept to himself and no one called him friend. Now and then he visited with one of the house girls.

One day he heard someone say Christmas was two weeks hence, and he was astonished to realize how long he had been in this land of perpetual sunshine and greenery and soft seawind, where there were no seasons to mark time's passage.

The next day he started back.

He arrived in Kansas City on a night of wind and bitter cold. He recalled the last time he had been here and the hard rain falling and the three who were with him and now all of them dead. He supposed that many of the men who had been here that night were now dead. He went into a crowded saloon and stood at the bar and drank whiskey in the clamor of men and women in desperate chase of pleasure. At every opening of the door, the sudden draft fluttered the lantern flames and the yellow light quavered on the walls. The place was hazed with smoke. In the heavy heat of the various potbellied stoves glowing red, the chief smells were of men unbathed and the cloying perfume of the whores.

The saloon grew louder and smokier and more crowded, the bar now packed four deep. He had just received a fresh drink when someone jostled his arm and most of the whiskey sloshed onto the bar. The man who did it had his back to him and wasn't even aware of the accident. A Federal sergeant in the company of two comrades.

"Hey, you!" He thumped the sergeant on the back with the heel of his hand. The man whirled with a glare.

"You owe me a drink." He gestured at the spilled whiskey.

The Fed regarded him closely. "I'll be go to hell," he said, his words barely audible over the din of music and song and loud talk and laughter. "I thought we'd killed all you bushrats or run you out of Missouri."

"He's one for sure, Silas," one of the other soldiers said, showing a yellow grin. "Look at the hair on him. Longer than my big sister's."

"Oh, he's one, all right," the third soldier said. He affected to sniff the air. "Nothing stinks like that but bushwhacker."

The soldiers were close about him and his back was against the bar.

"You still owe me a drink," he said.

The sergeant grinned. "Oh, I owe you something all right, bush-whacker, but it's not a drink."

"I'll wager it is," said a man who pressed up behind the sergeant and spoke over his shoulder. It was Coleman Younger. He grinned and said, "Hello, Jim. Good to see you."

The sergeant had lost his smile and stood fast, and Jim knew that Cole was surreptitiously holding a pistol to the man. The other two soldiers also stood wide-eyed, one of them with Frank James' Colt in his ribs, the other with Jesse's Smith & Wesson hard against his spine. Frank showed a small smile and nodded. Jesse was grinning like a lunatic.

"Get the man his drink," Cole said.

The sergeant shouted and waved hard for the barkeep's attention and signaled for a whiskey. When it came, Jim picked it up and looked at it and then poured the drink in the sergeant's shirt pocket. He looked at Cole and the James boys and said, "Let's get away from the smell of these Union shitbags."

Cole stripped the sergeant of his pistol. "You want this, come on out and get it," he said.

They swiftly snaked their way through the crowd and outside. They went to their horses and swung up on the saddles and came together in the middle of the street, reining their mounts in tight circles and all of them laughing. The wind had quit and their breath plumed blue in the bright light of a high full moon.

"I swear you got some luck, Jimbo," Cole said. "If we hadn't stopped in for a drink, those Yankee assholes might be dancing on your head right now."

"The door!" Frank said. The sergeant had come banging out onto the gallery, and the shotgun in his hands had likely come from behind the bar. It took him a moment to spot them and start to raise the weapon—a moment too long. Jesse shot him in the mouth and he staggered back against the door jamb and the shotgun fell and he pitched forward on his face.

They heeled their horses hard and sprinted away into the darkness of the wildwood.

They went ten miles at full gallop before they were sure of no pursuers, then reined up on a bluff overlooking the Missouri. Their horses blew great smoky exhalations. The trees stood darkly skeletal in the stark moonlight and the river shone like a silver ribbon. Cole uncorked a bottle and they handed it around and all took a drink in turn but Jesse, who simply passed it along every time it came to him.

They sat their horses under the moon and drank and caught each other up on things. Frank had been with Quantrill in Kentucky. He said Quantrill's mean-ass horse Charley threw a shoe one day and Quantrill took him to a blacksmith who wisely put leg restraints on the animal to keep from getting his brains kicked out, but the horse kept trying to kick him anyway and broke a leg in the trying. Quantrill had to shoot the beast. He wept when he did it, and he said it meant the end was near for him too. He was right. A week later a gang of hired Union manhunters caught up to them, and in the fight that followed, Quantrill was shot in the spine and paralyzed from the chest down. The Feds carried him away to Louisville and it took him a month to die. The way Frank heard it, he'd left a goodly sum of money to Kate King, and the story held that she'd used it to buy herself a fancy whorehouse in Saint Louis.

Last spring Jesse decided to take up the Federal offer of parole to all bushwhackers who turned themselves in. Together with a bunch of other rebels worn out with the bush life, he'd ridden into Lexington under a white flag—and the Yankees had opened fire. He was shot in the chest for the second time in a year, and for the second time was thought to be a goner—and for the second time beat the odds. He was now engaged to wed the woman who nursed him back to health, his cousin Zerelda.

The word on Arch Clement was that he was raising hell in Texas. Dave Pool had been granted amnesty and was now a lawman in Lafayette County. W. J. Gregg was a carpenter in Independence, had a wife and two children and another babe on the way. . . .

After he and Cole compared their California adventures, Jim said, "Well, what do you boys have in mind to do now?"

On an afternoon of driving snow, they robbed the Clay County Savings Bank in Liberty of $60,000 and made their howling, shooting getaway.

An hour later and twenty miles to the west—the storm now abated and the countryside white and still—a one-armed farmer wearing a ragged Confederate cap was searching for a lost calf near the Liberty road when he heard singing at a distance and coming down the trace. Soon there appeared a band of riders on prancing steaming mounts. As these horsemen passed by, they returned the man's smile and touched their hatbrims to him.

And as they rode into the national imagination and the legend it would make of them, they kept on with their song:

Oh, I'm a good old rebel, that's just what I am.
And for this Yankee nation I don't care a damn.
I'm glad I fought against it, I only wish we'd won.
And I don't want no pardon
for anything I've done.